THE
HONEST
LOOK

ALSO BY THE AUTHOR

Experimental Heart

THE HONEST LOOK

JENNIFER L. ROHN

COLD SPRING HARBOR LABORATORY PRESS
Cold Spring Harbor, New York • www.cshlpress.com

All Cold Spring Harbor Laboratory Press publications may be ordered directly from Cold Spring Harbor Laboratory Press, 500 Sunnyside Blvd., Woodbury, New York 11797-2924. Phone: 1-800-843-4388 in Continental U.S. and Canada. All other locations: (516) 422-4100. FAX: (516) 422-4097. E-mail: cshpress@cshl.edu. For a complete catalog of all Cold Spring Harbor Laboratory Press publications, visit our World Wide Web Site at http://www.cshlpress.com/.

Library of Congress Cataloging-in-Publication Data

Rohn, Jennifer L.
  The honest look / by Jennifer L. Rohn.
    p. cm.
  ISBN 978-1-936113-11-8 (pbk. : alk. paper)
  1. Scientists--Professional ethics--Fiction. 2. Netherlands--Fiction. I. Title.

  PS3618.O486H66 2011
  813'.6—dc22

                          2010026036

10 9 8 7 6 5 4 3 2 1

***Poems Quoted in* The Honest Look**: 5, Alfred Lord Tennyson, *Oenone*; 26, Walt Whitman, *30—Poem of The Propositions of Nakedness*; 32, Alfred Lord Tennyson, *In Memoriam A.H.H.*; 35, John Keats, *Bright Star;* 39, William Wadsworth, *The Prelude;* 46, Emily Bronte, *The Prisoner;* 55, Percy Bysshe Shelley, *The Revolt of Islam;* 63, Robert Herrick, *A Meditation for His Mistress;* 68, James Thomson, *The Seasons;* 76, William Shakespeare, *Cymbaline;* 87, Henry Wadsworth Longfellow, *The Arrow and the Song;* 88, Carolyn Forché, *The Garden Shukkei-en;* 102, William Blake, *Cradle Song;* 143, Miroslav Holub, *The Moth.* Translated from the Czech by D. Young and D. Hábová. *Intensive Care: Selected and New Poems* (© 1996 Oberlin College. Reprinted by permission of David Young and Oberlin College.); 173, Sir Thomas Lovell Beddoes, *The Second Brother;* 209, T.S. Eliot, *The Burial of the Dead;* 243, Oliver St. John Gogarty, *The Image-Maker;* 250, Edna St. Vincent Millay, *Dirge Without Music* (© 1928, 1955 by Edna St. Vincent Millay and Norma Millay Ellis. Reprinted by permission of Elizabeth Barnett, Literary Executor, The Millay Society.); 256, José Angel Buesa, *Poema del Amor Ajeno*, English translation by the author; 276, Margaret Atwood, *More and More.* (Reprinted by permission of Margaret Atwood.)

To my parents, Mary and Dan:
two artists who
unwittingly but graciously allowed
a young scientist to evolve and
thrive in their midst

Acknowledgments

⚜

The manuscript was read in various forms, and with varying degrees of tough love, by too many people to thank here. But for their honest look, I would especially like to thank David Weinkove, Francesca Pagnacco, Helen Cole, Clare Isacke, Vicky Long, Marilyn Lucas, Sally Leevers, Adam Lauring, Richard Grant, Sheila Pearce, James Pearce and Armand Marie Leroi. Emma, an intern at my then-literary agency (whose surname was never revealed), made some wonderful suggestions at the very beginning. Special thanks are due to Eva Amsen and Charles Kooij for checking my Dutch, and to Monica Iglesias and Daniel Bosch, my Spanish—any remaining mistakes are entirely my own. The regulars at LabLit.com and the Fiction Lab book group have been an unstinting and invigorating source of discussion and camaraderie. This novel was written on the dole in Amsterdam, in the wake of a catastrophic biotech bankruptcy, so I feel it only proper to thank the Dutch government for its generous social services, and the city of Amsterdam for its inspirational beauty. I am grateful to Mary Cozza, Jan Argentine, Denise Weiss, Mala Mazzullo, and Sarah Beganskas from Cold Spring Harbor Laboratory Press, and to John Inglis at the Press for his continuing support of my work in general, and of lab lit fiction in particular.

I own a tremendous debt to Professor Gustavo Perez Firmat of Columbia University for being kind enough to check my translation of *Poema del Amor Ajeno* by the nearly forgotten 20th century Cuban poet José Angel Buesa. The sole slight liberty I have taken with one of the lines, for literary effect, is my own responsibility.

Finally I would like to thank my "scientific grandfather" John F. Cairns and his wife Elfie, who provided many unforgettable conversations about the stories behind the world of science, both past and present, and whose continuing friendship has enriched my life.

Prologue

⊰❦⊱

Precisely ninety minutes before dawn, a commotion broke out in the far corner of the laboratory. Claire's head jolted up from her keyboard, ears full of the strange noise. And then an alarm on the console joined in, chiming in synchrony with the display as it flashed 06.00 in cool blue. She silenced the alarm, but the unknown noise carried on behind her—a rhythmic stopping and starting like a metal brush scraping along a fence.

Whatever it was would have to wait. As her hands moved automatically over keyboard and control panel, soliciting information and giving instructions, she listened to the alien scraping with a slow burn of curiosity.

The false-colour image on the computer screen was replaced by a string of numbers, then by a green progress bar, filling up from left to right as the command was executed.

Five minutes remaining, noted the task bar calmly.

Claire stood up, rolled the kinks from her shoulders and began tracking the noise to its source. It was mechanical in some respects, organic in others—either way, oddly familiar. She took a few steps, forgetting to breathe in her concentration as she tilted her head one way, then the other.

The acoustics of the room were misleading, thanks to its strange contents. Formerly an office, the room had been refurbished as a lab to house the great machine. Taking to its new environment, the apparatus seemed to sprawl into every available inch, a tumble of grey cubes jewelled with screens, dials and indicator lights. During the hushed pause between night and day, Claire was often seduced into suspecting the impossible: that the thing was growing steadily larger week by week, sending out new

1

tendrils of cables and tubing like jungle vines trembling towards the canopy.

She exhaled. The sound was issuing from the opposite corner, underneath the tower of incubators. She knelt down and peered into the dark two-inch gap. No movement was apparent, but there was no doubt about it: Machinery, even malfunctioning machinery, didn't make that sort of sound.

Something was alive back there.

She squinted into the space between the incubator and the floor, turning the sound over and over in her memory. Then she had it.

"Crickets," she said.

The scraping paused a microsecond at the sound of her voice, then carried on, neither confirming nor denying the accusation.

"The game's up," she persisted. "Come out with your legs in the air, nice and easy."

She saw nothing—no shapes, no motion, only a few puffs of dust. Where had they come from, and what food was keeping them alive? And why would summer insects be so active now? September was well advanced, and the climate was even colder here in the Netherlands than it was back home in England. Everything about them being there was wrong, which she rather liked.

The machine chirped reprovingly, jealous of rival distractions, and Claire returned to confront the beast. Its official name was the Interactrex 3000. A ludicrous name, she thought, like a bristling chrome skullcap designed to hoover the souls out of helpless female Earthlings in an old science fiction B-movie. Its actual function was nothing so dramatic, but it was the best way scientists currently had of peering inside living cells. In other words, the Interactrex was *a must-have tool for those dedicated to finding cures for the killer diseases that have plagued mankind for centuries*—or so Claire had been amused to read when she'd liberated the instruction manual from its shrink-wrapped cover.

Because names in general, and words in particular, were very important to Claire, she had privately christened the machine *Raison D'être*, and publicly, "the Raisin." Her coworkers, who weren't privy to the pun, thought her odd for it. Or more accurately, it became another oddity to add to the collection of things they knew, or misunderstood, about their new colleague.

There was no doubt about it: the Raison was the only reason she was here. It certainly wasn't on account of experience—she was the youngest

2

senior scientist on the payroll at NeuroSys. And it wasn't for any particular brilliance, either: that much had been made eloquently clear to her by the attitude of the other senior scientists. The truth was that she was one of the few people in the world who knew how to operate such machines. In fact, aside from the original invention and the Raison itself, the only other working model had recently been installed in the Danish Cancer Institute in Copenhagen, coaxed along by an equally patient and misunderstood postdoctoral scientist called Mads.

⚜ ⚜ ⚜

The first Interactrex prototype had been invented by Claire's former PhD supervisor, Maxwell Bennett, at the University of Liverpool. Maxwell had nicknamed his invention the *Lady June* soon after the Head of Biochemistry banished the monstrous prototype to the basement where it wouldn't scare off prospective students. Privately, Claire didn't blame the Head: the Lady Jane was five times the size of the Raison and nowhere near as attractive. Her PhD thesis had revolved around working out the machinery's quirks and demands in near solitary confinement, with only Maxwell for occasional company. Unfortunately, the biological process she discovered during her thesis work was nowhere near as exciting as the technology that had illuminated it, so she had spent most of her stint worrying about where her career was heading.

But then, while writing up the last stages of her thesis, Claire had received a mysterious phone call from the Human Resources officer of NeuroSys, a British-owned biotech company based in the Netherlands. The woman seemed to be encouraging her in the most indirect way possible to apply for a position. Putting the phone down afterwards, not entirely sure what had just happened, she leafed through the back pages of *Nature* until she found the advertisement.

"I don't think it will come to anything, guv," she said to Maxwell after sending off her application, "but I thought I'd warn you to expect a reference request."

Maxwell and Claire shared a similar brand of humour, and irreverent address was one of the habits they'd fallen into over the years. They knew better than to do this when anyone else was around.

He squinted at the advertisement in the folded magazine she'd thrust out, his fine fingers accepting it like a specimen.

"NeuroSys," he pronounced, drawing out the syllables. "Such an unfortunate name. But now it all makes sense—I was chatting on the phone with their CEO, Stanley Fraser, not five minutes ago."

"About *me*? But I only just e-mailed off my—"

"Nope—about the Lady Jane."

"Really, what about?"

Maxwell studied her with his watery-blue eyes, bloodshot from too many hours tinkering with circuits and wires. Claire noticed for the first time an undercurrent of self-satisfaction in his usually laconic manner.

"They've just purchased the first factory-ready model of our little beauty," he said. "And now it looks as if they're going to purchase you as well. The ultimate accessory."

"Very funny. But are you sure they'll want me? Read more carefully."

His gaze returned to the magazine, scanning the text and then going thoughtfully distant.

"Well?" she prompted, when it looked as if Maxwell were about to drift seamlessly back to whatever technical problem he was currently worrying about in his head.

He smiled faintly. "You're being *headhunted*, love. And surely you realize that my reference letter will elevate you to goddess-like proportions."

"They want an *ideas* person, Maxwell." She pointed to the relevant passage in the job description. "They didn't mention that over the phone!"

"*You*," he quoted, putting on an appropriately silly accent, "*will have a PhD in a relevant field, be self-motivated and ambitious, and possess the creativity to realize a self-conceived programme of basic research*"—he rolled the *r*'s, making her giggle—"*into the mechanism underlying neuronal diseases*—who writes this stuff?" He made a face. "So what's the problem?"

"Don't play dumb, guv. It clashes with the Obi-Wan beard."

She knew he was intimately familiar with what she thought of as her "ideas problem," as familiar as only a PhD supervisor could be. Claire, once briefed on a scientific mission, could track an elusive prey to the remotest foxhole, but coming up with the innovation—the brief itself—seemed beyond her.

Maxwell sighed, put down the magazine. "Listen, we can't all be Charles Darwins. And who'd want to be? There's a crucial place in the

4

scientific food chain for people like you, to provide the solid basis for all those mad dreams. Besides. . ."

"What?"

"I expect that's all corporate mumbo-jumbo. They just want someone who can make their expensive new bird sing. And as for the ideas. . ." He leaned back in his chair, stroked his beard with his spidery fingers before meeting her eye. "You might just surprise yourself one day."

❦ ❦ ❦

Exactly ninety minutes after the crickets first began to sing that September morning, the Raison sounded off another warning— 07.30—just as a shaft of sunlight knifed into the room, filling the lab with a shell-coloured haze. Simultaneously, the chorus snuffed itself out.

Claire suppressed the alarm and looked out the window, the sudden silence pulsating against her eardrums. The sun wavered like a molten bubble on the perfectly flat spirit level of the Dutch horizon. Some deep understanding made her realize that it was the light and not the alarm that had frightened the insects.

"*The grasshopper is silent in the grass*," she quoted softly—Tennyson, her father's favourite—before returning her attention to the keyboard.

Later, Claire consulted the Internet on the dietary requirements of crickets and began laying potato peelings underneath the incubator as daily offerings. Over subsequent weeks, she worked out the details of the insects' circadian concert schedule: always beginning ninety minutes before sunrise, inching incrementally later each day, and going mute the moment the sun rose. That the experimental alarm, the crickets and the sunrise were all in sync that morning might seem like a tremendous coincidence, but she was used to such flukes, both the trivial and the deeply consequential. Coincidences had dogged her since she was a small child. In her lifetime, she had run into an aging midwife on the summit of Ben Nevis who, upon further conversation, turned out to have assisted at her birth; found a soiled National Lottery ticket on the pavement that won £500 in the next draw; and narrowly missed a flight to Gran Canaria that had subsequently plummeted into the sea, killing all 115 people aboard.

Claire had not been exposed to crickets in her British urban upbringing, but she knew their songs from summer trips to American scientific conferences. So, at first, the morning serenade stirred up pleasant

5

memories: the smell of cut lawns, glittering green fireflies, heat lightning strobing behind clouds on a breathless night, ice tinkling in steamy cold glasses of tea. Colleagues gossiped and networked on the terraces during the evening coffee breaks, forging useful political alliances, while Claire wandered off by herself, leaning over the railings and dreaming into the darkness, allowing chains of words to illuminate her mind like fairy lights.

It was only later, after the accident, that the cricket songs began to warp into something uneasy. As any animal trainer knows, sounds are powerful associative tools, a convenient way to correlate stimulus with response. In the same way that a whistle can call up an irresistible equation in a dolphin's brain—*leaping through hoop* equals *fishy treat*—the crickets reminded Claire of that fateful morning when she'd dreamt up her first real scientific idea, unasked for and entirely innocuous. And as associations can be linked to produce a chain of neat dolphin tricks along the length of the pool, so the brilliant idea brought to mind the accident that had resulted, a lone poison apple when she'd been expecting a summer's crop of sweet berries.

Before the accident, the crickets had been her early morning companions. They had amused, even comforted. Afterwards, their reedy voices only stirred up fear.

The crickets, of course, were entirely innocent. They were what they had always been. Only the association had changed.

Part I

THE INTERLOPER

Chapter 1

⁓❧⁓

Claire stood at the front of the auditorium on her first day, feeling faint at the blur of faces staring back. Virulent static seemed to crackle in her ears: *Go home, little girl. You're not wanted here.*

When she had pictured working in a start-up biotech company, her active imagination had breathed life into the shiny brochure from the welcome pack: white-coated scientists labouring earnestly toward a common goal, suffused in a glow of camaraderie and far from the every-man-for-himself mentality of the university she had just left behind. Far too late, she realized her foolish error.

Marjory Dupres, head of Human Resources, was introducing the assemblage to its newest colleague, and in her tone Claire could detect a counterchallenge, a warning that any open insubordination would be punished.

"I'm sure you will all join me in making Dr Cyrus feel *welcome*," she said, before launching into an explanation of Claire's expertise.

The new title still sounded alien to Claire's ears. What had she got herself into? Maxwell was right: It had been flagrantly naïve to accept the job without an interview. There was a potent back-story here, some crucial problem with office politics. It couldn't be that she'd beat out some internal candidate—there wasn't anyone else in the world qualified. Maxwell would never leave his academic post, and Mads Thor Ahrenkiel had already accepted the position in Copenhagen.

Nobody could possibly blame her for this.

Claire looked away from the hostile sea and became entangled in the glare of a blond man in an acid-green shirt, lounging against a wall with arms crossed as if he were too important to commit to a seat. He was beautiful in the way of those poisonous jungle frogs: angular, jewel-like, and breathtakingly repellent.

Face burning, she forced her eyes forward as Marjory continued to speak, words devoid of meaning. She began to lose focus; nausea and racing heart following close behind. The panic attack had been coming on all morning, ever since she'd landed.

To fend off the fatal miasma, she attempted her usual trick, focusing on images to tether herself to reality. She chose her lifelines at random, just as quickly discarded when they proved insufficient: the panes of rainy window glass, writhing at her like tentacles in a drive-through car wash. The digital projector, its limpid eye resembling the open mouth of a shotgun. A tall, strikingly pale man sitting at the back of the room, watching her with the attention of someone who is trying to place a face, or memorize a bus timetable.

Silence. Marjory, Claire realized, had finished her bored little speech and was apparently waiting for Claire to say something. *How long?* Claire wrestled with the panic attack as the seconds stretched out like soft clay, focusing again on the pale man in the back row, his black slashes of eyebrow stark, almost vibrating, against that albino skin.

And just like that, the panic inexplicably dispersed in an elastic-band twang.

"I'm sure the weather at least will be familiar," spoke up a stocky, dark-haired man in the front row. He had a Spanish accent. When Claire looked over at him, he winked. "I can assure you that leaving Madrid was a far bigger sacrifice."

He flicked his hand towards the window's evidence and a few others chuckled, dispersing the tension.

"I'm Ramon," the Spaniard introduced himself afterward, with a firm handshake, as the others streamed out around them. Then, to Claire's surprise, he added in an undertone, "Come have a coffee and I can explain what the bad vibes are all about, no?"

She looked over at Marjory, who'd been shepherding her around all morning, but she seemed busy, exchanging words with the man in the acid-green shirt. At that moment, he glanced over at her, and Claire felt again the full force of the room's inexplicable resentment.

"Don't worry about them," Ramon said, taking Claire by the arm. "I already volunteered to show you around after the meeting."

He led her through a maze of corridors and stairwells, narrow and far too bright. Marjory Dupres had informed her that the light was a special wavelength proved scientifically to lead to a happier, more productive work force—a fact Claire found rather sinister. She had never been in a place so shrouded in paranoia. CCTV cameras swivelled over every doorway, security guards patrolled with expressionless faces, and only a few hours in the place had been enough to infect her with the general suspicion pulsating from the walls.

"*Bienvenida*," Ramon said, ushering her through a doorway. "Welcome to the Home of the Zapper."

She had no idea what he was talking about. Looking up at some peripheral movement, Claire saw a grainy, miniature version of herself pass in a ceiling-mounted screen, slim and insubstantial and jerky with slow frames. A few white-coated researchers eyed her as Ramon led her through the lab to a small office appended to the back.

They sat, wordless, with Ramon not bothering to disguise his lengthy inspection. She had to look away in the end, to the window on the far wall. Through the smears of April rain, the fields bled watercolour green into the slate sky.

"You're lucky to have a view," she finally said, just to fill the air with sound.

He glanced over at window before restoring his own steady gaze, crinkled now with humour. "Define 'view.' The flatness gets to me almost more than the weather—in fact, I often close the blinds altogether."

"At least you're above sea level up here," she said. "Might come in handy one day."

Ramon emitted a short laugh, his keen eyes taking on a conspiratorial warmth. At the same time, he appeared to be reappraising her.

"You mustn't let yourself be intimidated by people," he said. "But I apologize for their terrible manners. That was no way to treat a new person."

A flicker of anger, now, and Claire saw that Ramon, despite his evident kindness, was not the sort of person one would want to cross. She reinterpreted his earlier joke about Madrid as an oblique warning to the others, and remembered how many had taken his lead. A truly astute politician would have noted whom, and filed that information away for future skirmishes.

"Thanks for rescuing me. I'm not normally this..." She paused, searching for the perfect word. "...incapacitated."

He nodded, the sharpness doused as quickly as it had flared. "I had a feeling you weren't. Listen, it's not easy here—in Holland, or at

11

NeuroSys. You've got to bash your way through, *comprendes*? No one else is going to do it for you."

He reached over and poured two mugs of coffee from a thermos on his desk.

"My wife roasts her own beans the Spanish way," he said, sliding a mug at her with capable blunt hands, "so you may find it a bit green. She's convinced that Dutch coffee doubles as industrial lubricant."

"I like Spanish coffee," Claire said. He didn't know the half of it. Her mother, Pilar, had always prepared coffee the same way, from beans sent monthly by her relatives in Las Palmas. She felt too shy to do the obvious and decent thing: inform Ramon that she was half-Spanish, address him fluently in that tongue. It seemed somehow presumptuous. Instead, she just said, in English, "God, this is delicious."

"Wait until you taste her cooking," Ramon said. "We'll have you around some evening soon." Though the bluish happy lighting caught flecks of grey in his hair, she guessed that he was only in his early forties. "Now, I thought you might have some questions for me before I throw you back to the lions."

She put down the mug. "I do, actually. What did you mean by 'the Home of the Zapper'?"

"How many things haven't they told you?" he said, shaking his head. "The Zapper is the company's nickname for our key drug, NS158—and its scientific basis was discovered in this lab."

"*You're* Dr Ortega." Claire said, remembering the company prospectus she had been sent. She sat up straighter at the realization of his rank in the company.

He nodded briskly. "And before you meet my partner in crime, Alan Fallengale, there's something I have to warn you about."

❧ ❧ ❧

NeuroSys was a one-trick pony. At least, that had been Maxwell's opinion, shared with Claire as she stood stunned in his office, still clutching the job offer.

"Don't get me wrong," he added. "They're doing great stuff, and the pony's one trick happens to be pretty damned impressive. You could make a real contribution there, you and Lady Jane's daughter. But they only have the one drug. What if it doesn't pass its clinical trials?"

"They published it in the best journals," Claire said, already feeing defensive about her future employer. "And the mouse trials looked really promising."

NeuroSys had been founded ten years previously to develop treatments for neurodegenerative diseases such as Alzheimer's. Its scientists, headed by Alan Fallengale and Ramon Ortega, had discovered a key vulnerability underlying these disorders and designed the company's first key drug: a compound called NS158, otherwise known as The Zapper. Patents were filed, NeuroSys was floated on the stock market, and it was rumoured that patient trials were just around the corner. Emboldened by these successes, the company was expanding into other brain disorders, including stroke, and had recently convinced venture capitalists to fund their next phase. Hence, the purchase of the Interactrex 3000 and the hiring of Claire.

Maxwell shrugged. "Big difference between mice and men, love—many a hyped cure has bombed in patients. But I can see your mind's made up."

"We're not as rich as you might imagine," Ramon was telling her. "Has Stanley given you the corporate spiel yet?"

She nodded. "I met him briefly when I first arrived."

"I'm sure he raved about things like stock value, burn-rate and profit margins, but the truth is that the basic research budget is still quite tightly controlled—especially when it comes to expensive equipment."

He regarded her with mild brown eyes.

"The Interactrex 3000," Claire said slowly, "is a very expensive piece of equipment."

"You've got it in one. And not everyone at NeuroSys thought it was worth it."

"Did you?"

"Absolutely." His head bobbed with genuine enthusiasm. "All our competitors already have the equipment that Alan and the computer people wanted to buy instead, real brute force stuff."

"Brute force?"

"You know, the next generation of robots and arrays. Equipment where you don't think, you just trawl aimlessly through the human genome, hoping to stumble over something interesting."

"And Dr Fallengale—Alan—is that sort of scientist?"

"God, no." Ramon grinned. "He's about as old-fashioned as they come. Only something as revolutionary as the Interactrex could've driven him to side with the computer folk."

He paused to refill both their mugs. "But the Interactrex is more *elegant*, and better still, it's practically unique. Can you see anything clinically relevant coming from the Danish group?"

Claire shook her head. Mads, her former colleague, was lost in the abstract.

"And we'll be in a unique position," he said. "The sales rep told us they're not going to produce any more Interactrex models until it's clear that the first two prototypes work. We're guinea pigs."

"If Maxwell could hear you. . ."

"*Sacrilegio*?" He smiled. "Of course the Interactrex works—but it will never be marketable until it's been made more user-friendly—or so I understand."

"Try user-possible," Claire said.

Another bark of laughter. "Anyway, the bottom line is that we need more products. Alan is as anxious as any of us to ensure that NeuroSys discovers something else besides the Zapper, so if your machine performs as advertised. . ."

"It's settled that I'm not to be working on Alzheimer's?" *That* was an established idea—a clear brief—that Claire could have played with for years.

"I'm afraid not. If it were up to me, I think there's still a lot to be learnt, and the Interactrex could be invaluable. But Alzheimer's is well covered by the Zapper, and we need to target new diseases with new drugs—new baskets, not more eggs."

"New ideas," Claire murmured, but Ramon didn't appear to notice her unease.

"Exactly. We're putting you on the stroke project, which has got off to a miserable start—although you didn't hear it from me. Stanley hopes that you and the Interactrex will inject some new life into that project, make it worth the investment."

But I have no idea what I'm doing, she wanted to say. Instead: "So it was just the money that made everyone so angry?"

Ramon scratched his sheep-shorn head. "No—only the high-tech crowd. Some of the other long faces I put down to old-fashioned jealousy."

14

"Towards *me*?"

He shrugged. "You're young, you've been slotted into a rare Senior Scientist position over some of the local favourites, and frankly, you're a hotshot—you know how to run one of the most finicky pieces of apparatus ever invented."

She didn't reply at first, just sat and absorbed the liquid patter against the window, the murmur of the lab workers on the other side of the office door.

"I'm not so sure I can handle it." She looked up at him appealingly—they both knew she wasn't referring to the machinery.

"You'll be fine," he promised. "Alan will come around. They all will, once they see what your baby can do."

Whatever Marjory DuPres had said to Alan Fallengale after the welcome meeting must have been effective, or else he was an extremely skilled dissembler.

"Sorry I'm late," Claire said, standing before the desk of the blond man with the acid-green shirt. His eyes were a pale peridot green. Up close, he was all prince and no frog—*God, the lines of his face.* She felt that vacuum in her lungs again.

"So we meet at last," he said, like the impeccably mannered rogue in a period drama. "Has Ramon been regaling you with horror stories about me?"

She blinked.

"Don't believe a word he says," Alan said. "I'm sure we'll get along splendidly. Now sit down and tell me about this hideously expensive machine of yours—I'm afraid I don't quite see the appeal."

As she took a seat and opened her mouth to parry, he cut her off.

"It looks to me," he said, all innocently reasonable, "like a standard microinjection apparatus connected to a mass spectrometric device, bulked up by marketing hype and wishful thinking."

"I think you'll find it's a bit more sophisticated than that," she said, smiling. She may have been temporarily pithed by the disastrous welcome, but she was damned if she'd let this condescending man and his upper-class accent intimidate her, no matter how important he was.

"So you collect proteins from inside the cell with a needle, zap them into a box, and the proteins that bind together get identified, right?" He was mocking her, no question. "I stand by my original description."

"You've identified those proteins from *living* cells," she said. "Where interactions between proteins are highly active and often transient. But maybe you're not interested in obtaining an accurate snapshot of reality."

There was a long pause as the jibe registered. She thought she'd gone too far, until she recognized the amusement on Alan's face. And something else—she had his full attention now.

"The girl bites," he said. "Point taken. How sensitive is it, though?"

"Very." She filled him in on the pertinent information.

"You'll forgive me if I ask to see the numbers before I believe you?"

"By all means," she said. Her numbers were the most solid things in her universe, much more reliable than she herself. Truth and precision created by an imprecise human mind—this was one of the paradoxes of experimental science that had attracted her in the first place.

"And the interactions you can measure—how tight do they have to be? I presume only really strong binding will show?"

"Actually, we're measuring low-affinity interactions without much of a problem," she said. "It's all down to the enhanced collection programme."

"You designed that feature, I believe, in your PhD work?"

An oblique compliment, she sensed, accepting that description with a dip of her head.

"Listen, Dr Cyrus—Claire." He sat forward, hands braced spread-fingered on the table. "You've been hired for the new stroke project"— it was clear he thought little of this endeavour—"but Ramon and I have a few niggling questions about Alzheimer's that your machine could probably clear up—*if* what you say is true. Should you find yourself with any spare run-time, I do hope you'll think of us."

"Is that. . ."

"Permitted?" Alan smiled with a cryptic movement of mouth and jaw. "Stanley has probably told you how committed he is to inter-project collaboration. And he is not likely to be bothered about the details. At least, if I were you I wouldn't feel the need to keep him . . . closely informed."

After Alan dismissed her with a clipped, regal gesture, Claire was herded around for the rest of the afternoon to various people in turn. Like Alan, Stanley, and Marjory, nearly all of them were British. Perhaps because the company had started in London, the only Dutch people in evidence were young: technicians and PhD students. None of the lab heads showed any of Ramon's warmth, keeping themselves barricaded behind scientific facts.

Worst of all was Zeke Bannerman, the scientist in charge of the new stroke project. Thankfully he wasn't her manager, but of all the people at NeuroSys, it was with him and his team that she'd be working most closely.

"I see you have absolutely no experience with any aspect of stroke, or even neurological diseases," he said, scowling at her CV—which set the tone for the rest of the brief interview.

Last of all, she was shown to her new laboratory space and abandoned there without even a goodbye from Bannerman's postdoc. The Interactrex 3000 was waiting for her, gleaming pale silver in the afternoon sunlight—an unexpected friend in alien territory.

"God, you're a beauty," she whispered, putting a hand on the machine's heavily redesigned and downsized main panel. "I hardly recognized you. Have you lost weight?"

She dropped into a seat, suddenly worn out. For the first time, she internalized that she was actually here, in the Netherlands, in her first real job. She was a proper scientist at last. In many ways she still felt like an impostor—up until her eighteenth year, she'd been convinced that she was going to become an English professor like her father, and a famous poet if she were lucky. But that hadn't worked out as she'd planned, and here she was. It was too late to go back now.

Looking at the machine, Claire felt a surge of stubborn pride. Together they would visualize proteins joining and parting in their ephemeral embraces, and maybe cure stroke in the process. She didn't need the others to like her—she knew what she had to do.

Chapter 2

꧁

Joshua mounted the broad steps three at a time and passed from the rain into the main reception of NeuroSys.

"*Goeie morgen*, Marta," he said to the Dutch woman on the desk, lost in her *Telegraaf.*

"Good morning, Dr Pelinore." She didn't even look up.

Bitch. Marta knew full well that he spoke fluent Dutch, but it was the same every morning. Their little bilingual power battle had been going on for years, so long that he almost enjoyed it. But he was living for the day she got careless and actually replied in kind.

He smiled to himself as he keyed his way through the turnstiles, nodding at an unfamiliar person coming through on his way out. New students seemed to sprout up every day. The young man looked up at Joshua, startled, then quickly rejigged his expression.

Another familiar situation. Joshua never fully relaxed until he'd made it to the stairwell leading downstairs to the Bioinformatics Department. Nobody ever called it that, though—it had been known as The Pit for as long as anyone could remember.

Two flights down into the subbasement, then along the corridor, awash with muted music growing louder by the step. What was it Zeke Bannerman had said the other day, when he'd come down to ask about Protein Z homologies? *This place is a disgrace, Pelinore.* His tone making it clear exactly where he thought the blame lay. Joshua loathed Bannerman, but he'd kept his polite façade firmly in place. An old tactic from the playgrounds of long ago: no reaction, no emotion; no ammunition for the enemy to exploit.

Opening the door, Joshua registered immediately that something was up.

He shrugged out of the wet jacket and hung it on a peg, trying to work it out. On the surface, it was chaos as usual: music blasting, his team rushing about from terminal to terminal, chattering and laughing as they interacted. But Joshua picked up something additional: the undercurrent of excitement that only urgent gossip can impart.

A foam projectile appeared in his peripheral vision and Joshua ducked just in time: The boss's arrival had been noted. A chorus of morning greetings and hand-raisings, then, and Roz bustling towards him with an unmistakable glint in her eye.

"I'm glad to see you've stopped sulking," Joshua said.

Roz made a face, the glint fizzling out. "It still makes me ill, thinking how many decent arrays we could have bought for the same price as that weird machine. I don't know why you're not more upset."

"And that new girl," Matt said, not looking up from his terminal. "She doesn't exactly inspire confidence, does she?"

"Doesn't look old enough to have a PhD," Roz said.

"And so full of herself," someone else said, further along the row. "Acting as if she was better than everyone else."

"The way you lot were behaving yesterday, you could hardly blame her for being a bit aloof," Joshua said. Then he raised his voice a notch. "Don't you all have work to do?"

Roz elevated a pierced eyebrow at his tone—it was not like him to actually exert his authority.

Joshua sat down at a free terminal and booted it up as Roz perched on the table next to him, purple-fishnet legs crossed.

"Compared to Bannerman's group, we were pretty tame," she said, on the defensive. "And Alan was practically spitting blood."

"If you want to blame anyone, blame Stanley," he said mildly, calling up his morning's task log onto the screen. "He's in charge of the hardware budget."

She sighed. "I know, boss. Listen, forget all that—I've got some news."

"I rather expected you might."

She leaned forward. "I went up to Ramon's lab this morning to talk with Frederica about her new gene, you know, that nightmare one with the 95 introns I was working on last week. And I overheard Klaas and Ramon talking in the office—the door was ajar so I got the gist."

He suppressed a smile. "And?"

"The clinical trial," she said, "it's happening."

Joshua stopped typing and slowly looked up at his head technician.

"In the UK," she went on. "Probably at Addenbrooke's Hospital. Sometime next spring."

"You're sure?

"Positive. The MHRA's representative said that our proposal was top of the independent scientific review's list. We passed the ethical committee as well."

"Your hearing is astounding, Roz." He kept his voice calm—so many years, so much hard work, all leading up to this one moment. "I assume everyone else in the Pit knows?"

She shrugged. "I wasn't going to blab 'til after I told you, but by the time I got down here, it was already old news. Klaas is like the Al Jazeera of NeuroSys."

"I expect we'll get formal notice sometime today."

"Sort of puts the whole Interactrex thing into perspective," she said, sliding off the table. "As much as I hate to admit it."

Joshua had been as against the Interactrex's purchase as any of the other bioinformaticians, but their attitude offended him on principle. It was obviously not the new woman's fault. Nevertheless, he had sensed Roz's surprise when he'd stood up for Claire. Normally, he kept well clear of office politics and allowed his team to rant on against whatever scapegoat happened to be in fashion. In fact, he had turned down a promotion to upper management many years ago precisely to avoid such conflicts. Roz would have figured it out if she hadn't been distracted by her news; after working closely with Joshua for a decade, she knew his ways and quirks better than anyone.

The truth was that he understood only too well what it was like not to fit in. It was bad enough that he'd been born with albino skin. Even though he'd somehow ended up with black hair and brown eyes (a genetic mystery in itself), his appearance still shocked people. But after adolescence, he'd kept growing and growing, only stopping when he'd hit six foot eight. These two seemingly simple physical facts had shaped his entire life and how he interacted with the world.

But he'd found a home of sorts in the Pit, where he was respected as a supervisor and admired as a scientist. The experimental biologists upstairs didn't know much about what went on in the Pit. Only other computer folk could understand the innovative way Joshua blended instinct with hard mathematics to infer biology from DNA code. Camouflaged by so many other misfits—the eccentric and colourful characters drawn for various reasons into the world of bioinformatics—his appearance didn't seem to matter.

✤ ✤ ✤

As people continued to file into the meeting room, the buzz of voices grew steadily louder. The contrast from last week's gathering, row after sullen row punishing Claire Cyrus for her very existence, couldn't be more obvious.

Joshua studied everyone from his usual vantage in the back row, the rest of his department filling up the spaces around him in an unconscious protective shield. He was an astute people-watcher. It had all started when he was a child back on the Yorkshire farm. His family had raised horses, and his father had taught him how to sense internal stress through a palm placed against a warm flank. There were so many tricks: how working out *where* an animal was physically stressed could help you extrapolate what was wrong; how applying pressure on certain muscle groups could calm an animal down; how modulating tone of voice and one's own body language could engender respect and trust. Later, after years of close observation in the stables—far too tall to become a jockey, yet too enamoured to stay away—he didn't even need physical contact to understand what the horses were feeling. Becoming an avid observer of his own species had been the next logical progression.

When he'd told Roz all this, one drunken night down at the Onderwater, she'd howled with laughter and called him the Horse Whisperer.

"Maybe you can work out why Matt is such a fuckwit and sort him out," she'd suggested, wiping the tears from her eyes in a violet mascara smear across her face. Later, though, he'd caught her watching him calm down a hysterical undergraduate intern in about five seconds, and she'd looked thoughtful and never brought it up again.

"Such creatures of habit we are," he said now to Roz on his right.

"How so, boss?"

"Well, we always come first and colonize the back. The labs arrive in clumps and sit in the same general place every time—except the chemists, who pride themselves on their individuality—when they bother to show up at all."

Roz entered the spirit of the game. "The occasional mixing on the fringes..."

"Catalysed by the most social PhD students with friends in other camps." He paused, watching two people battling it out for the last seat in a particular sector and noting who had given way to whom. "Can you spot the key difference between Alan and Ramon's labs?"

"It's so unfair, boss, you've got nearly two feet on me." Roz was the only one who ever teased him about his appearance, something he secretly cherished.

"Ramon always sits in the middle of his group, one of the hoi polloi. But Alan..."

"I never noticed before, but you're right. Too busy licking Stanley's arse in the front row."

"You might want to keep your voice down," Joshua said, watching Alan and Stanley exchanging words, blond and grey heads close together.

"Here comes the new girl," she said, poking him painfully in the ribs. "Where's *she* going to sit?"

Good question. He watched Claire Cyrus pause on the threshold as others jostled around her: Was it his imagination or did the buzz dip a notch at her entrance? She was perfectly expressionless, serene—and this time the serenity went all the way though.

He had watched her with growing interest at the welcome meeting the previous week, standing in front of the group like a virgin sacrifice. He had been fascinated by the contradiction between her surface calm and the subterranean waves of desperation emanating from her, a desperation that no one else in the audience seemed to notice. It had only taken him a few moments to work out what Claire reminded him of: a panicked, feral thing, about to bolt. He had instinctively wanted to lay his hands on her, to probe the root of her fear with veterinary care.

Today she was a different person. Gone was the cheap first-day suit, which her thin frame had worn with the awkwardness of unfamiliarity. Instead, she sported jeans and a crisp black T-shirt, her long black hair brushed down her back, not primly pinned up as before. Despite her composure, there was something fragile about her slimness, as if she were hardly there at all. A good-looking woman, with her delicate features and vaguely Mediterranean skin—though Joshua preferred his women strong and substantial.

After scanning the room, expressionless, Claire walked down the side and took an aisle seat about halfway back, nowhere near anyone's sector.

"I'll bet you ten euros nobody's going to sit next to her," Roz said—not cruelly, but with a scientist's curiosity.

"No thanks—I don't fancy my chances." Joshua was careful not to get drawn into taking Claire's side, this time, though he felt that anger stirring again. "Wait, what's this?"

Ramon was standing up, working his way out of the row as he looked back in Claire's direction.

"I do believe it's the cavalry," Roz said, and they both watched as Ramon walked down the aisle and slipped into the empty seat next to Claire. She turned to speak to him, a small but radiant smile transforming her face. "Good old uncle Ramon—never afraid to go out on a limb to make a point."

Joshua silently disagreed, convinced that kindness was the main inspiration, but then Stanley was standing up, making his way to the podium as the roar trickled away into expectant silence.

"I'll cut straight to the point." Stanley's head protruded from his stiff white collar like a tortoise as he scanned the room over his glasses, partially askew as usual on the end of his pointed nose.

"I rather doubt that," Roz murmured.

"I'm sure you have all heard by now why I have called this meeting. But before we go into details about the trial, I think it's important to put this momentous achievement into *historical* context."

"I'm going to lie back and think of England."

"Roz," Joshua mouthed. "Shut *up*."

"Nearly fifteen years ago," Stanley said, "I was running an established academic research lab in London. Hands raised now, for the benefit of our newer members, those of you who were there with me. Don't be shy."

So few left, Joshua thought as half a dozen arms reached for the ceiling—Ramon and Alan, of course; Verity, Simon, Li-Liang. Curious faces turned around to stare at the back row, some looking surprised to see Joshua's own hand raised. He felt a mixture of pride, irritation and defensiveness, locked behind the placid white mask.

Stanley went on: "My contributions towards understanding neurodegenerative diseases up to that point were solid yet . . . I suppose *uncelebrated* might be the most charitable description. But then Alan and Ramon entered my life. Two new postdocs—young, brash and. . ."

"Virtuoso," Ramon suggested in mock-aside, precipitating a wave of laughter.

"I was going to say *uncontrollable*," Stanley said. "But I am so glad that they stubbornly refused to listen to a word I said." More laughter, sweeping through the room and ramping up the excitement. "Instead, they rolled up their sleeves and produced our first real breakthrough. You all know the tune: a revolutionary theory explaining the pathology behind Alzheimer's disease. The Universal Aggregation Principle, whose mechanism immediately suggested the possibility of intervention."

Joshua had been a new PhD student at the time, and he could still remember the excitement when the *Nature* paper came out—reporters and cameras in the lab for days on end. Two years later, Stanley broke the news: venture capital was available to spin off a company. At that time, in the early Nineties—ancient history by the accelerated scale of the biotechnological age—Stanley's initiative was more than eccentric. It was practically unheard of. The sort of behaviour, people muttered, that one might expect from a *Californian*, not a respectable British professor of hitherto impeccable credentials. Still, Stanley was undeterred, even though the only funding he could secure was from a Dutch multimillionaire, and part of the deal was that the company had to be located in the Netherlands.

"But an obvious intervention," Stanley said, "is a long way from a cure. It has taken all of us, working together, to come to this point. And now, having reached this momentous milestone in our evolution, I would like to thank Mr Herman van de Laan, the founder of our feast, who most graciously rearranged his schedule today to be with us." Stanley bobbed at the white-haired gentleman in the front row, on Alan's other side.

The philanthropist rose slowly to his feet, turning around to acknowledge the applause with magisterial grace before sinking back into his seat. Van de Laan had been eager to avenge his wife's death from Alzheimer's disease, and had offered far more than money; in addition to a new building in a rural village north of The Hague, he pledged exclusive access to a private Alzheimer's hospice whose patients consented to donate their diseased brains to science after their deaths. Then, as in the present day, human tissue was difficult to come by, and Stanley found the offer irresistible: it would give his company a significant edge over the competition.

"In about a year," Stanley said, "NS158 will enter Phase I clinical trials." Another murmur—everyone already knew it, but it made it somehow real to hear it from the CEO's mouth. "To some of you, this may seem like a long time. But in reality, there is so much to prepare.

We need to plan our protocols, assemble a team of clinicians, start enrolling the healthy volunteers. Produce bucket-loads of suitably purified product. The time will fly, I guarantee it, and before you know it, NS158 will be introduced into humans." He paused as his words settled into the silence. "We cannot predict what will happen. We can only hope that our little miracle drug will perform as advertised and come that one step closer to defeating for all time one of our most terrible diseases of old age."

"And if it doesn't. . ." Joshua identified the mocking whisper off to his right as belonging to Matt.

"We're fucked." Roz, in a rare moment of seriousness, had spoken only loud enough for Joshua to hear.

Chapter 3

⚭

Claire fell in love with Amsterdam straight away. The evening after her unfortunate introduction to NeuroSys, she checked into her temporary accommodation, dumped her luggage onto the mildewy carpet and ventured out into the carnival throng of tourists along the streets and canals of De Walletjes. She was transfixed by the women for sale in the windows, at the way their perfect doll-like skin glowed in the violet lighting. They seemed pure compared with the customers scrabbling outside their doors like rats, with the beggars and dealers whispering the universal language of need and oblivion along the piss-scented alleys, with the roaming packs of foreign lads powered along by alcohol and sheer bravado. All of this human drama, back-dropped by a Renaissance-era stage set of unearthly beauty—it was a place of contradictions more suited for poetry than science. *Let murderers, thieves, tyrants, bigots, unclean persons, offer new propositions!*

In this messy, worldly neighbourhood, her distressing day narrowed to a microscopic speck and dispersed in the cool spring breeze funnelling down the canals. Nobody was glaring at her—nobody was paying her the slightest attention. On impulse, she abandoned her plan to find a room in the country village close to NeuroSys and asked a newsagent for Amsterdam rental listings instead. The train ride, after all, had been quick, and at that moment, the idea of living as far from the company as possible was appealing.

She sat in the window seat of a café, sipping a beer, scanning the paper and occasionally looking out at the passing scrum. At one point, a fashionable woman with lustrous blonde hair went by, struggling to push a pram over the uneven cobbles against the current of tourists.

When her stare met Claire's through the glass, it broadcasted scathing dismissal: to the woman, Claire was just another intoxicated foreigner, getting in her way, leaving litter and vomit in the streets and making too much noise under her open window at night. Despite her relative innocence, Claire wanted to exonerate herself: *I'm different. I'm a scientist, looking for cures!* But the woman disappeared into the crowd, none the wiser.

And so in this way Claire arrived at the insight made by thousands of ex-pats before her: these streets huddled around Centraal Station weren't for the Dutch. Real Dutch people flocked to fresh herring and flower stalls, not coffee shops, rode on bicycles with helmetless, white-haired toddlers in purpose-built seats in the front and back, headed home at six for their *stamppot*. Yes, they were tolerant, but tolerance didn't equal approval, and open-mindedness didn't necessarily preclude disdain.

✤ ✤ ✤

A few days later Claire abandoned the tourist hotel for her new flat on the Tweede Jan Steenstraat in De Pijp, a graceful neighbourhood in the Oud Zuid quarter just south of the old city boundaries. On her first Saturday morning, early, she ventured out in a random direction to explore her new environment. The residential neighbourhoods were quiet, the spring air mild, almost liquid. She eventually encountered canals. The streets were sparsely populated, narrow and cobbled, pedestrians relegated to a small corridor between bollards and gaping stairwells leading to subterranean entrances along the house rows. Alien signage chided her with inscrutable ciphers: *Inrit*; *Verboden toegang*; *Hier geen fiets plaatsen.*

On a humped bridge over the Herengracht, a sharp odour drifted across her path: a childhood smell, something familiar but impossible to place. Pausing, she closed her eyes and tried to remember, but the smell had already dispersed—something botanical, some whiff of moss or the wriggling space under a rock. She looked down at the water, where a single green leaf drifted on the surface, slowly inching over her reflection. As it slid under the bridge and out of sight, an insistent command formed in her mind, its tone soft yet challenging. A command from the era of that odour, newly awakened.

Tell me the shape of that leaf.

27

Claire felt a warmth spread over her skin. Her dead father's voice, as clear as if he were speaking inside her head. As clear as if the last six years of failing to remember exactly what he sounded like has never occurred.

Claire's father, Edward Cyrus, had been an English poet, living in isolation in a village on Gran Canaria with his IBM Selectric typewriter and his dreams until Pilar, who ran the local *panadería*, seduced him with one dark look.

When Pilar became pregnant with her first and only child, the couple returned to England to escape the scandalized glares of her large Roman Catholic family. They married and settled in London, where Edward became a lecturer to supplement the meagre income he pulled in from more creative endeavours.

Edward was a gentle man, so his weapon of choice was propaganda by total immersion. From the moment Claire emerged from the drugged, milky world of babyhood, he started reading to her. Not children's books, much to Pilar's dismay, but essays, articles, stories, plays, novels, histories, and above all, poetry, the words bombarding her during the boundary of non-comprehension and easing her into linguistic awareness. Whereas Spanish became the tongue of corporeal comfort—food, sleep, song and mother love—English took over as the language of the imagination.

She began to read a full year earlier than most other children, her head full of a cast of millions, sets and costumes swishing on and off in a colourful parade. She disdained, with the stubbornness of a self-righteous toddler, the stale medium of television, which regimented what things and people should look like and could not tell you what the characters were thinking. But though she loved stories, reading poetry, and eventually writing it, became a father-worshipping obsession that would persist into her late teens.

It was Edward's wish that his daughter end up in a profession involving the art of words. And though he fought nobly, she surprised everyone, including herself, with a last-minute swerve into the sciences at University, falling back on biology and maths courses she'd done to stretch herself at school.

Claire didn't remember when her father had first started playing the game with her. It was something she had always known, like language itself. It invariably happened when they were taking one of their walks, and one unspoken rule was that they never played it when her mother was around. The game, Claire had grasped quite early on, made *Mamá* unhappy. Or angry. Claire couldn't tell which, because both states could produce the same heavy lines across her brow, heralding a storm that no right-minded person would want to evoke.

When the three of them walked, her mother would do most of the talking, with Claire, in Spanish, about things that she liked talking about: what to prepare for dinner; tasks that needed doing around the house; how awful the weather or how boorish her husband's latest new friend. Words that didn't require much of an answer, or certainly any imagination. Her father would be far away—no doubt, Claire would speculate resentfully, playing the game in his own head without her.

The child Claire loved her mother, but it was somehow always *easier* when she wasn't around.

❦ ❦ ❦

The game was always initiated by her father in the imperative mood.

"Tell me the colour of the parked car we just passed—eyes forward, young lady, no cheating."

Claire would have been in a state of high preparedness, already soaking up her surroundings in anticipation. She was always surprised by how tiring it was just to *see*—to see everything. So much of life flowed past unnoticed. But observation, her father was fond of saying, was the poet's best friend, and she was determined to be the best possible assistant.

"It was red," she might say.

"That's right. Now tell me three other ways to describe the colour red."

This was more difficult. Their strides would match in silence for a few moments, her legs stretching further than was natural, his more restricted, each unconsciously compensating for the other. Nearly twenty years later she could still call up her canvas shoes placed onto the pavement next to his brown leather ones: scuffed and repaired indefinitely by the cobbler.

"Crimson?"

Crimson was a written-down word, not really in the *vernacular*, but these were admissible.

"A bit on the orangey side, but we'll let it pass," her father might say charitably. "What else?"

"Ruby?"

"Well, yes . . . but how about something original now?"

Original meant something that she hadn't read, or heard her father or his friends say when they came round for dinner with their laughter and cigarette smoke. *Redness* would flicker past her eyes—the scrape on a knee, the shower of petals when her mother would bin spent dog roses, the velvety feel of her grandmother's curtains. And from these images, she would struggle to concoct something: not just a word, but a description. Her father liked descriptions best of all: *Berry-stained. Bruised. Blushed.*

If her father swept her up in his arms and tickled her until she squealed, she knew an answer had been original enough. She could still see him, his upturned face below her as he swung her around, winter sun glancing off his freckled skin, with its wonderful configurations: the slight cant of his regal nose, broken from a youthful motorcycle accident in the South of France; the haze of blondish stubble on his angular chin and cheekbones; the generous smile from well-formed lips; the translucent blue of his eyes, squinting then with good humour, but equally dramatic when doused in melancholy; the cherubic hair, nondescript of colour but fantastic with wild, loose curls that one could grab in great soft fistfuls. (*Nondescript* was a word that annoyed him: *No such thing, my darling: it's a shortcut for the lazy wordsmith.*)

He cuts a dashing figure, she had overheard one of her father's female friends confide, the woman who always sat closest to her father during the parties. Edward's friends spoke as if the child Claire was not there, reading calmly at their feet, as if she were a shadow, a stone, an insensate cat. Claire-the-invisible heard all sorts of interesting things. The woman had used a tone of voice Claire had already learned to identify as *ironic*. *Dashing*, though not *original*, was appropriate, though, with his bronze-coloured silk scarf, with his long black coat flying behind him, like the boy on the cover of *The Little Prince*, never mind that there was always a button missing or the lining was ripped and mended, bearing a thousand stitches from the point of Pilar's long-suffering needle. *Stitches*, she used to murmur with irritation to Claire in Spanish, that would soon outweigh the original fabric, no?

On that Saturday morning in Amsterdam, nearly May, seventeen years later, the wall had somehow come down. Claire could finally see her father again, and hear him, feel the dizzy sensation of being whirled about.

But one couldn't pause to enjoy the sensation; one had to be alert, because more imperatives were to follow:

Describe that tree. What is its essence?

Now imagine how it would look in the sunlight and describe it. Now at night . . . no, Clair de Lune, you can't see colours in the dark, remember?

. How would it look underwater? Yes, trees can so be underwater . . . what if there was a great flood and we all drowned? The tree would still be there, and would still look like something.

What would that fence feel like if you were blind?

What would those church bell peals feel like if you were deaf?

Make something beautiful sound ugly.

Make something ugly sound beautiful.

Claire didn't know it, but these exercises had done far more than hone her linguistic skills: they had also released in her some ability to see the truth about objects or people that no one else seemed to notice.

And so the new immigrant wandered the streets of Amsterdam with her father's voice, so long dormant, newly awakened in her head. There was something about the enveloping feel of the air that made her want to weep.

Those canal houses, now, leaning forward at that crazy angle. Tell me a simile for how they lean.

Claire had been disappointed to learn that the tall, skinny houses were purposely canted to facilitate the winching of possessions through the windows during a move. She had found more charm in the thought that the ancient structures were sagging in their foundations, listing like bewildered widows at a funeral.

That's a very nice simile, Clair de Lune, I might buy it off you. How much are you charging today?

But this wasn't Venice—blowsy, neglected, sinking into decrepitude. This was Amsterdam, where the Dutch seldom let things take their natural course.

The further she walked, the more quiet and beautiful the canal neighbourhoods became.

Aren't those elms magnificent? And the way their seeds are falling? Describe them.

The canals were lined with the great trees, which the Dutch prized more for the shoring-up properties of their roots than for aesthetics. Their branches were misted with new leaves, forming a mosaic against the blue of the sky, and that particular week, they were shedding winged seeds in profusion. The coppery translucent disks fluttered in the wind, clogged the canals, heaped up against kerbs and buildings like drifts of snow. Somehow, the elms with their false-autumn charade made her urge to weep even stronger.

"And gathering freshlier overhead/ Rocked the full-foliaged elms..."

(Her father had been fond of belting out Tennyson in public, a habit that had delighted his young daughter, mortified his wife and heartily confused or frightened passing pedestrians.)

The radial streets of the Western Canal Ring were cobbled together with bars, *eetcafes* and quirky boutiques selling second-hand clothing more expensive than their new counterparts, or devoted to a sole eccentricity: artistic toothbrushes, say, or dried flowers. Or vast wheels of cheese, stacked in the window and out on the pavement with dusty red or yellow wax rinds, stamped with words: *Edam, Gouda, Leerdam, Maasland.* Names that were cheeses everywhere else, but places here.

God, Claire, the smell of this shop! What is its essence? Essence of well-lov'd running shoe, that's what!

There was always the next corner, the next curve, just beyond. Amsterdam could go on forever—not outward, but infinitely subdividing, folding in on itself with fractal abandon.

Chapter 4

❧

Once Claire's father had returned to haunt her, his voice was never far away. He even followed her off the streets of Amsterdam and took residence in her den at NeuroSys, quoting poetry in her ear and generally made a nuisance of himself as she tried to concentrate on work.

Claire was an insomniac, so the occasional all-night sessions with the Raison that her experiments demanded were not as difficult as she'd expected. She appropriated an old armchair from the common room, wedged it into an awkward position behind the door and took to napping there during experimental lulls. On those occasions when she did make it home, she left for work before dawn anyway, a habit formed years ago in Liverpool when a failing relationship made her feel like a stranger in her own flat. Somehow, this routine persisted long after the young man in question had fled.

She would lock the door behind her every morning around five, cycling through the empty city to Centraal Station. On windy mornings, the hanging street lamps would swing back and forth, scattering pendulous shadows; traffic lights would blink off-duty amber and the gusts would thrum harmonics in the tram wires. On still mornings the city lights floated in perfect reflection on canal surfaces. Sometimes the stars would arch overhead, summer constellations in the winter morning, and when her eyes watered in the cold, the pale points of light would blur like a late Van Gogh.

The feeling of pleasure ended at the station, where she would slip past junkies, drug dealers and *daklozen*—the "roofless"—all drawn by the gods of shelter and spare change to this unlikely cathedral. Never make eye contact, a guidebook had advised, lest you be mistaken for a customer, and Claire observed the rule almost superstitiously, fantasizing about being erroneously *chosen* and dragged under by some lazy-lidded pusher slouched against a yellow ticket machine.

On to the night train, then, full of glam-clad flagging ravers dozing home towards suburbia from clubs or after-hours venues, clashing with the erect perfection of flight attendants in KLM blue on the way to Schiphol Airport. And in amongst them sat strange commuter Claire, lost in a battered book of Shelley or Skelton, Holub or O'Heaney.

Next stop: the dark provincial platform, air full of hyacinths in the spring, manure in the summer and rain in the autumn and winter. The glam-clad ravers would slump off in various directions, sparkling faintly under the station lights, while Claire found her second bicycle locked in triplicate to a lamp-post. The ride to the industrial park was a brisk thirty minutes of skimming past sleeping swans moored in canals, the cube of NeuroSys looming on the horizon.

An hour and a half, door to door. Living in Amsterdam, another strike of oddity against her when she could so easily have rented a flat in the village like everyone else.

On the first day of her second week, Claire made her way through the deserted, pre-dawn building. The patrolling night-shift security gorillas, thank goodness, had finally stopped challenging her. She keyed her way into the lab, flipping on the lights to reveal the brooding beast: dormant but purring almost imperceptibly in standby mode.

"It's all your fault," Claire reminded the Interactrex as she switched on its main power. "I'm only here because of you."

It chirped back, unrepentant: the server starting its lengthy boot-up process.

After donning a pair of gloves, she took a few plastic dishes from the incubator and looked down the microscope at the cells she'd seeded before the weekend.

"They look good," she called over to the Raison. "You ready for breakfast?"

Right on cue, the Interactrex's air filters began their self-cleansing routine, the flow of bubbles gurgling deep inside its main module.

Talking to herself already, Claire thought. Not good.

She put one of the plastic dishes under the Raison's main microscope lens, sat down and flicked on the computer screen. After a twiddling of the focus knob, faintly warm and smooth against her fingertips, the mouse brain cells appeared on the screen, gossamer forms scattered across the clear surface of the plastic dish—dark-dwelling entities that were never meant to have been exposed to the light of day. A trick of the optics made them glow with their own internal illumination, margins shimmering in white-hot lines. They looked like mutant starfish, with a round middle and a wild sunburst of too many spindly arms stretching outward. Or fireworks, in the act of exploding.

Bright star, would I were steadfast as thou art/ Not in lone splendour hung aloft the night.

Claire could still remember the first time she saw living cells under the microscope, in her introductory undergraduate biology practical. Textbook photos had not prepared her for the reality. How could this strange carpet of luminous bubble-wrap equate to the smooth surface of someone's skin, or the curve of a heart or the cornea of an eye? It was as if she'd walked on the featureless expanse of the beach for years before bothering to kneel down and notice that the sand was actually a chaotic mix of impossibly tiny rocks and shells and bits of organic matter, as rugged as a boulder scree to an insect struggling across it. It was this miracle of *scale* that had grabbed her by both shoulders, shaken the sense out of her and made her fall in love with biology. With the vast and unknowable beauty of life, if she was honest. Corny and romantic, perhaps, but she didn't care.

Further practical work with the cells in the classroom lab had only increased her zeal. It was like presiding over an orphanage of helpless babies that split into two once every eighteen hours. You had to feed them pink fluid, remove their wastes and put them in a new plastic dish when they outgrew their old one. You had to keep them warm in the incubator and, if you neglected them, they drew in their outstretched baby arms, shrunk to tiny bright balls and died. Those classroom cells were a strain that had been growing for more than fifty years, derived from the tumour of a woman who'd died before her parents had been born. *Immortalized*, the professor had called them. Miraculous, more like.

Not taking her eyes off the mouse cells, Claire manipulated the joystick until a needle appeared in the corner of the screen. She chose a cell and began to stalk it, moving closer and closer until—*zap!* She hit the collection button and the needle harpooned into the cell, pierced its membrane and sucked up a tiny sample of the fluid inside. The cell, unconcerned with this invasion, sealed up as if nothing had happened.

An invisible droplet, a billionth of the size of one raindrop but packed, Claire knew, with hundreds of proteins. Proteins, another miracle of scale, as small to a cell as a cell was to a person, invisible Legos which, in intricate, infinite combinations, seemed to be able to construct absolutely anything: a claw, a hair, a toenail, a leaf, an ear of corn, a blue whale. Proteins, which were currently streaming through the Raison's hungry gullet, transported from needle through tubing into the main routing area, whizzing around tight curves and loop-de-looping on a wild roller-coaster ride. The Interactrex was designed to find pairs of proteins, to shunt these up for identification while letting the solo proteins go by. It was able to make the decision—*shunt pairs or discards solos*—in a fraction of a second. Before Maxwell's invention, this sort of analysis could have taken a seasoned biochemist months—missing many of the most fleeting pairings in the process.

Almost everything that happened in the human body involved, at some moment or another, the pairing and communication of proteins. Including the body gone wrong: disease. With the optimism of youth, Claire felt it was only a matter of time before the protein pairings of stroke disease gave up their secrets to the Raison's hungry innards.

It had been a strange time to arrive, just a week before the Zapper's clinical trial was announced. She felt detached from the excitement—it was so clear this triumph had nothing to do with her and, in the meantime, who else cared about stroke with Alzheimer's at the top of the company's agenda?

Claire had spent her first week getting used to the Raison's sleek new controls and practicing on the cultured mouse cells. Getting in early made it easy for her to circumvent the morning coffee routine, which in turn somehow exempted her from the subsequent social obligations. The Raison's demands and frequent breakdowns were a good enough reason to avoid the canteen for lunch, to dribble sandwich crumbs over the keyboard on her own—to stay holed up in her lab most of the day, as it turned out. She'd been assigned a proper desk down the corridor with the others, but had never once sat there; instead, her papers, files and laptop were stacked in a cramped corner and she used the window ledge as a bookshelf.

Claire was the sort of person who enjoyed solitude, sometimes craving it as others longed for companionship, but she'd never before been so isolated. Even after her parents had died, six years previously, there had at least been friends, neighbours, colleagues, minor relatives. But there was something about NeuroSys that made her wary of interaction—not just the company and the people, but the conspicuous way she had first landed amongst them, like a parachutist hopelessly tangled in trees. Aside from a few curt experimental suggestions from Zeke Bannerman's postdoc (a hard-faced Frenchman who would never quite meet her eye), she found herself going the entire week without speaking more than a few words to anyone, so by the time her second Friday rolled around, the ringing of her mobile felt like a message from outer space.

"Maxwell!" Claire tapped the glissando that would put the Raison on standby, phone wedged between ear and shoulder. "It's so good to hear from you."

"How's our baby performing, love? I still can't say the word 'Inter-actrex' with a straight face—sounds like a particularly kinky mistress of bondage."

"She's OK . . . a bit tempestuous still."

"You'll tame her eventually. And how's corporate life treating you?"

"Not so great, to be honest."

"Why, what's happened?"

"Almost everybody hates me, guv."

"Don't be daft."

"It's true. Nobody wanted me to come in the first place."

"Are you making an effort to win them over?"

The line hissed faintly, parcels of empty information crisscrossing the North Sea.

"I'm completely out of my depth," she said at last. "I'm meant to work on stroke disorders, and I haven't the faintest idea about it."

"So do some reading, make yourself an expert." He paused, and she could imagine his gruff, sympathetic expression. "It's normal to feel overwhelmed in your first postdoc position, love. You were at the top of your game here, and now you're starting from the very bottom in a strange new environment. It's bound to take time for you to settle in."

"How can you be so sure I ever will?"

She imagined his sea anemone fingers, rippling thoughtfully against the surface of his messy desk.

"I remember a certain scared rabbit creeping into my office a bit more than four years ago," he finally said. "Fresh from Uni, just moved up North, some of the natives not terribly friendly. And look how much she developed, how bold and self-assured she turned out to be underneath that shyness. Look what marvellous things she achieved."

After he hung up, Claire decided she owed it to him to be patient.

❦ ❦ ❦

Claire soon opened up her laptop with the intention of downloading all the papers that the company had published on stroke diseases. Five minutes of searching the public databases brought her to a dead end—there weren't any. The work was either too preliminary to publish, or too shrouded in corporate secrecy.

What she really should have done next was to look up the most recent papers published by other labs on the biochemistry of stroke diseases, to give herself the edge that only wide knowledge can impart. Instead, she got distracted by a review article about Alzheimer's disease.

Nearly thirty million people worldwide, she read, suffered from dementia, and this was caused by Alzheimer's in more than half of all cases. So-called 'senile plaques' showed up on scans many years before people started to slide away, dark lesions stamped across the brain in ominous foreshadowing. The plaques were made up of a protein called amyloid beta—an imposing word, Claire thought, appropriately sinister. *Attack of the Amyloids—in full Technicolour.* A normal protein gone rogue, scrambled together like an egg and coating the brain in nonsensical gunk.

The review article referred to 'seminal research' first published by Fallengale *et al.*—Alan, she realized, and colleagues. Studying the bibliography, she looked up the list of articles that Alan and Ramon had published on Alzheimer's over the years, eventually tapping her way through the crucial experiments that had revealed the Universal Aggregation Principle. Such a simple idea: a common way that proteins involved in human senility diseases stuck together to form those plaques. A beautiful idea that had eventually given birth to the Zapper. An idea, in short, that might end up curing Alzheimer's. What must it feel like to be the originator of such a powerful discovery?

"This is so cool," Claire said wistfully, inspecting yet another graph on the screen.

The Raison's standby light caught her eye with a petulant blink.

"I know," Claire replied. "And ten times more suited to your talents than boring old stroke." Nobody was ever going to respect her unless she came up with some interesting experimental results. But interesting meant Alzheimer's—which was strictly off-limits.

Or was it? At that moment Claire remembered Alan Fallengale's suggestion of an illicit collaboration. The problem was, she had no idea how to go about it practically. No doubt he expected her to come up with some brilliant idea for how the Interactrex could be used to learn more about Alzheimer's and bring it to his attention. But despite having spent more than an hour reading up on the topic, her mind was, as usual, a blank canvas.

This was ridiculous. Alan wanted her help, and someone that arrogant wasn't likely to want to take her advice anyway. What she really needed to do was just go upstairs and ask him straight out if he was still interested, let him take the lead. But her memories of the intensity of his patronizing scorn at their first meeting still burnt like a scalded finger.

Yet everything was wanting that might give/ Courage to them who looked for good by light/ Of rational Experience.

"That's easy for you to say, Dad," Claire said. "You're dead."

Resolute, she went up the stairs to the Home of the Zapper. But just before she reached the door to Alan's office, she was alerted by angry voices and stopped herself just in time.

"—impossible now. We're stuck with it—and *her*." Alan, unmistakably.

"You shouldn't be so bloody-minded, *hombre*." This from Ramon, his reasonable tone only thinly covering a core of irritation. "I can't believe how impatient and intolerant you're getting in your old age."

"If we'd bought those arrays, we'd have the answer by now. Instead, that . . . unreliable *machine* is propping up Bannerman—for all the good it will do. You mark my words, the whole venture will be one big, money-sucking black hole that won't make a blind bit of difference."

Alan, she realized, was talking about *her*. Her and the Raison. He didn't want her help—he didn't believe it was worth it. The offer had just been a pleasantry, a game. She turned and sped back the way she'd come, only just picking up Ramon's rejoinder as she sped out of range:

"*Por Favor!* How on earth do you expect a biotech company to survive with just one drug? We'll be dead in five years if we don't diversify into. . ."

Back in her lab, seething with humiliation, she regarded the Raison, placid and patient before her. She'd come up with a brilliant idea, then show them all what her money-sucking black hole could really do.

Chapter 5

&

The complex waterways of Amsterdam, threading through the city in interlocking skeins, were partly to blame for its aura of infinity. In particular, it's the concentric semicircular nature of the canals that throws off the wanderer, semicircles pierced at irregular intervals with radial canals and roads like the spokes of a wheel. Walking along these subtle curves, south can eventually become north—reality can do a surreptitious one-eighty.

The canals didn't fool everyone. The natives, of course, felt the curvature in their blood. And Joshua Pelinore, after ten years of living in Amsterdam, had absorbed the city's layout by herd immunity. He co-owned a motorboat, and moorage rights, with five of his Dutch friends. On hot summer nights, the dark arteries of the town would whisper with hundreds of boats, slipping under lit bridges in the ancient centre or braving the choppier waters of the Amstel or the depths of the IJ: lovers, families with children, elderly spinsters swapping gossip, stag parties, groups of young people in satin frocks and dinner jackets drinking champagne on their way to the opera. Joshua once saw a boat containing a plush striped sofa and Tiffany lamp, its four occupants lounging around swigging Heineken as if in front of an invisible television.

"That's an installation," his girlfriend Hanneke had said of the sofa loungers as she reached over him to help herself to more strawberries, the boat rocking gently in response. "I read about it in the *Volkskrant*."

"Art," his friend Marco clarified, at Joshua's bemused expression. "I heard they got a two thousand euro grant from the government."

"Two thousand *euros*? To boat around on a sofa looking like idiots?" Joshua adjusted the rudder slightly to allow a passing group of picnickers more room. Across the gleaming skin of the Amstel on the opposite bank, the Saturday market at Waterlooplein was in full swing, music spilling out over the stalls.

"Laugh all you want, *jongen*," Marco said, grin expansive in his sensible, sunburnt face. "It's a pretty clever way to get a free boat. Comfortable too, by the looks of it."

Joshua had met Marco, Hanneke and all his other Dutch friends through the rowing club. His extraordinary height made him an excellent addition, and he'd been welcomed into the club eagerly, eight years previously, in a way that he had seldom been welcomed anywhere. The feeling of belonging was so strong that Joshua didn't mind the sacrifice of having to be on the water by 6 a.m. nearly every day of the week.

After the initial discomfort of quitting his warm bed, there was nothing quite like the joy he experienced in those early morning trainings before work, skimming across the water in perfect muscular communion with the other seven men. Hanneke would call out rhythmic encouragement from her cox position in back, her clear voice carrying far up- and downriver, mingling with other voices from other boats. Wind, water, reflection, birds, bridges: Joshua didn't have to be anyone or think about anything except the push-pull of the oars. He wasn't too tall; he wasn't too pale; he was just part of a larger organism, subsumed into the whole. The water, beneath him, was a surface that spread through the entire city in a watery web, connecting everything with everything else, and by extension, his own body with that of the city.

🌿 🌿 🌿

Gone native.

Joshua knew what the people at NeuroSys said about him, especially his longer-term colleagues. And he had to admit the description wasn't far off. Foreign languages came naturally to him; thanks to an attentive tutor in childhood, he already spoke several, and after a few years he was able to pull off the sounds of his adopted country without a trace of accent. Even his Dutch friends, normally grudging of compliment, had to admit as much. Eventually, Joshua began to dream and think in Dutch. Yet he maintained the ability to stand outside the language, too—when he was in a certain mood, he amused himself by mentally translating Dutch, real time, into the glorious Shakespearean overtones that its scrambled syntax and archaic vocabulary so resembled.

A typical morning exchange might go like this:

Conducteur: "Tickets, my lord?"

Joshua (showing his pass): "If you please, my lady."

Conducteur: "Hearty thanks. Know you not that it on the verge of expiry be?"

Joshua: "Alas, my lady, I know it well."

It had not always been so easy for him, though. After Stanley's lab migrated from London to the Netherlands, his expatriate euphoria had soon deflated, as it did for so many others. Looking back, he thought the painful process of settling into a new culture must be similar to what happened after ice ages and meteor impacts: lots of things died, but new things took their places. Just as with the language, his cultural awareness was so finely balanced that he could see both the before and after: the inexplicability of Dutch culture from an ex-pat's perspective, co-existing alongside his insider's view of the complicated society he had eventually infiltrated. He understood well why his British colleagues were frustrated as they struggled to understand the ways of these amiable giants: why were they incapable of queuing? Why didn't they let old ladies off the train first or give up their seats on the bus? Why, after having arrived across the North Sea with the idea that the Netherlands was a free-wheeling and hedonistic country, did they find themselves slamming into a wall of deep Calvinistic conservatism?

Instead of struggling through, most gave up, allowing the British enclave of NeuroSys to close ranks around them. Attempts to learn the language or to penetrate the protective, close-knit society by making Dutch friends were quietly abandoned. But Joshua had escaped the fate of his colleagues. Pushing his way through to the next stage, he'd achieved an understanding with his environment.

Perhaps the reason was superficial: ostracized all his life for his height, was it any wonder that he felt drawn to one of the tallest races on the planet; that among them, he could find the solace that conforming can bring?

Joshua enjoyed his job. Although he was a department head, nobody Above Stairs (as the Pit referred to the rest of the company) bothered him with any of the corporate decisions, which was just as he liked it. His managerial tasks were limited to making sure his kids took fair turns making the tea and microwave popcorn, that people were reasonably sober on a Monday morning and that none of the friendly rows spilled over into anything that would harm the atmosphere of the group. Probably because he seldom told anyone what to do, his occasional commands were heeded with remarkable alacrity. And when bums needed kicking, Roz was only too happy to do the dirty work.

Joshua's feel for the patterns of DNA code, meanwhile, was as instinctive as his affinity for the moods of living creatures, and just as difficult to explain. Coincidentally, people in his profession were often called 'gene jockeys'. The Gene Whisperer—definitely not a moniker to share with Roz, or he'd never hear the end of it.

He'd started out as a biochemist like everyone else in Stanley's London lab, but it wasn't long before the intricacies of bioinformatics had sucked him in. He had always been strong in mathematics and statistics, and had done a few evening courses in computer programming during the first year of his PhD. Unlike biochemistry, which seemed to be mostly like cooking—mashing up cells, boiling them, baking them, nuking them with radioactive isotopes and messy dyes and stains—bioinformatics was clean, pure, virtual and infinitely untapped. It all lay before him, back then, like a vast Rosetta Stone: the Human Genome Project launched only a few years before, data already starting to pour in. There suddenly weren't enough gene jockeys to go around, and Stanley had been more than happy to support Joshua's new obsession.

If you knew what you were doing, Joshua discovered, you could find out more about a protein in an hour by studying its code than by mashing it up twenty-five different ways over the course of a week. While Alan, Ramon and the others slaved away all night, floating white-faced down the morning corridors clutching paper cups of bitter coffee and squinting against the light like troglodytes, Joshua would work civilized hours in the sunny computer nook next door to the lab, spinning out reams of code from the printer and trying to get most of his work done before 3 p.m., when researchers in the US would come online and slow down all the genomics servers. Then home to a decent meal. Scientific research, for Joshua, wasn't an all-night slog of manual labour; it was like sinking into a good novel with a glass of brandy.

Yes, the Universal Aggregation Principle had been solved by a triumph of biochemical tricks, but Joshua's algorithms had guided their ideas and given hints that would never have occurred to the others. Joshua didn't begrudge Alan and Ramon the glory, but he sometimes wished they had at least acknowledged his contributions to the television cameras.

"Your name is on the fucking paper," Alan had retorted, eleven years ago when Joshua confronted him after the big news report. "And you can thank Stanley for that—I was outvoted."

So the 'real' scientists worked all night and made headlines, but it was Joshua who had become the troglodyte, down in the Pit with the other nameless, faceless gene jockeys.

Chapter 6

❧

Although Claire's social situation at NeuroSys remained unchanged, she soon reached an equilibrium of sorts. The Raison still threw spectacular fits, but she was getting better at dealing with the machine. And the experiments were finally starting to work. She found being an expert at something so much more gratifying than her lowly PhD student experience. The Raison wasn't some prototype, cobbled together with gaffer tape and aluminium foil into a massive rattling *thing* that the rest of the department laughed at behind her back. It was a gleaming, state-of-the-art machine, and the whole world was watching its first paces to see how it fared.

Still let my tyrants know, I am not doom'd to wear/ Year after year in gloom and desolate despair.

She liked presenting her results to the stroke team at the weekly meetings. Even though they remained cool, Claire's work was obviously so helpful that it was clear that they needed her, even if they didn't like her. And the best part was that she didn't have to think of any revolutionary new approaches. Dr Bannerman told her (with his characteristic self-important tone) what the company had decided to do next, and within that framework, Claire would make it happen. She didn't have to innovate, only creatively realize.

After the meetings, Claire would give instructions to her Dutch technician, Marieke, a capable older woman who, presented with only a rough sketch of what Claire needed, could fill in the gaps independently—rather like what Claire did with Bannerman's briefs, but to a simpler, less creative and more technical scale. Maxwell had been right; there were different sorts of scientists, from visionary Darwins (like Alan and Ramon) to people like Claire, all the way down to the Mariekes of the world and every shade in between. In the scientific community, everyone had their value.

Claire would have liked to know Marieke better. She was direct and friendly and didn't seem to hold anything against Claire—the political intrigues apparently took place at a higher level. But Marieke needed to do all her work in a wet lab one floor up, so the two women hardly saw one another. Besides, from the few clues she'd managed to pick up, Claire sensed that Marieke's social life, like that of most of the Dutch people in the company, revolved entirely around family and friends outside. Which left only the others.

Are you making an effort to win them over?

A different voice this time, Maxwell's.

She had tried several times to chat to Ramon in the corridors, but though he was friendly on those occasions, she'd never get more than a few words in before someone would rush up with a sheaf of printouts, demanding his attention, and he'd throw her an apologetic look before allowing himself to be dragged off. And that was downright approachable compared to everyone else.

It was too late; she was officially a loner. The stand-off had completely congealed.

✤ ✤ ✤

Just when Claire thought she couldn't bear one more second of solitude, someone dropped down next to her on the sofa like a radiant dark angel.

This someone was a woman, a few years older than Claire and dressed in well-cut black clothing: velvet trousers, silk blouse, pointed boots. She wore striking jewellery: a few wiry bracelets, blunt-cut stones on her earlobes, her swept-up hair pinned carelessly with antique silver pins. She gave off a faint pleasant smell, too, like expensive powder.

Claire absorbed all this in one shy sideways glance before refocusing on the party, dancers moving in an affable crush. She didn't know a soul, not even the host, whose number had been provided by the friend of a friend back in Liverpool and resorted to only in desperation. She wouldn't have bothered if she'd realized it would make her feel even lonelier than if she'd stayed home. Although with such an odd assortment of guests—ex-pats and natives lumped together and interacting in interesting ways—she had to admit that the people-watching wasn't bad.

"You were smiling to yourself, just before I sat down," her new neighbour observed suddenly, in a well-bred English accent.

Claire glanced over again in surprise. The woman's shadowy eyes seemed wisely amused.

"It's this herding instinct," Claire replied. "The Dutch guests, I mean. They'd been sitting in the far corner all evening, keeping to their own. But as soon as one of them decided to dance, suddenly they all were."

The woman smiled. "Like wildebeests to the waterhole. Are you an observer of the human condition?"

"I am tonight," Claire said. "Normally I specialize in inanimate objects, but I've run out of material, and I don't know anyone here."

"You do now." The woman held out her hand. "Rachel May, graphic designer and professional party crasher. What do you make of me, then?"

Describe this woman. What is her essence?

Claire shook Rachel's hand, feeling the smooth curves of rings pressing into her flesh.

"You're out of my league," Claire said.

Rachel started to laugh, a liquid peeling that intensified when Claire introduced herself with the tag description of *ex-poet scientist misfit*.

"This party is dire," Rachel said. "Let me buy you a drink somewhere more lively."

❦ ❦ ❦

Claire and Rachel became friends with surprising ease—surprising to Claire, that is. She often wondered what it was about herself that Rachel liked. As a central player in Amsterdam's English-speaking ex-pat scene, Rachel had her pick of companions. It wasn't possible to go anywhere in town without running into crowds of her admirers—not down the strip of trendy bars along the Nieuwezijds Voorburgwal, not in the smoky candlelit cafés of De Pijp, not in the obscure clubs sprinkled among the islands northeast of Centraal Station. Claire couldn't keep track of these Toms and Damiens, these Julias and Annas, a loose community of artists and actors, administrators and accountants, publishers and petroleum salesmen, united only by the arbitrariness of language.

Many of Rachel's friends were fellow graphic designers. An odd folk, Claire found: relentlessly curious; tactile. When Claire brought Rachel's birthday present along to the usual Friday night bar session at the Blauwe Vogeltje, a set of jade-coloured Japanese cups and saucers, the assemblage spent more time admiring and exclaiming over the cunning construction of cardboard box than the actual gift inside. Everyone wanted to *touch*: the box, the glazing on the porcelain, the way the bottom of a cup was engineered to dock onto its saucer. Things were passed around the table, opened and closed, docked and undocked, murmured over.

This gave Claire a belated explanation for Rachel's own behaviour. When the two women had coffee together, Rachel was subconsciously restless: feeling the tabletop with the pads of her fingers, weighing the cutlery, eyeing the logos on sugar packets, silently critiquing the layout of the menu, all without losing track of the flow of conversation. Claire was not certain that Rachel even realized she was doing it. Maybe, Claire thought, Rachel filtered the world through crafted objects just as Claire did so through words.

❧ ❧ ❧

Rachel's company was like a magic key into the heart of Amsterdam. They attended outdoor concerts in the Vondelpark and evening exhibitions in Nieuwe Spiegelstraat; they went dancing in clubs with strict and enigmatic door policies that Rachel never failed to negotiate. They regularly frequented a *bruin café* in the Jordaan where a Frank Sinatra impersonator, locally famous in those days, wowed the mostly Dutch, middle-aged female crowd with his crooning. And on Queensday, when the entire city donned orange, drank from green cans of Heineken and danced in the streets, Rachel lent Claire an outrageous silver lame frock and white feather boa and told her that they had less pedestrian things to do.

"Literally, darling."

"Where are we off to?"

"It's a surprise, but I promise you'll love it. Let me do your face first—with such lovely bone structure, it's a crime you're such a tomboy."

Rachel's surprise turned out to be an exclusive party boat presided over by a flamboyant DJ. Losing her friend just seconds after boarding, Claire took up a position near the prow as they embarked from a pier on the Browersgracht, taking it all in. The waterways were jammed with craft of all sizes. Never very strict with safety on normal occasions, the Dutch seemed to have gone mad, completely abandoning the rules of

49

right-of-way in honour of the monarchy. Claire watched nervously as boats cut one another off and collided with good-natured shouts and insults. The shores were lined with people—millions, it seemed, a blur of orange, pockets of music thumping from every intersection. On their own boat, people danced on the roof, stowaways joined their party from other boats and a chain of smaller craft tagged behind to enjoy the music. Inevitably, drunken revellers fell into the water and had to be fished out. Whenever a low bridge loomed, warning shouts would resound and the roof dancers would flatten themselves, the bridge under-belly calcified and dripping as it whizzed over just inches above.

"There you are—have you seen that beautiful man in the pirate costume?" Rachel joined her, looking sleek in a midnight-black dress fashioned entirely of feathers. Claire had noticed many men, back on the pier, giving the pair a second glance. "Shall we flip a eurocent over him?"

"Not my type," Claire said. "Besides, his hat clashes with his parrot."

Claire didn't like to admit it, but she was enjoying how it felt to be admired in the silver dress. She found Rachel's confidence in her own femininity enlightening too. Rachel was the sort who walked around her flat in bra and underpants with the curtains open, not caring who might see. She even cooked half-dressed, glass of rosé in one hand, tossing in fresh rosemary, basil, chilli peppers, crushed garlic. And she was an ardent gossip, drawing Claire into the world of men she sparred with like a hardened military general.

Why had Rachel taken her in? Perhaps she enjoyed having a real-life scientist in her entourage, spicing up the dinner party conversations and highlighting the eclectic tastes of the patroness. But that was an ungener-ous hypothesis, for Claire sensed nothing opportunistic in Rachel's regard. Maybe, as in science, the simplest explanation was the closest to the truth: she was the only friend who didn't have unrealistic expec-tations, and this took the pressure off Rachel, allowing her to relax and be more mortal.

That wasn't the right reason at all. But Claire wasn't as good at seeing herself as she was at seeing the rest of the universe.

Chapter 7

❧

Although later, Joshua would not be able to pinpoint the exact moment his disillusionment crystallized, the truth was that it all kicked off with the incident involving the fork.

He was eating dinner with friends on the riverside terrace of the IJsbreker one cool April evening. As the sun set, the evening filled with bronze light, glowing off skin, hair, wine glasses, and yes, even that momentous fork as it gestured in air. Frequent laughter punctuated their swift clippy Dutch—a language that, if an ear could squint, might be mistaken for incomprehensible English. After a discussion about politics, they picked over their ice creams and apple cakes and downed the dregs of their thick coffees as the talk turned to a popular topic: work-life balance.

"I just can't cope with the load," Saskia was saying. "I'm not sleeping as well as usual, and it's making me anxious."

Joshua examined her tanned face, clear eyes and the dozen other microscopic signs of health and relaxation.

"Some girls in your office work part-time, don't they? Why don't you try to arrange something?" Marco asked.

Saskia shook her head. "Already asked—not an option. But I've found a doctor who's willing to write a letter saying I'm heading for burnout."

Burnout was one of many English words that the Dutch had commandeered into their own language in the way of savvy traders.

"Are you?" Joshua asked, very carefully. Saskia had always struck him as being solid and stable. But the social services in the Netherlands were generous, and *burnout* was remarkably frequent in this country.

She shrugged. "Probably."

"Why don't you just have a baby, like Lisse?" Hanneke said. "That would solve everything."

Lisse smiled and placed a hand over the swell of her belly. "You make it sound like I had an ulterior motive."

"Solve what? You're going to keep working after the baby, aren't you?" Joshua tuned to Lisse, who was an assistant professor of archaeology.

Lisse exchanged glances with Hanneke. "Actually, I'm thinking of dropping out."

"You can't be serious!" Joshua said. "What about your research?"

"The chances of me being promoted are practically *nul*," Lisse said serenely. "There aren't any female professors now, and I don't get a sense that change is in the air anytime soon. Besides, somebody's got to stay with the baby."

"Doesn't the university have childcare facilities?" Joshua asked.

"Nominally," she said. "But the waiting list is long, and they don't keep very work-friendly hours there. Besides, I don't like the idea of my kid growing up in a crèche."

Joshua knew better than to ask why her boyfriend, who was a shop assistant, and rather repugnantly lazy in Joshua's opinion, couldn't look after the child. Hanneke was nodding sympathetically at Lisse.

While they were waiting for the bill, Marco looked at Joshua's plate. "Didn't you enjoy your meal?"

"I did, actually. Why?"

Marco gave him his slow grin. "Your fork, *jongen*. It's pointing upwards."

Joshua looked down his plate, where he'd carefully arranged his cutlery on the right hand side. Marco loved catching him out, and seldom succeeded.

"*Rot op*, Marco."

"No, seriously," Marco said. "That's rude, how you've got it. It means you didn't like it."

"Your fork is up too," Joshua said.

"Yeah, but I'm not as polite as you, *jongen*. And my chicken was overdone."

"He's right about the fork," Hanneke said, squeezing Joshua's thigh under the table. "Didn't you know?" Something in her tone sounded more smug than fond.

"Something slipping past your eagle eye!" Marco crowed. "An historic moment, *dames en heren*."

Joshua looked around the table where indeed, everyone else but Saskia had carefully averted the points of their fork.

Saskia smiled self-consciously. "It's all bullshit," she explained. "I never bother with that old-fashioned stuff—unless I'm eating with my *oma*."

"Just think," Marco said, "of all those waitresses you've been inadvertently insulting over the years!"

The others laughed. Joshua joined in, but inside he was rattled, all out of proportion for such a mild patch of cultural ignorance. Even later, when Marco took him aside and told him they'd played a trick on him, that the cutlery etiquette in question was decades dead, along with most other forms of basic courtesy, the damage had been done. Something had flickered and flipped in his brain, like those optical illusions that start out looking like protruding cubes but transform to receding steps on longer inspection. His place in the grand Dutch scheme of things had subtly altered, so much so that he would soon find it difficult to force the original picture back into place.

❀ ❀ ❀

"If your girlfriend was pregnant," Joshua asked Marco later when they were fetching drinks at the bar, "would you want her to stop working?"

Marco shrugged as he rooted around for euros in his jeans. "At the rate I'm going, *jongen*, this is never going to be an issue."

"Hypothetically, you pessimist."

Marco looked at Joshua thoughtfully. "I guess I would. I mean, if she was dead set on working, of course she could carry on, but frankly, it would make me feel better if she stayed home—or at least worked part-time."

When he told Hanneke later about Marco's comment, expecting solidarity, she said instead, "I think Lisse's doing the right thing, *schatje*."

"But she's well-known in her field, making important discoveries. Whereas Evert is a deadbeat nobody."

"It's all about priorities," she replied. "Lisse wants to be a good mother."

53

Hanneke didn't like conflict, the saying of the unsayable, so Joshua said nothing.

"That's her right," she added, slipping her hands under his shirt and seeking the mode of communication that they negotiated best.

Of course it was. Afterwards, he watched Hanneke as she slept. He realized only then that he had been suppressing a fundamental uncertainty about her for weeks. Little incidents and snippets of conversation, harmless in isolation and unremarked at the time, now manoeuvred into new patterns, fortifying his conviction. The closer he got to her, and to his other Dutch friends, the further away they seemed to slip; there appeared to be no way to get beyond certain concepts, to penetrate the surface skin of their nationally shared experiences. He was just as much of an alien as any of his work colleagues—who had he been kidding? Yet to admit it was to face the uncomfortable fact that, yet again, he was fundamentally alone in the world. Far better to convince himself that this was nothing, just a bad mood, a rough expatriate patch, a theoretical notion of loss that could be rowed away at the next session of sweat and exhaustion down on the Amstel.

Hanneke cried out softly in her sleep and turned, her glossy hair sliding over her bare neck and shoulders. Joshua thought the expression on her face was oddly complacent and suddenly, he felt nothing for her.

Chapter 8

❧

As the summer deepened, Claire too began to detect a change within. Her first conscious awareness came one evening as she leaned against the stone rail of the Nieuwe Amstel Bridge. She was feeling good at the time: the stone was still warm beneath her forearms, the air was cool against her skin, the sunset was divine—and her mind was swarming with words.

Ever since she'd started to play her father's word game again, the urge to write poetry had returned too—something she hadn't felt for years. Claire didn't know whether her father's voice had brought back the urge, or whether the urge to write had brought back her father's voice— or whether the two things were actually the same.

She was distrustful of this new development at first. She'd made her choice, so why allow an old childish passion to reassert itself? Especially as it was associated with a lot of other complicated issues she didn't want to revisit.

But as she absorbed the day, the desire itched against her skin. Would it really be such a bad thing? She stood there, wondering whether she could even pull it off anymore. And just like that, her stubborn streak rose to the challenge.

Keep it simple, Claire thought. Utilitarian. Rose streaks against pale blue, warped reflection in the water below. A sense of intensity, of things glowing that ought not to . . . of. . .

Bad subject choice, Clair de Lune: sunsets are difficult. They are hackneyed in and of themselves. It's nearly impossible to describe one without sounding tedious.

It could be done, though, Claire thought. Like Shelley: *I watched until the shades of evening wrapped Earth like an exhalation. . .*

She would approach it from the periphery, catch it while it wasn't looking: boats and birds, a fine evening's bustle, laughter from the terrace tables lining the east bank. An absolute euphoria of light.

And then a male voice; not her father's but an actual person's, right next to her.

Claire jumped. She was doing well in her Dutch lessons, but was so surprised that she missed most of the words produced by the smiling young man who had paused beside her, and those that filtered through somehow made no sense together.

In a flash, she hated being in a place where she was not fluent with the currency of easy human interaction: humour, flirtation, jibe, small talk.

"*Nog een keer, wat langzamer?*" she said, hopelessly crippled: *Can you repeat that more slowly?*

Of course he could have, but Claire had made this request enough times to know that the man would inevitably switch to English instead. That's just what Dutch people did.

"I beg your pardon," the man said, stiff and stilted, the gloriously strange vowels transformed into an ugly staccato monotone. He was crippled too, Claire thought, not in meaning but in aesthetics. "I asked you if you know what the man said when he came out of the Van Gogh Museum?"

The man waited for her response, embarrassed. The joke, of course, was already ruined. But once a Dutch person committed himself to something, he would follow it through—even a picnic in a heavy downpour.

Claire shook her head, mystified. "No, tell me."

"He said that the real sunset was a bit of a disappointment."

As he moved off, Claire thought that only the Dutch could take the joy out of something so amiably yet with such surgical precision.

✤ ✤ ✤

After this odd interaction, she crossed the bridge and sat down on her favourite riverside bench. The water looked unusually bloated, its mirrored skin milling about with ambivalence. Did the Amstel actually have a current, or tides? She doubted it: such movement seemed like something disorderly that the Dutch would have squelched centuries ago with their clever gates, sluices and *dijks*, like a spontaneous tendency or a rash moment of serendipitous joy.

She decided to carry on with her plan to write something, even though the sunset and the incident with the man were now so firmly linked that they could never be teased apart. What she'd wanted to write was spoiled.

Or maybe just made more interesting, her father's voice contradicted sourly.

"Shut up," she whispered.

Poems about sunsets, for pity's sake! Come on, let's see what you're really made of.

Rummaging around in her bag, she found a notebook and pen.

❧ ❧ ❧

It always starts with words and phrases, Claire, spilled onto paper with no plan, no inhibition. Maybe ninety percent of this stuff is useless. Don't let that stop you. Don't be afraid. It's only the first step. It's not a poem yet, just a dumping ground of arbitrary ideas. Imagine a door in your brain where the real poem is waiting. The words unlock the door.

Claire began to write, trying not to analyse or worry too much. She imagined the colours in her mind: baked amber, cooling lavender blue, the gilt tinge of the fading sky. She remembered the smoothness of the stone bridge, how it had felt skin-warm. She didn't screen out her residual irritation with the young man, but allowed this to tinge her palette too.

Eventually the chill in the air brought her to herself, and she inspected her crude list. It was suddenly difficult to make out the words in the dusk. Maybe ten percent of it was usable; maybe less; maybe none. Nevertheless, she looked, and felt the stretching feeling of a door about to open, just as it had used to do when she was younger.

But ink on paper is dangerously misleading, Claire. Written words are only a substitute for sound. You must never forget that your medium is the voice: you have to be able to hear the words. And if you start doing that out here, people will think you're a nutter.

Back home at her desk, she progressed the list into a finished poem. It came in a rush, a mixture of writing and speaking softly, crossing out and testing, several hours passing before she finally surfaced, neck aching and hungry from a skipped meal. She felt the weariness, the pride, the emptiness that she remembered from before but had forgotten in the interim.

Her first, in more than six years. The sky hadn't fallen, the earth hadn't swallowed her up.

Chapter 9

❧

Summer peaked and began to erode. The elms lost their magic and became mere trees again, leaves dusty and contemplating a drop. Roses and poppies gave way to hollyhocks and cow parsley in the bank-side gardens of the houseboats, and the constellations shifted subtly on Claire's early morning cycle rides to the station.

One October morning in the lab, a routine day like any other, Claire sat at the Raison's console, presiding over a routine cleaning of the machine's complex digestive tract. Later, she thought it was noteworthy that her mind was so completely on other things when it finally happened. With one keystroke, she fed the Raison a few sips of buffered saline, then twiddled a knob to burp the air out of its labyrinth of flexible latex micro-tubing—routine stuff, a child could do it half-asleep.

It was at that point that a brilliant idea occurred to her, out of nothing.

Well, not completely out of nothing. She had been turning the knob and watching the monitors as the stream of bubbles deep within the machine's innards worked their way out of the system. She had part of her attention on a line of poetry she was worrying in her head, and part of an ear on the crickets, whose song this morning sounded a bit different, a bit muffled, a bit shifted towards the right of the room. She was wondering if the group—herd? swarm? school?—was in the wall itself, and if so, whether that space had different layers or compartments, spaces within spaces within spaces, cul de sacs formed by insulation or ductwork, each with its own unique acoustics.

And then something about this possibility reminded her of the complicated three-dimensional set-up of spaces and tubes within cells, with their wonderfully old-fashioned yet evocative names: the *endoplasmic reticulum*; the *Golgi Apparatus*; the *mitochondrial christae*. Not full of migrating crickets, but of proteins, shuttling in and out of the vast micro-scopic motorway system, slip roads and roundabouts and tunnels and bridges, keeping everything running smoothly.

And there, just then: the idea was born. Not about stroke, but about Alzheimer's disease. And not just a filling-in-the-gaps idea, but a *trail-blazing* idea. An idea that, if true, would kick off an entirely new avenue of research. And it was so simple, and so suited to the Raison's strengths, that she was surprised she—or Alan or Ramon—had not thought of it before.

⚜ ⚜ ⚜

Claire and Rachel sat at corner table in a bar on the Kinkerstraat, safely south of the tourist wasteland of Leidesplein. Well past midnight, the room was saturated with the babble and bulk of fashionable Amster-dammers. Claire, who was of average height in England, always felt nervous amidst a sturdy forest of locals. The men's heads often brushed against the ceilings of older rooms like these, and some of the more spectacular specimens of Dutch womanhood were not far off. Both sexes were impressive with their expensive clothing, shining hair and energetic laughter; the bar vibrated with sound and vitality, so far removed from her staid and suspicious work environment. For the hundredth time, she experienced a surge of relief at her decision to live in Amsterdam.

Over the past half-hour the DJ in the corner had gradually turned up the volume of the ambient music, and it had become increasingly difficult to follow the conversation.

"—may be time to resort to covert operations," Rachel was saying, probing the stem of her wineglass with slender fingers. "Especially after I heard what Lucy found out. . ."

Claire made the appropriate encouraging noises and Rachel launched eagerly into this fresh piece of news, deflected in patches but still gener-ally understandable if she kept focused on her mouth. Claire loved watch-ing Rachel talk, with her dramatically smudged eyes and vast repertoire of facial expressions, almost as much as she enjoyed the absurd stories themselves. But tonight, she kept drifting off—the new idea about Alzheimer's was bubbling up inside her head, demanding to be viewed at all angles.

"What's up with you?" Rachel finally asked. "I've been blathering about myself for hours, and you're obviously distracted by something."

She smoothed her auburn hair back with a graceful hand, as if exposing her ear for maximum gossip absorption.

"Just something work-related," Claire replied.

"Is Bannerman being beastly again? Or has your Raisin blown another fuse?"

"No . . . I've had an idea, is all."

"A cure for stroke already? Darling, you've only been at it for half a year. Should I be buying stocks?"

"It's not about stroke, actually. It's about Alzheimer's. Strictly speaking, I'm not supposed to be thinking about it, but on my first day, Alan asked me to consider a side-project."

"Who's Alan?"

Claire filled her in.

"I know the type well," Rachel said. "Too beautiful for anyone's good, and about as welcome as a venereal disease." She put her index finger to her temple and pretended to pull the trigger.

"At first I didn't have any ideas . . . I'm not good coming up with hypotheses."

"Maybe you just needed some space," Rachel said. "I can't be creative when I feel it's expected of me."

Claire shrugged. "Maybe. But then a couple of weeks ago, I thought of a way to use the Raisin to address one of the remaining mysteries about Alzheimer's disease."

❧ ❧ ❧

In the middle of October, about a week after she'd come up with the idea, Claire had climbed a few flights of stairs to the Home of the Zapper—not Ramon's domain, but Alan's adjacent territory. Warily, it had to be said. She had not spoken to Alan since that first edged encounter and, in the meantime, she couldn't help having absorbed the rumours flashing through the building like electrochemical impulses. NeuroSys was almost sentient with gossip, and the consensus was that Alan, though brilliant, was a womanizer, and capable of spectacular tempers far worse, it was said, than the mild bitchiness she had so far experienced.

But her new idea was the very thing she needed to prove herself, and the Interactrex, to everyone. And Alan's initial offer of surreptitious collaboration, even if insincere, was the only way she could think of to secure permission to divert some of her time. But it had been half a year—what if he didn't even remember?

She found both Ramon and Alan sitting in Alan's office, backs to the door, absorbed by a display of colourful neurons on a monitor.

"Claire—do come in, sit down." Alan Fallengale looked over his shoulder in surprise. Not an expression, Claire thought, that his face was used to adopting. This suspicion gave her a surge of secret triumph.

Ramon, on the other hand, swivelled around and greeted her with a ready smile.

"I've got some free run-time on the Interactrex next week," Claire said, slapping a sheaf of papers on the desk between them. The new idea had enhanced her confidence like alcohol. "I've written a proposal."

"Have you now?" Alan's drawl was too obviously designed to provoke to have any effect on Claire.

"That's great, Claire." Ramon frowned at Alan before leafing through it.

"I had rather hoped that I might request my own series of experiments," Alan said. "Subject to your full approval, naturally."

"*Jesús*, Alan, don't be such a pompous arse. Why don't you at least look at what she's come up with?" Ramon said. "It seems clever to me at first glance . . . but of course, I'm no expert on the Interactrex."

He put particular emphasis on the word *expert*, and it was Alan's turn to make a face.

"Very well. We shall read it through."

"Don't take too long," she said, standing up. "I'm getting a load of new stroke samples next week, so the window of opportunity may be quite narrow."

She knew Alan would bite: her idea was too beautiful to resist.

❦ ❦ ❦

"Diseases like Alzheimer's are caused by proteins clogging up the brain," Claire told Rachel. "Proteins sticking together that shouldn't. They form these dense clumps that interfere with normal brain function."

"Where do the proteins come from?"

"The brain cells spit them out into the spaces outside the cells . . . lay them down like bricks."

"And then these proteins just stick together?"

"No," Claire said. "That's what people used to think. But Alan and some other scientists discovered that the sticky proteins in Alzheimer's and a few other neurodegenerative diseases all require an operative—like mortar—to help them aggregate. They call it the Universal Aggregation Principle."

"*They?*" Rachel smiled. "Interesting choice of pronouns, darling."

Claire let it pass. "In Alzheimer's, the brick proteins are called amyloids, and the mortar operative is called SCAN—that's short for Scaffold Neurodegenerative. So they ... *we* designed this drug—the Zapper—that stops SCAN from mortaring the amyloid bricks together."

"How does it work?" Rachel studied the cocktail napkin between them, which Claire had covered with scribbled circles and boxes.

"The Zapper is a chemical drug that"—she fumbled for an analogy—"melts the mortar."

"Okay ... so why do some people get Alzheimer's and others not?"

"Because both the amyloids and SCAN have gone wrong in Alzheimer's patients," Claire said. "Neither is supposed to be roaming around loose outside the cells—in healthy brains, amyloids sort of ... stick close to cells, and SCAN can't even be detected." Claire filled in one of the boxes absently with her pen. "But I had a feeling that SCAN might be hiding somewhere *inside* cells, doing something else altogether."

"Doing what?"

"I don't know—that's what my whole idea was about. I thought if we could *find* SCAN, we could work out what its normal job was." Claire looked up from her drawing. "And if we could do that, then we could figure out how it went wrong, and come up with more drugs like the Zapper, but even better ones—ones that would prevent the disease earlier."

❧ ❧ ❧

The day after Claire gave Alan her proposal, she was lying on her side underneath the Raison soldering a loose connection with pocket torch clenched between teeth when a throat cleared at the door.

"Hi," Alan said, looking down at her as she emerged. He had her proposal in one hand and, for the first time since they'd met, a real smile. "This looks like a bad moment."

"This is nothing." She put down her tools and wiped her hands on a rag, self-conscious about her dishevelled appearance. "Last week it almost set off the fire alarm—I had to take apart the entire front console."

"Is it terminal?" He eyed the Interactrex 3000 warily.

"It would only like us to think so. What did you think of my idea?"

"I love it," Alan said. Gone was the studied neutrality, the veiled boredom. He looked open and eager as an undergraduate, an impression enhanced by his untucked aquamarine shirt and jeans. "Ramon was right, Claire. It's a completely new angle—it might even lead us to another Alzheimer's drug."

They discussed a few specifics, Claire marvelling all the while at the change in attitude. She had apparently been promoted from juvenile annoyance to peer as a result of five pages of typescript. Having frequently noted this strange power of ideas people in the past, she basked in the intensity of her own first experience.

He had paused on his way out.

"Listen, Claire. I wanted to apologize for how I acted before."

She opened her mouth, but he carried on before she could speak.

"Really." He leaned against the door frame. "You never know at first what people. . ." A resigned, dramatic sigh. "There are so many idiots at NeuroSys. I can't abide idiots. I had a preconceived idea about the Interactrex—and you, to be honest. I was wrong."

After he'd left, her lips crept into a smile.

Gotcha.

❧ ❧ ❧

"It sounds typical of the man from what you've described so far," Rachel observed. "Started being friendly the moment he realized how much you could help him."

"It's not like that." Claire didn't expect the prickle of irritation. "He's just cautious."

"You're the one who should be cautious—you might end up getting exploited." Then, observing Claire's reaction, she added, "Good heavens, you're not attracted to him, are you?"

"Of course not!"

"Don't glare at me, darling. You *did* describe him as cold but handsome—what was that lovely quotation again?"

Claire thought a moment before accessing the verse. " *'You are like balm encloséd well/ In amber or some crystal shell.'* "

"Elizabeth Barrett Browning?"

"Robert Herrick."

"So back to your story," Rachel said, exerting her usual habit of dipping a toe into the water and feigning oblivion as the concentric circles spread further and further outward. "Do I have this right so far? Your big idea was essentially to look for this SCAN protein in various places inside the cell to see what it gets up to when it's not wreaking havoc outside?"

"Basically, yes—it wasn't something that Alan could easily have done with traditional techniques."

"So what happened next?"

"We decided to give it a try."

❧ ❧ ❧

Claire slowly nudged the needle with the joystick, wishing for the hundredth time that she hadn't backed down and allowed Alan and Ramon to observe. She could feel their scrutiny making her self-aware and clumsy. Worse, the men's ignorance obliged her to keep up a running commentary, preventing her from entering the trance-like state she normally slipped into during Collection.

"I'm going to aspirate material from the nucleus as a control," she said. "It's always good to include a sample where you don't expect a positive."

On the main screen, the mass of mouse neurons glistened like transparent insects under the phase-contrast light microscope, their inner structures enhanced by the innocuous red tracer dye. Her gossamer needle resembled a tree branch at this magnification, lumbering in from the left side of the screen, but its terminal nano-tip narrowed down to invisibility.

"First I'll position the tip. . ." She nudged the end of the tree branch over the round sac welling up in the middle of a fat, healthy-looking cell, guessing where the very end of the needle must be. "You have to be careful with the z-axis here . . . getting gummed up in the chromosomes is a nightmare."

A few more nudges, then Claire tapped a button and the branch recoiled with a convulsive movement. The nucleus puckered with the impact, then filled out again as the Raison emitted a self-satisfied bleep and a sprinkling of flashes on the console.

"That's got it," she said, checking the numbers on the screen. "Now let's cruise over to the Golgi, take another sample."

"This aspect of the procedure is essentially just like standard micro-injection, isn't it?" Alan asked.

Claire nodded absently, spinning the dial to finesse her needle a tiny bit closer to its target. "Except it's much, much finer. Traditional needles can't access the smaller organelles."

"What's happened to that nuclear sample you just took?" This from Ramon.

"It got sucked into the main sorting zone of the Interactrex, and now it's in the queue for Purgatory."

"Very droll," Alan observed.

"Don't blame me—Maxwell named everything. Purgatory is the central processing area of the machine where the Ra—the Interactrex decides what goes up the Ladder, and what gets flushed down the Snakes."

Ramon snorted with amusement. "Your Maxwell seems like an interesting guy."

Taking another sample, she explained how SCAN proteins would be captured by a microchip-sized filter of antibody-coated beads, then—after a critically-timed keyboard intervention from Claire—how any solo SCAN would get rejected down the Snakes, whereas SCAN sticking to other proteins would be shunted up the Ladder and into the identification queue, where its mystery partners would be revealed.

"How long until a positive ID?" Ramon wanted to know.

"It gets trypsin-digested and processed, blasted into the mini-MALDI-B, and crunched through the peptide fingerprint databases ... about twenty minutes altogether."

"Unbelievable—when I was a PhD student, this would have taken—" Alan began, just as the Raison began to ping in panic.

"Oh, no," Claire said, then invoked a fluent curse that would have shocked her mother. She didn't realize she'd said it out loud until Ramon pounced.

"I had a *feeling* you were one of us," he said triumphantly in Spanish. "It was only a matter of time before you betrayed yourself. Although after what just came out of your mouth, young lady, you might get excommunicated. Why didn't you tell me before?"

"What's happening?" Alan asked, annoyed.

"I'm only half-Spanish," Claire told Ramon, pointedly in English, "and the collection tubing's jammed. Show's over for now."

"Are the samples you've already collected safe?" Alan's voice was nonchalant, but Claire could hear the concern underneath. She found the fact that he cared intriguing: her performance had obviously gone a long way toward alleviating his scepticism.

"Perfectly," she said. "The blockage is upstream, but Purgatory and beyond are isolated in separate modules. I'm going to have to open her up, though. Why don't you two get a coffee, come back for the results?"

"In other words, get out of your hair so you can fix that beast in peace." Ramon said with a smile. "Come along, Alan, quit hovering."

❧ ❧ ❧

"It was an amazing result," Claire told Rachel. "We *did* find SCAN in healthy cells, just as I thought we might."

"Where was it hiding?"

"In the nucleus—in the centre of the cell, where the DNA sits. A small amount, but definitely real—it wasn't surprising that nobody had ever noticed it before using standard techniques."

"What does is all mean?" Rachel asked. "Why is SCAN hiding in the nucleus?"

"Well, the Raison couldn't tell us that. But it did give us a clue. When the target protein, SCAN in this case, gets shunted up the Ladder, it's been chosen because it's sticking to another protein."

"How does the Raisin choose?"

"If the target protein is sticking to something, it's bigger than it should be," Claire explained. "Like a person could fit just fine through a narrow door, but if she was holding hands with someone else and they tried to go through together, they'd get stuck. After the pairs get stuck, whatever is holding hands with the target protein gets identified."

"Okay..."

"Anyway, the Raisin told us that SCAN in the healthy nucleus was binding to a sort of . . . chaperone protein. Unfortunately this chaperone is very mysterious—we haven't worked out what it is yet. Or what it's doing."

"Any ideas?"

"Well," Claire said. "We know it's bad when SCAN escapes from cells, so maybe this chaperone is keeping SCAN inside where it won't do any harm."

"Like a prison warden, making sure SCAN can't escape and start mortaring bricks together?"

"That's exactly what Alan thought. Although at that point, it was only a guess."

⚜ ⚜ ⚜

"Remarkable." Ramon was shaking his head at the Raison's final analysis.

"Why didn't this nuclear chaperone ever show up in our pull-down experiments?" Alan demanded, also transfixed by the screen.

"Or the fact that SCAN is in the nucleus at all? We never saw it there with any other method." Ramon reached for the mouse and scrolled further down the screen, as if the answer might somehow be hiding at the bottom of the report. "And how on earth could a secreted protein get into the nucleus—or vice versa?"

"Maybe an alternative splice that edits out the signal peptide?" Claire ventured.

"Maybe," Alan said, dubiously. "The RNA is stable, but we always assumed SCAN protein was broken down in normal cells. We had no idea it was sequestered somewhere."

Claire's heart was still thrumming. "This is where the Interactrex really excels. It can detect tiny amounts that you can't see by other methods. And you would never have picked up this interaction in a mass population, like a cell lysate. Only a small percentage of the population is in the various compartments at any given time."

"It's like a zoom lens," Ramon said, "on a crowded street." His face looked like it was witnessing a stage curtain, gradually drawing apart to reveal a whole universe of possibilities.

"You do realize what this means," Alan said slowly. "If we could interfere with SCAN before it even gets exported, then we could prevent the *onset* on Alzheimer's."

"Which is definitely an improvement on the Zapper," Ramon added.

"It's only a pilot experiment." Claire's face was suddenly hot at the prospect of raised hopes and mistaken identities. She could already imagine the knowing smiles of the other Senior Scientists—and the renewed scorn on Alan's Apollo Belvedere face.

"So we repeat it," Ramon said, with a shrug.

❦ ❦ ❦

"Well, it all sounds terribly exciting," Rachel said.

"*If* it's true," Claire said, gloomily.

"Isn't this all part of the joy of discovery?"

"Hmmm." Claire wasn't sure it was joy she was feeling these days. More a bipolar ride of exhilaration knocked down every now and then by a solid dose of pessimism.

"If this was a good experimental result, I wouldn't want to see you after a bad one."

"Very wise. You probably won't have to wait that long, either."

"If it's any consolation, I already think you're a genius."

" '*O thou pervading genius, given to man/ To trace the secrets of the dark abyss!*' What do you reckon, Rach? Is my genius pervading, then?"

"No, I'm afraid we'd have to reserve that superlative accolade for Alan."

Chapter 10

〜❦〜

Joshua sat down at a free terminal and called up his task log. Usually the music and chatter of the Pit's morning bustle energized him, stoking up his anticipation for the mysteries that might be thrown at him that day. But for the first time in as long as he could remember, he was not looking forward to digging in. The ongoing chores on his list seemed routine, unimaginative—which is why he sat up straighter when a new task, with its flashing icon, appeared at the top.

Joshua always admonished the others to do each task in the order it arrived, no matter how routine. But being the boss had its privileges.

He clicked open the message, anticipation dashed as he saw the account-owner's code: Alan Fallengale.

"Great," Joshua muttered. Since Alan only trusted things he could touch with his own hands, ghostly computer-generated predictions offended him on principle, and requests from him were correspondingly rare—and often couched in the most dismissive possible terms. And of course, when the bioinformatics team provided him with any helpful clues, he never thanked them, let alone bestowed formal acknowledgement.

"I *said*, do you want a cup of coffee, boss?" Roz boxed him gently round the ears.

"Mmmm? Sorry, Roz. Yes, I would."

"What planet were you on?" She slipped into the adjacent terminal's seat, attired in a short denim dress and thigh-high shiny black boots that would not look out of place in the Red Light District.

"You can get me some too while you're at it, Roz." This from Matt, at the next terminal, fingers blurred over the keyboard and eyes transfixed by his monitor.

"Not in my job description," she replied sweetly. "I only fetch coffee for intelligent life forms." She peered at Joshua's screen. "Anything good?"

"Task request from Fallengale," Joshua said, his tone making the others chuckle.

"Send him off on a wild goose chase," Matt suggested.

Joshua clicked open the associated e-mail:

```
Hello, folks—and apologies in advance for the uninspiring
nature of this request. Just a simple homology check, I'm
afraid.
```

"Hang on," Joshua said. "This can't be right."

Alan usually just typed in a few curt lines of explanation. In fact, most people never bothered with pleasantries. Not to be deliberately rude, he suspected, but because they were under the impression that their questions would somehow get magically translated straight into computer code with no human interface to help it along.

Roz pointed to the signature line at the bottom of the lengthy note. "It's not from Alan—it's from Claire Cyrus. Silly girl must've typed in the wrong account code."

"Not necessarily," Joshua said, scanning through the rest of her sentences—well-formed, dynamic, infused with a wry humour. And all about SCAN. "This is an Alzheimer's request."

"Alzheimer's?" Roz said slowly. "Claire and Alan, collaborating? First I've heard. Must be on the sly."

"I guess you can't blame her for going off-piste," Matt said. "If I had to work with Bannerman, I would've flung myself into a canal by now."

"And you think Alan is any better?"

"Children, please," Joshua said. "If Dr Cyrus is up to something, nobody's going to hear it from us, understood? I don't want anyone to stop her—this looks like the most interesting thing I've had in weeks."

Roz read a bit more from Joshua's screen. "A new binding partner for SCAN, eh? Intriguing."

"Back off, Roz, it's mine, all mine . . . *Mwoo-ha ha ha.*"

"You have all the luck," Roz said, heading off resentfully towards the coffee room. "How come you get that, and I'm saddled with Frederica's ninety-five bloody introns?"

"Punishment for her sins," Matt said in a low voice. "And speaking of which, boss, can you help me hack into the task log so I can re-route Li-Liang's stupid two-hybrid request into Roz's list?"

"I heard that!" Roz yelled from around the corner.

"You're on your own, mate." Joshua clicked open the annotation fields, hoping Claire was conscientious enough to have filled them out correctly. He hated badgering people for information they'd forgotten to record in the first place.

Cell type: primary mouse neurocytes.

Protein isolation technique: It was a multiple choice question, but Claire, understandably not finding her fancy new machine on the list, had ticked '*other*' and filled in '*Interactrex 3000*' then a string of jargon he didn't understand. Commendable, recording all the conditions properly. He went to the next field, *Cellular compartment (if applicable)* and blinked at the answer she'd chosen.

"Coffee," Roz said, putting the mug next to his keyboard and taking the empty terminal on his right.

"Thanks, Roz. Look at this, will you?"

"*Now* he wants my help."

"She says she's pulled this SCAN-binder out of the nucleus."

Roz stopped with her mug a few millimetres from her lips, put it down and looked at his screen. "That's a mistake, surely. Wouldn't be any SCAN in the nucleus to bind to."

"Exactly."

"That's not the only mistake," Roz said. "Look what she's entered for the disease state."

He read: *Disease status: healthy control.*

"There wouldn't be any SCAN in a healthy mouse, full stop," Joshua said.

"It's probably that machine of hers," Matt said. "Some artefact or contamination. Nobody really knows if it works properly anyway."

"Is this Claire's first query?" Joshua asked.

"No," someone else piped up down the row. "I've done about a dozen of her stroke proteins already."

Joshua pulled up Claire's account and looked through all the documentation, both her original queries and follow-up data that Bannerman's biochemists had filled in as they learned more.

"To be fair," he said, "most of her hits have turned out to be real so far. So the Interactrex can't be completely useless."

In fact, he was impressed by how many hits she had managed in such a short time. He clicked the query follow-up button to send off an automatically generated request for confirmation about the nucleus source and the mouse's disease-free status. In the meantime, he invoked Claire's unknown protein, its neat grey lines of single-letter code filling the screen. A few keystrokes and he'd submitted it to all the public protein databases.

"A hit," he said, scrolling down the page. "Hypothetical product from a mouse EST. They've called it 'ESTA-333'."

"Rolls off the tongue, doesn't it," Roz said.

"It's completely unknown to date," he said, scanning the screen with disappointment. "No studies published, in any species. A big zero."

In the gene jockey's world, hypothetical proteins were still a daily occurrence, despite everything that had been learnt from the Human Genome Project and the sequencing of the genomes of a number of other organisms. He thought of the human genome as a library of about 21,000 books, each book corresponding to one gene. All the genes that people knew about from studying them in the lab over the years, only a few thousand to date, would be the books that people checked out, read, flipped through, poured over in search of enlightenment. But what about the other 19,000 or so genes predicted to exist? These were the brand-new books, never opened, patiently waiting in their slots on the shelves for someone to want to read them. Claire's protein was one of these: she had pulled it down and cracked apart the stiff new pages to see what was inside.

"Bad luck," Roz said. "Look like anything?"

Joshua performed a few more manipulations and fed it into his own home-grown domain-finding software.

"What do you know. . ." He scrolled down, checked a few statistics. "This guy is predicted to be in the nucleus—it's got a cryptic consensus import domain. Exactly as advertised."

At that moment, a dialogue box came up containing Claire's response.

Yes, I got it from the nucleus—and the mouse didn't have Alzheimer's. I know it's weird, but humour me.

Joshua smiled and went back to his domain report, but there was nothing else to see. Aside from the transport domain, the protein was a blank slate. For now, at least.

"And the track goes cold," Joshua murmured.

Roz looked over sympathetically. "Playtime over?"

"Maybe." Joshua looked more carefully at the original sequence. There was something bothering him about a region of the code in the centre of the protein—it reminded him of something. He could tell from his odd feeling—like *déjà vu*, or a glimpsed movement snagged by peripheral vision—that it wasn't the sort of pattern that was obvious enough to emerge from a database search. The merest whiff of familiarity. Joshua knew from experience that the best way to capture this elusive hint was to think *around* it, not directly at it.

The answer would come, in time, as it always did.

He logged his preliminary report, closed Claire's file and started reluctantly on the day's chores.

❧ ❧ ❧

Joshua's bicycle was in the shop with faulty brakes, so when he reached Amsterdam Centraal Station that evening, he decided to walk home instead of taking the tram. It was already full dark, with clear skies and a half moon, the chill of late autumn edging the air. He shouldered through slow-moving crowds along the Damrak under a haze of grease and grass, his least favourite stretch of the city: fast-food outlets, coffee shops, tourist restaurants, grim hotels, souvenir stalls selling clogs, fake Delft porcelain, wooden tulips, orange flags. Past the bulk of the Beurs van Berlage, past the Bijenkorf lined with lit picture windows full of eyeless mannequins and into the Dam, its cobbles slick and oily with recent rainfall, people crisscrossing with heads down, rattling cyclists and clanging trams streaming through the plaza in all possible vectors. The stark and utilitarian Royal Palace on the right, the Grand Hotel Krasnapolsky on the left, lights glinting off the wet pavement and everything somehow imbued with the sadness of another year's ending. Down the Rokin, a left swerve at Muntplein and eventually right down an alley into the Rembrandtplein and its crowds of revellers, music thumping from bars and casinos. And then finally the escape into the Utrechtsestraat, the place where tourism stopped and the real city began.

He slowed down as the noise and light faded behind him, passing boutiques on the left and right, upscale restaurants and bars lit only by candlelight, old men out for walks with their dogs. It was so quiet that he could hear the whirring of spokes as cyclists shot by. In the distance, the ancient bell tower atop the Oude Kerk began to strike the hour, the peals floating over the silence like mist. Two canals later and his house came into view up ahead, its tall white bulk gleaming faintly in the night. But something made him walk right by, another canal crossed and then a right turn into the street where Hanneke lived. He had told her he was busy tonight and wouldn't be available, but he knew she would be at home, watching television with her flatmates. Her routines were almost invariant these days.

He hadn't planned it at all, but standing in front of her door, he decided that what he had to tell her couldn't wait any longer.

Chapter 11

❦

O ver the next few weeks, Claire began to work harder during the day on her obligatory stroke experiments—almost thoughtlessly, and certainly with little enthusiasm—to free up the nights for the new Alzheimer's side-project. The finding that SCAN was hidden in the nucleus of healthy cells in a tight embrace with the chaperone ESTA-333 opened up far more intriguing avenues than Claire could possibly pursue. She had been disappointed that her bioinformatics query had unearthed only a name (and such an uninspiring one, at that) but was sure that she and the Raison would be able to work around this setback.

One night, late, after the building had emptied out, Alan dropped by to check on her progress—and lingered. She was surprised, but found she didn't mind the company. Then it happened again, and a third time, until his presence began to feel natural. Sometimes he chatted, theorizing about Alzheimer's disease and what mysterious role SCAN and ESTA-333 might be performing in the cell nucleus. And other times he just sat quietly, watching her hands flow over the equipment, so still that she could fall into her characteristic trance and forget he was even watching—so still that she forgot to wonder why he *did* stay, silent and watchful and serving no conceivable supervisory purpose.

On one occasion, while the Raison was busy noisily purging its network of artificial arteries and veins, Alan roused himself from nearly ten minutes of brooding to ask, "Did the original prototype make such an unholy racket?"

She looked over at him, suspicious. Small talk wasn't normally in his repertoire, but his expression seemed mild, unthreatening.

"This is nothing compared to the Lady Jane," she said. "When I first started at Liverpool—before I got used to it—I used to wear earplugs."

"And the rest of the lab too? It doesn't sound very social."

Claire looked away from the bright curiosity in his eyes and examined the progress bar on the main screen. "There was no 'lab'. The Lady Jane was in the basement under the department. A damp, dark, smelly basement with no central heating and a serious mildew problem. I felt like Circe down there, languishing in my cave."

"Well, you certainly look the part with that long dark hair of yours," he said, gaze lingering impersonally over the hair in question. "Did you ever feel the urge to enchant the other students into pigs? I know I do, most days."

"There wasn't anyone to enchant," she said, surprised he'd caught the literary reference, and a bit flustered by his comment about her hair. "Just me and Maxwell."

"No postdocs? No technicians, even?"

"Well, there was Mads," she said, "but he was just a visiting fellow, only trained with me for six months."

"That's a bit odd, isn't it? To run a group of only one person?"

The Raison produced a raunchy belch and she ran a comforting hand along the side of its main casing before she realized she was even doing it. The hand quickly returned to her lap.

"Maxwell is odd," she said. "And so was the project."

He's going to say that I'm odd too, she thought.

"And quite daunting, I've been told," Alan said instead. "You had a number of colleagues in the department though, I take it?"

"I didn't mix with them much."

She had grown uncomfortable with the line of questioning, but then Alan stood up, murmuring, "That explains a lot," before bidding her a brusque goodnight.

Great, she thought. If he didn't think I was a loser before, he surely does now.

A few evenings later, their scientific discussion had escalated into a heated argument.

"We'll try the ER inhibitors next," Alan said, with the tone in his voice than meant everything was settled. His ordering-about-the-servants voice: *Do as I bid thee: there's no more to say.*

"Haven't we been over all this before? It's never going to work."

He flashed her his feudal look again as she explained her point of view, after which he countered with a few insightful but ultimately insufficient lines of reasoning, his own voice both louder and slightly less reasonable than hers had been.

"Forget it, Alan. I'm not wasting time and resources on something so misguided."

"Might I remind you that your time and resources don't, strictly speaking, belong to you?"

"Well, *you're* not exactly authorized to order me about," she said. "And nobody's paying me overtime the last time I checked either!"

There was a charged pause, and then Alan began to laugh, palms upraised in surrender. "I'm not going to brave *that* glare. Very well, Dr Cyrus, I concede that I have no right to tell you what to do. But I propose a wager. If you perform my *misguided* experiment and I'm proved right, you have to buy me a drink."

"And vice versa when you lose?"

"Precisely. Not that it's relevant in this case."

"You're on." She laughed too, feeling the hum of power in his ironic handshake.

After he was gone, she realized that she had enjoyed his company that evening. Alan was very different from Maxwell. She had bantered with Maxwell, but it had all been open and gentle, full of absurdity. Even when they disagreed, which wasn't very often, it was with the fondness of a family spat. But Alan was more of a challenge. All the meanings and intentions were under the surface, like an elaborate word-game. She never knew quite how far she dared to go without eliciting some explosive consequence. And in learning the rules, she was growing to enjoy taking that risk.

Word-games, after all, were her speciality.

Two nights later, Claire was pointing at the numbers on the Raison's screen with rather rude triumph, while Alan was conceding defeat with remarkably good grace.

"As my idea is now officially misguided, I'll be back to fetch you in half an hour."

"Fetch me?" She felt a funny lurch in her stomach.

"Your victory drink, Claire," he said. "I'm a man of honour, despite what you may have heard."

It was close to midnight on a Sunday evening, and they found the Onderwater, the local bar convenient for NeuroSys, shuttered and dark and belatedly realized the time.

"Is it normally closed on Sundays?" Alan leaned over on his bicycle, trying to peer in through the slats. "I've never tried it on a weekend—too many students for my liking."

Claire shrugged. She couldn't possibly admit that she'd never been to the popular hangout on any night, having never been invited. Rain misted against her face, coalescing like tears and trickling into her collar. He would cancel now for sure.

"There's nothing decent open in the village," he said. "We could slog over to Leiden, but that's a half-hour ride, and in this weather. . ."

He's definitely going to cancel, Claire thought.

"Let's go back to mine," he said suddenly. "It's just around the corner. Hurry up, before we get soaked."

It's not what you think, Claire chastised herself as she sat on what appeared to be a vintage Le Corbusier sofa, listening to Alan open and close drawers in the kitchen around the corner. What she had seen of the place so far showed expense and the same measure of taste. The style was largely Bauhaus, emotionally spare but pleasing to the eye. Everything in the room was black or white except for a striking painting, positioned such that anyone on the Corbusier would have to confront it head-on: brilliant colours slashed across the vast black canvas like wounds: scarlet, tangerine, acid-yellow, electric blue. It looked like a Gerhard Richter—was that possible? Surely it was only a copy.

She focused on the slashes, trying to force her hands to stop shaking at the absolute absurdity of finding herself in Alan Fallengale's house.

No, being here wasn't the absurd part. It was the half-fear, half-excitement of the possibility that he might be attracted to her.

The trouble was, she wasn't even sure if she wanted anything to happen. She was certainly drawn to him, but couldn't work out why. Their evenings together in the lab hadn't provided many clues to his character other than reinforcing the shrewdness of his scientific thinking—the lost bet notwithstanding. Since she'd been at NeuroSys, she'd had a chance to see both Ramon and Alan give scientific presentations on their research. While Ramon was dreamy and idealistic, releasing theories that ran ahead of him like wild animals, Alan's practical edge tamed them, honed them, forced them to plough straight lines into the earth. It was precisely this complementary nature that made the two men such a good team. But what other good did she know of him? Although he could put on a show of civilized behaviour, the overwhelming impression was one of arrogant dismissiveness, with an occasional streak of downright nastiness.

Of course, he was beautiful. Like a slab of polished marble, she always thought: gleaming, smooth and chill to the touch. It would be silly to deny that she wasn't affected by it. Poets, unfortunately, are especially susceptible to the charms of beauty—it's an occupational hazard. And what Claire didn't realize was that it wasn't only his beauty she was attracted to, but the challenge of his coldness. It's the same reason why a climber is aroused by a sheer cliff.

So she waited, second-guessing her current sexual situation on the sofa. Alan had been matter-of-fact as he ushered her inside, took her soaked coat and rucksack and asked her what she wanted to drink. There was nothing calculated about the invitation, no telltale charge to the circumstances. She was clearly the only one who was feeling self-conscious—so she was determined not to let it show.

Alan came into the room with two glasses glinting purple-red under the halogen track lighting.

"I assumed you would approve of Rioja," he said, settling into a handsome armchair at right angles to the sofa. "Why didn't you tell Ramon straight away that you had Spanish blood? He was incensed." Alan took obvious pleasure in the hoodwinking.

"I'm not sure." The flavour of the wine bloomed in her mouth, as expensive as everything else in the vicinity. "I always find it odd when people claim kinship like that. It's confusing for half-breeds: We're not convinced we're welcome in either club."

"Your other half is?"

"English—I was born there."

"Well, it certainly turned out to be a harmonious genetic mixture."

The compliment, she noted, was scientifically impersonal, but she felt awkward nonetheless.

"This room is lovely," she said. "Do you do the collecting yourself?"

He nodded. "Thanks. My hobby's not exactly cheap—in fact, one of the main reasons I stayed with Stanley when he started the company was the prospect of financial opportunity."

"Not many people would admit to that."

"I see nothing wrong with it," Alan said. "Good scientific ideas don't come easily."

"That is so true."

He looked surprised at her vehemence. "*You* seem to have little problem producing them. And non-misguided ones at that."

He raised his drink to emphasize the point, and their glasses connected with a shimmer of sound.

"It's just been a recent fluke," she said, shifting her weight. "I'm not really that scientifically sharp."

"Are you sure?" He paused, looking intrigued by her reaction. "Listen, you may not know this, but as a member of upper management, I've seen your reference letters."

"Oh, God." She blinked, put a hand to her warm face.

"Hardly sporting, is it?" he said. There was a laugh somewhere, hidden behind the habitual sour curve to his lips. "It gives me a tremendous conversational advantage."

"If you've read Maxwell's letter," she said bitterly, "then you *know* it's a fluke." Maxwell would have been complimentary but ruthlessly honest. Everything seemed to be conspiring to take away what little appeal she had won.

"*Au contraire*," Alan said. "I won't go into details, but NeuroSys was amply reassured of your creative potential. As you grow older, you'll learn to appreciate how a change of environment can do wonders for the inspiration."

She sat speechless, completely exposed. What on earth had Maxwell said?

"Anyway," Alan said, "ideas, be they easy or not, ought to be adequately rewarded. Cash suits me just fine."

"Is NeuroSys generous on that front?" She latched gratefully onto the new topic.

"Didn't you read your contract, Claire?" Amusement ruffled across his features. And perhaps something else: disbelief? Exasperation? "Or have a solicitor examine it?"

"I'm not particularly interested in money," she said. True, but not strictly relevant: actually, she'd only skimmed that section because she assumed she'd never have an idea worth patenting.

"Well, the bonus system's not bad." A grudging nod. "It's is based on achievements, or *milestones*, as Stanley insists on calling them. You get token compensation if your discovered drug target is validated in tissue culture; there's another milestone bonus if the resulting drug passes pre-clinical testing in animals. But the real money comes when the clinical trials begin." He paused, eyes going faraway for a moment. "When The Zapper goes into Phase I, I'll have it made. I might even retire."

He must be joking, Claire thought. But it's so difficult to tell with him.

"That's one of the reasons I wanted to talk to you tonight," he said, putting his glass down. "This new aspect about SCAN that we've discovered with the Interactrex..."

Claire was careful not to react to the unexpected plural pronoun.

"I think it might be time for us to write a patent application," he said. "We need to discuss our strategy."

"A patent? Already?" There it was again, that impostor feeling.

"We have twelve months to add more data once the initial application is filed, so it's always best to initiate things as soon as you've got a whiff. And we'll have to come clean with Stanley about the side project—but don't worry, I'll make sure you're not in trouble. He'll be thrilled when he finds out our results."

"So nothing happened," Rachel said, relieved, as the two friends sat at a terrace table on the bustling Albert Cuyp Market the following Saturday.

"What do you mean?"

"You know what I mean, darling."

"The prospect hadn't even crossed my mind!"

"Liar."

A silence fell over the table—more unspoken rings expanding across the glassy water. Claire looked away, at the people moving between the stalls, at the sunshine spotlighting random assortments of items for sale: coral-coloured roses, sausages dangling from hooks, a perfect pyramid of grapefruits. Eventually, Rachel spoke up, dispersing the rings. "So does it bother you? Alan's proprietary manoeuvring over your big idea?"

Claire's fingers moved compulsively back and forth over her throat, feeling the fluttering heartbeat trapped within.

"No," she said slowly. "Yes. I don't know."

Rachel waited patiently, and then Claire added, "It's a real achievement for me to be on a patent application so soon. But I keep worrying that something will go wrong."

"What could go wrong?"

"I don't know; the whole thing could be a wrong turn, a big misunderstanding. And then Alan will. . ."

Rachel smiled, took a sip of her coffee. "And why would you care if he did?"

Chapter 12

ᘒᘒ

Claire was now completely captivated by her research. For the first time in her life, she was experiencing the crushing momentum familiar to a certain class of scientist who, once they sense the nearness of truth, cannot rest until it is captured. Yet this truth, safely in hand, only leads to more questions and further truths demanding to be revealed in turn. It is the momentum that wins Nobels and destroys relationships; the mind drives the body far beyond the limits of physical endurance. Sleep, food and companionship become secondary pursuits, sublimated into the need to do just one more experiment.

In fact, most life scientists no longer do just one experiment at a time: hypothesis, experiment, conclusion, taking the luxury to ponder the next step before beginning the cycle anew. Instead, they multitask a dozen independent hypotheses at once, each spawning yet more possible experiments. The scientist knows that only one of the dozen is likely to work, but twelve experiments in one week eliminates eleven bad ideas much faster than the same tests spread sequentially over twelve weeks. Through the blur of moments speeding by, one might hear one's wife say, *you'd be much more efficient if you got some sleep*, or one's husband murmur, *what difference will twelve weeks make in the grand scheme of your scientific career?* One might know these questions to be wise, but one simply cannot heed. One is in thrall. Claire was in thrall.

Ramon, if he ever stayed in the lab late enough to realize how many hours Claire was working—if he didn't retire nightly at a sensible hour—would have put forth some stern wisdom of his own. As it was, only Alan witnessed her late nights, and Alan was a kindred workaholic spirit who said nothing. This wasn't out of the desire to exploit; it just wouldn't have occurred to him. And as the huddle of smokers on a cold rainy balcony knows well, addiction is much more fun in numbers.

Ramon, though, was made of different stuff. Like most senior lab heads the world over, his career had been one long inevitable ascent (although some, like Ramon, secretly viewed it as a decline) from lab-rat to desk-bound supervisor. His powerful brain commanded twenty-five pairs of hands now, fuelled by younger bodies. Bodies that Ramon encouraged to leave his laboratory at six p.m. sharp. (In the lab next door, Alan's troops often cast wistful glances as their neighbours decamped one by one, filling the corridor with laughter as they headed for the local pub.)

In the resulting quiet, and freed of his supervisory and administrative obligations, Ramon would abandon his paperwork and putter around in the laboratory for one more hour, working, as he put it, *con las manos, no la mente*: with his hands instead of his head. He did small experiments, he did them lovingly and painstakingly, and he did them one at a time. Of course, at this rate his results were months in the making, and the others indulged him like a crazy uncle tinkering away at an invention in the garden shed.

"It's not so much about generating data," Ramon once explained to Claire. "I've got the others to do the important work. It's more about keeping my hand in, keeping my instincts sharp. Trying out new techniques—you wouldn't catch Alan using the latest kit or short-cut. It gives me fresh ideas; it keeps me young—and flexible."

He uses experiments like Rachel touches objects, Claire thought. *Like I worry words.*

"He's in denial," was Alan's version, a scathing murmur in Claire's ear that did not disguise his underlying affection. "The scientific equivalent of mutton dressed as lamb."

Claire had found out about Ramon's designated puttering hour by accident one evening when she was searching for Alan to ask for advice.

"No, don't run away," Ramon said, looking up with a smile. He switched into Spanish and added, "I've been wanting to come visit myself, find out how it's going."

"If you're busy, I can—"

"Sit, *siéntete*." He pulled over a lab stool. "How's the patent going?"

"Slowly," she said. In Spanish too, then—God, was she rusty. How long had it been? "I think Alan and I have different ... philosophical styles."

"Ha! This sounds interesting—in what way?"

"Well." She thought a moment. "He already has a strong idea of what the final scientific answer will be, and just wants me and the Interactrex to fill in the blanks. Whereas I'm. . ."

"Not so sure, and want to keep the options open?" He was nodding sympathetically. "Sounds like Alan all over: the experiments are just the things that confirm what you already know to be true."

While still managing somehow to keep his full attention on her, his hands began to work again, dispensing liquid into a row of small plastic tubes: open lid, add fluid, snap lid shut, flick it to mix, pick up next tube.

"I don't mean to be disrespectful, but isn't that all backwards?"

He snorted. "Of course it is. But hardly anyone uses the scientific method properly these days."

"Really?" In spite of herself, she was shocked—then just as quickly amused at her own callow idealism. "What about you?"

"I'm in your camp, *querida*. Preconceived notions can blind the eye to things that don't quite fit, to signals that are trying to tell you you're on the wrong track. Before you know it, you're completely lost."

"So are you saying that Alan isn't—"

"Definitely not!" Open, add, snap, flick. "He's as sharp as a eagle. Unlike most, he's clever enough to both have a preconceived idea and not miss the warning signs when he's wrong—which hardly ever happens, I hate to admit. But the rest of us mortals would do better not to count our hypotheses before they've hatched."

Claire started visiting a couple of times a week. He didn't seem to mind her company, and she told herself that it was helpful to talk about her experiments with such an experienced researcher. But really, she was drawn by his soothing influence, by his kindness and by the rare opportunity to indulge in her mother tongue. As Ramon's hands manipulated tubes and pipettes, and his voice spun colourful, amusing and often bizarre hypotheses in his comfortable Spanish, she would experience a peculiar sensation she had not felt for some time: *home*. A sensation that she instinctively mistrusted.

☙ ☙ ☙

After weeks of working with cells derived from mice, Claire had finally convinced Alan that she was ready to be entrusted with human material. Soon she had her chance, when an unfortunate young man slipped into an irreversible coma after a car crash in Maastricht. As the hospital representatives discreetly negotiated over his heart and lungs, kidneys, livers and eyeballs, as patients on the donor lists were weighed up, called in and tested for operability, the company's skilled lawyers had won the bid for his brain, narrowly beating out an irate team of neurologists from Groningen University.

The brain had been airlifted to NeuroSys on ice. The cells were then dissociated and put into temporary culture by the experts from the third floor In Vitro department, using patented methods and a secret cocktail of growth factors perfected at NeuroSys over the years. After a ritual flurry of acrimonious political manoeuvring, allocations of the coveted cells were distributed to departments all over the building. And Alan, of course, had secured samples for Claire with brutal efficiency.

Despite the many advances the company had made in neuronal culturing techniques, these cells, once allocated, would survive only a few days in their artificial environment. Alan had urged Claire to perform as many tests as she could squeeze in, as healthy brains became available only rarely.

Claire's results with the car-crash victim mirrored what she had been seen in the normal mice: a tiny amount of SCAN was imprisoned in the cell nucleus, locked in an embrace with ESTA-333 and doing whatever mysterious job it normally performed. She didn't know what felt better: her private joy at a hypothesis bearing out, or Alan's own openly jubilant reaction.

❦ ❦ ❦

Two days later Alan exploded into Claire's lair, electrostatic with news and a cerulean shirt and key-lime tie that somehow, as always, only just managed not to mismatch.

"I suppose in Holland, one ought to expect pouring instead of merely raining," he proclaimed, throwing himself into her napping chair.

"Non-cryptic statements only tonight, Alan—I'm trying to concentrate." Claire kept an unwavering gaze on the cell splayed in the centre of the main monitor. A few taps to the left, a few more, until the needle's tip hovered right over its nucleus, dark and round like a still pond at night.

"Don't you, and I quote, *relish a challenging puzzle?*" Alan had recently dug up the cover letter of her NeuroSys application with the express purpose of torturing her with her own obsequious statements.

"Know what the night porter told me?" She tapped at the z-axis key, feeling her own centre of gravity lower along with the needle. A few steps down, a few to the left . . . perfect. "If I ever ring the panic button, he'll come up here and sort out any molesters personally. Or something roughly translating as such."

She fired off the needle and admired the way the nucleus bulged in response.

Long, long afterward, in an oak/ I found the arrow, still unbroke.

"Now that's something I'd pay to see," Alan said. "Listen, Claire, a stroke of marvellous luck: one of the senile old Alzheimer biddies down at the Van de Laan Hospice has finally popped her clogs . . . no Dutch slur intended."

"Marvellous," she echoed, remembering how her Gran had looked, lifeless against greying institutional sheets.

"And I've secured you a large portion of her cells . . . no need to hide your enthusiasm, by the way."

"Sorry—that was nice of you."

"*Nice?* Good God, Claire, it's a *priceless* opportunity to confirm our rodent data in humans—do you realize how rare it is to get a normal and diseased human brain all in the same week? Do you realize how many arses I had to kiss to win this bid?"

Claire risked a quick look from the screen, but he was grinning at her, not glaring. And then before she could reply, he leapt up and shot out the door.

✤ ✤ ✤

Claire's interactions with Alan Fallengale during the past month had reflected some characteristics of the science of their collaboration. His inner workings were mysterious, but every so often, one of her probings would reveal a facet of this mystery, realigning all of the previous data to fit in with a subtly altered hypothesis. During some sessions, his architecture would be resistant, gumming up her needles and neatly deflecting any attempts to gain access. Then, he would be his usual brisk, sometimes callous self, concerned with superficial topics—typically money and how best to acquire it—and hardly requiring Claire's presence at his monologues. And other evenings, the road might inexplicably open, giving way with thoughtless ease—although only up to a certain point.

The first time this happened, she hadn't been at all prepared. It had been during a late night session with the Interactrex when, uncertain how to proceed with the experiment, she put the Raison on standby and went upstairs to see if Alan were still around. Finding his lab deserted, she walked slowly through the shadowy space towards the glow of the inner office.

He was sitting at his desk, head in hands and unaware of her approach. His posture, normally sketched in vibrant lines and brash shades, seemed dull and melancholy. She hesitated in the darkness, taking his likeness with a rush and spatter of silent words: *alone, aloof, alluring, alien.* Words that charged the air—as unspoken words tend to do—and brought his head up just at the precise moment she had decided not to disturb him.

Alan Fallengale's troubled gaze met Claire's with such an impact that she took a step backward, unprepared for his unexpectedly violent reaction. It wasn't that she had startled him—in fact, it was almost as if he'd been expecting her, with a strange mixture of yearning and fear that Claire instantly and instinctively knew was directed towards somebody else.

Confused, Claire found herself unable to speak or look away as the electric silence stretched out and the odd recognition in his eyes slipped into bitterness.

"Circe has left her cave," he observed viciously. "What is it that you want?"

After a few mute seconds, she turned and fled, as fast as she could propel herself without actually running. The harsh corridor lighting further inflamed the skin of her face, and the robotic motion-sensitive CCTV cameras craned their necks to watch her erratic transit.

The matsu trees brush her hair as she passes beneath them, as do the shining strands of barbed wire. . .

She had mostly composed herself by the time Alan tapped on the doorframe of her lair. Or more accurately, her humiliation had transmuted into the more controlled emotion of nascent anger—not quite exploded, but liable to do so any moment.

"Claire," he said, when she didn't turn to face him.

She tapped a few keys, cool plastic patter in the stillness.

"Why do you have to be so nasty?" She kept focused on the fall and dribble of numbers down her screen. The truth was that she half wanted him to provoke her temper into full life, just to see where that might lead.

"That's a very complex question," he said.

A long pause ensued. She didn't want to turn to face him then, but there had been something about his voice that was impossible to resist. Her head moved, and then her wary gaze: she took in his long grey overcoat, the briefcase, the renewed confidence, the enigmatic green eyes and expressionless face. He was back in control, too.

"I only went up there," she finally said, "to ask you something about *your* experiment."

"I realize that," he said mildly. "And I've come to apologize—yet again. I'm a twisted soul, you know."

No, she thought. I *don't* know. Why did she have the feeling that he wanted her to? But her usual facile tongue felt paralyzed.

"Are you aware," he said, cutting bladelike into that silence—for he was not a man to be intimidated by either silence or its ending—"that besides Ramon, you're the only one who ever calls me to task for it?"

The moment hung suspended, when things could have gone a number of ways.

"Apology accepted," Claire finally said, a defensive non sequitur, and asked him the question she'd gone upstairs to answer. After their brief discussion, she waited for him to invite her for a drink—something that had been happening with increasing frequency of late—but he only murmured good night and disappeared into the corridor dazzle.

Contrast that encounter with their most recent after-hours encounter, a week previously, when the tone couldn't have been more different.

"If material gain and prestige are that important to you," Claire had ventured, "then why didn't you become a neurosurgeon?"

She leaned back, making herself more comfortable—she had long since lost her awe of the Corbusier sofa—and he smiled, emanating the mischief that had infected him the entire evening. "You must have the most unfortunate impression of me, Claire."

"I'm a scientist—I observe."

"Indeed. Well, I suppose there's no point in trying to hide anything from your incisive eyes." A bob of the head, not necessarily ironical. "There are two salient points here. First, money is important to *almost* everyone"—another nod, this time to her quaint confession to the contrary during their first drink—"but most think it's too vulgar to admit it. Which makes me. . ."

"Refreshingly non-hypocritical?"

"Precisely." More unuttered laughter in the configuration of his features. "And secondly ... medicine is the mere *execution* of the innovations of scientists. I have no doubt that it is fascinating and fulfilling after a fashion, to those of a certain temperament, but I am not a lowly follower of—what is it, Claire?"

"I'm trying to imagine a roomful of neurosurgeons reacting to that assessment."

"Do they have bone saws and scalpels?" He laughed outright this time. "But why should I have to compromise? I've always been a gifted and hard worker, so why can't I enjoy the creativity of science and the pleasure of earthly rewards at the same time?"

"So money isn't everything, then. No thanks, I'm planning to return to the lab." She moved her glass out of range of the poised bottle.

"Not everything—only one highly essential component. But better not let that get out—it might ruin my heartless reputation, which I find, for many reasons, useful to cultivate."

"Why?"

He studied the glass in his hand, measuring the heft of the sturdy crystal. "Actually, I'm more keen to discuss what you were telling me earlier about your poetical upbringing. I find starving artists particularly fascinating."

"It sounds a lot more romantic than it really is, trust me." There was no way she was going to say any more about her father besides the barest biographical sketch he had already coaxed out of her.

"Here's what I find baffling and inconsistent," Alan said. "You say that money is wholly unimportant—"

"Not unimportant—just not a major focus, beyond the minimum amount required to live comfortably. I'm not *that* principled."

"Okay, noted." He was peeling a satsuma, teasing away the loose rind with meticulous fingers. "But if your first love is the literary—a notoriously ill-paid profession—why are you here at NeuroSys taking home an attractive remuneration package?"

She was quiet a moment, watching the exposed fruit materialize in his palm. "I'm not so sure I can explain." *That I want to explain*, was what she meant.

He looked up from his activities and gave her a small smile. "Of course you can. Your articulate nature is one of the most interesting things about you."

Was he teasing? It was impossible to tell.

"My father's teaching was meaningless to him," she said at last, "but worse, it sucked away the time and energy he needed for his real work. This would have been acceptable if he had succeeded as a poet, but. . ."

Alan began to pry apart the individual wedges of the satsuma, releasing a fine aerosol of juice, and kept a courteous silence while she gathered her words.

"Eventually," she said, "it became obvious that devoting your life to something that means everything—and then to fail or burn out on it— could break your heart. Far better to make a career out of something you merely respect and admire, and keep your passions as a hobby."

"It makes hard-headed sense," Alan said, his face unexpectedly sympathetic. "Not at all an attitude I would have expected from someone like you—or someone your age. But, forgive me for observing that it also seems a bit uncourageous. Why go through life keeping yourself one step removed from the things that truly matter?"

Claire only shrugged as she accepted a sliver of fruit, its bitter edges cutting into her tongue. It wasn't a question of removal: words were closer to her than anything else, regardless of how she earned her money. But she didn't think that Alan would understand.

"Try me," he challenged.

After that strange conversation with Alan, she had steered her bicycle slowly back to the lab. A full moon hung between the scanty winter trees, reflecting off the ice-glazed canals. The air was as cold as iron, and the environment was absolutely devoid of people, wind or any movement whatsoever. She was the only one alive in the entire universe.

It hardly seemed possible, in the sensible chill of night, that she had just spent the past hour discussing her passion for poetry with the likes of Alan Fallengale. It hadn't seemed odd at the time: he was interested and reasonably knowledgeable on the subject, and the conversation spun out easily, without self-consciousness.

But now that she was alone, she felt a confused sensation that she had given too much of herself away. Why had he pressured her into revealing all of those things about her father? Fortunately, she had caught herself before telling him the worst of it. Why, when it seemed at the time that the flow of information had gone both ways, did she realize in retrospect that she had done all of the revealing and he, all the digging? What did he want with her? Just friendly conversation? Could someone like him ever be someone she might call a friend? How long had it been since she'd had a friend she felt comfortable enough with to share such personal information? As fond as she was of Rachel, she had never told her about Edward's bitter life or her own private obsessions. Of course Rachel knew Claire "liked" poetry, and enjoyed hearing her quote it, but that was about as far as it went.

And what was this trembling raw feeling that infected her whenever she experienced, or even just thought about, Alan's mercurial face, flashing from scorn to humour to delight to menace in rapid succession, and was there any chance that it was, or might one day be, mutual? What was the reason for his sympathy towards her, when she knew he showed everyone else, with the exception of Ramon Ortega, impatience and disdain, and why did this sympathy make the raw feeling even more intense?

Of all these questions, she found one especially disturbing: was Alan correct, that her choice of a scientific career had been the act of a coward?

"It is important," Alan had said, near the end of the visit, "to recognize exactly what it is about life that makes you happy, and then to pursue it with unwavering commitment. There are no second chances."

Chapter 13

❧

Claire sat in her chair at the Interactrex, preparing herself like a concert pianist about to delve into a sonata. But this wasn't a mere practice session. The rarest of all cells sat waiting beneath the Raison's watchful eye: cells that had only a few days before resided inside the head of a terminal Alzheimer's patient. This was the actual performance, and the audience was hushed with silence, waiting for her to raise her hands.

It was about eight o'clock at night, and Alan had just left—a distinct relief, because he had been tense and irritable. At the same time, she couldn't help but resent that he'd gone home, whereas she was fated to spend another night battling endless rounds with the Raison. In the past few weeks, she had gone home only a handful of times, forcing sample after sample into the bowels of the machine with only the crickets for company.

But it wasn't just Alan driving her forward: it was the science itself. The closer she got to the fundamental core, the more glimpses of truth were obscured in seductive layers, like a reverse striptease.

She told herself, sternly, that Alan was using her. But then, he used everybody: it was nothing personal. She remembered her analogy about Alan forcing ideas into straight furrows; naturally, this strategy relied on beasts of burden to make the miraculous crops grow. She knew that the hours she had been putting in recently were far beyond what Stanley would expect, and even Ramon, normally reluctant to criticize or interfere, had taken her aside and suggested that she ease off, that her health was bound to suffer. She wasn't sure how he had found out the extent of her overtime, but the truth was that her exhaustion was noticeable to everyone—except Alan. In fact, most of the company knew of her long hours thanks to the night porter's penchant for gossip and, assuming she was trying to make everyone else look bad in comparison, resented her for it.

But there were benefits to staying on Alan's good side. There were those confusing off-site sessions at Alan's house. They were impregnated, at least for her, with some unspeakable charge, even more so because the invitations were impossible to predict, leaving her in a grip of anticipation right up until the moment he walked out of the lab. Why last weekend, and not tonight? Were there other assignations, other women? More than likely, if all the rumours were true. Claire told herself it was none of her business.

Possibly the most significant effect of Alan's patronage was the striking change it had effected in her colleagues' attitude—at least to her face. At the weekly staff meeting, people treated her with new respect, no longer doling out ritual harassment thinly disguised as scientific criticism. Everyone knew about the unofficial collaboration, and of Alan's enthusiasm, and while it had done nothing to make the others friendlier, it had at least created a sort of truce. No, truce wasn't the right word. It was more like keeping up in an arms race, the peace tottering under the aegis of mutually assured destruction.

But none of that was important now. Claire sat with her back perfectly straight, waiting. All was silent except for the pneumatic sighs and moans of the Interactrex 3000 going through a self-cleaning cycle. The multiple screens gave off a lush blue glow, throwing silhouettes into the corners and creating a disconcerting impression that the machine's rat-nest of tubing and cables was reaching out for her, trying pull her under like one of Hylas's nymphs.

I am half sick of shadows.

Suddenly, Claire decided not to submit to another all-nighter, Alan be damned. She would process this one last sample, then go home and get some sleep.

❦ ❦ ❦

Claire glided like a noiseless bird over the field of neurons, choosing her next prey with care. She was trying to slip into the half-trance, half-daydream of Collection, nudging the needle forward with infinite care, but it wasn't happening tonight. Awareness of the importance of this particular sample made it impossible to block out reality, prickling against her concentration like an annoying mosquito whine on the edge of sleep.

Maybe that was why Alan had decided to let her work in peace. She had come to recognize that despite his abrasive manner, he was not insensitive to its effects on others. Nevertheless, she didn't look forward to his reaction when he discovered that she had only performed one experiment this evening. But, she rationalized to his imaginary green-eyed glare, an exhausted operator would be error-prone, and there wasn't enough material to waste on stupid mistakes. Besides, there was still plenty of time left over the next few days to complete all the runs he could possibly desire before the ephemeral cells lost their potency.

"And anyway, you don't have to justify your behaviour to *him*," she said aloud.

The Raison chirped in sisterly agreement, and Claire tapped a glissando on the keyboard before approaching her chosen cell. These neurons looked different from those of the car crash victim. Although the brain's diseased architecture, with its plaque-like Alzheimer's lesions, had been lost after its cells had been teased apart, the individual cells themselves were odd—rough and flimsy, as if they'd been through battle.

"Let's see what we've got," she murmured, aiming her arrow towards the heart of the nucleus.

※ ※ ※

The sonata had reached its final movement, and the pianist was struggling.

She wasn't satisfied with the sample she had just taken; the preliminary numbers at the beginning of the Ladders indicated that the amount of protein was too low to expect a good signal. The Raison wasn't happy about it either, its warning light winking a petulant amber. Despite the ache in her neck and the telltale tremor of her hands, she resolved to make one more attempt.

Another alarm went off.

"Christ, what now?"

The Interactrex, reminding her that all eight units of the disposable Purgatory filter pack were used up. Gritting her teeth, she took a fresh pack from the refrigerator and snapped it into place before returning to her seat, willing herself to concentrate this time.

She zeroed in on her victim, the needle sliding inexorably past the thready network of ducts and vesicles on the edge of the axon body towards the dark centre.

And then it happened: an accident. *The* accident. Science, of course, is riddled with them. People usually think of research as planned, predicted, executed in a straight line from hypothesis to experiment, experiment to conclusion, conclusion to solid new fact, progressing smartly from *eureka*! to Nobel in one purposeful flow. But of course it doesn't always happen like that. Mistakes get made: weary PhD students forget to turn off their Bunsen burners, come in the next morning with a hangover to find that an interesting chemical reaction has occurred in the charred goo at the bottom of their flasks.

But what most people still don't appreciate is that the accident itself is not enough. The bleary-eyed lad must pause in the act of disposal, hand poised on the tap to rinse out the ruined remains of the previous day's work. He must have the observational skills, the foresight and, most importantly, the curiosity, to say to himself, *I wonder what those odd crystals are, shimmering against the curve of the glass?* The truth is that the majority wouldn't notice, and if they noticed, wouldn't bother. Instead, they'd grumble, rinse out the flask, set up the experiment anew and this time, remember to take it off the burner before going off to the pub. And therein lies the difference between mistake and serendipity. Between a rote researcher and a real scientist.

And so it was that fate fudged the numbers and changed the paths of a number of lives forever. As Claire held her breath and began lowering the needle, a weary muscle misfired in her hand. Her thumb, poised above the injection button, spasmed downward. She swore and tried to hit the abort bar, but it was too late: the needle fired off and sucked up a sample, the Interactrex emitting its beep of confirmation and its show of falling stars across the console.

"Idiot!" She hit the "pause" button to override the sorting programme. The needle hadn't yet been positioned correctly over the cell, so the sample it had drawn was useless, just the liquid medium bathing the cells.

The chips in those filter packs took hours for her technician to assemble, costing hundreds of euros in antibodies and coupling reagents—and one unit of it was ruined, just like that. She was half out of her seat to yank out the first unit of the filter pack and throw it in the bin when she stopped, remembering something Maxwell had been fond of saying:

"Everyone makes mistakes, but do try to make yours *useful*."

She sat back down, hit "play" and let the sorting programme continue where it had left off. There was no harm in completing the analysis; after all, it could serve as a useful positive control. The space outside of these diseased neurons should be loaded with excreted SCAN, roaming around and mortaring together the Alzheimer disease proteins with ruthless efficiency.

Ten minutes later, when the sorting was complete deep inside the Raison, with binding pairs zooming up the Ladder towards the identification queue and the non-binding proteins rejected down the Snakes, Claire activated the next unit of the fresh pack and went back, for the third time, to collect the proper sample.

❧ ❧ ❧

Claire headed for the coffee room to stretch her legs and wait for the final results. When she stepped back into the darkened room twenty minutes later, buzzing with caffeine and the anticipation of an impending result, The Interactrex was just formatting the final data.

She slung herself into the chair and scrolled to the top of the main screen, interpreting the columns of numbers with ease. The data looked good. No SCAN in the nucleus, just as she would expect from the diseased mice experiments. Just that long queue of SCAN heading towards the outside world to wreak havoc in the spaces between the cells.

Claire felt a rush of triumph. Just because Alan had vanished didn't mean she couldn't celebrate. She would ring up Rachel once she got back to Amsterdam.

She was about to start tidying up and shutting down the systems when she remembered the fluid she had accidentally taken from the space outside of the Alzheimer's cells. Turning back to the screen, she navigated back to the previous reports to see how it looked.

But the columns were empty of numbers. Instead, a sparse dialogue box:

Error number 15: No target detectable.

The Raison had failed to find any SCAN binding to the amyloid brick proteins in the space outside of cells; if it had, the binding pairs would have been measured in Purgatory, shunted up the Ladders, and the screen would have been full of numbers and statistics.

"This is odd," Claire said to the Interactrex, which did not deign to reply. According to the Universal Aggregation Principle, the space outside of these cells should be packed with SCAN/amyloid clusters. Maybe the death of the patient had slowed down its secretion—but

Alan and Ramon had performed many biochemical studies on similar brain cultures, and that would not be expected. Maybe the clusters were just too dilute to be detectable when they were loose outside the cell—although that didn't seem likely either. But it was true that she had never tried to test fluid outside of cells before, and did not remember Maxwell ever having done so either.

She'd give Maxwell a call in the morning, see if he'd ever performed any calculations about detecting proteins outside of cells. Maybe there was some technical problem in seeing proteins this way—she had never intended to do the experiment anyway.

She initiated the final cleaning protocols, hitting an affirmative YES to each of the Interactrex's routine questions:

"Purge MALDI-B?

"Purge Ladders?

"Purge Purgatory promenade?

"Purge Snakes?"

Claire paused over the last question, finger poised a millimetre from the appropriate key. It was impossible for the missing SCAN proteins to have gone down the Snakes, because that was the route that proteins took when they were solo, not binding to a protein partner at all.

And yet . . . it wouldn't be that difficult to run a routine ID on what had been rejected down the Snakes on that mistaken run. Just to be certain. All she'd have to do was re-route the ID queue tubing from the Ladders to the Snakes—a matter of ten minutes of fiddling under the cover. And then the normal twenty minutes for MALDI identification.

Undecided, Claire looked at her watch: ten past ten. Plenty of time to do the procedure and still get back to town for that drink.

Do try to make your mistakes useful.

She picked up a screwdriver and got to work.

❦ ❦ ❦

Claire came back into the room, called up the report and had a look.

And looked again. She tapped a few keys, but the numbers stubbornly remained.

"This is impossible," she accused the Interactrex.

The machine's red standby light winked back, on and off into infinity: *I'm only the messenger.*

A coldness seemed to creep into the lab. There *had* been SCAN proteins in the accidental sample, all right, so much SCAN that the initial histogram had gone off the scale and the machine had been forced to dilute the input material one hundred fold and reanalyse it.

And the implications were as clear as the rest of that evening's results. All the SCAN collected from outside the cell had been routed down the Snakes by the Raison's sorting programme because none of this SCAN had been binding to anything, least of all to the amyloid brick proteins. There simply hadn't been any Universal Aggregation at all.

Experiment, result, interpretation, the three links in the chain of this tidy, ordered profession that had seduced her. A conveyor belt of logic that only flowed in one direction, if you set up your experiments properly. No Universal Aggregation, no target for the Zapper: no cure for Alzheimer's.

Reason tried to assert itself. Surely someone would have noticed this fatal flaw by now. After all, an entire company had been working on nothing else for years, whereas she was just a green recruit. But then she remembered that her machine could study molecular interactions in real time, in a way that hadn't been feasible before. Had nobody seen this fracture in the company's central hypothesis because nobody had had the means to look?

It must be an error, a technicality. A fluke. She would repeat the experiment, and the second time all would be well. Or Maxwell would explain exactly why protein binding might not be visible when tested in liquid medium under these particular conditions. There had to be a logical explanation.

Celebration forgotten, Claire spent the rest of the night doing the same experiment over and over, using the unusual conditions she had accidentally discovered, numb rote movements in an exhausted trance. She probed the spaces outside of dozens of diseased brain cells, looking for amyloid and SCAN and any evidence that they stuck together. She had let the needle drink twice, ten times, and then a hundred times the normal amount of liquid, until the Raison, bloated with fluid, protested with a host of warning lights and chimes she had never had a chance to see in action before.

But the results remained the same, no matter how many times she rammed it through. SCAN existed as a solo protein once it reached the outside of the cell—it did not bind to anything, not even to the amyloid protein, which was clearly present in abundance. The Zapper, in that case, would be useless.

Chapter 14

❦

The next morning, Maxwell was delighted to hear from her, and then just as quickly distracted by her question.

"Direct sampling from the fluid *outside* of cells, did you say? Now there's a coincidence: I was speaking to Mads about this issue only yesterday."

Claire was curled up in her napping chair in the lab, trying not to weep. It was about nine o'clock and her head felt full of painful grit.

She made an effort to keep her voice level. "What does Mads know about it?"

"Funnily enough, he recently initiated a project to test cerebral spinal fluid from epidurals ... something about meningitis, though why the Danish *Cancer* Institute might be interested was beyond—"

"So did he get any signal?"

"Shocking waste of the Interactrex, if you ask me ... not using its functions to the full potential, might as well be a glorified aspirator. I told him—"

"Maxwell! Was he able to detect proteins from outside of cells?"

"Oh yes—handily. In fact, if anything it's apparently much easier without the distraction of intracellular material. Very clean, almost zero background—he e-mailed me the numbers."

"What was the protein concentration?"

"Hold on, love. . ." Claire could hear faraway tapping over the crackly line, before he pronounced a number.

Her hope plummeted—it was a good thousand times lower than the concentration of SCAN she'd picked up in the Snakes last night. So if Mads had had no problem seeing proteins in such scarcity, it was more difficult to believe her results were anomalous.

"And did he mention any problems seeing his protein bind to things that it should bind to, under those conditions?"

"I didn't ask, love." She could almost see his shrug. "But I can't envision it could cause any difficulties."

❦ ❦ ❦

A few minutes later she had Mads on the line from Copenhagen, as timid and stammering as she remembered.

"Problems with b-b-binding?" he asked, after she had outlined the situation in general terms.

"Yes, like a failure to see protein A bind to protein B when sampled from outside of cells instead of from inside a cellular compartment."

"How could that m-make a difference?" His tone sounded reasonable, which for some reason infuriated her.

"I don't know, Mads . . . different osmolarity? Different pH? Different specific gravity? Use your imagination!"

"It shouldn't matter, Claire. If that's the environment the p-proteins are normally in, they should just bind, right?"

"But you have to admit it's theoretically possible that they couldn't."

The line hummed for a few seconds. "You know what Maxwell would say?"

"I *told* you, I already talked to—"

"*He'd* say that your hy-p-p-pothesis was wrong, not the Interactrex. Oc-c-cam's razor." Another static-filled pause. "The simplest explanation is that your protein A just doesn't bind to protein B outside of the cell. Full s-s-stop."

Mads had been her student, in a special apprenticeship to become an Interactrex operator. She was stung, hearing him say the words that she had probably chided him with on any number of occasions in the past. It stung even more because they were absolutely true.

❦ ❦ ❦

After Mads hung up, she sat in the chair, watching motes of dust hang in the light. She saw them as single units of SCAN proteins outside of cells, hovering like clouds of solo gnats. She visualized the Zapper, NeuroSys's miraculous drug, as a flock of angry gulls, searching for mortared bricks and being unable to find any prey in the clear afternoon sea air. She saw swarms of solo SCAN getting flushed down the Snakes, gleeful with the deception. She heard the purging of the Snakes, or maybe it was actually the waves, soaking against the shore with oblivious repetition, the same as it had been doing for billions of years . . . she felt the warmth radiating off the sand. . .

"I *told* you we were pushing her too hard."

A voice penetrated the golden air, and then a hand landed gently on her shoulder.

Claire, confused, made out the silhouettes of two men against the blinding glare through the crosshatch of her eyelashes. The gnats and gulls had vanished, and the sun's angle was significantly lower.

"Are you all right, *querida?*" Ramon was bent down, face near hers and brown eyes concerned. Alan stood just beyond.

" '*Sleep, sleep, beauty bright. . .*' " Alan, a quickly adapting creature, had lost no time starting to tease her with lines of poetry. Not as well-versed as she, he tended to restrict himself to famous first lines. "Relax, Ramon, she's only dozing. We would have checked in earlier, but we were trapped in the meeting from hell."

Claire passed a trembling hand over her eyes, trying to orientate herself.

"How did yesterday's experiment go?" Alan asked.

"Can't you give it a rest for two seconds?' Ramon said sharply. "Let the poor girl wake up. How late did you work last night, Claire?"

She took a calculated risk that, underneath her white coat, neither man would remember what she'd been wearing yesterday. "Eleven or so. But I didn't sleep well."

"When was the last time you did?" Ramon's voice was relentless.

"I'm perfectly fine, honestly."

Claire struggled to sit up, the memory of recent events flooding back like a nightmare patching itself together. She had been ambushed before coming up with a plan. Part of her thought it was far too soon to be drawing any conclusions, that it would be better to say nothing. Her experiments couldn't possibly be right.

But she felt honour-bound to tell the men immediately. She had told little lies her entire life, as most do, but never about an experimental fact. To do so would be despicable, and would violate every code of the profession. And if she was right, what about the Alzheimer's patients who would soon receive the new drug? Giving them such false hope would be a crime—especially if they could have received a more effective drug instead.

"Let me show you the data," she said to buy time, standing up so rapidly that her head yawed with vertigo. Alan whipped out a hand to steady her, warm and powerful on her back. Caught off guard, she wanted to fall against him, to fall at his feet.

Instead, she reached for her notebook, which had not been updated since the accident.

"Is it good news or bad?" Alan asked, as his hand dropped back to his side.

She wasn't fooled by his offhand manner: he cared about the outcome, as much as he cared about anything. *When The Zapper goes into Phase I, I'll have it made.* Her heart began to thrum, the heat of her physical reaction to his presence slowly overwritten by the chemicals icing into her bloodstream. She could not lie, she could not possibly lie.

"It can't be good news if you're so reluctant to say," Alan said, eyes narrowed and searching her face. He had this way of closing down, warm flesh turning to stone. After she confessed, he would lose interest in her altogether.

"No," she said. "It went really well, just as we predicted." The words were somehow out of her mouth with no instruction, no permission—no thought. And impossible, now, to take back.

As Alan and Ramon exhaled relief, she felt like a boulder, wavering on the top of a pointed cliff and hanging there, just a microsecond, before toppling over the other side. The journey downward, from this moment on, would only get easier.

Part II

❧

THE DECEPTION

Chapter 15

﹏❧﹏

Precisely ninety minutes before dawn, the crickets began to sing. Claire didn't even look up from the screen. Although she had not been keeping track of the time, her subconscious had cocked a virtual ear and was prepared. And when the raspy chorus arrived on schedule, her brain responded with a reward of chemical satisfaction at nature successfully predicted, just as her caveman ancestors used to get a buzz from postulating tigers from broken twigs or trout from shadows in still pools. The only distinction important here was that a modern human like Claire could afford to waste her highly evolved intellect on whimsy.

But Claire wasn't thinking in such prehistoric terms. It was January, and a lot had already happened. The primitive reward was no match for the second reaction that followed: violent uneasiness, washing over everything she'd been feeling only moments before. She had long since grown used to a gnawing sense of wrongness, a persistent ache in the vicinity of her spleen whenever she remembered what had happened.

The association had become indelibly fixed.

❦ ❦ ❦

The New Year had come and gone in a smear of grey skies and cold rain. Typical of the national character, the Netherlands celebrated with their communal display of individual firecrackers, collectively sending up a midnight roar louder than any official display. On the afternoon of January the first, the streets of Amsterdam became coated in thick red mud as the papers from millions of spent ammunitions liquefied in the rain. The tyres of Claire's bicycle and the soles of her shoes became impregnated with the stuff, which would take many days to finally wash down the sewers.

Rachel had gone back to Brighton for the festive period, and the corridors of NeuroSys were nearly empty as well. But Claire wasn't close to any of her remaining relations, so she had no home to return to. For her, the New Year was a welcome return to normality: being in a foreign city without a real Christmas had increased her sense of isolation. The Dutch greeted their *Sinterklaas* with ginger *koekjes*, cunning poems and gifts the recipient had to sweat to receive: packages baked in cakes, suspended from trees, encased in concrete or otherwise hidden behind a string of clues. These ritual activities culminated on December the fifth—the rest of the month was just denouement.

And in the meantime, Claire was several weeks into a terrible quandary. After being unable to tell Ramon and Alan what had happened straight away, each day of silence had made the prospect became more difficult until now, it was impossible.

In the space of three seconds, when her hand had slipped on that needle, her life had completely altered. But Claire found it almost more disturbing that things continued on more or less as normal. Somehow, she hadn't been punished. The other experiments went on, the company went on, the clinical trial preparations went on, Alan and Ramon and their large team of researchers went on as if her pernicious, undermining little slice of truth about the Zapper did not exist. True, the crickets continued to sound a touch reproving to her guilty ears, but there was no sudden halt to the planet's revolution. The only physical reminder was that ache in her gut, which flared up with increasing frequency whenever she started thinking about her deception. A parasite, a *guilt*-parasite, sent to goad her into confessing.

❦ ❦ ❦

Finally, Claire couldn't bear it any longer. She had to tell someone, so she decided to tell Rachel. It was an otherwise unremarkable Friday night in a crowded, noisy bar in the Jordaan, mid-January. The rest of their crowd had gone to see a film, so they were alone.

Normally, Claire's resident parasite receded during the weekends, but as soon as she made the decision to confess, her gut began to ache and her

108

heart hummed with adrenaline. And was that a whisper of panic, brushing against her brainstem?

"So I'm dying to hear your big news, darling." Rachel looked at her levelly in a manner suggesting that she had long since registered her internal distress. Knowing Rachel, she might even have been patiently waiting for weeks for Claire to come out with it.

"It's about work," Claire said. "About the project."

"Your official project, or your big-idea project?"

"Neither," she said. "It's about something, Alzheimer's related, that I wasn't supposed to test, but that ended up. . ."

"Something's gone wrong, hasn't it?"

Claire couldn't help smiling. "You could say that. I'm in serious trouble, Rach."

Rachel sat up straighter. "What do you mean, trouble? I thought you were just talking about *science*. You haven't broken any rules, have you?"

"No, not exactly. Or . . . sort of. . ."

Slowly, reluctantly, Claire began to explain.

She told Rachel about the hospice and about the dead woman whose diseased brain had become available. She told her about the accident, how she had unintentionally analysed a sample of fluid from outside of cells, and found that SCAN existed solo under those conditions, and did not mortar together the amyloid brick proteins as the Universal Aggregation Principle dictated. She reminded her that the Zapper was meant to act by dissolving SCAN/amyloid clusters—clusters that she now believed did not exist at all in real Alzheimer's patients.

"Christ, Claire." Rachel swayed a bit. "But are you absolutely sure your company's drug is not going to work in people?"

"No, not absolutely. I mean, there's a chance it works against Alzheimer's, just not in the way that it was designed."

"That sounds like wishful thinking."

"Well, it did work in Alzheimer's mice, so the Zapper obviously does something."

"How can it, if this SCAN thing isn't acting like glue?"

Claire rubbed her fingers over her brows, feeling a prickle of headache beneath. "I've been trying to work it out, Rach. Mice and humans aren't always the same. Maybe SCAN works like glue in mice, and does something else in humans."

"You don't look very convinced."

"Occam's Razor," Claire said, thinking about Mads. "The most likely explanation is the simplest—and the most convoluted is the least likely. I mean, its pretty far-fetched if mice did one thing and humans the other—it happens sometimes, but not very often. It seems simpler that the company just got it wrong. Though I don't possibly see how that could be either."

Both women lapsed into silence, and Claire looked away at the press of humanity around them: push and shove, cigarettes and alcohol, flirtation and avoidance. The flickering lights captured expressions in dramatic still shots: a woman in a red dress with hard eyes, frozen in the act of rearing back her head in laughter; a man, his sliding hand arrested on the small of his lover's back; a bar worker, poised with a column of empty nested glasses curving dangerously near its pinnacle; an old man, incongruous and alone at a table, tobacco and papers arrested between gnarled fingers.

And then beyond. A man, even taller than the giants around him but obviously not Dutch. He looked familiar. There was something Celtic about the way his weirdly pale skin warred against the black hair, like the doomed hero of a tragic poem, although she could tell by the way his mouth moved that he was speaking rapid Dutch with his companions. She was struck, too, by his posture. She had observed that most very tall people slouched in a subconscious effort to blend in, but this man stood almost defiantly straight, shoulders thrown back and head high.

Out of context, it took her a few seconds to recall who he was: the intense albino-skinned man at the back of the welcome meeting on her first day at NeuroSys, the one who had not been hostile, but who had not joined in the laughter at Ramon's joke about the weather either. The one whose striking image she'd used as a prop to ward off her panic attack. She had seen him around the building since, but had never had a need to interact with him. She didn't even know his name.

While still speaking, the man's gaze intersected her own. The connection jolted her equanimity; even though he didn't nod in acknowledgement, she was certain he had recognized her. *Made a note of her*, utterly unperturbed, as his lips continued to form words she couldn't hear.

She jerked her head away, just as Rachel complained, "Claire— you're not listening."

"Sorry." Claire pawed in her handbag for some painkillers, liberated a few tablets and washed them down in a gulp of beer. She was angry; not only had it been stupid to be caught staring, but seeing him had ignited other grievances. She hated the idea that NeuroSys—in the guise of one of its employees—had violated the one last place she could escape from work.

"I said, how did Alan react when you told him about this?"

"I didn't tell him," Claire said. "I haven't told anyone."

"What!" Rachel stared at her, open-mouthed. "And this happened when? Before Christmas? What on earth are you playing at, Claire?"

She looked away from her friend's shock and outrage. The tall pale man was ignoring her now, speaking into the ear of a sleekly feline woman, who smiled in response. The entire party looked trendy—a good ten years older, up in the social stratosphere compared to Claire. She felt adrift, dislocated, the noise of the room dampening down into a numb bubble of unreality.

What on earth are you playing at?

Chapter 16

Joshua wasn't as surprised to see Claire in the Jordaan bar that Friday night as she obviously was to see him. He already knew she lived in Amsterdam, as they occasionally sat in the same train carriage coming home in the late evenings. Not that she had ever noticed him, the way she was so thoroughly lost in one old book or another, or in the spiral-bound notebook she frequently scribbled into. He had once watched with amusement as the *conducteur,* after repeated verbal demands to see her ticket, had been forced to shake her by the shoulder to get her attention.

He hadn't been entirely sure that Claire even knew who he was, but her reaction on spotting him from across the bar, moments before, settled the question. Claire was one of the most oblivious people he had ever met—or had repeatedly failed to meet, in her case—not counting their anonymous bioinformatics exchange several months ago. *Fey,* his Irish mother would have called her. She scurried through the corridors of NeuroSys with her head down, clutching her notebooks like a spinster church organist late for the Sunday service. He had never seen her in the canteen for lunch or in the local pub after work. He knew, like everyone else, that she was a genius with the Interactrex and that she spent most of her time in its lair. And it had become common knowledge that she was working almost exclusively with Alan and Ramon these days—Zeke Bannerman's mutterings about her neglect of the stroke project were getting louder by the week. And Alan's lavish attention wasn't exactly a safe situation either. Somebody ought to take her aside and warn her on both counts.

As a behavioural subject, Claire had him thoroughly stumped. Socially, she had never bounced back from the hostile initial reception— —but how did this jibe with the skill and confidence she would have needed to finagle a high-profile collaboration with a company director nearly twice her age? And more intriguingly, why had her fear returned in the past few weeks, evident to him even from chance sightings around the building?

He watched her lean towards her drinking companion, a sensible-looking, elegant woman with an emotional state that didn't even twitch on his psychometer. When Claire began to speak intensely, Joshua was hit again by her anxiety, lapping against him like a strange sea. As his friends carried on chattering around him, Joshua couldn't resist one last look. The mystery of an unusual pattern, begging to be solved. And maybe something more, something about the way she put down her glass, placed fingers against her throat, ran an unconscious palm over the curve of her dark hair. She seemed to be cloaked in secrets, yet too insubstantial to possibly bear their weight.

🌱 🌱 🌱

Over the next few days, Joshua tried not to think about Claire and her burden of fear. After all, it had nothing to do with him, and the last thing he wanted to do was get involved in anything outside of his comfortable domain within the Pit. But one night, he had a vivid dream involving a poisonous green serpent stalking Claire through a jungle dripping with blood-red fruit. In the dream, Claire was blind, and when the snake transformed into Alan Fallengale, Joshua woke up with a start.

One for the Jungian textbooks, Joshua thought to himself as he scraped a razor over his pale skin, and one that didn't exactly require a shrink to interpret. But the disturbing image stayed with him, so much so that at the end of the day, he took a detour on his way out to see if Ramon were still around.

"I've been meaning to come down to the Pit to speak to you," Ramon said, looking up amiably from a transparent confection of plastic columns and loops of tubing on his bench. The lab was otherwise empty, lit only by a small lamp next to Ramon's elbow.

"Why are the lights out?" Joshua said in Spanish, because Ramon was usually more expansive in his native tongue.

"I can't stand that damned blue frequency," Ramon replied in kind, accepting the change of language without appearing to notice. "It makes me suicidal. *And* gives me a headache." He turned a tiny knob

113

on the column, arresting the flow of droplets into the collection tube and giving Joshua his full attention. "But I did have a bioinformatics question for you, unless you're in a hurry to get home. . ."

"Always happy to help," Joshua said.

"It's about our new SCAN binding partner."

"ESTA-333? Yes, I dealt with that personally when it was first discovered—I was sorry I couldn't have been more helpful."

"We've pulled out a few unexpected mRNA variants, which might lend a few more clues. Here're the details. . ." Ramon rummaged through his notebook and passed over a printout. "I'm no expert, but one of my postdocs thinks there might be an interesting dominant isoform. I'll e-mail you the file in a minute."

"Interesting." Joshua scanned the lines of code, unable to prevent himself from searching for patterns. "Well, I'll blast it into the databases tomorrow morning and see if anything new pops out."

"I've already tried the standard searches, so you needn't bother with those. But I'd be obliged if you could put it through one of your special algorithms. And maybe check a few of the more obscure databases to see if anyone else has made any progress on this."

"I know this is all hush-hush," Joshua ventured, "but are you at liberty to say how it could be that the Interactrex could find SCAN in a healthy cell, and in the nucleus no less?"

"Consider our paradigm officially shifted," Ramon said with a grin. "Alan didn't believe it at first, so you can imagine how thoroughly we've confirmed the initial findings. But it's rock-solid now, so I'm fairly certain this won't be a waste of your valuable time."

"Definitely not—I always suspected that there was more to SCAN than met the eye."

"Exactly—it was all a bit too tidy for biology, no? Now, I'm being rude—did you come for a particular reason?"

"Just passing by and saw you working late," Joshua said. "But to tell you the truth, I've been hearing rumours about the Interactrex, and I'd been wondering how the machine was performing."

"Why?" Ramon looked distinctly uncomfortable. "Did Stanley send you to spy on us?"

"Of course not!" Joshua said. "It's only . . . you know our department was supporting the rival equipment purchase, so I knew you were involved in a side-project with Dr Cyrus and I was merely . . . curious if the investment was paying off."

"Oh." Ramon relaxed. "Well, I can't speak for the stroke project, but Claire's been doing miraculous things with our Alzheimer mouse samples in her spare time—although I'm not sure Stanley knows just how *much* of her time Alan is taking, so you didn't hear it from me, *hombre*."

"What's Claire like? I haven't seen her down in the Pit."

"She's great," Ramon said, genuinely enthusiastic. "Young, of course, and a bit insecure about her not inconsiderable intellect, but getting more confident by the day. She actually contradicts Alan on a regular basis now, which is something my own postdocs are still afraid to do."

"He's not too hard on her, then?"

"I will admit I've been worried that she seems a bit stressed lately," Ramon said. "I was thinking of asking Alan to back off a bit."

"She does seem a bit fragile, and he can be. . ." Joshua trailed off, aware that Ramon, unlike most, was fond of Alan. What he wanted to say was, *he can be vain, violently temperamental, arrogant . . . and frankly predatory when it comes to pretty young women.*

"A real pain," Ramon finished serenely. "But after a rough start, they're getting along surprisingly well. They seem to have reached some sort of understanding."

Joshua headed down the stairs, disturbed more than comforted by this revelation.

❦ ❦ ❦

Joop, the night porter, looked up from his magazine as Joshua passed.

"You are early away, *hoor*," Joop commented in Dutch.

"Can't seem to focus this evening," Joshua replied in kind, pausing by the counter. The elderly porter often snagged him in conversation, probably because he was bored, his English was poor and there were only a few Dutch-speaking employees—although it was remarkable how much gossip the man managed to transmit despite this handicap.

"You and I have the same problem." Joop gestured at the CCTV composite spread out on the side wall of his cubbyhole. "Staring at monitors for hours and hours is not good for a person."

Joshua scanned the bank of screens, an eight by eight grid depicting scenes inside and out, most of them shuffling every few seconds to different camera feeds. The computers of the security system did not fall under the Pit's jurisdiction.

"How come some of the images never change?" Joshua asked, momentarily hypnotized.

"Those are the most strategic areas . . . the main entrances, the really expensive equipment." Joop stood up, clearly delighted at the opportunity to speak about his world. "See here. . ." He squinted through his half-moon glasses and pointed to each in turn. "The servers in your Pit . . . the capillary sequencer room . . . the confocals . . . the mass spec facility." He stumbled over the harsh English words for which there was no Dutch equivalent.

"What about that pricey new machine NeuroSys bought last April?" Joshua asked casually. "The Interactrex?"

"Oh, that!" The porter laughed softly, pointing out the square at the extreme upper right-hand corner of the grid. "Dr Fraser insists it gets continuous feed, not an intermittent, because the thing is so expensive. But that girl is in there all the time, so I tell Dr Fraser it is not necessary, but does he listen? *Nee*."

Joshua looked more carefully at the corner screen, as murky as a foetal ultrasound. Then he decoded the shapes: a person dwarfed by the bulk of the Interactrex 3000, back to the camera, dark hair spilling down and hands splayed over its console.

"Why is the picture quality so poor?"

"She never turns on the lights," Joop said, shrugging. "Worse than Ramon—at least he has a lamp, eh? She will go blind one day—I tell her so. I can't see her clearly until dawn. Someone could sneak in to attack her and I wouldn't—"

"Dawn?" Joshua frowned. "What time does she normally get in?"

"Oh, about six in the morning." The old man rubbed his nose, a prominent beak in his broad farmer's face. "Two hours before I go off shift. Or rather, she used to . . . she has been working right through the night a lot nowadays."

That would explain, Joshua thought, why he never saw her on the morning train.

"But she always has a friendly smile, and a cheerful *goede morgen*," Joop said. "Unlike the most of others, she actually tries to speak Dutch. I like that, *hoor*."

"When does she sleep?"

116

This was rhetorical, but Joop answered readily enough. "Sometimes she naps up there—I can see her on the monitor, dozing in the armchair. She's heading for burnout—has entirely too much hay on her fork."

❦ ❦ ❦

Joshua slouched in the corner of his seat as the train swept though dark farmlands, punctuated only by the lit bubbles of greenhouses—faraway outposts on a lunar landscape. The topic of Alan Fallengale was still lodged in his mind. Joshua was thinking back to when they had first met, when Alan had been almost likeable. He'd still been a womanizer, conceited about his appearance and fond of those vile colours of clothing he still favoured, but at least he knew how to have a laugh and wasn't so obsessed about being the best. One could share a pint with the man and have a reasonably decent time doing it.

At first, the move to the Netherlands brought Joshua closer to Ramon and Alan. Confronted with a confusing new environment, banding together seemed the best way to cope. The excitement of unravelling the Universal Aggregation Principle was like amphetamines, and the trio spent many late nights in the pub, discussing the experiments or the local women, indulging in soul-baring, expatriate angst.

But something had happened to Alan about a year into the new venture. He'd returned strangely altered from his Christmas holidays back in England. Joshua wasn't sure how obvious it was to everyone else, but he could sense a deadening of Alan's spirits, and something else lurking beneath—anguish or rage, possibly both.

One night in the lab when the two men happened to be alone, Joshua couldn't stand the tension any longer and made the mistake of asking Alan what was wrong. The other man reacted violently to the probing, several decibels louder than seemed warranted, and a verbal altercation ensued, further ignited by the airing of a number of older grievances and ultimately escalating beyond all proportion. Joshua had not been provoked to lose his temper in that way since he'd been a child and the result was—well, shocking, even to himself. All the more so considering his usual serenity.

From that day onward, the threesome deteriorated. Joshua never attempted to make peace, instead retreating into silence, which ultimately became habitual. Always ambitious, Alan started to be fiercely competitive and cruel. And though Ramon remained as kind as ever, his close intellectual collaboration with Alan meant that eventually, when the band blew apart, Joshua was the one who ended up on the losing side. Two further acts on Joshua's part made the separation permanent: giving himself over to Dutch culture, and stepping off the career ladder at NeuroSys, descending into the basement to found a department and start again in the newly-invented science of bioinformatics. Ramon and Joshua remained friendly—on the few occasions that they ever ran into one another—but Alan acted as if Joshua did not exist.

Joshua sat in the main room of the Pit the next morning, staring at the revised sequence of Claire's nuclear chaperone, ESTA-333. But he was far away, tangled up in something that had nothing to do with patterns of amino acids. Then he realized that Roz had addressed him several times.

"You've been in stand-by mode a lot recently," Roz observed.

"Day-dreaming about some native Amazonian beauty, no doubt," Matt said.

"Roz," Joshua said. "What's the prevailing feminine view of Alan Fallengale these days?"

"How do you mean?" Roz looked at him curiously. "If you're talking bedside manner, you know I wouldn't know."

"More his general reputation."

She shrugged. "Same as it's always been. He gets around, strictly on a scorched earth policy. Most of NeuroSys's women have wised up by now, but there seems to be an endless supply of fresh recruits— particularly the PhD students. Why?"

"He after one of your Amazons, boss?" Matt actually stopped typing, which he only did when he was really surprised.

Joshua turned back to the screen, but he could feel Roz's careful inspection of his profile. More than any other denizen of the Pit, Roz had a knack for knowing when a topic in the light-hearted repartee had suddenly gone serious.

"We're fairly isolated down here," she finally said, softly. "I'm usually about a day behind on the gossip. What's this all about, Josh?"

"Nothing. Really, forget it."

Sensing Matt's continued interest, Joshua began to tap at the keyboard, clamping work about him like a protective garment. What *was* it all about? It wasn't like him to be so non-specifically anxious about something so entirely peripheral to his own life.

He forced his attention back to the enigmatic ESTA-333. There was still something familiar about that centre stretch of code, and his frustration was mounting—especially when it became clear that Ramon's extra information didn't add anything to what he already knew.

"Still no leads?" Roz asked sympathetically. He could tell by the look in her eye that the subject of Alan Fallengale was only temporarily closed.

"Nothing," he said. "Any brilliant ideas?"

"Have you considered throwing money at it?" She regarded him thoughtfully. "I don't normally suggest outsourcing to my clients because of budgetary restrictions, but seeing as how this is Alan and Ramon's baby, and Stanley is probably in such a good mood about the clinical trial. . ."

"Roz—you're a genius." Joshua pulled down a bookmark and started tapping excitedly.

"Don't encourage her," Matt said. "She's unbearable enough as it is."

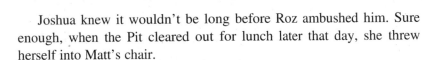

Joshua knew it wouldn't be long before Roz ambushed him. Sure enough, when the Pit cleared out for lunch later that day, she threw herself into Matt's chair.

"Not eating today?"

He shook his head. "I promised I'd crunch this gene for Salvatore, and I'm behind schedule. I'll grab a sandwich later."

"Anything I can help with?" She began to fiddle with her Fanta-coloured hair, recently hacked to fashionable dishevelment, with a restlessness that betrayed her true agenda.

"No, thanks."

"Listen, Josh. . ." She hesitated. "Did something happen between you and Hanneke?"

"Don't tell me you're actually considering one of Matt's theories?" Joshua almost laughed, but quickly saw that this response was inappropriate. "Although something *did* happen . . . but I put Matt's guess down to random noise, not his powers of deduction."

"You two break up, then?" She pressed her hand flat on her head, remorseful.

"Not so much that as drifted apart. And we're still friends." Joshua remembered how complacent Hanneke had been at the Jordaan bar that past Friday—a sure sign that their decision—brokered in the sensible, straightforward manner of all Dutch transactions—had been the right one.

"Why didn't you tell me?"

"It was no big deal." Joshua smiled faintly. "We seemed to have lost interest in each other simultaneously. Cultural differences."

"I thought you had been fully assimilated by the Nether Regions?"

Joshua considered her open, familiar face. "There's assimilation, and then there's true communion."

"Not sure that's got much to do with culture," she said ruefully. "But hang on . . . was Matt right that Alan was somehow involved?"

"No, that was the random noise bit. Completely unrelated question."

"I see." Roz's delicately pointed nose seemed to twitch at the air, trying to sense the direction of the wind. "Well, I made a point to journey Above Stairs earlier this morning and have a chat with Klaas about his project."

"Oh you did, did you?" He kept his face composed.

"Yes . . . and after a singularly fascinating discussion about the modular nature of transcription factor binding motifs, I let slip a casual interest in his boss's exploits."

"As one does." He knew she had something, or she wouldn't be so cagey. Getting gossip out of Roz was like birthing a foal—you had to know when to let the contractions do the work and when to use the forceps.

"Alan's been in a good mood recently, almost manic," she said. "But he hasn't had a conquest for a few months, which is unusual and also doesn't fit with the mood." She scanned his face for reaction, but he kept his expression bland.

"Anyone on the horizon?"

"Well, Klaas noted Alan's preoccupation with the Interactrex 3000. And he and the Black Maria have been spotted leaving NeuroSys together by bicycle several times, destination unknown. Nobody thinks it's serious . . . yet."

"Who's the Black Maria?"

"That's the Pit's nickname for Claire Cyrus." At his questioning look, she added, "As in, that annoying card that turns up just when you think the hardware budget is going to go your way."

"That's not fair."

"Sorry, boss . . . I didn't realize she was a friend of yours."

"She's not—we've never met. It's just a bit bitchy, don't you think?"

The lids of Roz's eyes closed almost to slits. "Since when has that stopped you from taking the piss out of half the building?"

He shrugged with eloquent disinterest. "Klaas say anything else?"

Chapter 17

⚜

Claire continued to distract herself from her distressing secret by picking apart the mysterious doings of SCAN and its chaperone ESTA-333. She let the stroke work slip as much as she dared, as it was too routine to lose herself in. Dr Bannerman was starting to harass her as the results dried up, and she knew the others were badmouthing her, but she didn't care.

Logically, she realized that pretending that the accident had not occurred was irrational and wrong, and she would contemplate telling Ramon (*never Alan, God no*) at least several times a week. Rachel, too, nagged her on nearly a daily basis to come clean, and the cricket song, some mornings, rammed the imperative into her brain until she wanted to scream. But the more time passed, the more difficult it became: how could she justify waiting one, two, four, eight weeks to confess? Instead, she would work long into the night on other things; she would shed fear into the bright-lit corridors. She would feel the now more-or-less constant ache in her insides, beginning to wonder whether this whimsical gut-parasite was actually an ulcer. Occasionally she would sense an incipient panic attack flutter suggestively at the base of her skull, but for some unknown reason these, like the secret, remained suppressed. For the moment.

🌿 🌿 🌿

A few days after Claire and Joshua had made eye contact in the Jordaan bar, Claire slipped into the Home of the Zapper at six-thirty in the evening to show Ramon her latest results. She found the man at his usual after-hours stool, in a pool of lamplight, applying stains to glass slides spread out all over his bench like debris from a vandalized shop window. The light glinted off the slides, fracturing into red, yellow and blue blobs that tangled in her eyelashes and made words stir in her weary brain. She was too tired to call up the old poem that the play of colours had reminded her of.

"*More* experiments?" Ramon put down his dropper bottle and took the sheaf of papers from Claire as she perched on a nearby stool. "How many times have I told you not to overdo it?"

"I'm not, honestly." The poetry was swiftly forgotten.

"Nobody could generate as much data as you do in a healthy work day."

"I've repeated the experiment with all the controls Alan insisted on," she told him, pointing out various columns of the Raison's printout and explaining what she had done. As expected, the numbers distracted him from his concern.

"That's very nice," he said, nodding as he scanned the page a second time. "Even Alan couldn't deny it now, the old mule."

"I heard my name in all that unholy jabber," Alan accused, sauntering into the lab. "I don't trust you two one bit when you've got your heads together like that."

"Claire was just telling me you'd lost yet another bet," Ramon said in English.

Alan sighed. "I'm going to swear off making them—she always wins. I suspect her of cheating . . . her, or the Interactrex."

"Blame it on anything but a failure of intellect," Ramon said. "It's like I keep telling you—you're losing touch with the common people, *hombre*. You ought to do an experiment now and then."

"Refresh my memory, Claire: What did I get wrong this time?" He made a face at her, but there was no rancour beneath it, only high spirits and bravado.

"If anything, the numbers are even more convincing under these conditions," Ramon said, still peering at the printout again before passing it to Alan. "I think it's time we put some more people on this."

"Good," Alan said briskly. Claire was intrigued by the way he never took it badly on the rare occasion when he was proved wrong—it seemed marvellously out-of-character. By all rights he ought to throw a glorious temper tantrum and stalk from the room. "Do we have any hints yet?"

"I've asked the Pit to take another look."

Alan made a face, making Claire wonder what he had against the Bioinformatics Department—too distressingly modern? But Ramon looked a bit uneasy as well.

Alan said suddenly, "Speaking of dubious computer miscreants. . ."

"Give it a rest, will you?" Ramon said sharply, baffling Claire still further.

The other man remained unperturbed. "Did you two read about that case of scientific misconduct at the Sanger Centre?"

They shook their heads.

"A postdoc actually faked database entries—invented an entire series of fictional gene variants—in order to beef up an article under consideration for publication in *Cancer Cell*."

"*Dios mio!*" Ramon said. "How on earth did he think he could get away with it?"

Claire's heartbeat seemed to stall for a second.

"*She*," Alan corrected, "must have had balls of steel—it was only a fluke that she happened to get caught. The news piece said she needed the paper to secure a fellowship and was desperate. I don't miss academia one bit in that respect, God knows."

Claire wanted to change the subject, but her throat was suddenly full of nausea.

"I don't get it." Ramon's voice was tight with emotion. "How can a *scientist* lie about the truth? Otherwise what's the point of doing science in the first place?"

She realized with bewildered horror that she was going to be sick. Dashing from the lab, she swerved into the nearest toilet and slammed into a stall. Teeth chattering, hands shaking, she waited for the dreaded resolution. She was as bad as that desperate postdoc—or even worse, because at least one could understand that other woman's motivations. In her own case, a failure to confess was far less comprehensible.

How can a scientist lie about the truth?

Afterwards, she leaned trembling against the sink, washing her face. She heard footfalls and then the door swinging open. In the mirror, she found it was not Ramon who had come to check on her as she'd expected, but Alan. She felt dirty, ugly, unfit to be seen. She felt *guilty*. The air still smelt faintly acrid from bile, and the artificial light seemed even brighter in here, glancing ruthlessly off the mirrors, stainless steel fittings and bleached-white tiles, smearing purple shadows under the eyes of her reflected counterpart.

"Okay?" he asked, coming over and putting a hand on her shoulder. He looked almost as curious as he was sympathetic. "Was it something I said?"

"Of course not." More vehemence than the joke called for, and Claire turned away from his perceptive stare to toss crumpled paper into the bin. "A bad sandwich, probably. I need to get back to work."

"Easy there. You're not going anywhere." He grabbed her arm as her escape turned into a wobbly lurch, and she felt too spent to resist as he helped her slump against the wall, keeping a firm grasp on her upper arm. The muscles in his hand felt bright, too, composed of the same material as the shining metallic surfaces around her, bands of tensile strength radiating energy and fire. Her vision darkened momentarily in a vice of vertigo.

"I'm sorry," Claire said, when it passed. "I know you've got better things to do than. . ."

"Look after an ill colleague?" His anger was swift. "Like any decent human being would? I take it, then, that you believe everything people say about me?"

"I. . ." She closed her eyes against the white dazzle, felt tears film underneath her lids. "I wouldn't know what people say."

"Why not?"

"Because nobody but you or Ramon ever really talks to me."

Alan swore softly and, after a few seconds of hesitation, put an arm around her. Claire, as if in a dream, leaned her head against his shoulder and breathed in the deep forest mossiness of his cologne. It was a moment that should have been awkward but wasn't.

"Is it that nobody ever talks to you," Alan said, just a voice in the darkness behind her closed eyes. "Or is it actually the other way around?"

There was a long pause.

"After a while," she said, "it's difficult to tell the difference."

She felt a mutinous tear sliding down her cheek.

"I've been aware of the situation," he said. Then, unexpectedly, "You had a hard time in Liverpool, too, didn't you?"

As she nodded, she had one of those reality-check moments: *I'm weeping in a woman's toilet with one of the managing directors of the company, talking about my strangeness. If anyone walks in, I'm finished.*

"Why do you keep yourself so removed?" he asked. There was that curiosity again, as palpable as heat.

She did not answer: how could she?

"At first I thought you were just shy by nature," he said, "but now I know you can be about as retiring as a high-speed chase. It's an active decision on your part, isn't it? What's causing it?"

Enough. She made herself step away, look him in the eye. She wasn't going to reveal anything more to this man who never gave anything back, no matter how kind he seemed at the moment. Especially on this particular issue.

Alan, to her relief, moved away as well, polite and respectful, but still with that supportive grip on her arm as if she might swoon at any moment.

"I don't know," she said, forcing herself to maintain eye-contact.

He did not appear to be convinced but, disarmed by her tears, didn't have the heart to go in for the kill. After a few more moments of studying her, he spoke again.

"I think I understand, better than you." An element of surprise had slipped into his tone. "I think you're a lot like me, Circe. And frankly, I'd like to know why."

Later, sitting before the Raison with unseeing eyes, her mind was full of questions. *Is he really a lot like me? Am I a lot like him? And if so, what have I become?*

Later that night, Claire woke from sleep and knew that she wasn't going to be able to return. It had all started, as it usually did, with an initial period of deep unconsciousness. Getting to sleep wasn't usually a problem—it was staying there. After a few hours, some inner impulse would throw her awake, sometimes into moonlight, more often into the pattering of a rainy night. Or when she slept on the armchair in the lab, it was frequently the crickets that roused her, serenading her off to the women's locker room before the daily cycle began again.

Her downfall was her restless mind, which tended to veer off given the slightest opportunity. Recently, since she'd started writing poetry again, words were the main culprit, fluttering before her open eyes in the darkness.

Claire kept her notebook and pen by her bed and was a practiced hand at writing in the dark. She had no way of knowing that her father had had a similar talent, borne of a wish not to disturb his wife. He would snake a long arm over the faint rise and fall of her sprawled curves to where his materials lay waiting on the bedside table, sometimes temporarily arrested by the peace of Pilar's expression in the half-light, more peaceful that he would ever see it by day. If he was troubled by this comparison, the pressure of unwritten words would not let him dwell on it for too long.

Claire had no one to disturb except herself; but light, she found, would often scare away a particularly shy idea or chain of words. In the morning, the dreamy vision would be captured in surprisingly neat rows, with scarcely an overlapping line.

When even after discharging the night's cargo of words Claire found she could still not sleep, she would dress carelessly and walk the streets of Amsterdam, hands deep in the pockets of her old black coat. She did this without anxiety or frustration as some might, but imbued with a deep sense of patience and inevitability. Beyond exhaustion, everything was deadened, including her fear.

Amsterdam was a different place in that suspended moment between three and five in the morning. Claire lived a good distance from areas where tourists could still be found making a nuisance of themselves, and all would be still. She felt no fear, although such carelessness was probably naïve. She would walk brazenly through Sarphatipark, through bushes rustling with wind and unidentifiable nocturnal beings, past the fall of water into a pond, past slumbering ducks with their oiled necks curved into their wings. Willows dipping into water silvered with fragmented moonlight; the breeze carrying the scent of damp earth, or algae, or the excrement of dogs.

Describe what you see without colour words. Now do it without shape words.

Tell me what that fountain looks like without using an adjective.

Describe your passage through this park without using the words I *or* me, *or the verb* to be.

She walked the parks, she walked the streets, she walked the riverside, she walked the canals. One night without knowing it, she walked right past Joshua's house, leaning in refined elegance over a perfectly still canal, its sole inhabitant lost in a sweaty jungle dream of fruit and serpents for the third night running—in a dream about her, coincidentally enough.

Claire, the blind writer-in-the-dark, walked by, as oblivious to this coincidence as she was to so many others.

Chapter 18

❧

It was a Saturday in late February, and Joshua slowed to a walk after his hour-long run along the Amstel River. Still breathing heavily from the exertion, he passed houseboats full of women hanging laundry in the unseasonably warm air, chiding unseen children or partners vigorously. He passed one of the rival rowing clubs, its piers full of fours and eights loading and unloading, and more boats skimming up and down the river, coxes bellowing and coaches throwing amplified instructions from the far bank. A number of acquaintances on the docks raised their hands in greeting, and he waved back. He passed pigeons swarming by the pavement where an old woman scattered breadcrumbs, the one moment in her day when she could exert any influence over another fellow creature. Sun glanced off the surface of the water, dazzling his eyes and filling his heart with a sense of indefinable expectation.

He blinked, and saw a familiar figure resting on a bench up ahead. Long black hair, delicate profile, slouched and staring peacefully at the sky. Not an ounce of tension was evident in her posture, in the languid way one of her arms draped across the back of the bench.

Without thinking too much about it, Joshua kept walking until he reached the bench, then sat down and greeted her by name.

She looked up, surprised but otherwise untroubled. He didn't know what he had been expecting, but it hadn't been that bold, unwavering glance—especially after her reaction in the Jordaan bar. She wasn't, up close, as fragile as she appeared from a distance.

"It seems impolite that I don't know your name as well," she said, voice soft but as direct as her gaze. "Though I do recognize you." A pause. "How do you know mine?"

"You're notorious," he said. "And I'm Joshua, head of Bioinformatics . . . a distinctly unnotorious position."

"Maybe so, but you're one of the most unforgettable people I've ever seen. Have you always been so pale?"

"I'm afraid so." Joshua was silently amazed. Most people danced around his appearance for months, pretending that the obvious wasn't staring right at them. But her question reflected the unapologetic curiosity of a child.

"You're not a true albino though, being so dark otherwise."

"No . . . the medics are baffled."

Her smile intensified, light off water. "I'm sorry, am I being rude?"

"Not at all," he said. "It's quite a coincidence running into you here."

"Coincidence? This is nothing." She laughed, but he had no idea what she was referring to. "And of course it's not the first time."

"True." He watched the subtle alterations in the set of her jaw, a ripple of tension creep over the outstretched arm and shoulder. It suddenly seemed wrong to have barged over and disturbed her rare peace.

A silence ensued, background sounds encroaching: children shrieking with pleasure, traffic and trams lumbering across the bridge, bicycle bells ringing. He wanted to say something: when would he get the opportunity again? But he couldn't exactly start off with, *I couldn't help noticing how terrified you are half the time and, by the way, Alan Fallengale is going to swallow you whole.*

"Most people from NeuroSys," she finally said, "would have pretended not to see me."

"Are you finding it difficult?"

She shrugged. "Not really. Not about that."

"What, then?" Carefully, so carefully tugging at the unexpected thread.

"Whose side are you on?"

"I'm No-Man's Land, Claire. Neither side even bothers with me anymore."

"Why not?"

"Just look at me. It's. . ."

"Oh, I see," she said suddenly. "I understand."

And strangely enough, he felt that she actually did.

"Tell me," he said.

❦ ❦ ❦

129

Claire felt breathless, almost dizzy. It had been one thing to reveal her disturbing results to Rachel, who was too removed from the situation to do any damage. But it would be madness to confess to this stranger—no matter how friendly and harmless he appeared, no matter how ostracized from office politics.

She stood up abruptly. "I'd better go. I—"

"Please don't." He coiled out with his tremendous span and clasped her arm as she tried to pull away. It should have been a violent, objectionable manoeuvre, but somehow, it wasn't. In fact, she found herself sitting back down, docile and confused. Calmness seemed to emanate from the warmth of his hand, and then before she could really think about what she meant by this observation, he had let go, and the sensation vanished.

"I'm sorry." Her words, too, were obeying some other authority. "It's all a bit upsetting."

"Take your time." His gaze felt impassive, giving no footholds for any of her embarrassment to establish. In fact, it was almost hypnotic.

"It all started last October, while the crickets were singing." The last part, too, came out before she could censor it, but to her surprise, he just smiled.

"So they're visiting you now, are they?"

"You *know* about the crickets?" Curiosity made her forget her distress momentarily. "Where did they come from?"

He stretched his impossibly long legs out even further. "A few years back, one of the scientists had a crazy idea to use them as an experimental model—I can't even remember for what disease."

"Do crickets even have proper brains?"

"Evidently." His humour continued the calming process that had been initiated by his touch. "One night they all escaped, and now they appear sporadically, mostly down in the basement where I work."

"Why is their singing all out of sync with the seasons?"

"My theory is that they're confused by that motivational blue lighting Marjory inflicted on us," he said. "But I quite like their songs, whenever they choose to serenade me. I've never reported them because I don't want Stanley to call in the exterminators. They don't stay in one place for long, anyway."

"They do if you feed them."

He raised an eyebrow but refrained from further comment. Then he said, "Please carry on with your story."

She nodded, took a moment to work out exactly how to say it.

"The thing is. . ." She looked up at him. "What would happen to the company if the Universal Aggregation Principle turned out to be wrong?"

❀ ❀ ❀

Joshua experienced an eruption of shock, like a mighty clash of tectonic plates. A woman of secrets, indeed. If he ever had any colour in his face, he most certainly would have blanched, but as it was, he managed to keep his reaction to a blink. The girl was already spooked, and he didn't want to risk setting her off again.

"NeuroSys would go under," he answered, matter-of-fact. "Nothing else we're working on is even close to being marketable."

"That's what I thought." She looked out over the river, nodding unhappily.

"You'd better tell me the rest of it."

Drained of all spirit, she accepted the bridle with a meek dip of her neck and allowed herself to be led back to the stables. Over the next fifteen minutes, she described the accidental experiment, reciting the order of events and the evolution of her insights with commendable clarity. Ramon had been right: she was intelligent, her thought processes unusually mature. She did not seem the sort who would jump to flighty conclusions.

When she had finished, her body seemed to sag with the relief.

"But Claire," he said. "It doesn't make sense. Alan and Ramon's teams have done years of experiments on the same sorts of human brain cultures. They can clearly see SCAN binding to amyloid proteins outside of cells."

"Yes, but how were those experiments done?"

He recognized the note of challenge. "Well, extensive co-IP experiments and GST pull-downs on cell supernatants, for one thing."

"In detergent buffers," she replied, sounding almost scornful. "Out of all context, and probably at an abnormal concentrations."

"And there was the co-crystallization on recombinant proteins, when they solved the structure."

"Even less physiological," she said. "Maxwell and I spent four years exploring the differences between conventional binding assays and our real-time approach, where the proteins can come together in their

131

natural environment." Her gaze was infused with evangelical fervour. "Of course no experimental intervention is perfect, but given a choice between traditional biochemistry and the Interactrex, I know where *my* money would go."

Joshua rubbed his stubbly chin, weighing everything a handful at a time.

"Have you told anyone else at NeuroSys?" he finally asked. "Or Maxwell?" When she shook her head, he said, "Good . . . that's very fortunate." He sat up to his full height, so that she had to lift her chin to maintain eye contact.

"Are you sure? I've been eaten up with guilt, hiding all this. I should have gone straight to Alan after the first—"

"No! And you're not going to now, either." He made himself lower his voice. "Not yet."

"Are you sure? I mean, this is. . ."

"Yes, it is," he said grimly. "But there are a few things we've got to consider here. It could still be a technical problem. We *know* that the Zapper works in mice, so the first thing you have to do is—"

"Of course." She sat up too. "I've got to do the same experiment in diseased *mouse* cultures—and if I can see SCAN binding to amyloids, there must be an important species difference." She paused. "But I still don't understand why you don't want me to tell Alan."

"I'm worried that if you do, you won't have a chance to investigate things further."

"What are you implying? That Alan wouldn't be interested in the truth?"

As the full extent of her indignation became apparent, he saw how everything was, opening up like a book in his hands.

"No," he lied, floundering in the wake of his tactical error. It wasn't difficult to believe that Alan might be attracted to Claire, especially now that he'd experienced her at close range. But he hadn't bargained on the reverse . . . which in the present circumstances, was a complication that might prove difficult. "What I mean is: Not only can the Zapper heal Alzheimer's in mice, but the Universal Aggregation Principle has been confirmed by years of hard work using irreproachable techniques. Whereas the Interactrex is only a prototype, based on an elegant but untested new principle, and you're. . ."

"Just an inexperienced postdoc with zero clout." Her anger had died out as quickly as it had ignited.

He sighed. "I wouldn't put it like that. But who are they going to believe, Claire? Even I'm struggling, to be honest, and I don't have the personal stake, the near-religious convictions, of Alan Fallengale." He very carefully omitted to mention the significant financial interest, of which she was probably unaware.

"So what do I do?" She appeared to be resigned.

"Keep quiet a bit longer. Collect more data with those mouse cells. You've got to convince yourself before you can convince anyone else. It's too potentially explosive to go blundering around in the dark."

❦ ❦ ❦

Rachel poured out the tea into bone china cups decorated with tiny pink roses: like many designers, she embraced finely-made anachronisms as a sort of post-modern irony. Sunlight splashed into the flat and pooled over her portfolio, currently spread across the floor in overlapping slices of colour and texture.

Claire had wandered along the river for about an hour after Joshua had walked away, fretting and uneasy, and had finally washed up at her usual comfort stop.

On hearing her news, Rachel was more worried than Claire had expected, her eyes shadowed like a charcoal sketch. She set the teapot down and raised her cup. Then she put the cup back down on its saucer.

"I don't think you ought to have told him," she finally said.

"But you've been at me for weeks to confess!"

"To Alan, or one of the bosses. Not some random employee you don't even know!"

"He seemed . . . okay." She kept remembering the otherworldly spell he had cast over her. Why hadn't it felt malevolent?

"Claire! You work in an Orwellian nuthouse, remember? You must have been mad to just blurt all that out to a complete stranger—what if he turns you in?"

"He won't." Claire sipped at her tea, wondering how she could be so sure.

Rachel expelled a frustrated parcel of breath. "I guess it's too late anyway. But you have to tell Alan now. If this Joshua person tells anyone and it gets back to Alan, you could be in even more trouble for withholding important information. I can't believe you've kept it hidden as long as you have."

"Joshua did have a point. It could all be a mistake, and it's not too difficult to do the few experiments that will decide it."

"So you made a mistake—big deal! You're a *scientist*, you've found what you've found. How can that be your fault, even if it doesn't turn out to be an accurate reflection of reality?"

She had a point. But all that Claire could see was how Alan's face would look if she told him, like a door closing in her face.

Chapter 19

In the wake of Claire's disturbing revelation, Joshua realized that her mystery chaperone, ESTA-333, might somehow be a piece to the puzzle of her bizarre findings. If SCAN wasn't behaving as advertised, it made sense to find out as much about it as possible. In that case, working out what its partner ESTA-333 did for a living should be upgraded from entertaining side-project to full-blown quest.

So first thing Monday morning, Joshua poked his head into Ramon's office. Too late, he saw that the man was not alone; Alan sat just behind the door, wearing reading glasses and poring over a stack of printouts.

"I'll pop by later," Joshua murmured hastily, starting to back out.

"Nonsense, come in," Ramon said. "Anyway, if you have news about ESTA-333, Alan would love to hear it too."

"Naturally," Alan said, not even looking up.

Joshua took a seat, now unable to avoid viewing Alan through Claire's eyes. Joshua had stopped being envious of Alan's appearance and its intoxicating effect on women years ago, when he had come to terms with his own physical oddities and had learned that women worth having were not repelled by them. The last thing he wanted was to start being bothered all over again.

"It's taken so long because I've hit on something interesting," Joshua said.

"I like the sound of that," Ramon said.

"Interesting items appear to come all in a rush," Alan added, meeting Ramon's glance significantly. A comment calculated to exclude.

"I couldn't learn anything more about ESTA-333 from my normal suite of programmes," Joshua began, "but—"

"How sad to realize that you computer wizards are after all, alas, mortal," Alan observed, "and powerless without the input of *real* scientists."

"Alan," Ramon remonstrated quietly.

"But I filed an enquiry with Canadian Validation Solutions," Joshua continued, impervious. "Are you familiar with that company?"

The men shook their heads.

"It's one of the largest functional genomics outfits in the world. My department has recently started paying for access on a case-by-case basis. They're working their way through the human genome, expressing proteins *en masse* and then running them through various high-through-put functional assays."

"The post-genomic equivalent of watching paint dry," Alan said sourly.

"Shut *up*, Alan," Ramon said. "Did you ask them about our baby?"

"Yes. They've already run a number of tests on ESTA-333, and we could have the data . . . for a fee, of course."

Ramon leaned forward. "How much are we talking?"

Joshua took the e-mail printout from his back pocket, unfolded it and slid it across the desk.

"*Madre de Dios.*" Ramon cringed. "But you think it's worth it?"

"It could save you about six months to a year," Joshua said. "They do excellent work—my clients have been satisfied so far."

Ramon said, "It sounds good to—"

"We'll think about it." Alan overrode him, swivelling his chair around and returning to his reading. Ramon rolled his eyes apologetically, and Joshua smiled, but as he strode out of the room into the busy corridor, he had to clench his jaw to keep his real feelings from showing.

❦ ❦ ❦

A few evenings later, Claire sat in the lower level of the double-decker train speeding towards Amsterdam, pen poised over her notebook. If she had bothered to look out the window, to press her forehead close enough to the glass to swim beyond the yellow haze of the carriage's reflection, she would have seen flat fields, a dark horizon bare of all but a few trees and the odd windmill. They were traversing what the Netherlands referred to as *het groene hart*, its Green Heart, which the main rail line pierced like the exit wound of a bullet.

Claire was trying to fall into a quiet space, a space similar to the trance she adopted when collecting samples on the Raison. A poem wanted to form underneath her pen. At the moment, there was only her list of words and a theme—a rough-hewn mould into which her molten words would pour.

Not literally, though; Claire's poems tended to hint at only the remotest essence of the thing, like the aftertaste of something strongly flavoured. The brief, if the brief had been conscious, was not to describe, but to let the words become coated with layers of emotion and memory, to take on whatever shape might result. When the trance finally dispersed, her poems returned to her like children sequestered in far-flung boarding schools for years: sophisticated, fashionable, worldly entities she hardly recognized, who knew things Claire did not. *And all this came from me*, she would marvel, even as the evidence of that genesis could be felt like an ache inside.

"You remove a piece of yourself and transplant it," her father used to explain, "and when you're looking the other way, it roots and leafs out and scatters seedpods into the wind."

"What do you mean by the seedpods?"

"It's a metaphor, Lady Moon. The seedpods—that's other people, reading your poems and acquiring a bit of that piece of you." His smile would hint at secret worlds, worlds far beyond her limited knowledge. "Only there's an infinite amount to go around, and the seedpods aren't restricted by space or time, either—they might blow over to China, or up to the moon, or three hundred years into the future. That's why someday, when you're older and more courageous, you're going to have to show them to people. Otherwise they won't be grown-up poems."

After the first time Edward told her this, Claire could never again write a poem without feeling, at least for a while, the tender edges where the piece of herself had been ripped free. But unlike her father, she had never dared disseminate her words to another living creature. As a result, the completed poems, unseen, were somehow stunted. Even though the actual words would have been identical, she could not forget that they'd had no chance to become properly grown up.

Tonight, though, even the unwitnessed words wouldn't come. She was well practiced at screening out the noise of commuter life, but that wasn't what was foiling her. She had no idea what was. At a loss, she put her notebook into her rucksack and sat back against the seat.

That's when she noticed Joshua further down in the carriage—noticed him for the first time after dozens of near-misses over the past year. He was facing her, long legs sprawling into the aisle and focused on a paperback book with an intensity that Claire found compelling. Facing her unseeing, with her secret loose somewhere inside his head, one step closer to being released into the light. Yet safe there for the moment, she was still irrationally convinced, despite Rachel's warnings. His face, normally so devoid of expression, seemed at that moment to hold the barest whisper of whatever drama was unfolding on the pages beneath his fingers. She couldn't pin it down to any particular emotion, but there was something in the play of light and shadow about his mouth and eyes that gave it away.

Just then, he looked up with that disconcerting flash of black on white, just as quickly dissolving into a smile. She waved him over and he stowed his book and moved, with a grace at odds with his height, down the aisle to the seat opposite and diagonal to her own.

"What a pleasant surprise," he said. "Special occasion?"

"I take this train fairly often. Or at least, I used to."

"I know. What's special is that you actually looked up."

"Oh God, don't tell me." She put a hand to her face. "This used to happen to me all the time in Liverpool—inadvertently offending my colleagues on the bus."

"I'm not offended," he said. "I once fell asleep on the airport train and ended up in Belgium."

She laughed outright. "Seriously?"

"Well, Roosendaal. Close enough." They shared a little chuckle, and then Joshua asked, "So what have you been trying to write?"

Claire paused, aware of the extent of observation his question implied, and found that she didn't mind.

"Poetry," she said.

"Poetry." Not a question, but a statement, and instead of looking surprised, as most would, he just nodded. "Are you any good?"

"Joshua, what a question! Where are your manners?"

His eyes seemed to glow with humour. "I was raised by savages in the wilds of Papua New Guinea. So, are you?"

She shrugged. "I think so. One can't really judge one's own work, though. At least, I know I feel passionate about doing it."

In the silence that followed, she was grateful he didn't commit the tedious *faux pas* of asking to read them one day, as if her creations were some spent newspaper left on a train seat.

"You haven't been as prolific tonight as other evenings," he said.

This was a generous assessment; in fact, her pen had been hovering over a blank page since they'd pulled out of Leiden Centraal.

"Writer's block," she said.

"Do you get it a lot?"

"I never used to, but in the past few weeks it's been a real problem."

"Any idea why?" He was wearing that neutral expression again, the one he'd had on the bench by the Amstel that made it easy to speak. That would almost pull the words from her mouth, if she had any idea what they might be.

She shook her head.

"Maybe it's because you're so tired."

"What makes you think I'm tired?" she demanded.

He tilted his head with the faintest suggestion of a smile. "Trust me, it's obvious."

The train braked sharply then, and she pitched forward—like a shot, his hand came up and steadied her, dropped away seconds later as the driver sped up. A casual movement, instinctive and perfunctory, yet there was something about it that radiated safety; in his presence, the secret that threatened to undermine everything she was working towards didn't seem to command its usual grim potency. Yet at the same time, she wanted to rebel against this sense of being lulled.

Joshua had carried on speaking in the meantime: "I find it very difficult to be creative when I'm exhausted. If you're wearing yourself out at work, it's only natural that other aspects of your life will suffer. It's all a question of priorities."

Claire experienced the old memory then, as detailed and stark as always. Swallowing down the splash of nausea, she swerved into the safety of scientific chatter: her plans to carry out the mouse cell experiment they'd discussed by the river. Joshua politely accepted the change of subject without comment.

The two colleagues parted ways in the multi-storey bicycle lot of Amsterdam Centraal station: thousands of rusted conveyances glinting under the lamps, stowed in haste, at obtuse angles, never lovingly or carefully, the floor littered with the burglarized remains of chains and locks— a sobering reminder that no bike in this low land was safe or sacred.

As Joshua pedalled off towards Nieuwmarkt to meet some friends, he found himself wondering what Claire's poems were really like. If they were even half as intriguing and enigmatic the poet herself, he found himself willing to believe that they could be good. He'd seen the way she laboured on the train, month after month—why would such an avid poet be treating her lab job as an all-encompassing passion, subjecting herself to repeated all-night sessions? Why had she been so upset when he'd mentioned priorities, and tried to cover it up?

But who was he to criticize? His own career choice, which he so militantly defended, had been losing its veneer for some time.

Late on the following Monday morning, Joshua was sitting at a terminal in the main room of the Pit, immersed in a series of database searches for a biologist up in Cell Signalling. She had been ringing him every day for the last week to harangue him in French, and he had grown heartily sick of the entire project.

Roz came up to him with an odd expression on her face.

"There's someone come down with a request, boss. I thought you might want to handle it personally."

Joshua leapt up from his seat. "If it's Marie-Laure, I'm not here!"

"It's *not* Marie-Laure, it's—"

"I'm up to my elbows in amino acids here, Roz." He sank back down. "Can't you deal with it?"

"It's Claire Cyrus," she said pointedly.

Joshua forced himself to count to three before meeting her knowing stare.

"Tell her to wait in my office."

"In your *office*? Since when have you bothered—"

"Just do it, Roz."

She gave him another penetrating look, then spun on her heels and stalked out of the room.

Joshua found Claire huddled in his armchair, took one look at her face and violated an unspoken rule of the Pit by shutting his office door.

"I didn't mean to disturb you," she said. Her fear was close to critical, great washes and ribbons of it.

"Don't be ridiculous—why didn't you come to me directly?"

"I tried to, but that woman ... intercepted me. And she wanted to know what I wanted, so I got flustered and made up something about stroke, and she was looking me over like I'd just had one myself."

"Roz has an over-inflated sense of my own importance." Joshua smiled, trying to put her at ease. "Next time tell her to mind her own business. Have you done the experiment?"

"Yes, and it's bad news." There was something odd about her eyes, as if she had to exert herself to focus on him. "The SCAN from outside of the diseased mouse cells bound just fine to the amyloid proteins, exactly as you'd expect from Alan and Ramon's earlier data."

"It was clear?"

"Perfectly," she said, the evidence of her agitation growing more intense by the second. "This proves that the Interactrex *is* able to see such interactions . . . if they occur. And they just *don't* occur, in humans. The Zapper is going to be useless!"

"Claire, please keep your voice down—these walls are like paper."

"What if I don't?" she said. "Are you going to do your snake charmer trick on me again?"

Her words seemed to scorch the air. He just stared at her until she dropped her head into her trembling hands, then stood up and turned his back on her, holding back any number of sharp rejoinders. Not for the first time, he wished he had a window to look out of. As it was, he had to make do with the bookcase, crammed with computer manuals and, in one neglected lower shelf, the spines of faded biochemistry texts from his aborted career as a "real" scientist.

"I wasn't trying to manipulate you last Saturday, honestly," he said evenly. "It wasn't conscious."

"I know," she said, sounding contrite. "I could tell. How do you do it?"

He turned back, confronting this perceptive woman with her dark eyes burning out of the corner of the room. She kept blinking, too frequently, and her fear scraped at his brain like a headache.

"I don't know," he said. "It's just a knack."

After a moment of silence, he said, "Can you think of anything you might have done differently this time? Something trivial that might account for the discrepancy?"

"No, nothing." When he didn't reply, she said, "The company is doomed, isn't it? My God, how can I tell them now? How can I . . ."

Joshua watched her lips try to carry on, forming a shape from which no sound emerged.

"Claire?" He took an involuntary step forward.

When she began to shake, he realized belatedly she was having some sort of seizure. He crossed the floor in two great strides and put both his hands on her shoulders, the muscles beneath clenched like fists: a trapped thing with nowhere left to run. There was nothing his rudimentary vet talents could do against this sort of violent physiology, so he just knelt down and supported her as the convulsions rippled through his frame, keeping her from slithering off the seat.

After about half a minute the fit drained away, and he was letting go, backing away, and she was busy wiping her face with her sleeve, smoothing back the wild excesses of hair. Her body had gone completely lax in the past ten seconds, and the fear had vanished.

"Are you all right?" His heart was still rattling its cage.

"Yes—it helped that you were here."

"Epilepsy?"

She shook her head. "Panic attack."

"It looked more like a fit to me."

"That's just how I get them, Josh." Despite everything, she managed a smile. "I had about four neurologists fighting over the diagnosis, and that was the compromise. But whatever it is, epilepsy drugs don't help, and it's definitely panic that sets it off." She straightened her cardigan. "It's been coming on for hours."

"Do you get them often?"

The openness of her face flickered a moment.

"Not too many in recent years," she said. "I almost had one on my first day here, though."

"I remember that."

She looked up at him in surprise, but said nothing. Then, "I didn't mean to blame you, before. I was just upset."

"I know." He dropped into the other chair, oddly shaken.

"It's a bit weird, isn't it? How you can. . . ?"

"Yes." He was not used to so much honesty, this saying out loud of everything that normally should only be thought. "Yes, it is."

"What am I going to do, Joshua?" Everything about her seemed depleted, except for her eyes, which still glowed like black stars. "I've got to tell them now, haven't I?"

✤ ✤ ✤

Claire left the building at lunchtime, still feeling mentally bruised from the episode in Joshua's office. She took her sandwich down to the canal's edge, among the bare willow trees. It was very cold, and thc sky arched overhead, dull aluminium. A scattering of crocuses and snowdrops was the only sign of better days to come, and on the far bank, a heron was frozen on one leg, fixated on some underwater scene only it could see.

She took a small book from her coat pocket, a translation of Miroslav Holub, and let it fall open at random.

Freedom makes
the moth tremble
for ever. That is,
Twenty-two hours.

She closed the book, put it back in her pocket.

How had she got from there to here? Less than a year ago, she had been free: free of education, free of England, free of the pain of her first and only serious relationship, as free as she probably ever could be of grieving for her parents' deaths. She had been set loose in a new environment where she was unentangled by any thing, any person. But now, almost without realizing what had happened, she found herself bound up again, one tendril at a time. By circumstances—the appalling truth that she was going to have to reveal. And by people—Alan, primarily, who was fast making her feel that desperate need she had sworn she would never allow herself to feel again—not that way, not under those unequal terms.

And even Joshua, this odd man who she scarcely knew, had a claim on her now. He had earned it with that unintended moment of intimacy, an intimacy that had forced their acquaintance to the next level far too soon. She couldn't just discount him now. Although she sensed that her instinct to trust him had been correct, it was becoming clear that his *knowing* was going to weigh her down. In exchange for the comfort of confession and collusion, she had purchased an obligation: he was aware of her secret now, just as he would be aware if she chose to delay revealing it. And he had made his dislike of Alan plain, too—which was not an aspect that Claire, in her present state, could easily forgive.

And what, exactly, did she mean by "choosing to delay"? It shouldn't be something she was free to *choose*. NeuroSys was in the midst of arranging a human trial for the drug NS158. If she had any information that the drug might not be effective in patients, she was morally bound to make it known as quickly as possible, now that her mouse experiment had proven it without doubt. Hadn't she just promised Joshua that she would do as much, not five minutes before in his office?

But now that the panic had had its way with her, she felt her usual calm patience returning. She sat on one bank and the heron on the opposite, watching and waiting as one entity.

Staring past the reflection of the sky in the water at her feet, she saw another idea form, like a fish ripe for swallowing.

Chapter 20

ᘐᘗ

Claire pushed her way into Alan's lab, past the flurry of white-coated scientists scattering before her like nervous birds. It had become clear that none of them knew what to make of her, but they were at least used to her frequent appearances by now.

"He's in the chemical annex." Klaas, the broad-faced Dutch technician with the keen eyes, jutted a thumb as Claire paused to look around the lab.

Claire thanked him and tracked towards the side door in the back of the room, feeling the following stares hot on her back.

She opened the door and found Alan ladling a crystalline powder into a plastic dish on the analytical scales, a powder whose orange colour jarred badly with his clothing. She had never known there were so many shades of blue-green before she had encountered Alan's wardrobe. She had waited all her life for someone like him to raise his head and notice her.

"God, Alan—where on earth did you find that hideous tie?" she said, covering feeling with bluster. "It would probably register on a Geiger counter."

"There's a coincidence, Claire—I was just thinking about you." He gave her an uninterpretable smile. "Although I'm embarrassed to be caught out doing such menial labour—one of my technicians is ill."

"Menial labour is good for the soul."

"So Ramon keeps telling me, but better keep your voice down: You might inspire a coup d'état among the troops." His gaze roamed over her, spirited and enigmatic. "Now what can I do for you?"

"Two things."

"Only the two?" He tapped a last sprinkle of the Titian orange powder off the spatula, every movement tidy and unwasted on trivialities. "If you're going to be a *proper* woman, you need to learn to be more demanding."

"I need another brain," she said.

"Don't we all!" Alan emitted a bark of laughter. "Have you finally exhausted your own splendid specimen?"

"I mean, I need another human Alzheimer's brain."

He shook his head, capping the bottle of powder and placing it back on the shelf. "I take it back, my dear: that *is* suitably demanding. But you know we're at the mercy of the gods there. May I ask why?"

"I feel uncomfortable drawing conclusions from only one sample." Claire tried to appear unmoved in the wake of his careless endearment. "That patient could have been atypical."

"I saw the Path report," he said, shrugging. "It was textbook Alzheimer's. But I certainly agree that two brains are better than one, statistically. Your attention to detail is commendable—I have to beg my people to repeat an experiment even once, let alone two or three times. Naturally I shall be especially vigilant for all future opportunities."

"Thanks."

"You mentioned requests, plural?"

"I had another idea," she said. "Could I have a bit of the Zapper, to run a few tests?"

"Thank the lord, a request I can actually grant," he said. "But dare I ask what this is in aid of?"

"Actually, Alan..." She hesitated. "It's a rather silly idea."

"I sincerely doubt that."

"Can't I just tell you afterwards, if the results are good?"

"I don't see why not." Alan looked her over with amusement, and something else she couldn't define as she stood there, awash with relief that he had not pressed her for more details. "After all, anticipation can be such a turn-on."

Claire wrestled with insomnia all that night and then overslept, arriving at Centraal Station at the tail end of the normal rush hour. Dazed at this new perspective on urban existence, she half expected to run into Joshua on the train again and was relieved when she did not.

After all, he would be eager to hear how her confession had gone over—a confession she had decided to delay yet again.

As she stepped into the harsh lighting of the lobby, she was hailed by the day porter, a thin-lipped, unpleasant woman, the yin of Joop's yang.

"Dr Cyrus? People have been looking for you." The porter passed her a folded note.

"What for?"

The woman eyed her dishevelled state. "You have missed an appointment with Dr Fraser this morning."

For one terrifying second, Claire thought she'd been found out, that Joshua had informed on her.

"Your first assessment?" the woman added, as if she were speaking to an imbecile.

"Oh, God."

She took the stairs two steps at a time, scanning the brief memo.

If you are now awake and would deign to stop by my office at 11, I have managed to reschedule your evaluation.
—Stanley Fraser, CEO

She looked at her watch: only ten minutes until eleven. Dashing into the nearest toilet, she splashed water on her face before inspecting herself in the mirror. She thought she resembled one of those victims dying of consumption in an Edvard Munch lithograph. As her tangled mass of hair failed to stay smoothed down, she plaited it into a single thick braid down her back. It made her seem about sixteen, but at least she no longer looked as if she'd slept under a bridge. And thankfully her clothes were clean—she was even wearing a skirt, having run out of fresh trousers. Laundry was one of the many things she no longer had time to do.

"Good of you to fit me in," Stanley said as she sat down, nervous and apologetic. "Marjory will join us—that's routine."

"Were you ill, Claire?" Marjory bustled in with notepad and terrorizing smile. "You know you're meant to call if you're coming late."

"I'm really sorry. I overslept, and I'd forgotten about the appointment."

"Yes, well, I always say it's unfair to discriminate against those who choose to start work late," Stanley observed, giving her an unexpected wink. "After all, watching eyes aren't around to see what time you go home, hey?"

"Well, as long as you're working your full forty, we won't quibble," Marjory said, although she sounded doubtful that this could possibly be true.

Claire said nothing: to explain how she'd been racking up more than double that recently would probably backfire as *she doth protest too much.*

"You may have noticed," Stanley said, "that this meeting is taking place before the traditional twelve months."

"We had some *special* concerns," Marjory added.

Claire was suddenly completely awake.

"The good news first, though, Marj," Stanley said, harrumphing a bit as he fiddled with a flimsy pair of wire glasses and a sheaf of papers. "I've only just received. . ."—more fiddling and harrumphing, and a shower of paperclips raining onto the desk—"a set of glowing reviews from Alan Fallengale and Ramon Ortega about your progress on that side collaboration. Let's see now . . . I always like to quote directly from the sources. . ."

Claire was aware of Marjory's impatience, of the nervous pattering of her scarlet nails against the desktop. She was like a lower-ranking carnivore, anxious for the head male to finish ripping into his share of the carcass.

" *'Dr Cyrus has a keen intellect, bold execution, and innovative ideas.'* Remarkably complimentary, I'd say."

"Which one said that?" she asked faintly.

"Alan—I see you're surprised, hey? Not like him to be so full of praise, I can tell you. Except for himself, mind!" Stanley began to chortle. "Known him for nearly fifteen years now, always been full of himself."

"Stanley . . . the time."

"Ah yes, Marj . . . now where did that next bit go. . ."

Claire fidgeted in her chair, longing to read what else Alan had written about her.

" *'Claire is hard-working, usually arriving by 6 a.m. and often working right through the night. While her enthusiasm is admirable, I do have concerns about the possible effects on her health.'* That's from Ramon. See, Marj? I reckon you're getting your money's worth after all."

"I'm relieved to hear that," she said, looking as if the hyenas had just darted in and stolen a particularly tasty chunk.

"When I was a lad, I used to spend many a night in the lab grabbing the odd kip on a musty old camp cot. . ." He dwindled off, lost in nostalgia.

"Stanley. . ." Marjory poked his shoulder with one of her talons.

He roused himself. "And finally, one must not forget to mention the draft patent application"—he held up the folder with a flourish—"upon which Dr Cyrus is a co-inventor. Very impressive indeed after so short a time in our little family."

"Are we finished with the good news?" Marjory squared a stack of her own papers, and at Stanley's nod, she said, "While we are extremely grateful for all your hard work with the Alzheimer's team, which Dr Fraser has so succinctly outlined, we are a bit concerned about your progress on the project for which you were originally *hired*."

Stanley bobbed his head like a benevolent uncle and Claire felt her spirits sink as Marjory extracted a sheet of paper. She had known that this moment was inevitable.

"As you are aware, due to your special expertise, you were given Senior Scientist status straight away, which means that you have no direct supervisor," Marjory said. "But you should be liaising more intimately with Dr Bannerman's stroke group. You should be writing more reports, initiating more studies. Frankly, your activities there have shown a lack of leadership and a lack of output in the last few months. May *I* quote, now?"

Stanley waved magnanimous fingers.

She cleared her throat. " '*Dr Cyrus, while obviously skilled, is aloof and unapproachable. Our group has not been satisfied with her recent productivity, nor with the way she has failed to integrate with the various scientists on the stroke project.*' "

"Well, my girl?" Stanley was peering over his glasses at her, looking so kindly that she felt a sudden prick of tears.

"Actually, I hadn't quite finished with—"

"Let the girl defend herself, Marjory." The tone, though courteous, was backed with iron.

"I have tried," Claire said. "But they just don't like me. They never have done."

"Ridiculous!" Marjory exhorted. "Why, the Bannerman group is renowned for—"

Stanley whipped up a palm, stopping her mid-sentence. This violent movement was at strict odds with his expression, which remained sympathetic as he gazed at Claire.

"A moment, Marjory, please." And then to Claire: "Why do you think that might be?"

She looked down at the tabletop, extremely uncomfortable. "I'm young. I'm shy. They treat me like a technician."

"And I bet they're jealous, too," Stanley said, "you swanning around with Alan and Ramon, writing patents, while they can't seem to discover their own backsides."

"Dr Fraser!" Marjory said.

"An observation that goes no further than this room." His blue eyes took on an implacable tint. "I am prepared to overlook the negative report, seeing as how the others are so exemplary. And you, in turn, will put a bit more effort into getting along. Just show Bannerman that lovely smile."

Marjory closed her file, lips pressed together.

"And as fascinating as the Universal Aggregation Principle is to you, and all of us," he went on, "I'm going to have to insist that you devote more attention to the stroke project from now on. Do we have an agreement?"

He extended his hand, and Claire clasped it with the zeal of the converted.

❧ ❧ ❧

Claire went back to the Interactrex's lair, a child smarting from a headmaster's scolding. Knowing full well she had got off lightly, she was filled with a sense of reprieve, a fervent desire to justify Stanley's faith. She had no way of knowing that he had kept legions of scientists in line with precisely that same blend of tough kindness, from the lowliest of bottlewashers and undergraduates right up to the most senior of lab heads.

She would do some hard thinking about stroke straight away; later, she would wander down to Bannerman's lab and make peace. That would relieve a load of guilt that had been accumulating all year.

And there was another relief: If she was on some sort of unofficial probation, now was definitely not the right time to make trouble with any crazy-sounding confession. She would see out her new plan and say nothing to anyone about the disturbing results.

Resolved, Claire pulled down the binder full of Interactrex printouts from her abandoned stroke experiments and curled up with it in the napping chair. Looking at the date of the last entry, she was rather shocked to discover it was more than a month old. No wonder Zeke was furious. She removed the elastic on her braid and teased her hair loose to relieve the ache in her scalp, then settled down into intense concentration.

There were Alzheimer's mouse brain cultures languishing in the incubator across the room, but they would just have to wait.

❧ ❧ ❧

Joshua had managed to avoid Roz all of yesterday, but knew his peace was only temporary.

"Don't even try to escape," she said, approaching him in the early afternoon with two mugs of coffee. She bent down, whispered in his ear. "Now, we can either have this conversation in front of the entire crew, or you can come quietly with me."

Roz always had a light touch during any acts of extortion, but he was not foolish enough to underestimate her. Still, it was difficult not to smile as he followed her to his office.

"What in hell was that all about yesterday?" Roz said. "Shut up in here for nearly an hour with the Black Maria, who emerges, I might add, looking like a train wreck. Did you really make her cry, boss?"

He just shook his head, disturbed that so much had been witnessed. But how could he have expected anything less?

"*Please* don't tell me you two are an item," she said plaintively. "I will *so* never be able to live down being the last to know."

"Claire," he said, "is in love with Alan Fallengale."

"Oh! Poor thing." Roz looked genuinely remorseful for about a millisecond, before becoming distracted by more interesting prospects. "And I suppose that you're in love with *her*?"

"No. At least, I don't think I am." He had not meant to phrase it like that. "That is, I hardly know her. . ."

"Oh, dear." Roz looked grave. "This doesn't sound very convincing. So that's what yesterday was all about—her crying on your shoulder about Alan, and you hiding the fact that you'd rather be smashing his face in?"

"Actually, it was nothing to do with that. It was. . ." He trailed off, at a loss.

"Was it about her assessment, then?"

"Er, yes. Yes, it was."

Roz leaned forward eagerly. "She'd probably heard the rumours—some of the postdocs in Bannerman's lab are nasty pieces of work, crowing for weeks that she was slated to get fired this morning. But who's laughing now?"

"What happened?" Joshua looked up sharply.

"You're the official tear-mopper for the Black Maria and she never even *bothered* to let you know how it went this morning?"

"No . . . I've been busy with—"

"Got off with a slap on the wrist!"

"What for?" He was full of dread.

"For slacking on Zeke Bannerman's samples at the expense of Alan's, of course. People are saying that Alan stepped in directly—talk about divine intervention! Maybe it's not so hopeless for her, after all." She saw the look on his face. "Sorry, boss."

But Joshua was thinking there was no way Claire could have told anyone about her incriminating Interactrex results after all, as she'd promised, or it would have come out at the assessment and the whole company would be buzzing by now.

What was she up to?

❦ ❦ ❦

"What have we here . . . *Sleeping Beauty* strikes again?"

Alan's drawl pulled Claire out of a glorious dream, a dream where he had been holding her in his arms, touching her face with his hand.

As she fluttered to consciousness, she realized that Alan's fingers really had passed across her face with the light touch, if not the intention, of a lover.

"God, not again." She found herself in the napping chair and struggled to collect her scattered hair, an effort hampered by the heavy binder pinioning her against the scratchy fake-wool upholstery.

"Don't do that on my account." Alan was studying her, head to one side like a museum-goer examining an oil painting. "You look ravishing, all splayed out in abandon. And that skirt's an unexpected bonus."

Realizing only then that the item in question had hiked halfway up her thighs, she smoothed down the hem self-consciously.

"Here, let me take that," he said as she struggled with the binder. He peered into its pages. "And I come up to find you sleeping with another man as well!"

At her confused look, he added, "That idiot Zeke Bannerman, I mean."

"I just thought I ought to catch up a bit."

"Oh you did, did you? I take it your assessment went well, then!"

Claire just grimaced.

"Tell me," he said with morbid curiosity, "did you *really* sleep through the first appointment? That's definitely a company first for sheer cheek. I'd have given anything to see Marjory's reaction."

"I was told off severely. If it hadn't been for you and Ramon. . ."

"And that skirt, I shouldn't wonder—Stanley's a dirty old man, you know." Alan sat down at the Raison's main console. "Or at least he pretends to be. I'd been afraid something like this might happen, so I took special pains to tip the balance in my report. Bannerman's been on the warpath about you for weeks."

"Does that mean you didn't mean all those things you wrote?"

"Oh, I forgot . . . Stanley *always likes to quote directly from the sources.*" His passable impersonation made Claire laugh. "And I never say anything I don't mean—well, at least not in writing when a signature's required and lawyers abound. You know how highly I think of you . . . and Ramon as well. And it's our fault you're skiving off from stroke, so don't think we don't appreciate it."

"I don't," she said, unexpectedly subdued. She rubbed her eyes, trying to dispel her exhaustion.

"I am being callous and rude." Alan's voice softened. "I've come up here to find you sleeping on the job again, and it's made me realize that Ramon is right, that we're pushing you too hard. I want to make it up to you."

"Have you found me a brain?"

"Hard-hearted girl. No, I want to invite you out for a meal tonight—a proper one, seeing as how you're already wearing the skirt. You're not allowed to say no."

"Is Ramon invited too?"

Alan's smile was typically inscrutable. "Ramon, most unfortunately, had a prior engagement."

Chapter 21

⸎

For the rest of the day, Claire felt as if she were harbouring something wild that needed to be released, as if she should be running laps around the building. Instead, she vowed to stay on her best behaviour. She actually went into her floor's study room and sat at a computer with the others to work on some new ideas about stroke. At first, everyone looked at her askance, her presence was so unusual. But as lukewarm as their feelings for Claire were, most people actively loathed Bannerman's group. And on top of that, in the barnyard mentality of NeuroSys, there was nothing people liked more than the triumph of an underdog, even if she did happen to be a black sheep.

At first, nobody spoke to her, but news of her assessment seemed to be common knowledge, and eventually one of the PhD students couldn't resist asking her shyly for the coveted first-hand report. She soon had the whole room laughing with her description of the ill-fated interview, and when everyone went for coffee, it seemed only natural that someone should ask her along, and that she should accept.

Her initial reception in the stroke laboratory was a good deal cooler, but she insisted on showing Zeke Bannerman her new ideas, softened with smiles and flattery, and eventually he cracked as well. She found herself wondering why it had taken her this long to realize that she could influence people if she only made an effort.

Later, she returned to the Raison, who was clearly piqued at the neglect, and decided to give the machine a full tune-up. Maxwell would be horrified if he knew how long it had been since the last one.

She was kneeling on the floor, the machine's guts spilling out of a side panel all over her lap, when there was a knock on the open door.

Joshua stood there, backlit by sunlight from the corridor windows, an imposing seraph in a halo of copper. No matter how well she thought she remembered him in her mind, the first glimpse of his pale skin and dark hair never failed to affect her. He still reminded her of a lost poem, something good and old, definitely pre-Victorian. Possibly even pre-Donne.

He wasn't going to be happy.

❦ ❦ ❦

"You haven't told them yet, have you?" Joshua said, looking down at her. "You promised me, Claire—and your meeting with Stanley was the perfect opportunity."

"I couldn't," she said, eyes wide and serious. "I'm on probation."

"So I've heard. But that shouldn't—"

"And besides, I've had an idea. Several, in fact."

"I don't like the sound of that." He took a seat, watched her as she carefully finished replacing a wire-snarled circuit board before putting down her tools and giving him her full attention. There was something endearing about such a slight person attacking a vast machine with obvious expertise. He couldn't stand women who were hopeless about mechanics or electronics . . . and just like that, he could feel his irritation melting away.

"The thing is," she said earnestly, "it suddenly seemed foolhardy to jump to conclusions after checking only one human brain. I mean, what if it's an anomaly?"

"We've been through all this, Claire: that's not for you to decide alone. The burden of proof will lie with them. Besides, today's lecture from Stanley should have taught you where your priorities lie."

"But if that brain really was a fluke, and the Universal Aggregation Principle is still valid, my results could throw everything into disarray and clinical trial could get delayed."

"I suppose that's possible," he admitted.

"And if it *wasn't* a fluke, then the Interactrex might be the only way to discover the truth. Revealing things prematurely could actually jeopardize the company."

"In what way?"

"You said yourself that once I tell them the bad news, there's a risk they won't believe in the Interactrex anymore," she said. "If they think it's not an appropriate method to study Alzheimer's, maybe I won't be allowed to do any more experiments on it. Especially after this morning. Or worse—maybe they'll lose faith in the machine altogether and trade it in for something more reliable."

"But how could the Interactrex possibly help if the basic scientific principle is flawed? NeuroSys will be finished."

"I've been doing some reading." She looked up at him. "Lots of drugs have worked, historically, without people having a clue about the underlying mechanism. Isn't that right?"

"Well, yes. Up until recently, clinicians just tested random chemicals, and those that worked were used on patients."

"Exactly! They only figured out in *retrospect* what cellular processes were actually being targeted—and in some cases, we still don't know."

"What are you getting at, Claire?"

"I had an idea: Maybe the disrupted SCAN/amyloid clusters in mice are just a red herring. Maybe the Zapper *really* works by doing something else altogether."

"And?" He had thought of this possibility already—and there it was again, that funny *déjà vu* he'd experienced when he'd first looked at the patterns of the EST-333 code down in the Pit.

"*And*," she said, more confidently, "Maybe I can work it out, using the Interactrex. Maybe ESTA-333 is the key. I already managed to borrow some of the Zapper from Alan without arousing any suspicion."

"It might be very complicated, Claire—maybe you won't be able to figure it out. I mean, you don't even know what you're looking for."

"Yes, but can't you see that either way, whether that first brain was right or wrong, we can't lose by waiting just a bit longer? I've put my name on the list for the next Alzheimer's death . . . it's only a matter of time."

Their eyes met for a few seconds, and then Joshua sighed, extending his palms in surrender.

"Okay, you win," he said.

"So you won't turn me in?"

"Of course not." She doesn't, he thought, have the slightest idea of her power.

They were alerted in time by the whistling of a Frank Sinatra tune echoing down the corridor.

Alan stopped abruptly when he saw Joshua, before shrugging him off as an irrelevance. "Almost ready, Claire?"

The effect that Alan had on Claire, Joshua noticed, was instantaneous: she seemed to go up in a blaze.

"Fifteen minutes, while I close the patient?" Her voice was breathless, too.

"I've brought the car tonight—I'll meet you downstairs. Evening, Josh."

To Joshua, it seemed that Alan's final two words, with their particularly cheery emphasis, represented an obscene victory dance that only men could understand.

"I didn't know that you and Joshua Pelinore knew each other," Alan remarked, manoeuvring the car out of the lot, one powerful arm slung across the back of the passenger seat as he looked out the rear window.

"We're . . . friends." Claire hoped that the approaching dusk would hide the flush of guilt as the secret prickled beneath her skin.

"Instead of *Sleeping Beauty*, I walk in on *Beauty and the Beast*."

"That's a terrible thing to say. Besides, I *like* the way he looks—it's dramatic and romantic, somehow."

"Careful. You're going to make me jealous." He flicked on the windscreen wipers, smearing the streetlights into a blur of colour.

She didn't reply, her heart quaking against the shoulder belt with that same sense of wildness that had infected her all day.

"You should watch him, though." He kept his gaze on the road, his strong hands loose yet controlled on the wheel.

"What do you mean?"

"I've known Joshua for nearly fifteen years, and I wouldn't recommend trusting him with anything important."

"Why not?" Her heart seemed to squeeze closed for an instant.

"I don't want to tell tales, drag up anyone else's personal history—that's not terribly sporting. Just. . ." He threw her a quick glance before looking ahead once more. "Consider yourself warned."

The dinner in The Hague had been perfect. There had been no more talk about Joshua or work, or of things that reminded Claire of the secret. Instead, there had been tremendous conversation—a satisfying mixture of the introspective with the flirtatious, the inconsequential with the erudite. And there had been champagne, oh yes, and wine, and a lovely French meal of an expense that she would never consider indulging in—and no question about who was paying. When she caught a glimpse of herself in the ladies' room mirror, she looked different: not the tomboy anymore, but softer, more mysterious and desirable, with her hair loose and indolent around her face, her skin glowing with anticipation.

Now, back at his place, he had taken her coat and dimmed the lights, and she had settled in one corner of the Corbusier. For the first time in their acquaintance, he sat down next to her.

"Can I get you another drink?"

"No, thanks . . . I think I've had enough." But she didn't feel drunk exactly: it was more as if she wasn't getting enough oxygen.

"Good, because I wasn't looking forward to dragging myself away." With a strange twist to his mouth, he lifted a hand and tidied a strand of hair behind her ear. "Your skin is a lovely colour in this light, Claire."

Her breath came out more like a shiver. She had just been thinking that his skin was no longer marble, but burnished pine, and his hair, fields of grain in a Flemish painting. His eyes had softened from gemstone green into the hue of a new leaf. And far from being stony, the brief touch of his hand had scorched like an ember.

"You know why you're here, don't you?" he said.

She forced her gaze to stay fixed on the leafy greenness. "I'd been hoping you were going to seduce me."

"Who's seducing whom?" He laughed softly, ran a finger along her face again. "That's one of the things I like about you, Claire: your devastating directness, when most women would try to be coy."

"I've never been very good at coy."

His humour settled as if by force of gravity. "And I've never been very good at *not* being coy. And you're here because it's one thing to be coy over champagne and *escargot*, and quite another to keep up the act in the mundane environs of one's own home."

"You never say anything you don't mean . . . remember?"

"Clever girl—I keep forgetting that you never forget anything. But I was referring then to things that *matter*."

"Oh." She put a hand to her face, where it was still burning from his touch. "Are you saying that this doesn't matter?"

"Emphatically not." He took her hand from where it still rested against her cheek and enveloped it in both of his own. "That's the whole point . . . and the whole problem."

She looked at her wrist, at the point where her hand disappeared in his two. There was that feeling of old, the deep freeze about to clamp down. She had not expected it so soon. Not before things had even begun.

"I am almost twenty years older than you." His fingers began to move against her own. "Not, in itself, a significant impediment. But I am too old to say that I have never felt a certain way before. There have been too many experiences to expect anything but variations on a few well-worked themes."

She couldn't speak, caught between the looming deep freeze and the effect that his fingers were exerting on the rest of her body.

"The best I can admit to is a feeling which, in my life, has been . . . rare." He smiled ruefully. "A stingy, perhaps insulting concession, but your directness compels me to similar honesty. And because of this rarity, my normal behaviour would be unacceptable."

"How would you normally behave?"

"I think you can probably guess. Or you can ask anyone at NeuroSys: they would be happy to give you a forthright assessment, a distillation of the best and worst rumours. There are, frankly, a lot of data to work with."

He paused to let the words register.

"I see you are not shocked: good. So let me be perfectly plain. I find the prospect of a brief fling with you impossible—which is a surprising revelation at my time of life."

"But not because you don't want me?"

"Claire." He sounded impatient. "I've wanted you for weeks. Today, when you were sprawled in that chair, if I'd no reputation to maintain, and those damned CCTV cameras weren't installed. . ."

She trembled beneath another brush of his fingers along her face.

"And I could've had you on this very sofa any number of times—why do you think I've been holding back?"

"Because you like me too much to want to even try?" When he didn't answer, she added, almost scornfully, "That's like me becoming a scientist because of how I feel about poetry."

"You have a masterful way of fighting me with my own words." She could see the mineral aspect of his eye colour return. "But I have to make up my own mind, and for that, I need some breathing space."

"So I'm on probation with you as well?" Anger then, somewhere under the numbness. "Don't I have a say in any of this?"

"I'm afraid not. I can't trust you to consider your best interests. The last thing I want is for you to get hurt because I'm a jaded old fool."

"It's too late, Alan." She snatched her hand away, placed it out of reach.

"My dear girl, I'm so sorry." And he clearly was, which made everything worse.

"I'd better go, then." A bluff she was certain he would call.

He sighed. "I'll run you to the station."

When she was fastening her coat, he placed his palm on her face once more, made her look at him.

"This isn't necessarily the end, Claire, I promise. I just need . . . some air."

Chapter 22

Claire returned to Amsterdam on the night train, throat raw, head aching and heart sore. She slipped Alan's wad of taxi fare to an astonished beggar and rode her bicycle home in the lashing rain, hoping that it might somehow put out the fire that consumed her.

But the fire persisted. She thrashed around in bed, shivering and burning with confused, miserable desire. It was only when the sky began to lighten that she realized she was ill, and the heat was not shame or thwarted passion but a raging fever.

The next few days dissolved into a meaningless cycle of combustion and chills, of bitter aspirin eroding her gut and dousing her into a baptism of sweat before the cycle started all over again. She remembered some sort of impact, and being incredibly cold afterwards. Rachel, who had spare keys, suddenly appeared halfway through—Claire was not certain how or when. She grasped onto snatches of Rachel's beautiful voice, trying without success to hang onto consciousness.

"...let me just put this cloth on your forehead ... there, now, darling..."

"...thirty-eight point five."

"...you have to drink this, Claire. Please, you really must."

"...not coming into work again this morning. No, I'm afraid I *don't* know when she will be better. No, she really *can't* come to the phone..."

"...thirty-nine point four."

"...*he's* not here, Claire. It's only me."

"...forty point two."

". . .is Dr Huizinga, darling. He's going to take a look."

". . .appreciate your concern, but we are quite certain that that won't be necessary."

⚜ ⚜ ⚜

Then one day she opened her eyes to a room full of light and found that reality had righted itself. Her throat was stinging, the glands along her neck swollen and tender, and even the weak winter sun was enough to fill her eyes with moisture. Looking about, she saw Rachel sleeping fully clothed in the armchair by her bed, a faint frown on her face. When Claire extended an arm to touch her friend's knee, shocked at how difficult this simple movement was, Rachel's eyes flew open.

"Finally!" She leaned over and put a hand on Claire's forehead. "Thank God for that—the doctor said one more day of fever and you were to be admitted to hospital."

"How long?"

"Days, darling." She sat on the bed, stroking Claire's hair. "You were last seen at work on Tuesday. I got suspicious on Wednesday afternoon when you weren't answering my calls and e-mails, and let myself in. And it was a good thing I did, too—you were in a distressing state, lying on the floor halfway to the bathroom; I almost had a heart attack. And now it's Friday."

"You haven't been missing work on my account?" Claire, in her weakness, felt her eyes flood with more tears.

"Hush, darling." Rachel kept caressing her head with a benevolent hand. "I'm a senior designer, so I can work wherever I want. I'm camped out in your lounge with my laptop—it's such an airy space, very conducive to creativity. And so are the roses."

"Roses?"

Rachel bounded up and left the room, voice muffled through the French doors. "You thought *you* were feverish, darling—I've had to wait *two entire days* to find out who sent them."

She returned with a vase of long-stemmed red roses, which she placed carefully on the bedside table. "A proper lover's two dozen, I counted . . . and here's the note."

Claire opened the small white envelope, slipped out the stiff florist's card.

"Well?"

She had to make an effort to decode the beautifully swooping curves of ink:

You have no idea how much I'm wishing now that I had let you stay.
Please get better soon.
Love,
Alan

"Oh, God." It all came rushing back to her—the dinner, the conversation, the crushing shame of his rejection . . . Alan, with his fingers in her hair, telling her that he wanted her, that he needed to breathe. . .

"Who is it, the office nerd?" Rachel looked disappointed. "The leering old man in the post room? That vile Marjory person who's been on the phone every five seconds, finally giving in to a lesbian sadomasochistic crush that she can no longer deny?"

"It's Alan." Claire held out the card with a quavering hand.

"Alan?" Rachel's eyes darkened as she snatched it up, then something remarkable happened to her face. "Claire, what does he mean, *let you stay*? Is this why you've been calling out his name constantly in your sleep?"

Claire told her the entire story, and Rachel listened with astonishment. When Claire stopped speaking, Rachel picked up the card and read it two or three more times, shaking her head.

"But, darling, this is the most romantic thing I've ever seen."

"He refused to have sex with me, Rach. It was humiliating. Painful." She sneezed violently, her head spinning in its aftermath.

Rachel passed over a tissue and gave her a stern look.

"You've got it all wrong. That's precisely what's romantic—he doesn't want to mess you about. I have to admit it looks like I was completely wrong about the man."

Claire turned her face away, the idiotic tears starting again.

Rachel leaned over, tucked the covers more securely around her chin. "Don't let your silly pride obscure the possibility that he might actually be in love with you too."

Joshua slipped through the crowd, knowledge of the new telephone number in his pocketed phone making him edgy. He refused on principle to deal with it before he'd done his shopping, refused to allow it to derail his routine, as if such restraint would prove something important in his own mind.

The Saturday market on the Albert Cuypstraat was already bustling despite the weather, all the edges of the world blurred by a cold morning's mist. The Amstel, which he'd so recently quitted, had been a witch's caldron of fog hovering over mirrored surfaces as the boats sliced through, Hannah's calls strangely amplified and disembodied and the rising sun squelched to a muted sodium glow behind the overcast. Here, the air was warmed by the rhythmic patter of vendors mixed with the music of the regular buskers: the black-hatted, gap-toothed crooner slapping his string bass with jazzy aplomb, who people paid to play on, the doped-up Hendrix impersonator people paid to go away. He passed gelid-eyed fish, draped on crushed ice next to squid, thick eels, mussels and scallops pulled from the North Sea. (Later, when the market was empty, great blue herons would mince among the remains, otherworldly and fearless.) He passed stalls of meats and cheeses, flowers and fruit, cheap glittery clothing spiralling on hangers in the wind. The breeze was full of the sweet smell of *stroopwafel* and *suikerspin*, of frying onions and baking bread, coiling amidst the vapours.

As Joshua paused at this stall or that, exchanging money and humorous words, he was aware as always of being involved in a custom so deeply rooted in Dutch culture that it could explain everything you could possibly want to know about its society. Only the goods and currency had changed—the rest had been going on forever: the coins fingered and examined, the amiable, character-filled faces, the old women prodding the cabbages with suspicious intent. But he was distracted today, so much so that he even left a stall without remembering his meagre change—an unthinkable crime against commerce that impelled the vendor to chase after him with the handful of copper.

He couldn't stop thinking about Claire. And he did not understand exactly why, which annoyed him in itself and caused further distraction, iterations of analysis feeding back and bootstrapping into increasingly complex patterns. The disgust he'd experienced when she went off with Alan Fallengale last week had swiftly given way to worry when news of her severe illness had trickled down to the Pit. He was starting to wonder if Roz had been correct. Love was too ridiculous a word for someone he knew so little. But he could no longer deny that his initial concern for a fellow outcast had mutated into a much more specific feeling. Not love—not like the fiery need that Claire had been giving off in the presence of Alan that Tuesday night. But certainly something: the sensation that they shared a bond, some subliminal chemistry or new element that the alchemy of secrets had somehow forged between them. There was, too, an undeniable allure in the way he felt when she looked at him openly, without fear or censure, as if his paleness belonged comfortably in this world—as if there had never been any question. Meanwhile, the tenuous connection between them made him, irrationally, want to protect her from harm, whether the threat of Alan or the explosive ramifications of what her accident with the Interactrex had brought to light. Even though he was starting to suspect that she was more than capable of looking after herself.

Enough. He cut away from the market down a side street and soon was standing on the pavement outside a particular building, mobile phone to ear. Five rings. Six. Seven.

"Hello?" Claire's voice sounded clogged, and about half an octave deeper than normal.

"It's Joshua Pelinore. I abused my position and hacked your number from the NeuroSys staff database—I hope you don't mind."

"No, it's good to hear from you."

He shifted on his feet, hefting the grocery bag. "The truth is, Claire, that I hacked your address as well, and I'm standing outside your front door like a common stalker. It turns out I live just around the corner."

"Oh!" High above, a curtain parted, and Joshua made out a figure, waving at him. "Please come up, it would be nice to see you."

In true space-efficient Dutch style, the narrow wooden staircase was more like a ladder. She'd left her flat door ajar, so he pushed his way inside and found her curled up under a quilt on a sofa in a long room, a classic Amsterdam layout with high ceilings and a swooping rosette of decorative plasterwork at its crown. A vase of roses seeped heavy scent, and he sucked in his breath at the books: there was not an inch of wall space not covered by shelves, and not an inch of shelves not covered by books. Easily a thousand of them, many very old.

"Are you feeling better?" he asked.

"Did Marjory send you as an independent witness to take my temperature?"

"Please. As if that would possibly convince her." He set the bag onto the floor and pulled up a chair. "I brought you some juice . . . a few cans of soup . . . a box of tissues. . . ." He was glad he'd changed his mind about the tulips, because they would've looked paltry next to the roses.

"How kind of you," she said. He was startled to see that she was weeping.

"Claire—"

"Oh God, don't mind me . . . I've been an emotional wreck ever since I came to. It's just this 'flu. And also . . . realizing that I've got friends after all."

Joshua opened up the box of tissues and passed one over, and she blew her nose vigorously.

"The whole company is seething with rumours about you," he said. "One even had you airlifted to a London hospital."

"I think I slept through that bit." She giggled behind the wad of tissues.

"That was nothing. I had Zeke Bannerman down in the Pit on Friday, wracked with guilt and saying that he'd been wrong about you, that his negative report actually precipitated your collapse."

"Funny how even on my death bed, it's all about him."

They both chuckled, and then Claire struggled upright on her pillows.

"Joshua, about our little secret. I can trust you, can't I, not to say anything?"

"Of course." He tried to look into her eyes, but they were evasive. "I've already given you my word."

She nodded, but didn't seem entirely easy about it.

"Claire, what's this all about?"

She sighed, looking years younger with her nose so reddened and raw. "It's going to sound terrible. I really shouldn't say anything."

"But that wouldn't be like you."

"I suppose not. The truth is that Alan warned me not to trust you, and I'd like to know why."

"I see." The anger welled up, as easily hidden as always. "And this just came up in casual conversation?"

She thought about it. "Well, I suppose it was somewhat random. He seemed annoyed to discover that we were friends—he obviously dislikes you."

"I'm sure you've worked out by now that the feeling's mutual. What was the exact warning?"

"He alluded to some episode in the past, and said it wouldn't be gentlemanly to go into details."

"How very convenient." He stood up, took a few paces then turned to face her. "It's a bit difficult to defend myself if I haven't a bloody clue what he's talking about."

"You don't need to defend yourself," she said quietly. "I still trust you."

"Then how can you square that with Alan's accusation?" Joshua was beginning to form a suspicion about the origin of the roses, a suspicion that transformed their beauty into something sinister.

She sighed again, slender shoulders rising and falling against the cushions. "There must have been some misunderstanding. Have you two ever fought about anything tangible, or is it just non-specific animal loathing?"

"Well." He told her about the post-Christmas screaming match years ago—although neglecting to mention its final outcome. "But the worst you could accuse me of there was prying with good intentions."

"Maybe he didn't appreciate your snake-charmer trick."

"Claire, I'm really sorry about that. It wasn't—"

"Don't be, please." Unexpectedly, she reached over across the awkwardness between them and placed a hand on his arm, left it just a moment. "Whatever it is that you . . . do, it's. . ." She searched for the words. "It's compassionate. It's natural. And it's helped me on more than one occasion, so I really ought to thank you."

They looked at one another then, and even when Joshua was striding down the pavement afterwards, a cloud of sparrows streaming up past his shoulders towards the clearing sky, the heft of her words still lingered.

Joshua was only the first of three visitors Claire received that day. Soon after he departed, the door buzzed again. Ramon Ortega's voice materialized on the intercom, very sorry to disturb her, but he'd managed to convince Stanley to dig up her home address from the confidential files, and happened to have a few errands to run in Amsterdam. . .

"It's good to see your face, *querida*," he said, pausing just inside the room.

"I've heard a rumour that my funeral takes place tomorrow." It was a relief to speak Spanish, safe and warm under the quilt like a child. "I was hoping you could be one of the pallbearers."

"Your predicament has provided entertainment for many this past week . . . and significant worry for a few." He sat down, his eyes unusually emotional. "I've been feeling partially responsible for all this."

"*Dios mío*, Ramon . . . between you and Bannerman . . . haven't you heard the latest scientific discovery? It's called the Germ Theory of Disease. There're these little viruses, right, and—"

"Don't be impertinent." He couldn't help smiling. "Those are beautiful flowers, by the way."

"Alan sent them."

"Alan?" A peculiar expression gripped his face, and then he stared her down until she blushed. "Don't tell me it's like that with you two?"

"To be honest, I'm not entirely sure what it's like."

"*Tonto*! I must be blind not to have noticed. Listen, Claire, I've known Alan for a long time and I love him like a brother, but he's not what you would call the steady kind."

"*Oye*, Ramon, I'm not stupid."

"Hmmm." He looked her over. "No, you certainly aren't. In fact, most of the time you seem to know exactly what you're doing—which is probably why Alan has taken a fancy to you . . . still . . . you're such a lovely girl; it would be a shame if you let him break your heart."

"I'm not as fragile as I look, you know."

"I don't believe that for a moment," he said, almost bitterly.

"Ramon," she said. "You say you love Alan, so he must have some redeeming features, *no*?"

"Well." He looked down at his shoes.

"Ramon? Tell me, what is it?"

He shrugged, looking awkward. "How to explain? He's become . . . lost over the years. Sometimes I'm not sure how much of the Alan I love is really left."

"What a funny thing to say." She watched his bowed head, the bleak way he rubbed at the tight curls on his scalp. "What on earth do you mean?"

"Not for me to tell, *querida*: for you to discover, if you ever manage to get in that far. Lord knows I never could." Then he paused, raised his head. "All this reminds me . . . I offered to give Alan a lift today if he wanted to join me, and he said something strange."

"What?" She leaned forward. "What did he say?"

"He said he wasn't sure you'd want to see him." His forehead creased. "And then he asked me to try to work out whether you would, without asking you directly. And I said, *Jesús*, Alan, how in hell am I meant to—"

"Oh, Ramon! Tell him yes. Tell him as soon as you can."

Chapter 23

⚜

It wasn't until the evening that her buzzer finally rang again, just as she knew it must, and Alan's voice issued through the intercom, sounding short of breath. She wanted to greet him at the door, but couldn't find the energy, so she just collapsed on the sofa, filled with a trembling that was more trepidation than desire.

He came straight through, not bothering, like the others, to look around the room or gape at the canyon of books, or to waste a second with a word of greeting. With his anxiety plain, and some other element that Claire couldn't fathom, he exploded across the hardwood floor, knelt on the floor by the sofa and gathered her up in his arms.

"You really are all right? You really want to see me? I didn't dare believe it until Ramon..." His words were muffled against her throat, and then he was kissing her, with an urgency that stole all her limited strength and breath, even as she relished in the overpowering onslaught of it all. Kissing her, then pulling away to devour the sight of her. "I would never forgive myself if you had..."

"It was only influenza," she said, half laughing and half stricken at the look on his face.

"You were very ill—I don't think you realize." There was an edge to his reaction that was completely out of all proportion, but she was too distracted by the look in his eye to give it much credence at the time.

"How could you know?"

"I spoke to your friend Rachel on Thursday. She's as obstinate as a oil tanker, I can tell you."

"You ... how?"

"I broke into Personnel and stole your number. I told Rachel I was Stanley, concerned about one of my employees." His usual sly smile pierced her heart like a shard of joy.

"You didn't!" She had to laugh, and then just as quickly, to cough, and he held her until she was finished, with a tenderness that shocked her.

"I must say she seemed properly impressed by the hands-on, personal approach of your CEO." Then his smile faded. "Claire, she told me how she found you on the floor—you could have struck your head—head injuries can kill, you know—I couldn't get that image out of my mind, especially when I remembered how cruel I'd been."

"Alan—"

"And did you realize how high your temperature was? I couldn't convince her to call an ambulance, she said she'd had the doctor round and there was no need . . . these Dutch GPs, I don't trust them, I—"

She stopped his rant with another kiss, fierce and hungry and very much alive.

"It doesn't matter. I am so happy to see you, Alan. I'm so glad you came."

"I had to suffer through a humiliating lecture from Ramon before he would tell me whether I was welcome here." He looked both appalled and amused at the memory. "I had to swear on my mother's grave that I wouldn't break your heart—I don't think I will ever live that down."

"And did you mean it, when you swore? Was it something that *mattered*?"

"Oh, yes, my dear. God, yes."

The extent of Claire's physical malaise became apparent to Alan after only a few moments.

"I'm going to stop pestering you and cook some dinner," he said. "Don't look at me like that, wanton girl: it's for your own good."

Soon he was rattling around in her kitchen like a tornado of energy, whistling, singing, occasionally blurting out irrelevancies such as, "Oh splendid, you've got chives," or "Any objections to giving this aubergine the decent burial it deserves?" She lay on the sofa with her eyes closed, smiling at the sizzles and aromas of ordinary domesticity invading her solitary domain.

She must have dozed off, because the next thing she knew there were lit candles everywhere, Carl Phillip Emmanuel Bach on the CD player ("I'm glad to discover that your musical tastes are vastly superior to those of my postdocs"), and supper on a tray. He'd filled her wine glass with orange juice and helped himself to a bottle of Gewürztraminer. And later, after clearing up, he lay down on the sofa next to her.

"Feeling a bit better?"

"Mmmm." She couldn't get enough of the way it felt to bury her face under his chin. "I only wish I had more energy for dessert."

"At the risk of causing a relapse by rejecting you twice in one week . . . I think we ought to wait."

"Oh." She disentangled herself, confused. "Are you still breathing? I mean, am I still on probation? I assumed. . ."

"Shhh." He smoothed her hair. "Please don't taunt me with my own idiotic insecurities. I've learned my lesson—it only took a few days without you to realize that you had actually become my oxygen."

"Then why. . ."

"Trust an older man—it will be far better if we wait. You're in no fit condition." Then he said, "Don't give me that look again; I assure you it's futile. I'm going to have to distract you with words."

"Words?" Claire was unable to stop looking at him, at the way the candlelight was soft on his face. She could scarcely believe that he was here in her flat, holding her in his arms.

"I couldn't help noticing that we are absolutely swimming in poetry in here," he said. "Will you read to me?"

"Oh, Alan. . ."

"What, squeamish, are you?" He went up on one elbow, viewing her complicated reaction with interest.

"It's too . . . intimate."

"Intimate!" He burst out laughing. "The girl is perfectly willing to seduce me, but too retiring to quote a few meagre lines!"

"Words are much more powerful than sex."

"Now that's a *very* intriguing thesis, not to mention kinky. I simply must hear you now."

"Please, Alan. . ."

"You really won't? Don't upset yourself, I won't make you." He thought a moment. "Any objections if I read to you?"

"That depends on what it is." She wasn't happy with his cavalier attitude.

"What's to hand?" He looked about and snatched up the volume on the coffee table, parting its pages to where the ribbon lay.

"Oh no, Alan, not that. . ."

"Silence, please." He cleared his throat dramatically.

Love, do I love? I walk
Within the brilliance of another's thought,
As in a glory, I was dark before,
As Venus' chapel in the black of night:
But there was something holy in the darkness,
Softer and not so thick as other where;
And as rich moonlight may be to the blind,
Unconsciously consoling.

He faltered, perhaps realizing for the first time the privacy that he was trifling with.

Then love came,
Like the out-bursting of a trodden star.

Stupidly, Claire started to cry, part from true feeling, part from embarrassment, and part from physical exhaustion. Chastised and shaken, Alan put the book down and took her in his arms.

"I'm sorry, love," he said. "I promise I won't do that again. Not until you're ready."

Part III

❧

THE ENTANGLEMENT

Chapter 24

Claire had not thought that Alan would be the type of man who would want to spend the night. Then when he defied her expectations by asking to stay, she did not think he would still be lying in bed when she woke up. Finding him there in the morning, lit by a shaft of sunlight with church bells pealing from ancient churches across the city, she predicted at the very least a return to his brisk, removed persona on waking. But again, his continued affection proved her wrong.

This trend of foiled preconceptions carried on in the ensuing days, as Claire's health returned and she went back to work. There was no sign on Alan's part of losing interest; the deep-freeze seemed to have evaporated forever.

Claire was perceptive enough to tell that she wasn't the only one whose expectations had been thwarted. Alan began to wear a bewildered look that reflected some inner amazement, as if he had never dreamed he would find himself in such a situation again. Sometimes she would catch him looking at her as if he were trying to convince himself that she was real. She'd be sitting in the window seat of his bedroom, engrossed in a book, or looking out into the night in a wash of moonlight, and she'd glance over to find him arrested, unable to draw breath.

"Do you have any idea how deadly you are?" he asked one night, sounding almost panicked. "I hope you realize that I'm at your mercy."

Ramon, too, noticed the change.

"I'm not sure what you've done, *querida*, but I hope it lasts. I haven't seen him *not* acting like a pompous arse for years. It certainly makes departmental meetings more relaxing."

But Claire knew that he wasn't completely altered. Alan was a restless sleeper, voluble and energetic, and she could hear his past rising like a dark spring within him as if he were one of the damned roasting on a spit in a painting by Heironymus Bosch. When she asked him what he dreamt, he said that he couldn't remember and it didn't matter, but she had the feeling that he was hiding something from her. Occasionally she thought of what Ramon had said about him becoming lost, but despite their growing intimacy, she sensed that digging further was futile. Part of her thought she didn't really want to know.

As for the rest of NeuroSys, the news of Claire and Alan's relationship—not so much its inception as its stubborn persistence—exceeded all expectation as well, and caused a predictable sensation. But soon, the furore settled into the mundane acceptance of all steady couples, no matter how unlikely. Alan delighted in being formal with her in public—she suspected that the flex of mental powers required to flirt outrageously over other people's heads gave him a perverse sexual kick. She enjoyed the game, too, because it reminded her of the aloof confidence that she had fallen for in the first place—and eventually conquered.

And fortunately, her new status did not disrupt the fragile relationship she had begun to forge with her colleagues. The stroke programme blossomed under her attention, and she was content almost all of the time.

But the parasite in her spleen was not entirely vanquished. True, her memory of the results she had gathered about the possible problems with the Zapper had lost their potency, just as the horror of a nightmare gradually fades throughout the following day until one can scarcely imagine what the sweating fear was all about. In fact, sometimes she felt that she actually had dreamt the entire problem. But then she would glimpse the notebook containing the Alzheimer's brain results, growing dusty on her window ledge, or she would catch Joshua giving her his doomed knight look across the canteen, or something Alan or Ramon would say would bring back the prickling uneasiness. She couldn't bear to leave Alan before dawn, but the rare times she worked on an all-night experiment, the crickets rubbed at her conscience like a Greek chorus.

✤ ✤ ✤

"Post for you, boss." Roz sauntered by, dropping an interdepartmental envelope onto Joshua's keyboard.

"Hope it's not a redundancy notice," Matt said.

"What are you on about?" Josh stopped halfway through slitting the envelope open with his thumb.

"Don't be an imbecile," Roz said, glaring at Matt. "Besides, if it comes to downsizing, I know who *I'd* put first on the list."

"What's all this about downsizing?" Joshua released the envelope's content, just a normal memo. "Have I missed the latest, as usual?"

"Check this out," Matt said, with the eagerness of a newsreader revealing the body count. He clicked closed his DNA search window to expose a luridly animated stock market surveillance page. "We're in v-fib, boss."

Roz leaned over and peered at the column of numbers. "Down fifty-five. Not as bad as yesterday, though."

"It's all this terrorist activity," Matt said. "Venture capitalists have started to store their bankrolls under their mattresses."

"Pity we don't work on anthrax or smallpox," one of the other technicians muttered.

"There're saying that the Pit will be the first place to feel any cuts," remarked another person along the row of terminals. "Everyone knows we're the most under-appreciated department in this building."

"As if they could survive two seconds without computer back-up," Roz said. "Just try running a modern lab without it."

"Speaking of which. . ." Joshua had scanned the brief memo from Stanley. "My latest proposal to buy information from the Canadian database about ESTA-333 has finally been approved."

"Here that, everyone?" Roz said. "There's obviously some money left in the coffers, so no need to dust off your CVs just yet."

Stanley's memo inspired Joshua to call up the sequence file of ESTA-333, Claire's mysterious nuclear chaperone, and take another look. He ran a few routine database searches to see if anything had been discovered about the gene in the month since he'd last checked— at the current pace of science, entire theories could rise and fall in a matter of weeks. But unfortunately, he found that ESTA-333 had continued to be ignored, with no publications or related sequences reported in the meantime.

He was just about to close the window when he paused, snagged again by that odd cluster of amino acids that had been haunting him from the beginning. And then, suddenly, he had it.

"What is it, boss?" Roz had drifted over, attracted as usual by the intensity of his focus.

"Do you notice anything familiar about this region?" He pointed out a few scattered amino acids, filling with that slow burn of excitement.

She sat down and leaned closer, brow furrowing. "I don't see anything. Just an arginine here, and a phenylalanine and proline a bit downstream."

"Yes . . . but not just the amino acids themselves." It was always difficult to describe his instinctive vision, but after so many years working with Roz, they understood one another's thought processes unusually well. "It's the distance between them, and how the intervening sequence seems to. . ." He shrugged. "Seems to *look*."

"Hmmm. I'm afraid I'm not with you on this one, boss."

"Hang on." Joshua navigated through a few menus and pulled up the sequence of a wholly unrelated protein—beta-amyloid, the Alzheimer's disease protein—then performed a keystroke that would align the two strings of code, letter by letter.

Roz blinked, put her nose even closer to the screen.

"Wait a minute—that's the Zapper's docking site, isn't it?"

"Give the lady a prize."

She manipulated her thatch of hair until it was peaking in all directions. "That's a bit of a stretch even for you, wouldn't you say?"

"You're probably right. It's bound to be nothing."

But after Roz left, Joshua couldn't stop staring at the suspicious bit of code. He knew, with the solid feeling of a key sliding into a lock, that things were about to take a turn for the worse.

❀ ❀ ❀

Claire opened up her refrigerator in the lab and caught sight of a tiny, forgotten glass vial.

Frowning, she picked it up and rolled it around in her fingers to reveal the label. It was the sample of Zapper that she had borrowed from Alan ages ago and then forgotten about. Those five simple characters in standard black font, NS158, pierced her like an arrow. In the wake of its prick, she remembered the crazy plan she'd come up with just before her illness, to try to find some way out of the disastrous endpoint that her accidental experiment had spelt out. A plan that Joshua had advised her against, when he tried for the second time to persuade her to confess the whole story to upper management. A plan that, weeks later, seemed naïve and stupid to her as well.

She held the vial in her hand and, at that moment, standing there in the laboratory, the entire world seemed to shift. All of the implications of the suppressed experiment came back to her: not some dream, but a crisis, still very much ongoing. The unthinkable had happened: love had made her soft. What would Maxwell say if he could see her now?

She put the vial back in the refrigerator and took the lift down to the basement.

❦ ❦ ❦

Joshua felt a brief touch on his shoulder and, through that contact, a familiar sensation that had not been evident for some time.

"Claire." He looked up from his screen. "What can I do for you?"

"Can we talk?" Her voice was subdued, anxious.

So they found themselves back in his office. It seemed far longer than six weeks, Joshua thought, since she'd suffered the panic attack. For him, too, there had been a dreamlike quality to the hiatus. But unlike Claire, Joshua had known that she was going to wake up eventually. He'd kept mostly clear from her during what he thought of as her honeymoon period. During their occasional casual chats in the corridor, he'd been careful not to allude to her accidental experiment or the secret she was keeping about it, and certainly not to voice any concerns about her new relationship with Alan Fallengale. He had not wanted to ruin her happiness. For against all his expectations, Claire had been radiantly happy, and this state had showed no signs of flagging— until now.

"Tell me," he said, sitting down opposite her.

Claire took a deep breath, and he prepared, with triumphant anticipation, to hear that Alan had finally strayed.

"Why did you let me go on for so long?" she demanded. He was surprised to see that her anger was actually directed at him.

"I'm sorry?" he said, blinking.

"Why did you let me *forget*?"

"Oh." He felt the darkness of her gaze splinter off him. "I'm not your conscience, Claire."

She bowed her head, the anger slipping away as quickly as it had come.

"Besides," he said. "You weren't too likely to be receptive. We haven't really talked since that time in your flat, when you were ill."

"I know, I'm sorry. Have you resented it?"

"Of course not. I was glad to see you so happy." Strictly the truth, he told himself.

"But the problem didn't go away, just because. . ."

"No. I figured you'd come around eventually."

"Content or not, you could've given me a nudge." A little glimmer of the anger returned, but this time, it seemed aimed at herself.

"But you see, Claire, you actually made that very difficult."

She looked at him a moment. "How?"

"When you told me how Alan had called my integrity into question, you restricted my options."

"But you know I didn't take that seriously!"

"Yes, but let's be honest: you're in love with Alan, and I'm just a colleague."

"A *friend*," she insisted.

"But still, it made me have to overcompensate."

"I don't understand."

He sighed. "I'd given you my word not to tell anyone, but if I nagged you about it, you'd probably start worrying that I'd change my mind, that I couldn't be trusted to keep the secret. It put me in an uncomfortable position—I didn't want to make things worse for you."

"Okay, I understand. But it's not too late to carry on with my plan, now that I've come to my senses—look into alternative modes of action with the Zapper while I'm waiting for the next Alzheimer's brain to come along."

"So there's still no way you'll consider telling them the truth now?"

"No," she said, without hesitation. "We've waited this long—I might as well do the repeat when I get the brain samples and be really sure."

He could see there was no changing her mind—and there they were, right back at the beginning. Loops within loops, errors of judgement converging, compounding, amplifying. "What about your probation?"

She shrugged. "Everything's under control now. We're making good progress with the stroke work, and I do have free run-time. In fact, I have to start thinking about adding more data to the initial patent application anyway—the twelve month grace period is slipping away. It's the perfect excuse to ask Alan for more Alzheimer's cells."

"It's good timing, actually." Joshua reached out a long arm and retrieved his laptop, opening a few windows to display the comparison he'd performed for Roz earlier on. "Let me show you something weird I've just stumbled across."

After he explained the tenuous similarities he could see in the coding, Claire said, "If I'd brought this alignment to the bioinformatics people at Liverpool, they'd have laughed me out of the place. It's one of the reasons I avoided them—they were so scathing."

"We're not all that bad," Joshua said. "Although I do recognize the sort of mentality you're describing. My personal philosophy is that no idea is too crazy, no matter what the statistics say. I've been criticized for it in the past, believe me."

"It's crazy, all right." She took another glance at the lines of code. "Based on this, you *really* think ESTA-333 shares a region of similarity with the amyloid protein?"

"I admit it's only a very faint resemblance . . . more like a *shape* than a sequence, if you know what I mean."

"And this region of similarity just happens to be the site on amyloid which couples to SCAN—the place that the Zapper blocks."

"Yes," Joshua said. "So given that SCAN also binds to ESTA-333 . . ."

"The Zapper might interfere with SCAN binding ESTA-333 in the nucleus as well," she finished.

"It might . . . although it's a very long shot."

She looked at him a moment, shaking her head. "Not only is it a long shot, but the irony would be unbelievable if you're right. *I* think the Zapper's not going to work because the Universal Aggregation Principle is wrong, and *you* think the Zapper's not going to work because it's going to muck up ESTA-333. *Two* potential problems with the company's only marketable product!"

"Let's not jump to conclusions," Joshua said. "This second problem is very easy for you to test—just throw some Zapper on your healthy mouse brain cells and see whether the ESTA-333 and SCAN pairs break up."

She nodded, slowly. "Yes, it would be a breeze with the Interactrex. Have you mentioned this second potential problem to Ramon or Alan?"

"No, but I see no reason to keep it secret," he said. "If I'm right, its consequences are relatively minor compared to the Universal Aggregation Principle being wrong. It might just mean that the Zapper will

183

have some side-effects in patients—NeuroSys can work around that sort of set-back."

She nodded. "Okay, I've already got some Zapper in the fridge, so I'll tell Alan what I'm up to. But if the drug does disrupt SCAN binding to ESTA-333 in the nucleus, we'll need to know what effect that has on cells."

"We may be further along with that than you think," he said. "Has Ramon told you about our related bioinformatics project?"

"You mean with that company that tests proteins randomly?"

"Canadian Validation Solutions," Joshua said, nodding.

"Have they really done experiments on ESTA-333 without even knowing what it is?" She looked almost as skeptical as Alan had. "Or without caring, from the sounds of it."

"It's the future of science: vast high-throughput screens."

"In some ways, the prospect is sort of awful. Where is the creativity, the hypotheses, the scientific method?"

"But just look at what can be accomplished," he said. "The Human Genome Project is a wonderful example. In the beginning, everyone said it was mindless and would be a waste of time and money—"

"And now these same people are clamouring for the information?"

He nodded. "And companies like CVS are the next logical step in the post-genomic era. There are many thousands of genes sequenced, but we haven't a clue what most of them actually do."

"I suppose it's only natural that computer people would see things from the larger perspective," she said.

"I think experimental scientists get bogged down with their one little gene," he said. "But we like to think of gene families, networks, how everything is interrelated—finding patterns in the way things fit together."

"You seem quite captivated by our one little ESTA-333 gene, though."

"I know." He smiled at her. "Reformed experimentalist reverts to vestigial type."

"You haven't always been in bioinformatics?"

"No, I was a PhD student in Stanley's academic lab, as it happens, right at the beginning of the Universal Aggregation Principle work. Doing actual biochemistry. If you look at the fine print, you can see my name buried in the author lists of a few of the classic papers."

"I had no idea," she said. "Why did you abandon ship?"

Joshua thought about it a moment.

"Part of it was that sense of being obsessed by one tiny part of a vast whole," he finally said. "It seemed like a waste of brainpower. Part of it was novelty—bioinformatics was in its infancy, and I was thrilled by its potential. And part of it. . ." He paused, wondering how much he could say. "There wasn't a lot of . . . room in Stanley's lab. Intellectually, I mean. Some of the senior postdocs weren't too keen on giving up aspects of their territories to the students."

"Tactfully done, Josh, but I can tell from your face you're talking about Alan." She laughed. "Let's not let him come between us— you're free to hate him, honestly. It doesn't change the fact that I like you."

"You're a remarkable woman, Claire." He shook his head. "Actually, I ought to thank Alan for being so greedy—changing fields was the best decision I ever made . . . and one I hardly ever regret."

"What is it, Josh? What is it you do regret?" He looked up to find Claire studying him, and realized he'd let his mask slip. The unusual effect that Claire was having on him would have been scientifically interesting if it weren't so disconcerting.

"I love what I do," he said slowly. "But the set-up doesn't always seem optimal."

"The Pit, you mean." She was still looking at him with solemn eyes. "Is it the isolation you don't like?"

"Not exactly. More. . ."

"Is it that nobody gives you any credit for your discoveries?"

He nodded. "I know it sounds shallow, but it does get to me sometimes."

"So it should," she said. "At Liverpool, all the other PhD students looked down on me because I was helping Maxwell refine an invention, not solve some earth-shattering biological question like all the others."

Joshua wasn't fooled by her light tone: there was pain behind it, a long shadow stretching out across the ground.

"Nobody made much of an effort to hide their opinions, either," she said. "It was enlightening—I hadn't realized that science could be so snobbish and hierarchical. So it's not shallow at all. Who wants to work hard and then not get any glory for it?"

"If you put it like that. . ." Joshua relaxed. "And the other main thing is that I have no choice—I just have assignments, and I can't turn the boring ones down. I do like the variety, and there are a lot of interesting

185

projects on my desk, but sometimes, I miss the freedom of pursuing my own lines of inquiry."

"I don't suppose you've any other option," she mused. "Bio-informatics tends to be a service, not an independent discipline."

"Well, I've had this idea for a long time. . ." Joshua ran his fingertip over the trackpad of his laptop, watching the cursor loop wildly around his desktop. "I've always thought it would be great to start a bioinfor-matics company. There's increasing demand for what I do, and I could probably attract enough clients to make a profit by initiating collabor-ations myself, solely on projects that truly intrigued me."

"What's stopping you?"

What, indeed? The cursor completed a few more orbits and then plummeted downward, burning up in the atmosphere.

"I've seen enough corporate bickering at NeuroSys to last a lifetime," he said.

Chapter 25

❧

Claire paused in the doorway, watching Alan scribbling on a notepad—the bold lines, circles and squares of his indefatigable plans. Ramon, as he so often was, sat nearby, tapping at a monitor. Alan had told her that the two had shared an office for so long in the old days that neither of them had been truly happy to receive private ones when NeuroSys expanded. After finding themselves wasting most of their precious time trekking back and forth to bounce ideas off one another, they finally decided to treat both spaces like joint offices.

Claire was delaying the moment that would cause Alan to look up. She never tired of seeing the look in his eyes when he caught sight of her.

"Dr Cyrus—how delightful to see you." The glint in Alan's eyes transmitted a wealth of information.

"A moment of your time, Dr Fallengale?"

Ramon rolled his eyes. "You two are so weird." Just then, his mobile went off. "*Gracias a Dios*—saved by the bell." He wandered amiably out of the office, phone to ear.

"What can I do for you," Alan asked pleasantly, "that would not precipitate a shameful scandal were someone to walk in?"

"I need mouse brain cells, Alan. Lots of them."

"So you think you can cheat on me with Zeke Bannerman for *two entire* months and then just traipse back to my lab as if you'd never been away?" He reached out a stealthy finger and ran it lightly along her exposed forearm. "Alzheimer's mice, I presume?"

"Yes, and matched normal mice too, as controls. I've got some ideas about ESTA-333 that I'd like to test."

"Tell me." Alan put down his pencil, alert. Claire loved the way that their relationship did not impair his professional respect for her scientific ideas. A lesser man might condescend.

"I want to study the effect of the Zapper on the behaviour of ESTA-333 and SCAN in the nucleus. For the patent." The statement was true enough, so she had no problems delivering it.

"What makes you think the Zapper will affect that?" He frowned. "It's a very specific drug, tailor-made to disrupt SCAN's binding to amyloids."

"I know, but Joshua's done some more bioinformational modelling." It was a mark of Alan's new mellowness that this name caused only a mildly disdainful sniff. "And he thinks the drug has the potential to compete with ESTA-333 for binding to SCAN."

"Very interesting." Alan picked up the pencil again and tapped it against his chin before leaning forward. "And I am certain that your nimble mind has already taken this one step further. If by some miracle Joshua's wizardry turns out to have a basis in *fact*. . ." Despite her familiarity with his attitude, she found herself unexpectedly irritated. "It could mean that the Zapper might have unexpected side-effects in humans, ones not evident in our mouse experiments."

Claire felt sweat prick in the hollows of her palms and slipped her hands into the pockets of her white coat.

"Don't look so alarmed, my dear—you're making my testosterone levels surge," he said. "In that very unlikely event, we'd only have to pester the chemists to come up with a non-cell-permeable version of the Zapper, to keep it safely away from the nucleus. Drastic, but not the end of the company. And you'd be its heroine."

She tried not to flinch at this wholly inappropriate appellation.

"Tell Klaas to give you whatever you need," he said.

🙰 🙰 🙰

Joshua and Ramon were sitting in front of one of the common computers in the Pit, surrounded by the usual animation of bioinformaticians at play.

"The contrast of this place to my lab is remarkable," Ramon said, ducking as some sort of plastic aircraft zoomed over his head.

"It is rather like a crèche in here—I don't even notice the commotion any more," Joshua said. "It's quieter in my office, if you prefer."

"No, *hombre*, I wasn't complaining. Let's get to it."

Joshua navigated into the Canadian website and entered the password that he'd been sent earlier that morning. With agonizing slowness, the files began to download.

"Exciting, isn't it?" Joshua caught the older man's eye. This whole exercise was bringing back vivid memories of their London days, when he and Ramon had been real colleagues. He couldn't deny he'd missed the thrill of an experimental result about to be revealed, and the camaraderie of sharing that experience.

"Very. And Alan tells me that Claire is resuming some of her Alzheimer's work with the Interactrex, now that she's domesticated Bannerman."

"Yes, so I understand." Joshua fiddled with the mouse.

"If we're lucky, the information from CVS could dovetail very nicely with Claire's work—and I've got a new PhD student willing to follow up on anything that comes out." Ramon paused. "That reminds me—you're welcome to start attending our weekly lab meetings, as I think it's important that we keep each other informed. I've already invited Claire to participate."

"Thanks." Joshua was unexpectedly touched. "Does Alan know you've asked me?"

Ramon sighed. "Listen, Josh. I know it's difficult, and I apologize for his attitude, but believe me, he just wants what's best for the team. He's always been suspicious of new techniques, but if your collaboration with CVS is as helpful as we hope, I think you'll start to notice a difference. I told the same thing to Claire when she started here, and, well. . ." He shrugged, somewhat awkwardly.

"Say no more," Joshua said, grinning. "Okay, it's landed." He clicked on the first report, and both men moved their faces closer to the screen, reading as fast as they could.

❧ ❧ ❧

Claire was priming the Raison for its next run, but her mind was not on her work. She had been thrown of balance by her recent encounter with Alan. It wasn't only her half-truths—she'd already known those would be difficult. She was more unnerved by the reasonable way he had reacted to the possibility that the Zapper might not be ready for clinical trials. Of course it had all been based on a highly unlikely hypothesis, but one could not have hoped for a more measured response.

As a scientist, she could not deny the logical corollary: that if she had told Alan her real concerns back when they had first arisen in December, he would probably have reacted in a similar manner. That he would have faced the truth and done his utmost to ensure that any future clinical trials would be based on solid foundations. That this entire act of secrecy might have been unnecessary.

She kept going back to that pivotal moment on the bench by the River Amstel. She had been sitting there, gathering the internal momentum she needed to confess everything. And then Joshua had come along, draining the potency of her fear with his inexplicable powers and simultaneously planting the seeds in her mind that to come clean prematurely would be inadvisable. Joshua hated Alan; of course he had tried to convince her that Alan would not be able to handle the truth.

"All of this was his fault," she whispered.

The Interactrex chided her with a small beep, and she let go of both breath and anger in one rough exhalation.

"You're right," she said, entering a few strokes on the keyboard. "That's not fair."

True, she'd been on the verge of confessing that weekend, but she'd kept the truth to herself for weeks before that moment. And then, Joshua had only asked her to wait until she'd performed the key experiment in mice—which she'd completed in a scant few days. Afterwards, when she'd collapsed in his office, he had made her promise she would tell Alan straight away, and when she did not, his simmering disapproval had dogged her for weeks.

The blame lay squarely with herself.

"It's not too late, though." She spoke again to the soothing blue interface of the Raison's screen, hitting another key. "I could still tell Alan that the Universal Aggregation Principle might be wrong. I could tell him tonight."

But this time, the Interactrex's answering chime sounded ambivalent.

"Hmmm." Claire's hands clattered over the keyboard in autopilot execution.

She forced herself to be objective. It was one thing to react reasonably about a potential flaw that might make necessary a minor chemical adjustment in an established drug—especially a flaw that was almost assuredly not going to bear out. But it would be quite another to be faced with the destruction of a life work, a cherished theory and the entire reason for

NeuroSys's existence. This was not a prospect to be undertaken lightly, without complete and unequivocal proof.

"It looks as if EST-333 is an adapter," Joshua told Ramon. The bustle of the Pit seemed to have faded away in the excitement of the moment.

"An adapter," Ramon mused. "Linking what to what?"

"Well, we know it binds to SCAN. So it must be helping SCAN to communicate with some other protein in the nucleus."

"Do they already know what protein that might be?"

"Let's find out." Joshua moved his cursor to the appropriate button and clicked it. After a few seconds, a single page came up. "There's the culprit: RAJI-23. So SCAN binds to EST-333, and EST-333 binds to this RAJI-23. Our chain is getting longer, Ramon."

"I've never heard of RAJI-23," Ramon said, squinting.

Joshua scanned the report, and the underlying sequence, with an expert eye. "You're probably not the only one. Looks like it's another unknown orphan protein from the Human Genome Project."

"*Estupendo*! Don't tell me we've just dropped an unthinkable amount of money to fish out yet another mystery protein."

"It's not as bad as it looks." Joshua ran a finger under a suspicious-looking pattern in the middle of the sequence, and then another one near the end. "I'll bet you anything you like that this RAJI-23 is a transcription factor. These motifs are pretty incriminating."

Ramon brightened. "Now that's more like it—switching on genes! Something that even Alan would have to admit is tangible."

"Or switching them off," Joshua reminded him. "But that's not the best thing. Look." He scrolled to the bottom and clicked on a salmon coloured button marked "additional information available".

A new text box came up, informing them that further experiments had been performed successfully with RAJI-23—

"—and are available upon approval of further payment," both men finished in one voice.

"Shit," Ramon said, scratching his head. "Stanley's not going to like this."

"It'll be worth it," Joshua said, clicking back to the report on RAJI-23. "This is fantastic news, Ramon. They're bound to have done micro-arrays; it'll be the first thing they'd try, with those sorts of patterns.

They probably already know every single gene that this adapter helps regulate. CVS has amazing chips—you've never seen anything like it."

"You're sure it's not a scam?" When Joshua shook his head, Ramon sighed and said, "I'll see what I can do."

✤ ✤ ✤

Later that afternoon, Claire stood in the cavernous tissue culture suite shared by Alan and Ramon's laboratories, listening to the hum of the great stainless steel flow cabinets, feeling the prevailing wind of the air filters and watching Klaas's ample backside wiggle as its owner rooted around in an incubator.

"Ten dishes, you say?" The Dutchman's voice sounded muffled and disapproving. "I'm going to have to split these."

But as Klaas's boss was Claire's lover, that was all the insubordination he was likely to muster.

As Klaas took out some plastic dishes of cells and sat down in front of one of the flow cabinets, Ramon came into the suite, followed by a willowy blond girl who stared at Claire with wide eyes.

"I want you to meet Merriam, that new PhD student I was telling you about," Ramon said. "Merriam, Claire is the one who discovered that ESTA-333 binds to SCAN in the nucleus."

Merriam's eyes grew larger, if possible. "I saw that machine of yours on my welcome tour," she murmured. "I don't know *how* you manage to operate something so complicated."

Claire met Ramon's gaze over Merriam's shoulder, saw the apologetic humour there, then asked the young woman a few polite questions about her project. Meanwhile, she couldn't take her eyes off Merriam's appearance. If Joshua was a doomed knight, then surely this was the princess he was meant to meet his death rescuing. She had a helpless beauty from another era, with her long corn-silk hair and drowned Ophelia-blue eyes. She didn't belong in a white coat in a laboratory; she should be wearing a heavy velvet dress, imprisoned in a tower, braiding camomile flowers into her tresses and staring longingly out of the window.

Claire realized that Merriam had asked her a question, and that she had been too distracted to hear it. As Claire muttered something, the other woman's eyes took on a knowing acknowledgement. Not so helpless after all, then. She was aware, Claire thought, of exactly what effect her looks had on people, regardless of their gender, and took pleasure in that power. No, a princess in a tower was too passive an image: she should be sitting on a sea rock in a painting by John William Waterhouse, singing sailors to their demise.

✧ ✧ ✧

"I wish you didn't have to go tomorrow." Claire rested her face against Alan's chest, trying to memorize the feeling of skin on skin.

He gathered her more closely under the duvet and breathed deeply into her hair.

"I'm not looking forward to it either," he said. "But don't worry—with the schedule Stanley's got lined up, there's not an iota of free time when I could possibly misbehave."

His tone was teasing, but something about it made Claire recall a pair of drowned Ophelia eyes.

"Merriam Clark's very beautiful, isn't she?" she said suddenly, without having meant to say the words aloud.

Alan sat up on one elbow, more amused than startled. "What's brought this on?"

"Ramon introduced us today. She's mesmerizing . . . and she knows it."

Alan considered this, with the gravity of a true connoisseur, before speaking. "There is certainly great surface appeal, I'll grant you, but in all other respects I find her utterly vacuous. The sex would probably be great, but could you imagine trying to sustain a conversation?"

Claire rather wished he hadn't mentioned the sex.

"I prefer my women bold and impertinent," he continued, stroking her bare shoulder with his expert sense of timing. "But if you're that keen on her, I could probably suffer both of you in my bed at once . . . providing *you* do all the talking."

Claire sat up suddenly. "Stop it, Alan."

He looked up at her with surprise. "I was joking, obviously."

"Well, it's not funny."

"Don't tell me you're jealous?" He pulled her back down to him, chuckling at her stiff-limbed resistance. "My dear, you've nothing to fear from the wispy likes of her. Besides, you're the one who brought her up in the first place."

"I'm sorry." She looked away. "I'm just being stupid—I should keep my insecurities to myself."

"Why?" Alan wriggled around to interrupt her view, and his green eyes were warm and sympathetic. "Two things. First of all, don't believe everything you read in women's magazines."

"I never read women's magazines," she said, sulkily.

"I bet Merriam Clark devours them. She certainly flirts as if she's following a formula." He laughed at her chagrin and gave her a kiss on the nose. "The truth is, I don't mind a little jealousy, from you. With all the hundreds of women who've preceded you, and not a single question, not a word of resentment ever passing your lips—I was starting to think you were impervious. It's good for my ego to discover that you aren't."

Claire relented at last, relaxing into his embrace. "And what's the second thing?"

Alan didn't say anything for a moment, his breathing tangled in Claire's ear with the pattering of raindrops against the window. "I like to think that, one day, you can trust me enough to reveal anything. And vice versa."

"One day?" Claire felt a stab of fear, and an ache in her spleen that reared up out of nowhere.

"Don't look so terrified, dearest." He slipped careful palms down her back. "I promise that none of my skeletons is horrific enough to scare you away . . . at least, I very much hope not."

"What are you—"

"Shhhh. It's too soon. Later, I promise."

And with his subsequent actions, he left no more room for talking.

Chapter 26

⚜

The next morning, a Saturday, Alan left Claire with a kiss in darkness and headed toward Schiphol Airport, still under the spell of his nightly crop of disturbing dreams. Claire rose a few hours later, made coffee and wandered with her mug into the Bauhaus living room, its furniture all taut angles and geometric precision, poised predators waiting to spring from the shadowy undergrowth.

She was eager to write. As much as she knew she would miss Alan, she had been craving solitude for weeks, the extended isolation that would allow her to commit to paper the words that had been accumulating in her brain. Alan, now that he had found her, seemed reluctant to let her out of his sight. He wanted to talk with her, make love to her, guide her through the cultural nightlife of The Hague. She'd even lost those brief moments of writing time on the train, having spent most of her nights in Alan's bed. It was not that she didn't enjoy his company. But her loss of privacy was proving to be a much bigger sacrifice than she had expected.

She pulled her travelling notebook from her rucksack and sat down at the glass Van der Rohe table, the blank page an incitement to . . . what? Nothing seemed to be forthcoming. She felt Alan's presence in this room, watching her with a critical eye and making it difficult to sink into her usual reverie.

⚜ ⚜ ⚜

At first, Alan had indulged her literary habits with the fresh-eyed tolerance of the new lover. He allowed her to sit curled up unmolested on the Corbusier, reading verse, or to retire to the bedroom's bay window seat to inscribe her lists of words or the poems they might eventually lead to—though the lists never seemed to open as many doors these days, there being insufficient time for the initial ideas to crystallize.

As time went by, though, he began to manifest symptoms of impatience.

"If you spent as much time reading the scientific literature as you did poetry," Alan had observed one evening, standing in the door of the bedroom with a glass of port, "you'd be ten times sharper in the lab than you already are."

Claire tried to surface from the page, interrupted in the act of lovingly stroking out an exploratory phrase about the movement of water down a surface of glass: the way she felt when she sat in this particular seat on a rainy night, trying to screen out the environment and find her sense of self, which in turn might be a metaphor for her—

"Claire?"

"Sorry." The watery, glassy words scattered like coloured marbles across a carpet, and she closed the notebook. "I'm not really interested in that sort of reading—especially when I'm off-duty. It's a chore."

"A scientist is never off-duty," he said, sitting down next to her on the window seat, "When I was your age, I was devouring all the latest research. I couldn't get enough."

She could tell that he was settling into conversational mode, his eyes brightening with the challenge of an impending friendly spar.

"It's probably healthy for me to switch off sometimes," she parried.

"You're a good scientist, Claire, but if you devoted yourself to the cause, I think you could be a great one."

"Really?" She was intrigued despite herself. "You're just saying that. You're not objective any more, are you?"

He leaned over to put his glass on the bedside table and then picked up her hand, kissing her fingers until she felt weak.

"I hardly need flatter you to get into your underpants by now, my dear," he murmured between fingers. "I'm serious. You could be brilliant, if you only applied yourself."

She closed her eyes, using her arousal as an excuse not to answer.

"If you can't get excited by reading," he persisted, lips moving into the palm of her hand, inching toward her trembling pulse in a way that still allowed his words to be perfectly articulated, "then I could arrange with Stanley to send you to a few international conferences on brain disorders. There's so much going on in the field now—it's all terribly stimulating. I think you might find—"

"No," she said, opening her eyes.

Alan put her hand down, straightened up with a look she had not seen in some time.

"I'm sorry," she said hastily. "I didn't mean to be rude—it's lovely of you to want to . . . help me." *Improve* me, is what she was really thinking. "But honestly, I'm happier the way things are now. I *like* my job, but. . ."

"But what?" he asked. "It's just a day-job, and you'd rather be a poet?" Was that a trace of sarcasm? "I thought you didn't want to burn out on your passion."

"And I thought you said that one ought not be cowardly about pursuing one's passions!"

"Maybe so," he said, "But I don't see much evidence that you'd ever manage to commit yourself to such an endeavour."

She drew a breath in, rather shocked.

"Of course you do write," he went on, "but it's all dabbling—it's not a full frontal assault. You lack true commitment and, meanwhile, you're under-utilizing your scientific talents. It's a waste, Claire."

She looked out the window and did not answer. Alan, like Claire herself, knew exactly how to choose his words, and *dabbling* was about the most patronizing one he could have come up with.

His voice became gentle, and he took her hand again, though she refused to look at him. "I just hate to see you splitting your energy into two conflicting directions. I think you ought to become more passionate about the one field that I *know* you can conquer."

Claire, sitting there with her coffee and her blank notebook, tried to screen out this memory, and the few others it brought to mind, but she could not seem to enter her quiet space. Restless, she left the empty house soon afterward, got on her bicycle and rode through the sweet April air to the train station. She was suddenly anxious to get back to Amsterdam, to her flat and her books, to a place that was not so impregnated with Alan's helpful criticisms or watchful eyes.

At that precise moment, Joshua was also restless.

He was tired of waiting. The list kept getting longer: waiting for Stanley to approve his latest request about ESTA-333 while the truth hovered just beyond the reach of his cursor's click. Waiting for Claire to finish the experiments with the Zapper that would settle their most recent concern one way or the other. Waiting for the brain of the next terminal patient at the Van de Laan Hospice to succumb to the tangles and plaques of proteins that were slowly stifling it, so that Claire could finally re-address the crux of the matter of NeuroSys's existence.

And, in the back of his mind, waiting for Alan to break Claire's heart. He was certainly taking his time at it, Joshua had to admit, which would only make things so much worse when it finally happened.

Until any of these things occurred, he felt powerless and unable to focus on work. And, once his morning rowing routine was completed, he couldn't muster up much enthusiasm for any of his normal weekend leisure activities either—reading foreign language novels, running along the river, meeting his Dutch friends for a coffee.

Particularly the latter. In recent months, since his break-up with Hanneke and the sense of vague disillusion that had precipitated it, he had found Dutch company increasingly unsatisfying. Formerly he had taken refuge in the rare sensation of simply belonging, of being accepted by a group and moving with it. He had derived a thrill from even the most trivial instances of insider information, like knowing the precise etiquette for ringing a bicycle bell—one polite *ping* to alert a native on passing versus the rapid-fire volley reserved exclusively for tourists who had the effrontery to stray onto the cycle paths. But something was missing from the brightly-coloured fabric of conversation: beneath it, for him, lay only emptiness. He found himself craving deeper truths, things that normally never got said.

"What's with you, *jongen*?" Marco had asked Joshua earlier that morning as they towelled off from the shower, the laughter and jibes of the other men and the slamming of lockers echoing off the steamy tiles.

"What do you mean?" Joshua kept his voice mild as he reached for a clean black T-shirt.

"Why haven't you been coming to The Three Sisters with the rest of the crew?" Marco stood there, short blond hair in wet spikes, pale blue eyes unusually serious. "Has something happened between you and one of the lads?"

"No, of course not."

"Or have *I* done something?"

"No, really. I'm just . . . in a strange mood lately."

Marco pulled a sweatshirt over his head, and the muffled question emerged: "Is it because you've heard about Hanneke's new boyfriend?" The spikes protruded from the collar, and then the blue eyes, curious and hesitant.

Joshua smiled. "I hadn't heard, actually—thanks for the warning. But I think that's great."

And it was: Joshua detected nothing inside: no jealousy, no sadness, no regret. Marco did not press Joshua further, as Joshua knew he would not. Marco had a blunt initial approach, but it only ever went so far. Still, Joshua could tell from his body language that Marco was hurt and still fundamentally unsatisfied.

"I'm sorry I've been so useless," Joshua said. And then, speaking the magic formula: "Let's have a drink later."

Marco, as usual, responded with an insulting jibe, and that was that.

These were the thoughts and memories that occupied Joshua as he passed through the flower market on the Singel that sullen, late April Saturday, on his way to nowhere. He normally avoided the more touristy areas of town, but the restlessness had propelled him out of the house that afternoon, and then further beyond his habitual square kilometre of well-paced neighbourhood.

"You speak English?" A rotund Scot with a rucksack touched his shoulder.

"Like a native, mate," Joshua said, taking the proffered camera, an antique 35-millimetre.

The Scot arranged himself and his girlfriend in front of a triffid-like display of orchids, and a half a second before Joshua depressed the shutter, a familiar figure launched herself into the background.

Snap: Claire's absurd expression and laughing dark eyes were preserved for all eternity in the album of a stranger.

Joshua kept his own face impassive until the tourists had thanked him and moved on, then broke out into a huge grin.

"Think they'll notice?" she asked.

"That was naughty. What are you doing in Amsterdam?"

"I live here, remember?" She smiled up at him, hands buried in the pockets of a well-worn military coat.

"Nominally."

"Hmmm. But after a late night in the lab, faced with the choice of going 'round the corner or taking the long train ride home. . ."

"So what's the occasion, then?"

A ripple of emotion passed across her face. "Alan's out of town this week—some big pharma conference in Vancouver. I thought I'd better make sure my plants were alive—and that Rachel was still speaking to me."

"Rachel?" He remembered the elegant woman Claire had been drinking with that night back in January.

"My best friend. At least she was, until I went underground. I'm going to meet her now, for an appeasement drink . . . why don't you join us?"

❧ ❧ ❧

Claire stood on tiptoe, scanning the crowded terrace tables.

"She's not here yet," she said, starting to thread her way towards a free spot in the heart of the bustle of Leidseplein.

"Maybe she's inside?" There was still an edge to the air, especially when the wind gusted. Joshua glanced up as he followed, undecided as to whether sunlight or rain was about to burst through the brooding overcast.

"No chance—Rachel likes to see and be seen," she said, over her shoulder. "Do you mind?"

"Of course not."

Soon they were ordering their beers, Joshua noting that Claire had a good grasp of the language basics—although, predictably enough, the waiter replied initially in English. But Claire kept gamely at it, answering with clumsy but confident Dutch at every turn until the man finally surrendered. Persistence was the only way to handle the traditional treatment, and he was impressed that, unlike most, she had figured it out.

The drinks arrived, and they sat, waiting for Rachel and surrounded by the babble of dozens of languages and the trilling of tram bells scattering tourists in the centre of the square like confetti.

"I've missed Amsterdam," she finally remarked.

"It's good to finally catch up."

She put her glass down, meeting his gaze. "I should've made more of an effort. But you know what it's like, the first few months. . ." She put a concerned hand to her cheek. "Don't you?"

He smiled. "I'm not a monk, Claire. In fact, I've recently come out of a year of domestic bliss myself."

"Oh! I'm sorry."

"Don't be." He looked away a moment, at the determined crowd of pigeons scrabbling for cold, mayonnaise-smeared *frietjes*. "She had her reasons . . . as did I."

"What were hers?"

"I was stubbornly resisting the whole family thing."

"You mean she wanted a baby?"

"No . . . well, possibly yes. But what I meant was, the *extended* family. If you acquire a Dutch partner, you acquire an entire universe of social obligations. The birthdays alone are enough to kill you: coffee and apple cake, sitting in a circle talking about mortgages until you want to shoot yourself in the head."

"How many could there be?" Claire's eyes were shimmering with humour.

"Including the aunts and uncles, cousins, nephews and nieces, grand-parents, god-children, god-parents, work colleagues and friends—child-hood, school, university and current? Pretty much every weekend, and some weeknights besides. I had recently mutinied, told her it was time I broke the cycle. And she took exception."

"Oh, Josh. . ." She started to giggle. "I'm sorry, but what a reason! I hope yours was better."

"Much less tangible, I'm afraid."

She slipped a hand on his forearm, a warm surprise. "You don't have to tell me."

"It's not that I don't want to. I'm just not sure I can properly explain."

"Did you love her?"

"Yes," he said. "I think so. But it felt like we'd been married for thirty years, even at the beginning. It always seems to be like that with my relationships. I finally decided that comfort and congeniality shouldn't be enough."

"No," she said quietly. "They shouldn't."

There it was again, Joshua thought. The sense that everyone else in the world was sorted, while he inhabited his universe of one.

"Sorry I'm late," a voice said over his shoulder.

Joshua glanced up to find the elegant woman looking down at them, her sculpted face expressionless, her keen, shadowed eyes taking note of Claire's hand as it disappeared under the table.

"You must be Joshua," she added, a smile dispersing her severe expression as she collapsed into a chair, relieving herself of an unbelievable number of shopping bags.

"How did you know?"

"You may have noticed that our Claire has a way with descriptions." She reached down to unzip her high-heeled boots, sighing as she wriggled each stockinged foot half way out.

"You were probably expecting something much more extreme, then." He noticed that Claire was watching their interactions curiously.

"No." Rachel's gaze was critically appraising. "She's got you spot-on: *'tragically handsome, shadow and snow'*."

He couldn't tell if she was flirting or if this was just her normal manner. He had no way of knowing that an entire legion of expatriate men in the city were similarly baffled.

"A bit of poetic license on the handsome bit," Joshua said, smiling.

Rachel refused to bite. "That was a Claire Cyrus original, by the way, not a quote. But she's been driving herself frantic trying to track down the poem you remind her of."

"Rachel," Claire said quietly, intervening for the first time.

"Sorry, darling, have I betrayed a girly secret?" Rachel raised a graceful hand, and about three waiters fell over themselves to be the first to respond. After delivering her order in unabashed English, she turned to Joshua once more. "So what's Alan Fallengale *really* like?"

"Haven't you met him yet?" he countered, glancing at Claire. She lifted a rueful shoulder, giving him tacit permission for honesty— as if anything else could possibly prevail in this strange world of frankness that Claire and everyone associated with her seemed to command.

"As if. She's keeping him well hidden . . . although we have spoken on the phone, under false pretences."

Both women smiled but did not elaborate.

"Well?" Rachel demanded. "I was against him at first, but he seems to have improved. And what a priceless opportunity, running into a second opinion."

"Let's put Joshua out of his misery—they hate each other, Rach."

"How perfectly marvellous!" Rachel seemed truly delighted. "Conflict of interest?" Her charcoal gaze flitted over to Claire before settling back on him.

"Rachel," Claire murmured again.

"No, it goes back much further than that," Joshua replied, unperturbed.

"Oh, do tell!"

"Sorry, but I'm not prepared to say anything. It wouldn't be fair to Alan or to Claire."

"Spoilsport," Rachel said serenely. "I'll have to work on you later."

❦ ❦ ❦

Claire watched her two friends banter across the table as if they'd known each other for years. She'd had a suspicion they would hit it off, and was pleased, but the way Joshua had refused to complain about Alan had shifted her equilibrium. Nothing would've given Alan more pleasure were the roles reversed, despite any discomfort that Claire might have experienced as a result.

"If you ladies will excuse me a moment. . ." Joshua rose to his full six foot eight inches and made his way sinuously through the scattered tables.

"Darling, why didn't you tell me how absolutely charming he is?" Rachel was also watching his retreat, sipping at her Baileys with delicate appreciation.

"Did you *have* to mention the poetry?"

She ignored this line, mused, "And on further acquaintance, I think he is rather handsome—once you get over the shock of that white skin. Great body, too, very athletic . . . and he's got an expressive face, when he chooses to reveal what he's feeling."

Claire didn't say anything, still annoyed.

"Is he single?" Rachel asked, after a few more moments.

"Yes."

"He's definitely straight." This more question than statement.

"Definitely."

"Hmmm." Rachel drifted a bit, then looked up and gave Claire a petulant look. "You bringing along an eligible bachelor *almost* makes up for your neglect these past weeks. I've missed you."

"Oh, Rach . . . I'm sorry."

"But you *are* happy, Claire? Everything *is* going well?"

"Of course." For some reason, the concept of Alan seemed unreal, as if he'd been gone for months instead of just one night.

"I'm glad. But be careful with that one, darling." Rachel angled her head towards where Joshua had disappeared into one of the bars fronting the terrace.

"What do you mean?" Claire shifted uneasily. "Because he knows my secret?"

Rachel just looked at her. "As if someone like that would ever betray you. I *mean*—he's really nice, so just tread carefully."

"You've lost me, Rach."

"Never mind." She shook her head, disgusted.

Chapter 27

ₐ₈₂

It turned out to be one of those timeless Saturday afternoons. The sun eventually won the battle, bathing the terrace in warmth. Mobile phones went off sporadically, trays of *frietjes*, *bitterballen* and *vlammetjes* were demolished, and the group around the table expanded and contracted as various of their friends popped in and out for a drink and a chat.

Joshua observed the various social interactions with his usual attention to detail. As always, the Dutch and British contingents got on well at the superficial level. The Dutch tended to be masters at bold flirtation and the art of the friendly insult, and while they could seldom achieve the subtle humour of the British, they appreciated being subjected to it. Once Joshua's friends overcame the horror of finding themselves such a touristy locale, they relaxed out of their self-righteous blather and started to enjoy themselves. Rachel and her fashionable female companions certainly didn't hurt the atmosphere, and her male admirers seemed perfectly happy to discuss football with members of any nationality. Even Hanneke had stopped by, draped around the new boyfriend: to Joshua, she seemed almost like a stranger, and he marvelled at how quickly and cleanly they had repelled one another, like opposing magnets. Only Claire seemed out of sorts—her earlier high spirits had slipped, a state betrayed by the slowness of her smile, the cast of her arms and a few other physical cues that Joshua could not avoid cataloguing.

❀ ❀ ❀

Claire had opted out of conversation a few minutes previously: Rachel, on her right, had her back to Claire as she related one of her

205

outrageous stories to a cluster of rapt rowers, and Joshua, on her left, was speaking quiet Dutch to one of his friends, which she could only just about piece together.

Rachel: "And that was when I realized that this guy was actually a Dutch celeb!"

Marco: "En zij was zo ongelovelijk mooi, hoor. . ." *And she was so unbelievably gorgeous. . .*

Rachel: "Of *course* I'd never heard of him, darling. How on earth do you—"

Marco: "*Erg* mooi, met *gro-*te—" *Really gorgeous, with big—*

Love-struck rower: "You have actually *spoken* to Rob de Jong? Do you realize—"

Marco: "En dan . . . haar zus komt binnen . . . en zij is nog mooier!" *And then her sister walked in . . . and she was even prettier!*

Rachel: "No, we didn't speak. Get this: he was too *important* to actually ask me out in person."

Joshua: "Ik denk dat ik wel weet wat er gebeuren gaat. . ." *I think I know where this is heading. . .*

Rachel: "He sends his *PA* over to ask me out *for* him. She had a clipboard . . . and an earpiece, just like the Secret Service!"

Joshua: "Dat is zo typisch jij, probeer je twee vliegen in een klap te slaan, en mis je ze allebei!" *That's typical you—try to kill two flies with one swap, and end up missing them both!*

Claire eventually gave up trying to follow the disparate threads. She had been disappointed, earlier that morning, when coming to Amsterdam had not provided the hoped-for literary inspiration. After a few hours of flipping fitfully through this book or that, she had left her flat with the intention of going back to NeuroSys and actually doing some experiments. She had even contemplated taking Alan's advice and reading a few scientific articles in the company library. He was probably right that she ought to get more serious. *Splitting your energy into two conflicting directions.* She had invested a great deal of time and energy on her PhD, and now she was climbing a stable, predicable ladder, the speed of her ascent largely down to her own efforts—a most gratifying correlation. Hadn't stability been the one thing she had learned to crave at all costs?

But something had happened to her halfway to the station. Waiting for the traffic light at Muntplein, the old clock tower started to ring the changing hour, raining its ancient tones down onto the crowd funnelling down the *Bloemenmarkt*. She'd be damned if the thought of Alan's disappointment would force her back to the lab on a beautiful Saturday afternoon.

Sitting at the table, surrounded by happier people, she nursed her sudden resentment.

"You're a man of surprises," Marco said softly to Joshua, in Dutch, as both of them scrutinized Rachel's performance. "One minute you avoid us, and the next, you're Mr Social." After a pause. "Is she available?"

"I don't know," Joshua said. "But I'd be careful if I were you, *jongen*—she's got claws."

"Really?" Marco settled back in his chair, smirking. "All the better."

"Your naïvete is so refreshing. She'd have you for dinner, Marco."

"*Rot op, jongen.* I'd have her for dessert."

"If I weren't such a gentleman, I'd say that a wager might be in order."

"Ha!" Marco promptly leaned across the table and attempted to insinuate himself into Rachel's circle.

Joshua turned to Claire, who was smiling up at him.

"If Rachel gets wind of a bet, your friend is in serious trouble," she said.

He laughed. "You understand more Dutch than I gave you credit for."

"Not really," she said. "I just have an overactive imagination when it comes to words . . . I'm good at filling in the gaps."

"Speaking of which, how's the writing going?"

Her face settled to a neutral holding pattern. "Up and down."

"A bit more down at the moment?"

"Maybe."

When she didn't elaborate, he asked, "So what are your plans these days, on that front?"

"Plans?" She looked startled.

"You know—entering competitions. Giving readings. Trying to get published. Whatever it is that poets do to advance their profession."

"Oh." She shook her head. "No, I've never tried that sort of thing."

"Why not?"

A shrug. Joshua watched her mutilate a paper serviette, eyes down. This was clearly a no-go area. Just as he was thinking of changing the subject, she suddenly said, "Do you think being a scientist is more important than being a poet?"

"No." He sat back, considered. "I think they're two diffcrent activities with two separate values—although maybe a lot more related than either practitioner would care to admit."

"I know exactly what you mean. Sometimes I watch Ramon fiddle with his hypotheses and come up with some mad new idea, and I think to myself . . . this is art."

"Or black magic. My computer stuff is even more esoteric."

"But, Josh. Surely science is the more practical choice."

"Well, there's no doubt it's more likely to keep you in the manner to which you've grown accustomed."

"That's not what I meant."

"Practical for society, you mean?"

Another shrug.

Joshua took a sip of his *witbier*. "I once had an English tutor who was always bemoaning the lack of decent poets in the twentieth century. She was predicting that this century would be even worse."

"She was right, probably."

"Whereas we're up to our ears in scientists—more PhDs are produced each year than can possibly be absorbed into the system. I can't think of anything more pathetic than a postdoctorate flipping burgers, can you?"

"How about a poet using a pipettor?" She had a sad little smile on her face.

"You're twisting my meaning," he said. "The point is that you shouldn't decide what you want to do based on some self-conscious impression of what's expected of you. You should do what *you* want to do, full stop. And everything else will fall into place."

"Is it really that simple?"

"No," he said, giving her a pat on the knee. "Not even remotely. But you've got to start somewhere."

They lapsed into silence, and Joshua pondered the wisdom of his own advice.

"Joshua was right," Rachel said. "This club is so kitsch, it's actually cool."

"It's a fine line, though, isn't it?" Claire replied, adjusting her position against the wall to get a better view of the dancers. They were in an obscure place on the outskirts of town. Aside from their own friends, the clientele were Dutch—rich, well-dressed professional types who threw themselves into both the music and the drinking with enthusiasm. Claire was standing out this number to catch her breath, having lost track of the number of times she'd nearly been knocked over or jabbed in the kidneys by Louis Vuitton handbags in the past hour.

"Look at Joshua with Viv," Rachel said. "I wouldn't have thought someone so tall would be such a good dancer." Then, with a sigh, "Darling, what's the matter with you tonight? Are you pining after Alan?"

"Sort of," Claire admitted.

"You're not worried about him and other women, are you?"

"Yes and no."

"Any cause thus far for legitimate concern?" Her words were light, careful.

"Only if you take his previous reputation into account. But how can you not? People don't ever really change, do they?"

"So the urban myth goes."

"Do you believe it?"

"No. Are you the same person you were last year? Five years ago? Ten?"

Claire made another noncommittal noise in her throat. Then she quoted, *"And I will show you something different than either; your shadow at morning striding behind you; or your shadow at evening rising to meet you; I will show you fear in a handful of dust."*

"Oh, Claire. Can't you just relax and hope for the best like the rest of us?"

⚜ ⚜ ⚜

Soon after Rachel evaporated, Joshua appeared by Claire's side and passed her a bottle of lager, startling her out of a haze of thoughts. He *looks happy*, she thought, wholly unlike his normal self. *But what gives me the right to assume I would recognize his normal self?*

"What were you day-dreaming about so ferociously?" he asked.

"I was just trying to imagine what Alan would make of this place."

He smirked. "Eurotrash not in his repertoire?"

"Oh Josh, you know what he's like. He would entirely fail to see the humour. And even earlier, in Leidseplein. Could you picture him eating chips and talking trivialities with random strangers?"

"Does that bother you?"

"A little."

"He's quite a bit older, Claire. You've got to make some allowance."

"He's not that much older than you, is he?"

He paused to do the maths. "Seven years . . . it's a fairly significant difference."

"Josh—I appreciate your restraint earlier, but I'm surprised to hear you making excuses for him now that we're alone."

"I won't deny that I'm concerned. But. . ." He sighed.

"What is it?"

"There's something about you that always makes me say too much. And all the alcohol I've drunk isn't helping matters."

"I'm sorry."

"Don't be—I'm learning to like it." He placed a hand on her shoulder, and through it, she could feel his gentle force filtering into her, loosening her taut muscles and melting the top layer of her distress. She wanted him to put his arms around her, to make the rest of it go away too, and in a flash, she found herself wondering how such tremendous physical empathy would translate during an act of passion.

"What I'm trying to tell you," he said, "is that if someone like *you* loves Alan, then there must be something more to him than I can see. And I'm willing to be converted."

She felt the swift prick of tears behind her eyes. "I'm not a saint, Joshua. If you knew what a terrible thing I. . ." She stopped, moved away from his caress before it could draw out the rest of the story.

He dropped the rejected hand back to his side (when he could so easily have fought unfairly, she thought bitterly). "It's not like you to stop with a truth half told," he said.

"Even I have my limits."

"My apologies, this time." He looked out over the dance floor, the flickering lights colouring his face. Eventually he said, "I'd venture to guess that if you really had done something terrible in the past, there would've been good intentions behind it."

"You have no idea what you're talking about." Suddenly furious, she pushed away and into the crowd.

❧ ❧ ❧

Claire, if asked which of her dead parents she most resembled, would have replied unthinkingly: she possessed the body of her mother and the mind of her father. These two parts of her, she imagined, had segregated discretely according to the classic laws of Gregor Mendel, the monk who had stumbled across modern genetics in a tangle of peas and snapdragons in his abbey garden. Family photographs proved that Claire had physically mirrored Pilar at every stage of her development. But her intellect, her strange power over the written word, her love of solitude, her humour and sympathy, her sporadic shyness and insecurity—all of these bore the unmistakable stamp of her father.

Nevertheless, Edward Cyrus would have immediately recognized the set of Claire's features and the fire in her eyes as she fought her way through the grove of drunken giants obstructing the club's main entrance. Pilar, too, had simmered for long periods and then exploded into violent fits of fury. Although Claire had chosen not to enunciate her anger to Joshua on this particular occasion, if she had it would have been delivered with the loud, blunt and thorough efficiency she had learned—or inherited—from her mother; scientists are still debating the distinction.

For Pilar had not been a happy woman. It was one thing to run away with an enchanting foreign poet and quite another to live with the reality. They had arrived in England one frigid evening in November and Pilar hated it on sight. Further acquaintance did not improve her opinion. Her English was poor and everyone seemed reserved and inscrutable: the neighbours, Edward's university colleagues, the eccentric literary strays he was forever bringing home from bars and cafés, especially the females, who seemed to take no notice of his married status. She missed the warm arms and sweet songs of her sisters, the constant murmuring of the sea, the taste of *puchero*, *sancocho*, and her mother's banana tart. And she felt keenly the loss of her bakery, and the pride and responsibility of running it, the way it had placed her so squarely in the centre of her former community.

After Claire arrived, Pilar's joy was restored for a few years. But Claire's perfection, in her mother's eyes, began fading when her daughter, effortlessly bilingual, started to speak. English, this ugly language that Pilar could not seem to master, flashed like a spark between father and daughter, flaring up into passionate whirls and eddies and riptides of sound, creating an exclusive universe that Pilar could not share. With their books and words and games and secrets, it was probably inevitable that Pilar would grow jealous of Claire for having Edward's attention, and of Edward, for having Claire's.

Claire was sensitive enough to feel the underlying resentment, even as her subconscious memories of lost mother love would always shadow her. And though Claire had been quite soft-spoken while growing up, in recent years she had developed a habit of seeing and speaking the truth when others wouldn't dare, a habit that attracted certain types of people with irresistible magnetism. She had always thought it had come into being by spontaneous generation. But if she had known Pilar in better, happier days, or if her father had been around to point it out, she would have realized that this tendency, too, was something that her mother had bequeathed.

✤ ✤ ✤

Joshua didn't move after Claire left his side. In a way, it was a relief to see that honesty did have its consequences—and boundaries.

"Everything under control?" Rachel had come up beside him in the meantime.

"More or less. Maybe you ought to go after her, though."

"In a minute—it's always best to let her cool down first." She blotted her forehead with a sleeve—Rachel was the sort of woman on whom even sweat looked sophisticated. "Have you ever seen her temper in its full glory?"

"I don't think so."

"You'd know it if you had—things normally get thrown. You didn't make a pass at her, did you?"

"Please—I'm not stupid."

"I know. But I do feel sorry for you."

"Don't. We're all adults here."

"How long have you. . ."

He shrugged. "A few weeks? A few months? To be honest, I'm not even sure what it is that I do feel."

"Trust your Auntie Rachel on this one: you're smitten."

"Whatever it is, I'll get over it," Joshua said.

"Maybe you won't have to, if Alan de-evolves back to Neanderthal."

"I wouldn't wish that on Claire now, for anything."

She looked up at him, eyes shrouded. "You're a very strange man, Joshua."

"So I've been told."

She just looked at him for a time, a twitch of amusement at the corner of her mouth. Then she said, "Don't take this the wrong way, but can we exchange phone numbers? I can't seem to shake the feeling that something awful's going to happen to Claire at work. You know, because of this secret result she's been hiding."

"She told you about that?"

"Ages ago—what harm could I do?"

"I suppose you're right," he said.

"Anyway, it would make me feel better knowing we could contact one another."

Joshua pulled out his phone and passed it over. Rachel followed suit and they both entered numbers impersonally for a few moments, like passing moths imprinting one another's vital essences.

"Can't you *make* her tell someone?" She slipped the mobile back into her handbag. When he shook his head, she added, "And *you* won't, I suppose."

"I promised I wouldn't. I could never. . ."

"No, I suppose not. It wouldn't be like you, would it, even if you didn't feel the way you feel."

❧ ❧ ❧

Unbeknownst to Joshua and Rachel, something did get thrown—a mostly-full beer bottle, smashing into the empty lot outside the club and disintegrating into a million emerald shards under the moonlight.

❧ ❧ ❧

Later on, tangled in bed and spinning with alcohol, Claire suffered through horrifying nightmares. First she had the usual one about her father, although it had been many months since it had chosen to haunt her. The preliminaries often varied: subtle differences in her age, in the season, in the time of day, in the building. But whatever route it took, the dream never failed to culminate with the same graphic still shot—not a made-up image, but the actual memory, the memory which had been burnt into her retina before she could turn away.

Usually this scene was enough to blast her into consciousness, but this morning, the dream went on and on. There was a jumble of light and shadow, of anxiety and dread, of being lost in passageways or stuck in a falling lift or late for a maths exam, and then she was at NeuroSys, trapped in her lab and wearing a heavy velvet dress. The Interactrex 3000 had come to life, its grey tentacles—half steel, half brain-like matter—curling and sliding around her limbs, keeping her from the open window. Out on the flat plains of the Dutch landscape, Joshua was trying to reach her, head raised towards her tower, so focused on her plight that he was unaware of the vast pit that had opened up in front of him.

She had been wrong, she thought in the dream, an insight that she would not recall on waking. Merriam wasn't the princess, the siren, the *femme fatale* who was going to destroy Joshua. It had been herself, all along.

Chapter 28

❧

Joshua walked down the corridor to his office first thing Monday morning and came to a sudden halt just over the threshold. A bouquet of white tulips sat in a glass beaker on his desk, pointing to the ceiling like closed hearts.

He approached the alien life forms, slit open the small envelope with wary fingers.

> I tried to find ones the same shade as you, but they don't exist.
> Forgive me for ruining a perfectly wonderful Saturday.
> Love,
> Claire

"All the Pit is aflutter," Roz said from behind him. "Who is the culprit, and how did they manage to sneak by this morning without any of us seeing? An inside job, people are speculating."

The perils of leaving your office door open.

"Claire's an early riser," Joshua said, putting the card carefully into his wallet before dropping into the chair. Her honesty was obviously contagious, and he found himself completely infected.

"Claire *Cyrus*?"

"Are you here for a particular reason, Roz?"

She gave him that look. "Are you mad? You don't want to mess with Alan's woman, boss. He'll have your balls on a platter."

"At the risk of sounding clichéd, it's not what you think."

"Well, thank God for that. But he's going to find out about the flowers and draw his own conclusions."

"Not if you don't disseminate who sent them to me."

"Touché." She held out his pile of post. "One from Stanley, so it might be news about your project with Ramon."

He snatched up the interdepartmental envelope and demolished it.

🌿 🌿 🌿

After such a distressing weekend, it was a relief for Claire to be back at work, far away from nightmares and memories that she couldn't control. She had spent the night at Alan's house on Sunday; even though it was empty, she'd been soothed by the smell and feel of his bed and had finally slept, deep and dreamless. And then, at seven in the morning, the man himself rang from Vancouver, tired from a full day's session but so affectionate that her fears were vaporized.

"Only four more days, love," he'd said, "ones I'm not sure I can stand—Stanley is a wretched substitute for you."

She'd had to cycle all the way to Leiden Centraal Station to find a florist open so early, but this act of absolution eased another gnawing discomfort. It was a clear spring morning, the tree buds sprinkled like pastel stars, the birds warbling with only one thing on their minds, and the exercise pumping the final fragments of nightmare from her blood.

Now she was poised over the main console keyboard of the Raison, energized with a sense of purpose. Joshua had discovered a second potential problem with the Zapper, and she was the only one at NeuroSys who could find out if his theory was correct. Almost the only one in the world—she and the Raison. Bolstered by her soul-searching over the weekend, she suddenly experienced a rare pride in her career. She had never intended to become a scientist, but sometimes when she caught herself in the act it was like glimpsing an unexpected reflection in a shop window: grown-up, confident, not at all like the unassuming bookish girl she viewed herself as on most days. With Alan's recent advocacy of her scientific talents, she was finding it increasingly easy to believe in the role. Wasn't she almost ninety percent of the way already? Joshua's advice could actually apply just as well to science— if science was what she truly wanted to do, she should just make it happen. She should make it her *whole*.

Today Claire planned to test whether the Zapper truly could interfere with SCAN's binding to the chaperone EST-333, a situation that might cause any number of unexpected side-effects. In a few hours, she was going to attend Ramon and Alan's weekly joint lab meeting for the first time, and it would be appropriate to have some results to present.

She placed the first small dish of healthy mouse brain cells under the microscopic eye of the Raison, a dish that had been impregnated with a large dose of the Zapper. Calling up the image display on the main screen, she zeroed in on a cell nucleus and lowered the needle towards its final destination.

❦ ❦ ❦

Ramon was just looking at his watch for the second time when the door opened and Claire scurried in, arms full of binders and a fresh print-out fluttering on the top of the stack. When her roving gaze snagged Joshua's, her expression didn't change, but he could sense the hidden greeting.

"Sorry, Ramon, everyone," she said. "I only just finished my last run about a minute ago."

"That's the sort of excuse we like around here," Ramon said, smiling.

Joshua watched Claire look around the crowded room then deliberately choose a free chair next to him. She seemed tense—maybe the experiments had turned something up.

"Before we begin," Ramon continued, "I'd like to thank Claire and Joshua for joining our weekly meetings. As I'm sure will soon become clear, they are both engaged in interesting work on our behalf. Also I'd like to apologize for Alan's absence..."

"Thanks, by the way," Joshua murmured to Claire in the general furore as a PhD student began to fire up the digital projector. "Entirely unnecessary, but extremely beautiful."

"I hope I didn't cause a scandal down there." Her lips twitched as she gave him a sideways glance.

"Only enhances my general reputation as a man of mystery. I should be the one apologizing, though."

"Nonsense. I was out of line. Listen, you won't believe what happened this morning with—"

But the first speaker had begun, so she had to close her mouth. After giving a short summary of his most recent findings with a new mouse model for Parkinson's Disease, the student sat down, and Ramon invited Claire to the front to explain about her work.

"I don't have anything prepared," Claire said to the expectant faces in front of her. "And I think most of you already know the background of the original patent application, so I'll keep the intro brief."

As she turned to the flip chart and began to draw the outline of a neuronal cell in fluid strokes with a marker pen, Joshua became aware of restless movements to his right. The strikingly attractive blond girl, the one who had openly flinched when he'd sat down next to her, was suddenly flustered.

She doesn't like Claire, Joshua sensed. I wonder why?

"As we all know, the Alzheimer's brain deposits cleaved amyloid peptides outside of cells, which aggregate together to cause damaging plaques," Claire said. "And SCAN proteins are secreted from the cell and are responsible for inducing this aggregation."

She delivered the last line without tremor or waver, Joshua saw with relief, despite the fact that she no longer believed a word of it. She met his eye briefly before continuing.

"But up until this point, no one knew what SCAN might be doing in normal cells . . . what its proper job was. When Alan and I first initiated this work"—another resentful rustle from the blonde—"we discovered, using the Interactrex, that small amounts of SCAN actually reside in the cell nucleus, bound to an unknown protein called ESTA-333. The consequences of this binding are as yet unclear—I believe Joshua might be able to shed more light on that aspect in a moment."

She nodded towards him before making a few more marks on the flip chart.

"As I don't have to remind this audience, the Zapper disrupts the binding of SCAN to amyloid peptides by physically interfering with their coupling. But Joshua and I were concerned that the drug might also disrupt SCAN's binding to ESTA-333 in the nucleus of healthy cells."

"Hardly a likely prospect," one of the old-timer chemists spoke up from the back. "We designed it based on the crystal structure, against a stretch of unique amino acid residues."

"Nevertheless, a formal possibility," Ramon said. "Please continue, Claire."

"I fully *expected* a negative result, Peter," Claire said to the chemist, and a murmur started up in the audience. Joshua sat up straighter.

Claire accessed a file from the shared server via the laptop, and a dense column of numbers filled the screen. "I did the experiment three times this morning, and the results are clear. I know most of you aren't familiar with the Interactrex, so I apologize that these numbers won't be very informative. But I'm happy to stay afterwards and explain."

"Just tell us what you found, Claire," Ramon said, voice taut.

"The higher the number," she said, "the more proteins are binding together. Here's the amount of nuclear SCAN bound to ESTA-333 in the absence of the Zapper." She pointed out a six-digit number at the top of the column. "So that's the normal situation."

"Is that a lot?" somebody asked.

"Yes," Claire said. "In fact, I can't really detect any solo SCAN in the nucleus. As far as the Interactrex can say, it's pretty much all tied up by the pool of ESTA-333 . . . under normal conditions."

She indicated the next number with a fingertip.

"But when I started adding the Zapper to the cells, this number began to get lower. ESTA-333 and SCAN started falling apart. The more drug I added, the lower the number got." The fingertip swept down the column, where the figures were steadily losing bulk, plummeting to five digits, four, three. . .

Joshua's sensitive skin felt the tension of fifty odd fellow humans like a prickle of static.

"The maximum amount of Zapper I tested was analogous to the doses you deliver to cure your Alzheimer's mice," she said, pointing to the number at the bottom of the column.

Zero.

Ramon emitted a soft curse in Spanish, and another flurry rose up in the room. Joshua was shocked. He'd been so concerned about the Universal Aggregation Principle being wrong that he hadn't truly believed that his own speculative second problem with the Zapper could really be true. But suddenly, it was, and he felt like he was witnessing a dress rehearsal for disaster—how was everyone going to react to this relatively minor setback? For not the first time that day, he was fervently grateful for Alan's absence.

"To sum up," Claire said, voice steady and confident. "The Zapper prevents SCAN from binding to ESTA-333 in a dose-dependent manner. Therefore, using the regimen needed to cure Alzheimer's, you would expect that whatever SCAN normally does to ESTA-333 will no longer occur . . . for better or for worse."

"Preposterous!" A middle-aged woman was so incensed that she leapt to her feet. "I supervised those mice experiments myself, liaised with Pathology—practically slept in the animal facility. There weren't any side effects. We published it in *Nature Medicine*."

"Verity," Ramon said soothingly. "Nobody's questioning your beautiful results. We just don't know what effects to expect . . . especially in humans. Maybe nothing, *sí*?"

"If this stuff is true," Klaas spoke up, "how long will it take to design a modified Zapper that can't access the nucleus and cause trouble?" Thank goodness for Dutch practicality, Joshua thought.

"Peter?" Ramon said.

"God." The chemist scratched his head. "Maybe a few months. But then we'd need *in vitro* validation . . . to say nothing of repeating Verity's pre-clinical mouse studies. . ."

"It could set us back a year," someone muttered.

"As if the stock market would ever allow that!"

"Why should we believe *her*, or that machine, anyway? It's not as if it's an established method."

It took Ramon nearly half a minute to quiet the audience. "*Oye, gente* . . . I think it's important not to get ahead of ourselves. Why don't we hear what Joshua has to say about ESTA-333 first?"

❖ ❖ ❖

"Talk about a tough act to follow." Joshua was standing up at the front now, a grim smile on his face. "In fact, I've some news of my own. Apologies, Ramon, that I looked at the new Canadian data without you, but I only got the password about an hour ago, and you weren't available."

"It's okay, Josh—just get on with it," Ramon said impatiently. And indeed, the entire assemblage seemed to be holding its breath.

Claire sat motionless, clenching her notebook with stiff fingers so that no one, particularly Merriam Clark, would be able to tell how upset she truly was. The panic was coming, no question about it. She could feel it mounting inside like the deep warning twitch of a leg muscle under the bedclothes in the middle of the night—if she moved even a millimetre, the balance would tip and the cramp would explode into a spasm of time-less agony.

Please. Not now. Not yet. The room had already begun to swim, so she focused on Joshua, on the intelligence of those black eyes, lingering on hers with evident concern.

Joshua closed Claire's file and called up the first slide of his digital presentation: row after row of amino acids in single-letter code.

"This is ESTA-333, a protein of unknown function as of a few months ago," he said. "All we knew, thanks to Claire, was that it binds to SCAN in the nucleus. No known patterns or motifs that might be helpful— except the nuclear import signal here. . ." he indicated the relevant area of the sequence, "and here, where the sequence is reminiscent of the site where the Zapper docks with amyloid . . . hence the bioinformatical basis for Claire's latest experiment."

Claire heard a murmur behind her: Peter Klugg, whispering furiously with another chemist. She took another deep breath, and Joshua began to explain what sort of company Canadian Validation Solutions was and what services it offered. She allowed his voice, reasonable and calm, to exert a soothing effect. Suddenly, she saw him not as Joshua—her odd friend and confidante—but as everyone else must: Dr Pelinore, head of the Bioinformatics Department: older, professional, reliable, every sentence infused with assurance. She wasn't alone—and she couldn't have asked for a better ally. As his words flowed over her, her heart rate slowed and her visual focus began to track properly again.

Joshua clicked on the next slide. "Thanks to the expiring status of Claire's PCT patent application, Stanley generously agreed to expedite our license agreement fees for this project, so we now know quite a bit more than we did last week . . . or even this morning."

Claire saw Ramon's back stiffen in the front row. Should she have told him the news in private first? Should she have waited until Alan had returned? Should Joshua have?

"It turns out," Joshua said, "that the Canadians have performed GST pull-downs with ESTA-333 and isolated several binding partners. The most prominent partner, with very tight binding indeed, was yet another unknown protein called RAJI-23."

Joshua paused, his gaze sweeping the crowd. "But before I tell you about RAJI-23, I want to point out that, in light of Claire's data, I thought it prudent to delve a bit deeper into their numbers. I was given access to the primary information—and SCAN also came up as a minor binding partner of ESTA-333 . . . thereby corroborating Claire's initial finding. So it *is* possible to see this interaction with conventional methods, even without something as sensitive, or *untested*"—his glance settled briefly on the man who'd made the derogatory comment about Claire earlier—"as the Interactrex 3000."

The room erupted again.

"With all due respect," Ramon said slowly, voice raised over the furore, "I have personally performed thousands of pull-downs, and have never found *anything* binding to SCAN. Except for amyloid proteins in the diseased brains, of course." He paused. "Actually, Josh, I believe your own name is on one of those original articles."

Claire had never heard that tone of voice from Ramon before.

Joshua's face remained impassive. "If you look at their numbers, the binding of ESTA-333 to SCAN is very low-affinity. It could be ... missed, in the wrong detergent environment. And the Canadians use state-of-the-art fluorescence methods, high throughput robotics—they can test hundreds of conditions simultaneously."

"Okay," Ramon said, moderately appeased. "Go on."

"So SCAN binds ESTA-333 in the nucleus, and ESTA-333 binds to RAJI-23. ESTA-333 is acting as an adapter to link the other two together." Joshua clicked to his next slide, another string of amino acid code. "So what is RAJI-23? This time, the sequence told us everything straight away."

It's told *you* something, Claire thought. But to me it looks like gibberish. Her respect for Joshua's talents was growing by the minute.

"Although this gene was only pulled out by the Genome Project, and no one has published any papers about it, these motifs clearly indicate a transcription factor." He underlined two separate lines of code with a casual finger. "Fortunately, the Canadians performed full microarray analysis in cells and tissues from several species, so we now know exactly what genes are being switched on or off by it."

He went on to the next slide. "And the best part was that they've done analyses in primary brain cells from both humans *and* mice, so we can see what genes RAJI-23 is regulating in our relevant situations ... and how these might differ between species."

Claire glanced over and saw that Verity Arbingdon was biting her nails, eyes fixed on the screen.

"The news isn't good, I'm afraid," Joshua said.

Chapter 29

Joshua and Claire stood in the corridor outside the meeting room as people swept out around them. Joshua noticed that the others were avoiding coming too close, as if their dual bombshell had made them unclean. Within five minutes, the entire company would know what had happened.

"You're all right now, aren't you?" He spoke softly as he studied her face.

She nodded. "It was a close thing, though. You were magnificent in there."

"So were you, Claire. I—"

Ramon came up. "Can you two join me in my office, please?"

"I'm so sorry, Ramon," Claire said. "You must be furious."

"It's not your fault, *querida*." Ramon looked tired, resigned.

"I could've waited until we were alone," she said.

"That's not how it works in my lab—we're a team," Ramon said. "You were both absolutely correct to tell us this stuff as soon as it came to light, no matter how preliminary or unpleasant."

Joshua saw Claire flinch. And that's when the world shifted, for him. What in God's name had they done, suppressing the most incriminating evidence of all? He saw in a surge of perspective that it was too late. The secret had gone on so long now that there was no graceful way of revealing it—especially after today's complication. And it wasn't just Claire's problem: he was deep in it as well, entirely as guilty. Even more so, with his position of seniority. Claire was young and easily frightened, but *he* ought to have known better. Real fear began to rise up inside him, fear that he had to try to force back into a hole, but it kept seeping out between his fingers like mud.

That's not how it works.

The three of them went into Ramon's office, and Ramon shut the door. Through the Venetian blinds, Joshua could see that the technicians who hadn't been at the meeting were already looking at them, whispering, faces pale and uncertain. Team or not, Ramon flicked closed the blinds with one rapid movement.

"You're one hundred percent sure, Joshua, that the Zapper will switch on this harmful receptor gene in the human brain?"

Joshua shrugged. "I can't give you that level of certainty, Ramon. You know as well as I that RNA microarrays aren't perfect—you're going to have to back it up with solid protein experiments. But the upregulation was sky-high—in the area of a fifty-fold induction. Based on the bioinformatics, there's a pretty good chance that the Zapper will mimic this effect—but only in humans, of course, as mice don't have this particular gene."

"Claire," Ramon said. "Have you alerted Alan yet?"

"No," she stammered. "I literally just finished the last experiment, and it's..." She looked at her watch. "Four in the morning in Vancouver."

"I think you ought to wake him up," he said. "If he hears it from someone else first ... like Peter or Verity..."

"But..."

Joshua saw the fear in Claire's eyes, and without thinking, leaned forward to Ramon and murmured in rapid Spanish, "Don't make *her* tell him. He'll take it much better from you—or at least, there's nothing between you two that can't withstand the consequences if he decides to kill the messenger, *comprendes?*"

There was a moment of awkward silence, and then Claire began to cry, hands over her face, and Ramon was saying, angrily, "*Por Dios,* you idiot, she's a native Spanish speaker. Didn't you know?"

As Joshua stared at him, speechless with surprise and consternation, Ramon leaned forward and put a fatherly hand on her shoulder.

"Hush now, *querida* ... everything's going to be all right. *Cálmete, niña, cálmete...*"

Claire just shook her head, face still hidden as she heaved with sobs. How could he have been so stupid?

Ramon looked over at him, eyes bleak. "Tactless delivery or not, Joshua, your advice was dead on target. Of course I should be the one to break the news. He'll explode, naturally, especially being the last to know, but Stanley will calm him down, and by the time he gets back..."

Claire finally seemed to have herself under control, head raised and blowing her nose with the tissue Ramon passed her.

"I agree with Josh too," she said. "And anyway, I can't do it. I'm afraid that . . . I'm afraid. . ."

"Claire, I'm sorry I tried to go behind your back—I don't know what I was thinking," Joshua said.

"You were only trying to protect me . . . to protect me and Alan. . ." Her voice broke, and she started crying again.

Ramon stood up. "Listen, Joshua, could you do me a favour? I'm going to place the call in Alan's office before someone else musters the *cojones* to wake him. Stay with her, and when she's calmed down, take her off site for a few hours, will you? She's in no fit state to face anyone. Here. . ." He dug into the pocket of his jeans and tossed him a set of keys. "Use my car—it's the green Nissan station wagon parked at the west end."

When the door had shut, Joshua finally put his arms around Claire and she soaked against him like sea into sand. And then she began to shake.

Sea into sand, sand sliding back into sea, the delicate lines of foam shredding away in the fierce wind, tangling in the bottle-green bladders of algal jetsam. Joshua tightened his hold on Claire's hand as they walked along the shore, pummelled by air and microscopic particles. The North Sea was the colour of titanium, flecked with rabid white spittle, bleeding without transition into the overcast above. Far ahead of them, the lighthouse and pier of Scheveningen were black smudges on the horizon.

She hadn't said more than a handful of words to him since they'd left NeuroSys using the back staircase. She'd stared straight out the windscreen, limp from the aftermath of the panic attack, on the short drive to Katwijk aan Zee, then followed him obediently along the dune path with its scrubby pines and down to the water's edge. After she'd stumbled three or four times, he'd taken her hand, and she seemed content to cling to him and walk forever.

The ruthless, impersonal environment was doing them both good, but it was starting to get cold. Joshua turned in towards land until they'd reached a sheltered area abutting the bluff, and then they sat, backs against the rising earth and shoulders barely touching. They stared out at the sea and sky until Joshua was finally moved to speak.

"I think it's truly going to be okay. With Alan, I mean."

He turned to look at her, but she was still staring ahead, battered yet impervious. "I know that, now that I've had a chance to think." Her voice, too, was calm. "He and I actually discussed this possibility when I initiated the study."

"Really? How did he seem?"

She shrugged. "Reasonable. Measured. Said we'd just design a modified Zapper and I'd be the company's heroine." She uttered a bitter laugh. "What a joke. I can't believe how much I've misjudged him—and how thoroughly I've messed everything up."

They both breathed in and out for a moment, then she added, "But he won't be reasonable if I tell him the rest. If I tell him how long I've known."

"We'll have to decide the best way to do it."

"You know what? I think I'd rather hand in my resignation and go back to England."

"You can't be serious." He stared at her in disbelief. "What about the clinical trial? What about your relationship with Alan?"

For a brief second, Joshua himself saw the allure of escape. He could run away, too, to France or Italy, to some new country where he could begin the long, painful process of attempting to fit in again, where he could try to forget this flawed, unearthly woman who would never love him.

"They're both doomed," she said, "whether I stay or not, when it all comes crashing down. And I don't think I'm strong enough to see it happen."

"You're what, how old, Claire? Twenty-four? Twenty-five?" At her nod, he said, "What I was saying before about allowances for age . . . nobody's going to blame you for being terrified. Ramon treats you like one of his own daughters. Even Stanley knows what a rough time you've had of it, socially. And Alan . . . well, if he truly loves you, then he'll understand too."

She was shaking her head. "I can't get my head around it, Josh. It's doomed. It's over."

Far out to sea, a wan shaft of sunlight sliced through the clouds, illuminating the surface of the water like polished silver.

"How about this, then." Something had come into his mind. "This fluke we've discovered with ESTA-333 is probably going to buy us some time. Six months, minimum. There's bound to be an Alzheimer's death in that span. Do the experiment then, fake the same accidental sampling and pretend it was the first time." His voice was speeding up. "You can start again, Claire. Clean slate. Like it never happened. Then make it happen all over again, but this time go to Alan and Ramon straight away, like we did this morning."

She had raised her head to look at him and her eyes were becoming blacker and blacker.

"Destroy the data from the first brain, the data where you sampled SCAN from outside of cells," he said. "Destroy your notes and wipe the files from the Interactrex. I can take care of the back-up tapes—I'm the System Administrator, I can do whatever I want."

"Josh. . ." She couldn't go on.

"It's the perfect solution," he insisted. "Nobody gets hurt—not you, not your relationship, not even the patients. NeuroSys will probably go under, but that would've happened anyway, when even the modified Zapper failed miserably to have any affect whatsoever on human Alzheimer's patients. Or . . . maybe in the meantime, you and your miraculous machine can discover another drug target . . . you can find a cure for stroke. . ."

"My God, Joshua, do you realize what you're saying?"

"Of course," he said roughly. "And *you* know it's the perfect solution."

"It's absolutely out of the question! I'm tired of all the lies, Joshua. I can't stand them anymore. I'd rather *lose* Alan than lie to him another day."

"Okay, then look at it from my perspective." Joshua had no idea where all this dark mercilessness was coming from—probably from that hole of fear within, from underneath the seeping mud. "You can call Alan right now, tell him the entire story, but if your lying days are over, you'll also have to reveal that I've known everything as well— for months."

"But I don't have to—"

"The truth is the truth! You can't just pick and choose your confession as it suits you, Claire. If *you* won't tell him I knew, then I will."

Her eyes widened. "You wouldn't!"

"You'll probably be let off, on grounds of inexperience, but I'm a *department* head. I'll be fired so fast I won't even have time to clear out my desk. I'll never work in science again."

"You can't tell them—I won't let you!"

"Just try to stop me."

They stared each other down, breathing heavily, and then Claire transformed before his eyes, scrambling to her feet, eyes flashing, looking around at the sand until she'd found a sizeable rock, which she flung at the bluff wall with a furious cry. Joshua struggled up just as the rock smashed into the loose material, sending a spray of sea grass and pebbles and sand tumbling downward. Some of it got in his eyes, and he stumbled back a few steps, blinking at this fiery apparition.

"You know what *really* gets me?" she shouted at him. "Anyone else would've used that as a legitimate form of pressure, but you don't really care about your career at all, do you? You only care about *me*, God knows why! It's not *natural*! Why can't you be selfish like everyone else? What in hell is wrong with you?"

The world seemed to stall then, with nothing but the wind in his ears, and then Joshua felt his own anger begin to rise, a sentient anger mounting like thunderheads. He whirled around to walk away but she came after him, tried to wrench his arms and make him turn to face her—her own fury gave her the strength to make the motions painful. He whirled around and held her off and she struggled to free herself, all the while staring at him with those black, crazy eyes.

"You know full *well* I could never do that to you," she said. "How *dare* you blackmail me!" She was a runaway beast, galloping across a field. "I forbid it, do you hear me? Blackmailing me for my own good—what gives you the right?"

Suddenly, awareness unfolded on her face. She went slack between his fingers as all her violence sapped away. He released her, and she staggered back a few paces, her gaze never leaving his.

"You're in love with me, aren't you?" she said.

When he didn't answer, she started to smile, a half-mad smile that was horrible to behold. "Well? Aren't you?"

He shrugged. "Are you going to forbid that, too?"

There was a reverberating silence, and then she just shook her head. "I'm so sorry, Joshua."

"I don't want your pity. I only want to help you."

"But helping me will hurt you!"

"That's what love is, Claire. If you're under any other delusion, then come talk to me in ten years' time and we can compare notes."

"I can't . . . I can't bear this." She lurched against the bluff and placed one side of her face against the wall of earth. "It's too much."

More saltwater, soaking into the sand.

He stood and watched her for a while, then said, "I'll be waiting in the car. Take as long as you like."

❦ ❦ ❦

Claire walked across the empty car park and opened the passenger-side door of the green Nissan. Joshua's long limbs and slightly crouched head made the car into a child's toy. She got in meekly, pulled the door closed, and he kept his face forward, its blank, composed countenance, with its exquisite white cast, glowing in the dusk. It filled her with a cutting anxiety, the thought that he would never look or smile at her again.

But then, miraculously, he did turn his head, and he did produce a faint smile, and her clenched heart opened like a flower.

"I'm glad you're back," he said quietly, "I was about to go looking for you."

"I've got something to tell you," she said. "But first, do you know . . . despite how messed up everything else is . . . my biggest fear right now seems to be the prospect that I've ruined our friendship forever?"

"I've been sitting here thinking pretty much the same thing."

"I've got a terrible temper, that's all."

"I noticed."

She started to giggle, and then he was laughing too. She leaned against him, and he put an arm around her.

"Can I ask you one thing before the subject is closed forever?" he said. "You don't have to answer."

"I will if I can."

"I know you don't love me." His hand left her shoulder, brushed against her head, moved gently down the flow of her hair. "But do you find the idea of me loving you intolerable? Because if you do, I don't think I can stand being around you."

She hesitated, remembering what he'd said in the club: *There's something about you that always makes me say too much.* She had that feeling now, like she'd had one too many drinks, like she was intoxicated by an excess of dark emotion.

"I've been attracted to you since I first saw you," she said. "Your looks were what stopped me from panicking in front of that room. And your touch . . . I've thought about it, Joshua. How it would be if you . . . if we. . ."

She was suddenly aware of everything about him, barraging her with input as if she had just sprouted dozens of senses in addition to the usual five.

"Best stop there," Joshua said, clearing his throat. He took his hands off her and put a few centimetres between them. "And thank you for being honest. Maybe it's a stupid male ego thing, but it makes a big difference."

She didn't answer, still surprised herself at what had come out of her mouth.

"And speaking of honesty," he said. "I hereby withdraw my pathetic blackmail attempt—it was unspeakably awful of me. You're free to tell Alan whatever you like, hide my role in it to protect my career if that's what you want, and I'll support your story. We never talked about SCAN not binding to Alzheimer's proteins outside of cells. We never talked about anything."

"No," she said. "That's what I have to tell you. You were right, Joshua. Clean slates. We're going to erase the first experiment and start again."

Chapter 30

After Joshua dropped Claire off at Alan's empty house, she switched on her mobile phone to find four messages from Alan, each sounding increasingly concerned. Emboldened by this evidence, she rang him up in Vancouver with an erratic heartbeat. There were more tears, but Alan had been so compassionate, so absolutely refusing to lay blame that it was clear that all her earlier fears truly had been groundless.

She hadn't slept well, but that was more to do with dwelling on that strange episode by the seaside than with any concerns about Alan. She kept re-experiencing, as a physical memory, the touch of Joshua's hands. And she could still feel, too, the rush of conflicting emotions that his unexpected confession had elicited, and the naked intimacy of their subsequent conversation. If she hadn't browbeaten the words from him, how long would she have remained so completely and idiotically blind to his feelings?

(And, a small voice inside of her countered, if he hadn't eased the words from *her*, how long would she have remained blind to her own?)

When she decided it would be best to stop thinking about Joshua altogether, the prospect of the risky cover-up they were going to attempt slipped in to overwrite the sand, the sea, the wind, the pale face lustrous in twilight, the charge of an all-knowing warm palm against the back of her head.

❀ ❀ ❀

And as for Joshua, he returned Ramon's car and keys and finished the rest of his work (in his office, door closed, white tulips the only witness) before shooting off towards Amsterdam in the bitter darkness. He was now lost, but at least in being lost, he knew exactly where he stood.

Claire arrived at NeuroSys before dawn the next day. She told herself that she was reverting to her old tendencies because of Alan's absence, but the truth was that she was ashamed, and keen to avoid social contact. Ramon's technicians would have lost no time in reporting on her ravaged appearance when she and Joshua had finally emerged from the office, and it wouldn't look convincing, let alone professional, that she couldn't handle her own bad news.

"*Goede morgen.*" Joop the night porter peered at her over his glasses. "It has been a while, *hoor.*" He was speaking the slow, simple Dutch he knew she could handle.

"Yes, I haven't run into you for weeks." She used the formal form out of respect for his age—she had noticed that the other employees who bothered with Dutch at all did not seem conversant with this basic courtesy.

"I have heard about your big performance yesterday." Joop put down his tabloid abruptly. "I have heard we are in trouble. Is it true, *meisje?*"

"Maybe a little," she said. "Are people saying it's my fault?"

"Nay! I know it has not always been . . . but most people respect you now, Dr Cyrus. And some are really worried—like Dr Ortega, he looked awful last night. And Dr Pelinore too."

She didn't want to picture it. "I'd better get started, Joop."

"Look after yourself." He jutted a thumb over one shoulder at the bank of CCTV screens. "And I am always watching too, you know."

Claire needn't have worried about her reception. The atmosphere was unexpectedly supportive, and a number of people stopped by her lair throughout the day to see how she was coping.

"It went better than I'd expected," Ramon told her. "After Alan woke up enough to realize who I was, he was more dazed than upset . . . and, to be honest, a lot more concerned about your well-being than the company's. Which from him is pretty remarkable."

"Listen, Claire." Zeke Bannerman twisted the lapels of his lab coat with his wiry brown hands. "I know we haven't always got on, but I speak for my entire lab when I say that we stand behind the Interactrex and your results. It's a good thing you've found out about this before any clinical trials—I don't care what some of those idiot chemists have been saying."

"I wanted to apologize," Verity Arbingdon said briskly, "for my attitude yesterday. It was just shock, dear. Of course there are so many differences between mice and humans—I ought to know that better than anyone. I'm sure, with your timely intervention, we can make the best of a bad situation. Now, I was wondering if you could explain those numbers you showed us yesterday a bit more carefully. . ."

"Good news, Claire." Peter Klugg popped his head around the door-frame, ducking his bald pate in greeting. "We checked the chemical bank, and as luck would have it, we'd already isolated a non-cell-permeable variant of the Zapper in the initial screen last year. It's called NS3003, but folks have already christened it "Son of Zapper." I told 'em it ought to be Daughter, in honour of you. At any rate, the tissue culture validation people have all signed up for overtime . . . and I'll get you a vial for your own experiments, as soon as the synthesis crew have whipped up a big batch. . ."

In the canteen, where she'd been dragged off by some people in her department for lunch, Merriam Clark had wafted up to Claire at the salad bar.

"I heard you were pretty upset after the meeting," Merriam said, her marine eyes cool and innocent. "I bet Alan gave you a horrific lecture over the phone for springing it on us behind his back."

Klaas, who was queuing up behind Claire, said brightly, "On the contrary, Merriam, I spoke to him this morning and he had nothing but good things to say about Claire's brilliant discovery."

When Merriam turned away, Claire smiled her thanks at this unexpected ally.

"She's driving me crazy," Klaas admitted. "If she spent half as much time concentrating on experiments as on trying to steal your man, she might actually get something done. You watch her, Claire—she's jealous . . . and ambitious."

Roz, Joshua's ferocious watchdog, cornered her at the coffee machine after lunch. "You stick to your guns, girl. Don't let any of those old duffers tell you your experiments aren't real. You and Joshua are going to save this company whether it wants to be saved or not."

And then, in the afternoon, she'd received an e-mail from Joshua, requesting her presence in his office.

❧ ❧ ❧

"You wanted to see me?"

Joshua looked up with a grave face, and if he noticed her discomfort, he didn't show it.

"Shut the door, please." He closed his laptop and gestured for her to sit.

"Why didn't you just stop by?"

His face remained impassive, but his volume dropped significantly. "You may have noticed that there aren't any CCTV cameras in this room."

So it has begun. What else did she expect? Wasn't that what she had decided she wanted?

"Aren't people going to be suspicious of the closed door? Everyone was staring on my way in."

"We're collaborators, remember? And after our joint production yesterday, everyone knows it."

"Collaborators," she echoed. A word with many unpleasant connotations.

"Listen, here's what I want you to do about the files."

He pushed a piece of paper at her, containing several dozen lines of instructions written in a spindly hand. "After you drag them into the bin, I need you to perform a few extra steps to make it really untraceable. I'd do it myself, but your machine's not linked to the server, and it would be too suspicious for me to be working at your console. If I were you, I'd do it as part of a routine clear-up . . . you do have stuff you normally have to delete?"

"Definitely—my hard drive's always full."

"Such a bad habit, slows everything down," he said mildly. "No one would blink if you did some spring cleaning. Just to be safe, I'd do it in daytime. Your room's on continuous CCTV feed."

"Why daytime?"

"The lit screen's much more visible at night—I doubt the resolution's that good, but no point in taking any chances." He paused. "How do you back up your work?"

"DVDs, of course, but once a week I copy their contents onto the server."

"Okay, that's the easy bit. If you write down the full names of the relevant files, I'll take care of those for you—and the corresponding files on the back-up tapes in the archives. I wouldn't take any chances with the DVDs . . . copy all the files you need to save onto fresh ones, then destroy the originals. I'd do that back in Amsterdam. I find a hammer useful."

"Right." There was something reassuring about his matter-of-fact manner. "And the hard copies?"

"That's going to be more conspicuous on CCTV. I've been thinking that the best way is to take the entire binder home with you, and maybe another irrelevant one as a decoy." He paused. "Home to Amsterdam, I mean . . . so you'd better do it before Alan returns. Be sure to comment to someone, like Ramon, that you need to catch up, whatever. Then burn whatever you have to."

"Anything else?"

He leaned back in his chair. "You've probably heard that a candidate replacement drug for the Zapper already exists. I think we have to assume that our grace period might be significantly shorter than originally anticipated. The company's pulling together in a most unexpected way over this—we just have to hope that a new Alzheimer's brain becomes available very soon."

"I never thought I'd find myself hoping somebody would hurry up and die."

For the first time since she'd come into the office, a trace of Joshua's gentle sympathy returned. "To be brutally honest, Claire, it will probably be the best thing that could happen to them. And their family."

As she was standing up to go, feeling strangely incomplete, Joshua said, "When does Alan get back?"

"Thursday."

"I've got a departmental thing on this evening, but would you have a drink with me tomorrow after work?"

Well, and why shouldn't she?

❦ ❦ ❦

The next evening, Ramon stopped by Claire's lair just as she was putting on her coat.

"Good to see you leaving at a decent hour, *querida*," he said. "I was actually stopping by to see if you fancied coming round for dinner after I finished up in the lab. Carla's been nagging me to ask you again—and I've been worried about you being on your own after Monday's incident."

"*Gracias*, Ramon, but Joshua's already volunteered for tonight's shift."

"Oh, that's okay, then." He looked pleased. "You'll be in safe hands. Anything fun?"

"Just the Onderwater for a few beers." The thought of Joshua's safe hands sent an unexpected reaction through the hairs on the back of her neck.

❦ ❦ ❦

The bar was slow, just a few clusters of NeuroSys employees sharing a quiet drink. Many of them raised friendly hands when Claire and Joshua walked in, and each of the recipients felt a similar reaction: the happy surprise of misfits-turned-heroes, followed by the guilt of scheming co-conspirators.

"So how did it go at your end?" Joshua set her lager onto the table, relieved that she seemed relaxed and in agreeable spirits. It was good to have put a few days between the rawness of their Katwijk encounter.

"Sorted, Josh, although I felt positively ridiculous with that hammer. It's so much better in the movies, when they get to use the fancy shredder. And with you?"

"Sorted as well." He raised his beer. "To clean slates."

"Clean slates." She clinked his glass, added, "When all this is over, I'm never going to let anyone down again . . . at least, not intentionally." She gave him an anxious glance.

"If you're referring to me, it doesn't apply."

She sighed. "I hope that, after those ten years you mentioned before, I've managed to become even a fraction closer to being like you. I don't understand how anyone could possibly be so objective."

"Plenty of practice, Claire—I was a wreck at your age." He smiled. "If I could suddenly turn back into that younger me, I'd probably be poisoning Alan's coffee right about now . . . in fact, there nearly was a murder once, over a red-headed technician who preferred Alan's classic features."

She shook her head solemnly. "I'm sorry, but I just can't picture it."

"And for that I am infinitely grateful."

Claire looked up, smiling too, and then the smile turned into something else. "It's Alan," she said faintly, going instantly flustered. "How. . ."

Joshua glanced over his shoulder out of the rain-spattered front window and saw the man leaning over to lock his bicycle, lit dramatically by the overhead streetlight.

"He must've flown back early." Joshua kept his tone casual. "Worried about you, more than likely, nagged Stanley until he sent him away to get a bit of peace. Has he homed in on your location by sheer pheromonal instinct?"

"Ramon knew where we were off to."

"He's going to be upset finding us together."

"Let him be. I'm tired of him putting you down—if he wants me, he'll have to accept you too." There was a stubborn edge to her voice.

They both turned as Alan came through the door, drizzle condensed on his coat. He came directly over, heedless of the stares and murmurs of everyone else in the room, eyes so full of Claire that Joshua couldn't bear to look at him, nor at the way he just murmured a hello to her and slid a hand down her face—at the way her eyes closed in response. Then seeming to remember where he was, he turned to Joshua.

"Ramon told me what you did for Claire on Monday," he said quietly, without a trace of his normal arrogance. To Joshua's shock, he was extending his hand. "I wanted to thank you for looking after her for me."

"My pleasure." *But I didn't do it for you, mate.* Joshua accepted the firm shake, a shake steeped with a sincerity that Alan would not be able to fake with someone of Joshua's sensitivity.

Claire looked as surprised as Joshua felt. And something more . . . worried about his paltry feelings, no doubt, somewhere underneath the blaze of sexual longing that had kindled the moment Alan entered the room.

"And also for your work with Canadian Validation Solutions," Alan continued, "which helped to back up Claire's important findings. I apologize for my earlier scepticism. And I understand it was your bioinformatical research that pointed towards the problem with NS158 in the first place."

"That's right." Joshua cleared his throat. "Listen, I expect you two have a lot to catch up on, so I'd better push off."

"Are you sure, Joshua?" Claire's anxiety was even plainer.

"No, really, I wanted to buy you a drink," Alan insisted. Still unbelievably and utterly sincere.

"I'm sure," Joshua said firmly, saying his goodbyes.

As he was wrestling his bicycle out of the rack in the rainy night, he took one last look through the window and saw that Alan was already helping Claire on with her coat, that the drink Joshua had bought for her had scarcely been touched.

❦ ❦ ❦

Despite his jet lag, Alan pinned Claire against the wall as soon as he'd shut the front door, and she'd succumbed to him as explosively as the stack of incriminating printouts she'd set alight in her kitchen sink the night before. Somewhere in the back of her mind, she was thinking how strange it was that arousal could be so different with different men, as if constructed of distinct base elements. If the way she responded to Alan was all fire and electricity, then Joshua's influence was like the patient sea, working its way in an inexorable tide, ripples of water expanding out from a hand passed through flat midday doldrums, a storm in no particular hurry to go from force one up the scale to the final hurricane.

❦ ❦ ❦

Joshua felt about as bad as you might expect, huddled in the carriage on his way back to Amsterdam, a trip he felt he'd made thousands of times over millions of years, as ice caps formed and melted, as continents shifted, as species evolved out of the slime and then promptly went extinct. Just as the train shot out of the airport tunnel, and people around him started using their phones again, he had an idea.

He pulled out his own mobile and punched through the screens until he was looking at Rachel's details, sitting there in coy grey on white.

❦ ❦ ❦

Later, in bed, Alan and Claire talked long into the night.

"Stanley finally let me leave because I convinced him that the company needed me in its time of crisis," he said. "But that was a lie—I just wanted to make sure you were all right. Ramon told me you broke down in his office. Why?"

"I was just being stupid."

"Were you worried that no one would believe you?"

"No. I was worried that you would be angry with me."

"Whatever for, dearest? You haven't done anything wrong."

"I know how much this clinical trial means to you . . . and the milestone payments."

The silence between them made her feel ashamed, no matter how well grounded the comment had been. Alan, shaken, said, "Well, I suppose I have only myself to blame if that's how I've come across."

She could hardly stand the look in his eyes.

"If I can't acquit myself to you, Claire, then I am truly lost." He gave her that twisted smile. "No matter what foolish and egotistical things I may have said in the past to capture your attention—and so misguided, to believe that such machinations could possibly have worked with someone like you—the only thing that truly matters to me is the truth . . . and, recently, you. Everything else might as well not exist."

The truth, she thought, has been erased, but when it comes to life again after the next Alzheimer's death, I shall not be afraid of it any longer.

✤ ✤ ✤

"You're not even remotely all right, are you?" Rachel's smudged eyes studied him critically over the rim of her cocktail, its contents glowing a lurid cobalt in the lighting.

"No, but it's nothing a sub-lethal dose of alcohol won't cure."

Joshua was aware of the contrast between the comatose Onderwater and this place: brash with fashionably dressed people and the trendiest music, spun by a DJ slouching over his decks in the back, crushing head-phone to shoulder and caressing his vinyl. It suited Joshua's despair and the acidity of his jealousy to be lost in the nameless crowd, to be taking comfort from the presence of someone so wholly unlike Claire, even as he devoured every morsel of information about her that Rachel let fall under the table. He wondered how far that comfort might be persuaded to stretch. Of course he felt nothing for her, but that was part of the appeal at the moment.

"It somehow wasn't so bad when she didn't know I loved her."

"Any idiot could see you love her, Joshua."

"I've always prided myself on my opacity."

"It's normal to develop cracks when things start to pressurize." She shrugged. "You stare at her as if she's an angel. You take any excuse to touch her. I haven't the slightest idea why she never noticed. And personally. . ."

"What?"

"I wish she *was* with you instead of Alan. Even though I've never met him, I just don't trust him. Is he really as beautiful as she says?"

His stomach clenched. "And to make matters worse, she seems to be transforming him into a decent human being."

"Claire's a very potent individual like that," she said. "Is she transforming you, too?"

"I don't know," he said. "I can't see anything any more."

"What about this big secret? *That's* not like you, is it, all this subterfuge?"

"Has she told you the latest?" The vodka was making him expansive.

"No—has something happened?" She lowered her own glass with a clink onto the marble tabletop.

"Claire and I figured out that NeuroSys's lead drug compound is flawed on two levels. We told the company about one of these problems on Monday."

"Is this about the proteins not sticking together—the universal whatsit theory being entirely wrong?"

"No, that's the *real* problem. The one we brought to their attention is a new minor hitch—quite serious but ultimately surmountable. Our drug in its current form is predicted to seriously impair higher cognition in healthy brain cells—it may cause more problems than the Alzheimer's it's trying to cure. Everyone took it surprisingly well, which finally made Claire realize that the other problem—the real problem—ought to have been revealed ages ago."

"Well, obviously." Rachel shook her head.

"So I cooked up a plan to destroy all the evidence. . ." He outlined the scheme, taking peculiar pleasure in the shock that crept over her features.

"Are you mad? This was *your* idea?"

"Everybody wins . . . especially Claire."

"Unless you get caught, and you both get fired!"

"I never dreamed your experiment would really work," Alan confessed. "It is just another example of what a splendid researcher you're shaping up to be. I'm sorry I was so cavalier."

"You never were." She recalled his ready acceptance.

"But I wasn't exactly supportive either. And, I recall, I was pretty scathing about Joshua as well."

Again, amazement at the bizarre change of heart. "He's a really good scientist, Alan."

"I'm starting to realize that. I'm just old-fashioned, Claire. In my day, we didn't do experiments with computers and robots, high-throughput screens and machines like the Interactrex 3000. We used test tubes— and our hands."

"And he's not only a good scientist," she persisted. "He's a good man."

"Hmmm."

"Alan ... will you tell me why you dislike him so much?" She hesitated, not wanting to betray her knowledge. "Did something happen between you?"

"So has Claire transformed you as well?" Joshua allowed himself to move several inches closer.

Rachel gave him a sly smile. "Are you familiar with the old philosophical paradox about the irresistible force and the immovable object?"

Lights, rhythm, smoke, and a spectacular haze of anaesthesia. Joshua asked Rachel if she'd like to carry on the conversation somewhere more private, and she slowly raised her head, shadows gathered around her hazel eyes like gloaming.

"I think you ought to tell me whatever it is."

"You're right." Alan sighed. "But listen, Claire. I haven't slept for more than twenty-four hours. I don't think getting into it tonight ... this morning, rather ... is a good idea."

"Okay. But soon?"

"Soon. I promise."

Claire lay in his arms as he drifted off, haggard face relaxing into its perfect geometry. But later, his usual nightmares began to trickle up, gregarious and unrelenting, and she held onto him, thinking of her own past, her own nightmares, her own secrets.

Chapter 31

❧

Claire left work the next day and entered the rush hour of venous life flowing back to the heart of Amsterdam, drowning herself in the surge of tall, implacable commuters clotting the stairs and escalators of Leiden Centraal Station. The whistles were already shrilling as she pushed her way onto the platform and, after a swish of yellow doors, her usual airport train slid away without her in a hum of electric nonchalance.

Still breathing heavily, she crossed the platform and boarded the less convenient train that went via Haarlem, collapsed into a seat and leaned her head against the window. She felt very strange—nervous, anxious, as if something terrible was about to happen, or already had, if only she could remember what it might be. She had been tense all day, knowing that Stanley had flown in that morning. He, Ramon, Alan and the rest of upper management planned to be in conference until late, thrashing over all the options for dealing with the corporate crisis. Claire—worn out from her sleepless night—had felt the urge to go home, and Alan promised to drive up and join her when they'd finished.

But that wasn't the only thing troubling her. She couldn't seem to shake the memory of Joshua's closed face when Alan had interrupted their drink, nor the unexpected feeling of sadness she'd experienced when he left the bar. She was preoccupied too by Alan's fear later that evening, a trailer for something much worse that she'd always known she'd be unable to avoid forever. And then there'd been the little scene at breakfast.

"In all the excitement last night. . ." Alan, poise fully restored by the morning light, had paused behind her chair as she was sinking a knife into the soft green flesh of a pear. The knife arrested as his hand lifted the heavy hair from her neck, still damp from the shower, as his lips pressed into the bared skin beneath. She closed her eyes and, unconnected to any rational design or intention, her body responded in the usual way.

"I forgot to give you this," he said, dropping her hair and moving away, into the seat opposite her.

Claire opened her eyes to find that a square, rectangular package had replaced the now-vanished pear. It was wrapped in opulent magenta paper imprinted with a tapestry pattern and sealed with a golden oval bearing the name of a prominent Vancouver bookshop.

A childlike delight had ensued, overwriting the night's unease.

"What's this?" She put down the knife, still wet with juice, and began to open the gift.

But she already knew: Alan was aware of exactly the book she most wanted: the latest critical volume of Oliver St John Gogarty's complete works. She'd mentioned it while paging through the *Times Literary Supplement* shortly before he'd left. She hadn't thought he'd been paying attention at the time, but of course he never missed anything, did he? Fitting too that he should buy it for her; hadn't she been reminded of Gogarty the first time she'd seen Alan's eyes?

Hard is the stone, but harder still
The delicate performing will
That guided by a dream alone
Subdues and moulds the hardest stone
Making the stubborn jade release
The emblem of eternal peace...

The worlds fizzled out as she parted back the leaves of magenta paper. It wasn't Gogarty, or poetry of any description. It was a glossy, granite-coloured hardback entitled *The Molecular Circuitry of Brain Disease*, Second Edition, compiled by one Ravi Venkatu, MD, PhD. Revised, the cover informed her, with five new chapters.

"It's a classic," Alan said, spiriting the pear from under the table and taking a bite of it as she struggled to keep her great disappointment from showing, just as lovers given precisely the wrong gift have done since the beginning of time. "Of course textbooks are out-of-date by the time they're printed, but you're so lacking in the basics, it shouldn't matter."

"Thank you," she said, opening the book to peer obligingly at the table of contents, where Alan had inscribed something in bold swooping ink:

A little something to help nourish your true passion.

❦ ❦ ❦

Claire had no way of knowing that Joshua was on the same train, some four carriages ahead. While her presence was an accident, Joshua had deliberately let the airport train go by so he could see the bulb fields—an annual pilgrimage that he hoped might provide a badly needed distraction.

Claire, however, had been unaware that such a seasonal display even existed. The diagonal stripes of colour were already fleshing out, mono-chromatic daffodils and crocuses having given way to a thousand different shades of tulip in the past week. She was almost overwhelmed by the unex-pected sight. But even the most hardened natives allowed themselves to be as transfixed as any tourist or oblivious young scientist poet: businessmen looked up from their laptops; shifty youths from their gaming consoles; white-haired couples who probably spoke no English and might as well have come from another era, from their conservative newspapers; all gazing out of the window at the unfolding drama of another spring.

Troubles forgotten, she drank in the view. Flowers had always been a popular topic for poets, and she allowed centuries of examples to flow through her mind, a habitual game that both soothed and amused and that lulled her into feeling that everything was going to be okay.

She was making her usual head-down way through Centraal Station when someone jostled into her—an inevitable tourist, luggage-burdened and eyes raised towards the departure board. Claire muttered a rote apology as she rebounded, then caught sight of a familiar black-and-white figure, leaning over from a great height to inspect the bouquets on sale at the station shop.

Claire experienced conflicting instincts: she wanted to flee almost, but not quite as strongly as she felt compelled to draw near.

He looked over his shoulder in surprise at her greeting, but she could see that in all other respects he resembled the Joshua of old—calm, unemotional, giving nothing away. It was as if they had come so far together that they had somehow arrived back at the beginning. It was not, she thought, a particularly comforting prospect.

"Are you off to a party?" She indicated the flowers.

"Not exactly." He paused. "I behaved in a rather unsubtle manner last night, and I'm hoping to beg forgiveness from the woman in question."

Claire accepted the sick feeling that bloomed up inside her as an apt punishment for everything she had done.

"What happened?" *Did I cause this?*

"I'd rather not say."

"What does it matter? I wouldn't know her anyway."

He didn't answer, which was answer enough for Claire. As he stared down, everything shuttered and barred against her, she countered by letting it all show, flowing out of her pores and undulating towards the high ceilings of the station. Not hiding—giving him maximum satisfaction—was somehow part of her punishment.

"I'd go for red roses," she finally said. "They're her favourite. If you aren't particularly serious, make sure the number's not divisible by twelve so she doesn't get the wrong idea."

"Don't play games with me, Claire."

"I'm trying to be helpful."

"You're trying to be horrible."

"I'm just jealous, that's all."

Finally, she'd managed to inflict *something* on his face, just as quickly erased.

"You've nothing to be jealous of." He sighed. "She was having none of it—and in my drunken state, I seem to recall not taking it very gracefully."

"You could've let me go on believing something did happen."

"I know. But after seeing how much that would hurt you, it wasn't possible."

That's what love is, Claire. She was squarely put in her place.

"I'm sorry it didn't work out with Rachel."

"Are you?"

She paused. "No, I'm relieved, which really *is* horrible. But I'm also surprised—she told me she thought you were charming."

"It's not always such a simple formula. And she said something about not 'violating the sisterhood,' whatever that means."

"Oh, I see."

"Would you mind giving me the rough translation?" he said.

The decision wasn't even conscious: "She's figured out that I have feelings for you too."

245

This time, he didn't even try to hide his reaction, and she felt a spasm of distress, added, "I can tell her to forget all that if you want."

"Don't bother," he said. "I'm not interested in her, that way. I was just angry with you."

"Oh." The relief was like a rainstorm. "Are you still?"

"No." He sighed again. "No, I'm not. Although part of me wishes I could sustain it."

"Listen, Josh, I'd go for irises. She's very fond of them, and they'll strike exactly the right tone."

"Thanks." He picked a few bunches, dripping from the pail, and took them to the counter, and when he'd returned, she asked him if he wanted to have dinner.

"What about Alan?"

"He won't be here until around midnight."

"I'm not sure it's such a good idea." The purple and gold of the flowers seemed to vibrate against the pallor of his hands. "In fact, I've been thinking today that I ought to steer clear of you for a while."

"Please." She was making everything up as she went along—her whole life, it felt like. "Can't we just try to make this friendship work? I know it's awkward, and I don't even have the right to ask, but the thought of not being around you..."

His eyes seemed to perform some silent calculus.

"You do know," he finally said, "that if you push me hard enough, I *will* break."

"I know."

They stood there among the swirling crowd, bombarded by the whistles of trains about to depart, by amplified announcements in Dutch, French, German and English, by swooping clouds of station pigeons: a young woman with impossible hope and a giant of a man, careering completely out of control. A man who ought to know better.

"All right," he said. "If it means that much to you, I'll try."

❦ ❦ ❦

Rachel opened the door and raised an exquisite eyebrow at the irises.

"Peace?" Joshua said. "I'm sorry I acted like a thug."

"I'm surprised you even remember." She took the flowers, breathed them in with a smile. "Apology accepted. But you were hardly a thug. In fact, I was flattered ... and tempted."

"Still. It wasn't like me at all."

"I realize that, darling. Do you want to come in for a drink?"

"I can't really—Claire's waiting downstairs with our bicycles."

"Claire?" The eyebrow shot up again. "I should've thought you two would want to put several cities at least between your respective sexual tensions."

"She's got other ideas."

"Are you sure you know what you're doing?"

"No. I'm just in free-fall now."

"Well, you'd better be careful—the ground's pretty damned hard."

❦ ❦ ❦

Claire, like every other visitor Joshua had ever entertained, couldn't hide her initial reaction to his house.

"You must've been on a waiting list for years for a place like this." She took a few steps forward in awe, taking in the antique opulence and fine details of a different age. "And on a canal as well. How can you possibly afford the rent?"

He took her coat and hung it up next to his own. "I own it, actually."

She tilted her head. "Rachel and I like to look in the estate agent windows and fantasize about tall, skinny gingerbread houses like this. You'd have to be a millionaire."

"I am." He led her into the main space, indicated a cluster of comfortable chairs.

"Very funny." Then, "You *are* joking, aren't you?"

"My father owned one of the most prestigious and exclusive thoroughbred breeding concerns in Britain. Both my parents are dead, and I don't have any siblings—I inherited the lot."

She backed into a chair and fell into it as an afterthought. Then, almost accusingly, "You don't *act* like a millionaire."

"How am I supposed to act?"

"Well, not slaving away in the basement of NeuroSys all day, getting bossed about by supercilious biologists, for starters... Not using public transport. Not..."

She trailed off when he started to laugh. "Would you start acting differently if you suddenly had more money than you could possibly spend?"

"What a question. I think I probably would."

"Would you drive to work when you could be relaxing on the train with a book? Would you *stop* working, if it was something you loved doing?"

"Well..."

"I never wanted money, never aspired to it—it just landed in my lap. Hardly anyone knows about it, and most of the time it's a right pain in the arse. I only took this house because the lawyers were nagging me to make the investment." He sat down on the sofa. "It embarrasses me, to be honest, but you insisted on coming back here."

"When I think how some people would give anything to be in your shoes..."

"You're talking about Alan, aren't you? It's one of the things he's always resented about me."

She didn't reply, but she didn't have to.

"I'd trade it all in to have my parents back for one day," he said.

The old painted clock on the mantelpiece subdivided the silence in measured magnificence.

"I know how that feels. I'm an orphan, too. My..." She stopped, started again. "I still think it's unusual, Josh. Just because you didn't command all the money when you were growing up doesn't mean you wouldn't still act..."

"Rich?"

"You know what I mean."

"My father built it all up from nothing. Our family came from a long line of agricultural labourers, and hard work was the only thing tolerated. We lived on a farm, Claire, not in a mansion, and we were all expected to contribute. You think I'm slaving away in the Pit? You ought to have seen my childhood."

"Did you resent it?"

"Not at all. I loved the horses—much more than people, most times."

"What happened to the farm?"

"I sold it—and everything—to a close family friend. I didn't want all my father's hard work to unravel—I had a way with the animals but a lousy head for business. I miss it sometimes, but fortunately I'm welcome to visit whenever I want."

She smiled at him. "I like the image of you hiding in the stables as a child."

Joshua relaxed against the sofa. They had passed the critical period of revelation, when it became clear whether the person was going to treat him differently from that point onward.

"I think the only part of my upbringing that really reflected the money was my education. After about the fourth life-threatening altercation on the playground, my mother insisted I be withdrawn and given private tutelage."

"God . . . that's awful."

"Kids are cruel," Joshua said. "And I was even stranger-looking back then, before I'd had a chance to catch up with my height—gawky and clumsy and all out of proportion." He paused, trying to decide how to phrase it. "Also, I was quite strong—and I wasn't able to contain my temper in those days."

"Really?" Her eyes were wide.

"So I stayed home and learned to control myself. But I've always suspected that if Mum had just left me to it, I would've eventually found a way to be accepted. I still wonder how I'd be today if she had."

"I think you turned out wonderfully. I can't really picture you any other way."

"I'm not so sure. In many ways my life has been truly lonely. As if I've spent the entire time trying to make it back to the playground, to the point where I left off."

She was silent, the sympathy in her eyes filling him with an ache that could never be eased.

"Anyway," he said. "I loved my schooling. I had lots of attention, the best teachers. It's why I speak Spanish . . . in case you were wondering how I'd the means to be so appallingly rude the other day."

"Please don't worry about that, Joshua—I was going to break down no matter what was said." She reached over as if to place a hand on his knee, then apparently thinking better of it, put her hand back into her lap. "Do you mind switching to Spanish now? It always makes me feel more at home."

"*Vale*, if you prefer."

"And your Dutch is beautiful, too, I noticed last weekend."

"I speak a few others as well . . . French, Italian, German. I couldn't get enough of languages. For a while I thought I might become a linguist."

"But you ended up in the sciences," she said, an odd expression on her face.

"My father was really disappointed," Joshua said. "He always wanted me to be a vet, and when I got distracted by fundamental biology at University, he—"

Claire suddenly clamped down, like a flower pressed between pages. There it was again, that dangerous ground he kept blundering into. He rapidly shifted through the various past clues and patterns, but was still lacking a few essential pieces to make an accurate prediction. Remembering how she'd reacted to his probing at the club, he decided to let it pass.

"He gave me an earful," Joshua went on, mildly. "But he lived long enough to see me graduate, and I could tell that once he'd got used to the idea, he was very proud of me."

"A happy ending, then." Claire appeared to have composed herself.

"Yes. But enough of my blathering." He stood up. "Do you mind giving me a hand in the kitchen?"

Claire let herself into her flat around half past ten that night and, as had been her habit in the past few months, went straight to the bookshelves and pulled a volume at random. Finding the lost poem had ceased to be a game and had become an obsession. The more aspects of Joshua that were revealed, the more she wanted to revisit the half-recalled words that had been haunting her, as if with them, she might unfold his secret heart. More recently, she'd entertained the irrational feeling that the poem would help orient herself, to instruct her how to navigate these dangerous waters between the friendship she craved so inexplicably, and the rocks and whirlpools of attraction that were getting in the way.

The slim red book fell open:

Lovers and thinkers, into the earth with you.
Be one with the dull, the indiscriminate dust.
A fragment of what you felt, of what you knew,
A formula, a phrase remains, —but the best is lost.

Not at all helpful. Shoving the book back into the rest of her father's remains—the sole corpus of her own rich inheritance—she went over to the sofa and submerged herself in darkness.

At precisely the same moment, Joshua was also thinking about his father, the memories loose and swirling around after their conversation about his childhood. As he tidied up the kitchen, he recalled a particular episode when he'd been about eleven or twelve.

The man had climbed up into the hayloft, knowing exactly where his young son would have gone.

"No permanent damage, I trust?" He squatted down nearby, moved aside Joshua's hands to inspect the new bruise flowering beneath, bloodshot iris against the too-white skin.

Despite his rage, Joshua could feel the calming effect of his father's roughened hands as his scrawny, too-long leg was inspected, and he tried hard to hold onto his anger in the face of it.

"I think you'll live," was the prognosis, humour twitching just behind the solemn proclamation. "Are you ready to come down and make up with Beelzebub now?"

Beelzebub was the spirited yearling—formerly Joshua's favourite—who, faithful to his name, had just delivered a spectacular kick in the shin while Joshua had been trying to brush him.

"No. And you can't make me."

Joshua's father sat back on his haunches, regarding his offspring. "You know, son, you're never going to be a good vet if you take these things personally."

"I don't care. I don't like him anymore."

And true to his word, Joshua had never touched that particular horse again.

Claire's telephone rang, jarring her out of memories. Expecting an update of Alan's arrival time, she was surprised to find that it was Rachel.

"Are you decent, darling? I'm in the neighbourhood, and I was wondering if I could come up and have a word."

A few minutes later, Rachel swept in, pausing at the door to the lounge. "How positively funereal. Do you mind if I switch on the light?" Not waiting for an answer, she flicked the switch and came over and sat down on the armchair, body tensed and hands restless.

"You can help yourself to a drink," Claire said warily, blinking against the harsh fluorescence. It seemed as if she'd already had a few.

"What in heaven's name are you playing at with Joshua?" The question was tinged with unexpected venom. "I know you're confused, but I never thought you were the heartless type."

Claire opened her mouth, but Rachel cut her off.

"Do you realize how *nice* he is? How sensitive? He brought me *flowers*, Claire, just for the dubious crime of wanting to forget about *you* for one night." Rachel stood up, paced a few steps. "Don't you think you ought to leave him alone?"

"We're friends, Rachel. And I'm not forcing him to be."

"Please—you have absolutely no idea, do you? And what were you thinking of, extracting his confession like the bloody Inquisition? Let me guess—you threw something, didn't you? Had a tantrum? Forced him to lay everything at your feet?"

Claire pressed her lips together, feeling the heat crawl over her face.

"If you hadn't," Rachel said, "he would've kept it behind that mask forever, and then at least he would've retained his dignity."

"That's why I told him that . . . why I let him know it wasn't exactly one-sided."

"And you think that was a *kindness*? You think that didn't hurt the situation a hundred time more than it helped?"

"I gave a secret back to him. I gave him power, too."

"You gave him hope, when he hasn't a chance in hell next to golden boy!"

"Don't, Rachel. And trust me, he knows it's hopeless."

"Is it? What exactly do you want from him, anyway?"

It was the precise question she herself had been struggling with for days. "I want to be around him, talk with him. . . know more about him. . . I want him to be happy, I. . ."

"And you *want* him, full stop. Sounds strangely reminiscent of the definition of love, Claire."

"It can't be," she said faintly. "I'm in love with Alan."

"Well, you'd better make a decision one way or the other before someone gets seriously hurt. You don't even bother to hide all your conflicting signals—how long until Alan notices?"

She wanted to defend herself, but Rachel's words had held up a mirror, and Claire didn't like what she was seeing reflected back.

"There's more than just what *you* want at stake here," Rachel said. "I suggest you start thinking about other people for a change."

The door of the flat shut with heavy finality.

And five minutes later, the door of the gingerbread house opened to reveal Joshua's surprised face.

"Have you left something behind?" Then, on closer inspection, "What's the matter, Claire?"

She came inside and flung herself against him, breathing heavily from the run, and he put his arms around her, pushed the door closed with a foot.

"I've come to say goodbye." Her words sounded smothered to her own ears.

"What on earth are you talking about?" He sounded more amused than alarmed. He pulled her hair from where it was tangled against him and smoothed it back in a wave behind her, and she could feel each strand as it moved between his fingers.

"You were right, at the station, that I ought to leave you alone, but I bullied you into changing your mind. Like I've bullied you into everything else."

"Nobody's bullying anyone." The hand, moving from her hair to her shoulders, spread ripples in a circle down her back, both pacifying and awakening, mutually exclusive elements that should never co-exist in the same universe. "And I thought everything went fine this evening— we had a nice time, didn't we? Perfectly civilized?"

She was struggling to control herself and didn't answer.

"What's brought this on, *cariño*?"

"Rachel came over and had a go at me. She said some terrible things . . . but I think they were all true."

"I see." His voice was solemn, but she couldn't leave the comfort of his shirt to see what might be reflected in his expression. "And is saying goodbye what you really want?"

"Of course not! This is all about what's best for you."

"Listen." He pulled away, made her look up at him in the dim light of the corridor. His smile was both humorous and tender. "I'm sure she meant well, but I'm perfectly capable of looking after myself."

"She said you weren't. She said I had to choose."

"Well, I'd rather you didn't, because I know what side I'd end up on."

She paused, and the words came out of her mouth unplanned: "I'm not so sure about that anymore."

He dropped his hands abruptly and stepped back.

"I wish to God you hadn't said that, Claire."

"I'm doing it again, aren't I? Influencing you unfairly."

His eyes burned down at her with the intensity of a provoked animal.

"You'd better go," he said, "before I give in to the temptation to exert some unfair influence of my own."

Her heart caught inside her chest, a tiny engine that couldn't quite turn over, and she became aware of everything swimming around her: the drowned murk of streetlight through the leaded glass diamond on the front door, the glittering of his gaze under serious black brows, and above all, the ripples that had spread far beyond where he had touched her, threatening to override her better judgement.

"I can't decide," she finally said, faintly, "so you'll have to. Is it goodbye?"

At the angle required to look him in the eye, she had to bare her neck like a condemned person awaiting the scratch of the rope.

"Let's just call it goodnight, for now." His entire body seemed resigned as he herded her towards the door.

❦ ❦ ❦

He sat there in solitary splendour, surveying his domain with frantic eye and slamming heart. He was full of self-loathing. What a pair they were: Wasn't he just as guilty as she in the manipulation department? Standing there in the front hall, he'd been too clever and sensitive a lover not to realize how she would react to the precise and calculated efforts of his so-called comforting touch. Hadn't he accumulated all he needed to know during their embrace in the car, subconsciously measuring her microscopic reactions, testing the effects of subtle variations of pressure, of tension, of the way that withdrawing could intensify far more than continuing? He had pushed her until she was trembling on the edge, and tonight he could so easily have tipped the balance. She didn't weigh anything—he could have carried her effortlessly up to his bedroom, laid her down, and he knew, from the bodily knowledge so recently beneath his fingertips, that she would not have resisted—that she was hungering for him, and would have rejoiced in it.

At some point, Alan would have rung, and he'd have heard it in her voice, even if she tried to conceal it. And if she didn't answer her mobile, he would have found her flat empty, and waited, and when she finally returned, the truth would be imprinted all over her, the spoor and scent and shifting eyes of betrayal. And just like that, it would be over, and Joshua would have won, beaten his old rival at his own game, for the ultimate stakes, in a way that he had failed to do for more than a decade.

But this was nothing but an empty fantasy. Joshua could never take what could only be given, and even if he had, the taking would have made the experience something altered, something spoiled, and the essence of what he had loved would be gone forever.

He knew it, and so, he suspected, did she. It was probably the only thing that had saved them.

✤ ✤ ✤

And as Claire lay sleepless in Alan's embrace that evening, she felt resolve filter through her and slowly douse her hot blood. She would take the energy of her guilt and channel it into ruthlessness. She did not want to love Joshua, and she was determined to force the compass of her heart to swing away from its true pole. She was not, perhaps, to be blamed for thinking that she could thwart nature and the laws of the universe. After all, so many thousands of her predecessors had had the same aspiration: students of alchemy, would-be inventors of perpetual motion machines, biologists transubstantiating maggots directly from dead meat, explorers determined to find the jagged edge of the earth or lost civilizations drowned beneath the waves.

But Claire was undeterred. Until she managed to strangle her new feelings, Rachel's warning had come just in time. She would have to hide her turmoil from Alan as scrupulously as she had kept her data about the Universal Aggregation Principle from coming to light. Alan already clearly sensed that something was wrong, but from the few comments he had made, she knew he thought she was anxious about her role in the delay of the clinical trial and, perhaps, by the looming promise of his own untold secret. She would have to work hard to ensure that these suspicions did not stray toward the real source of her anxiety.

Chapter 32

❧

On Saturday, there was a white envelope in Claire's post-box in Amsterdam, unadorned except for her name. She immediately recognized the spindly handwriting, and her heart started to beat faster. Holding the dangerous thing by one corner, she thought quickly. Alan was upstairs, making lunch, and she had volunteered to buy some fresh basil from the Albert Cuyp Market. Instead, she took a detour to her usual bench by the Amstel River and sat down to open the envelope.

Dear Claire,

I want to be explicit: after several nights of sleep, I definitely don't want to say goodbye. I will subsume all risks and consider you blameless. I don't claim your expertise with poetry, but I thought the following was appropriate:

Puedes irte y no importa, pues te quedas conmigo,
como queda el perfume mas allá de la flor...

She slammed closed the piece of paper as if it were contaminated, but it was too late: the meaning of the first few lines had already soaked into her, transforming ever so slightly in the process, as particularly apt poetry will, to suit the precise circumstances. Where could he possibly have dug up such a thing?

Of course she could not resist unfolding the note and reading the rest:

You could say goodbye and it wouldn't matter,
because you'd still be there, perfume lingering far from the
*   flower.*

You know I love you, even if I don't say it,
And I know you're mine, even if your love isn't.

Life draws us together and time breaks us apart
like dawn splits night from day;
My thirsty heart craves your clear water
But it's another man's water that I dare not drink.

This is why I let you go, because although I don't follow,
You're never entirely gone, like a scar,
and my soul's like that furrow after they've mown down the
   wheat:
the heads of grain are lost, but the roots remain.

A wave broke over her head then as she realized the full extent of her tactical error. By confessing her attraction, she had revealed cracks that Joshua now appeared to be levering. Having deemed touch to be an unfair weapon, he had switched to her own sphere of wordplay—and in her mother tongue at that, a powerful combination that Claire was not accustomed to. He wasn't going to remain a static object for the taking or leaving—he was going to contest his fate.

Precisely because she had offered him hope, as Rachel had so astutely noted.

Winged elm seeds showered down on her, pennies from heaven. She knew she should rip the note into a million pieces and throw it into the river, among the coots and ducks, the wild irises and water lilies and the sparkles of reflected sunlight, but it proved a crime of which she was incapable. Instead, she took it home with her after her errand and hid it inside a particular blue book when Alan wasn't looking.

❧ ❧ ❧

On Monday morning, Ramon came by her lair.

"Group meeting's cancelled today," he told her. "Everyone's too busy preparing to test the new drug. And there's another piece of news, which Alan asked me to pass on, since he's tied up in a meeting."

Claire looked up from the console, alerted by the undercurrents of his tone.

"There's been a death at the hospice," he said simply.

"Oh." Claire blinked, and cold wings fluttered against her heart.

"There'll be a slight delay—I understand they're waiting for the daughter to fly up from Pretoria before they switch off life support."

She nodded, waiting.

"We would be very much obliged if you could test Peter's crude version of the modified Zapper," Ramon said, inevitably. "To make sure that the binding of SCAN to the Alzheimer's proteins is still disrupted."

"Of course."

"My lab will also have a look with our conventional methods, naturally." He leaned against the door. "It goes without saying that even Zeke Bannerman won't mind if you prioritize this."

"Of course." She seemed capable only of inane parroting.

"You *can* aspirate and test material from outside of cells?"

"In theory," she said faintly.

"Good. By the way, Merriam did some experiments over the weekend confirming that the old Zapper definitely switches on that inappropriate receptor gene, just as Joshua thought. And, also as predicted, it only happens in human neurons, not those from mice. I thought you'd be happy to hear that you'd both been acquitted on all counts."

"I'm happy, Ramon."

"That's what I like to hear, *querida*," he said. "Expect the samples on Thursday, then. With any luck, we'll be able to laugh at all of this one day soon, *no*?"

❦ ❦ ❦

As soon as Ramon left, Claire pulled out her phone and sent Joshua a text message: *big news—can I see you tonight?*

A few minutes later, her phone chirped, and she read his reply: *yes, but only if it's in public.*

❦ ❦ ❦

Roz and Joshua were eating a late lunch in the Pit's coffee room, having worked through the noontime period to beat a deadline on a joint project. Joshua was chewing his sandwich with automatic movements and a vacancy of focus when Roz toed him in the leg. She was wearing what she called her Jackbooted Thug Footgear, so the blow smarted.

258

"Ow. What was that for?"

"You are spectacularly bad company today, boss."

"Sorry. It's all this deadline stress."

"Bollocks." She eyed him. "May I have three guesses?"

"No."

"People are starting to talk about your moodiness. It's not good for morale—we've enough to worry about as it is."

"It's not as if I'm usually all sunshine, Roz."

"True. But honestly. . ." She wiped her mouth with her sleeve. "I'm concerned about you."

"Well, don't be."

"It's *her*, isn't it?"

He sighed. "I don't know what you're talking about."

She started folding fingers down. "The tulips, the moods, the closed-door office sessions, the joint heroics. . ."

The poetry, the fervent embraces, the secret assignations, the unquenchable desire. . .

"Is anyone else making this connection, or only you?"

"Only me, for the moment. But frankly, you've not been your usual unreadable self recently."

❦ ❦ ❦

Claire stopped by the Blauwe Vogeltje directly from Centraal Station, knowing that Rachel would be having her usual after-work drink. She was not certain she'd be welcome.

"Still speaking to me?" Rachel said, moving away from her group a little to give them some privacy.

"I was about to ask you the same thing."

"*Mea culpa* about the other night—no, this round's on me, I insist. I was beastly—one too many glasses of rosé while I was cooking."

"No, I deserved it—you were absolutely right."

"Does this mean you decided to leave him alone? How did he take it?"

"He didn't. He refused to be dismissed."

"I was afraid of that." Her eyes darkened.

"Not only that, but he's started to be more . . . assertive."

"Has he?" Rachel looked intrigued. "Well, good for him. Fighting is better than falling."

"What do you mean?"

"Never mind. But I know who *I'm* supporting in this match."

"Rachel . . . it's going to make everything much more complicated."

"That's what happens when you open doors, Claire. Things start coming in."

"But you're still on *my* side too, aren't you?"

"Of course I am, darling." Rachel put a hand on Claire's forearm in a rare show of physical affection. "I'm going to do my best to make sure that you don't get hurt. Although it doesn't look as if that's going to be particularly easy."

❧ ❧ ❧

A bit past the appointed time, Claire cycled through Museumplein then locked up outside the small café across from the park. It was a warm night, with a slim crescent moon, a sprinkling of stars and the scent of cherry blossoms in the air. She could already see him in a window seat, pale skin warmed by candlelight from a red glass globe. He was absorbed in a book, his large hands relaxed along the cover and an amused expression on his face, one solitary man amidst well-dressed couples enjoying a pre-performance drink before strolling over to the nearby Concertgebouw.

She went inside, and he looked up, faced composed and cool. The book was closed and secreted away before she could read the title on its sleek spine, although she had the impression it was in French.

"Sorry I'm late," she said. "I had a best friend to placate."

"I assume I'm in her bad books now?"

Claire sat down and wriggled out of her coat. "You may be acting inadvisably, but she still thinks you're wonderful. I wish I knew your secret."

"Everyone loves an underdog," he said shortly. "Listen, Claire, I heard about the Alzheimer's death. Your big news, I presume?"

She studied his face, feeling the feathery touch of fear return for the hundredth time that day. "I wasn't prepared for it to happen so soon, but it will be a relief to get it over with."

"I take it you got access to some of the precious cells?"

"I couldn't have avoided it if I wanted to. Apparently the Interactrex is now officially essential to test the Son of Zapper."

"What's the plan?"

She explained about the next-of-kin. "If the brain arrives on Wednesday as expected, the In Vitro department will propagate the cells overnight, so I'm scheduled to receive my samples on Thursday afternoon."

"How are you going to break the news, after?"

"I may not have to."

"What do you mean?"

"Alan sometimes watches me work, when it's an important experiment. I wouldn't be surprised. . ."

He sat up in his seat. "And Ramon?"

"It's going to be a late session, and he usually tries to eat with his family. But I'm sure Alan will ring him straight away."

"Hmmm." Joshua mulled this over. "I have a feeling the result will be covered up for a few days, while Stanley comes to terms with what he's going to do."

"I suppose you're right. I'll probably be asked not to say anything. I promise I'll let you know somehow, even though I'm sure the outcome will be the same as last time."

"Don't e-mail or text it."

"Of course not. I'll stop by the Pit, or safer yet, drop a note at your house."

"Did you want anything, by the way?" he said, still with that perfect composure. The previous evening, the love letter, might never have happened. "I can get someone's attention."

"Not particularly. I'm not here for the drinks. Or to discuss work, for that matter." She didn't let her own gaze waver.

He tipped back the rest of his beer and put some coins on the table. "In that case, let's take a walk. It's a lovely night."

❧ ❧ ❧

As they crossed the road and passed into Museumplein, Claire said, "I thought you wanted to be in public."

"It's a public park," he replied imperturbably. He could feel the wet grass sliding underneath the soles of his shoes and, bolstered by the solid grandeur of the spot-lit Rijksmuseum up ahead, became buoyed by an unstoppable confidence.

"I know exactly what you're doing, you know." She had switched to Spanish at last.

"Good. So do I, *cariño*."

They walked in silence a moment, then she said, "I thought we'd decided not to use unfair influence."

"There are many forms of influence. I'm weighing the fairness of each on a case-by-case basis."

"All perfectly civilized?"

"Something like that."

A pause. "It was beautiful, though. The poem."

"I thought you'd like it."

He sat down on the next bench, and she joined him, leaving a good foot of empty space between. The moon hung sideways over the imposing bulk of the American consulate with its barricades and bristling high fences. In the current climate, he wouldn't be surprised if there were snipers in its gables as well.

"I haven't found the perfect response yet," she said eventually.

"The poem Rachel was referring to in Leidseplein?"

"No, that's something entirely different." Her tone warned him off. "To keep with the rules you've already established, it would have to reflect me more than you."

"True." He had not anticipated this rather encouraging development.

"I'll probably have to write it myself."

His heart stopped mid-beat before carrying on at an increased canter.

"I'm looking forward to it, then," he said.

"You really ought to be on your guard. Love poetry can go horribly wrong." She smiled at him sadly before turning her attention to the night sky.

"Claire." He studied her profile, the way the ambient light touched it with a gentle hand. "I want to thank you for giving me a chance."

"Is that what I'm doing?" She wasn't mocking him—she just sounded bewildered.

"That's what it looks like to me."

"I'm just improvising, Joshua, all out of control. It will probably end in disaster." She turned to face him, and he could read everything there was to see.

"Please don't take this the wrong way, but I can't stand to see you upset." He put his arms around her and she melted into him, a shock of warmth and relief. "With all this fuss about my feelings, someone ought to be properly worried about yours."

She raised her head to him, and a new page had turned in her dark eyes. He leaned down to kiss her, an extraordinary kiss that seemed to go on and on. When they finally came apart, she said, breathlessly, "Was that what you meant by taking it the wrong way?"

"More or less." He had to laugh, to give some outlet to his surge of joy.

"That was about a million times better than I'd been imagining." She rested her head against him, running a hand along his chest underneath his coat, a small, curious movement that radiated down his nerves in all directions like a starburst of lit firecrackers. After a few more breaths, she said, "Are you angry?"

"God, no." He couldn't keep his hands out of her hair—it had nothing to do with fairness or unfairness. She closed her eyes and pressed her face into his coat, clinging to it as if to keep herself from being swept away by storm waters.

"Does a kiss count as infidelity?" she asked, voice muffled by cloth.

"*That* one certainly did."

"One more for my collection of dirty secrets, then." But she made no move to disentangle herself, and eventually Joshua had to be the one to move away. She seemed to accept this with equal measure.

"Now that we've demonstrated our absolute inability to behave in public as well as private," he said, "will you have to stop seeing me?"

"Just try keeping me away." Her hand shot across the bench, capturing his with fearsome possessiveness.

He hesitated. "Claire, have you ever written a poem for Alan?"

A considerable silence.

"That one's a bit on the borderline of fairness, wouldn't you say?" She paused. "But no, I haven't. Not for anyone, actually."

"I promised myself I wouldn't ask this next one. Do you forgive me in advance?"

She nodded tiredly.

"You do still love Alan. And want him."

"I'm ... I'm not sure any more. I might be. I'm sorry, but I'm a bit confused right now."

Despite everything, he felt sick disappointment and despised himself for it. Nothing had really changed—and his feeling of invincibleness had been a sham from the beginning.

"Do you suppose this is how Guinevere felt?" Claire said. "I never had much patience for her—I always thought she was a silly fool. But now I'm starting to see where she was coming from."

"Who am I, Arthur or Lancelot?" He sounded bitter to his own ears, bitter and petty. "I could never decide which was in the worst position."

She gave him that sad smile again.

"Everybody lost in that story, Joshua."

❦ ❦ ❦

Two very confused souls returned to their respective empty homes soon afterward, crushed with frustration, regret and a growing sense of dread. Yet somewhere beneath, there was also the idea that the world could be more terrifyingly beautiful than a heart could possibly stand.

Chapter 33

❧

On Tuesday evening, Alan and Claire were listening to Mahler and drinking port after dinner. She was leaning against him on the Corbusier, reasonably relaxed for the first time that day—as relaxed as could be expected under the circumstances. As time had passed, Alan's powerful influence had slowly pushed Joshua's to one side. If she kept it up, would it always be like that, she wondered; back and forth, one eating into the other, each having his just and proper zenith before being herded back into nadir, *ad infinitum*?

But to keep it up was unthinkable. What she was doing was wrong, and could not carry on now that she had allowed herself the heartless self-indulgence of drawing Joshua over the line. Joshua, who was entirely innocent, who had exposed the magnitude of her error in judgement simply by existing. At that moment, it suddenly seemed so clear: her feelings for Alan were misguided. He wasn't the person she'd imagined; and she certainly wasn't the person he wanted her to be.

As she sat there, thinking these thoughts, her blood went cold with adrenaline at the thought that she could broach the topic right this moment. She could take control and *make* it stop. She could tell Alan the truth: that she was having second thoughts about their relationship, that she needed time to think. That she was young and stupid, and not ready to commit herself. That she needed someone who could accept that she might be more poet than scientist after all. She could—

"I want to tell you why I have nightmares," Alan said without preamble. "I want to tell you now, before it starts giving you ones of your own."

Just like that, her resolve was shattered. Meanwhile, another shot of adrenaline topped up the initial cocktail. Despite her other preoccupations, she was still afraid of what he was going to say.

Alan himself seemed cool, sedate. "I had a very sporadic childhood, Claire. My mother left my father when I was three, and when she remarried I hardly ever saw her—she didn't want custody. Meanwhile, my father was with the Foreign Office, and we were always on the move. I never lived anywhere for more than a few years at a time."

"That must have been difficult."

"I suppose all the travel and varied experiences were good for me, but it was impossible to maintain relationships. I found it hard to put my trust in anyone. When you're a child, you don't see things logically. My mother's departure had to be about me—all those playmates and teachers disappearing one after the other, likewise."

"What about your father?"

"He drank," Alan said, and his tone drew a line under that particular branch of the story.

Claire put down her glass and slipped a hand over his.

"I focused most of my efforts on my studies, and found the sciences to be a very effective escape. I was good at it, and the steadiness of the physical laws, the robustness of theories, was such a contrast to my family life."

"Lots of theories turn out to be wrong," she said, soft fingers of fear brushing against her heart.

"Of course I know that now, dearest, but I was very idealistic in my youth." He moved his fingers along her face in his habitual gesture. "And I took solace in women, too. I've been doing that all my life, but even when I was younger, the liaisons didn't seem to matter and nothing lasted. I take full responsibility for that—I wasn't terribly receptive to commitment, after having been at the wrong end of it for so many years."

He took his gaze from the coffee table and peered at her a moment. "Will you find it too painful hearing about my other loves?"

"No. That's not you *now*."

"It most certainly isn't." He hugged her closer for a moment. "At any rate, when I was a little bit older than you, a postdoc in Stanley's lab, I met an incredible woman, doing a PhD in genetics in our department. Her name was Serena."

"Was she beautiful?"

He nodded. "In fact, she looked very much like you. She would've been only a few years younger than you are now when we met. The first time I saw you, I thought I was seeing a ghost—that's part of the reason why I reacted so badly to you."

Claire was silent, watching the memories flit across his face.

"She took one look at me and saw through everything, all the flimsy constructions I had built up over the years to protect myself. Again, in that way she was much like you. I fell deeply in love for the first time in my life. I never told anyone about our relationship—although it may seem odd to you, in those days, it wasn't the done thing for postdocs to be sleeping with the PhD students. Even Ramon didn't know about this."

Despite the years of elapsed time and her own diverted feelings, Alan's vivid descriptions were getting to her. He saw this, and paused in his story to kiss her. "Don't worry, you're not just a substitute for her. In many ways you are also wholly unlike her. Please don't think. . ."

"I don't. Go on."

"Well." He swallowed. "Stanley moved the lab to Holland, but Serena had to stay in London a bit longer to finish her PhD. I took the ferry over for some weekends and holidays. My first festive period away, I naturally went back to London to spend it with her. There was a very big party at someone's house on New Year's Eve—one of those affairs when there are hundreds of people and furniture gets destroyed. I got very drunk."

He was only half with her now. "Although I loved Serena, I was also terrified. How could I let someone get close to me after I'd been let down so many times in the past? When I drank, those fears would often intensify."

Claire felt a fresh stirring of coldness.

"I can hardly bear to. . ." He passed a hand over his face. "I started to flirt with Serena's friend on the dance floor. Just to prove that I still *could*, that I wasn't trapped. Serena tried to take me home—she was a sensible person, not given to jealousy; she knew me very well. I refused to go. She didn't have cab fare, and I wouldn't give her any—I didn't want her to leave, you see. In my intoxicated state, her *seeing* me exert my independence was part of the package."

He kept the hand over his eyes, now, as if trying to blot everything out. "I didn't find out what had happened until hours later. We didn't have mobiles then, all this instantaneous coverage. I stayed on with Serena's friend, and Serena finally persuaded another acquaintance to drive her home, but that person was drunk. There was a dreadful accident. . ."

Claire's hand had moved, too, involuntarily over her mouth.

"I made it to the hospital just as she was slipping away. Just in time to hear her forgive me. I think that was almost worse than if she hadn't spoken at all, if I hadn't made it there in time."

Claire wasn't able to speak, so shocked was she by the sight of Alan Fallengale weeping. She could only hold him as the past heaved out and eventually left him quiet and breathless.

"Are you still with me?" he finally said, subdued. She could tell he wasn't referring to the story.

"It wasn't your fault."

"It was." His eyes were at their most stony green, the spent tears crystallizing on his skin. "I assure you there is nothing you can say to change my mind. Everything that happened was a direct consequence of my hateful actions. And it turned me into someone else—someone just as hateful—from that day onward."

"No, of course it didn't." Her fingers in his fair hair reminded her of other fingers, other hair.

"Which brings us to the famous feud." Unexpectedly, Alan gave her a tight smile. "I'd never been very comfortable around Joshua anyway, but this is what we fell out over. I don't know if you've noticed, but he has a way of knowing things you'd rather he didn't."

She didn't dare answer, just kept moving hand over hair in automated movements.

"When I returned to NeuroSys after the funeral, he sensed that something was wrong and tried to worm it out of me. I ... well, *snapped* is probably the most charitable description. I said some fairly provocative things—we had a fight in the lab. A real fight."

"Real ... you mean ... with fists and everything?"

"Fists and everything. Broken glassware. Rolling around on the floor. The works. Obviously we were completely unmatched—the man is huge. And I've never seen anyone that angry in my life. He broke my arm, Claire."

"Oh, my God. Did you ... did you press charges?"

"No. Stanley and Ramon talked me out of it—the bad press, the fragility of the start-up at that point, et cetera ... and besides, when I cooled off I realized I had probably deserved what I got—I said some pretty nasty things."

Claire was silent, amazed.

"A few days later," Alan said, "I attempted to apologize, but he wasn't receptive. And that was the last time we really communicated."

"It sounds as if he was only trying to help." She didn't seem to be able to raise her voice much above a whisper. "Before the broken arm thing, I mean."

"I realize that, dearest." His eyes were studying her carefully. "And I'm going to make more of an effort in future, especially now that he's been so decent to you . . . and I know it will make you happy. Won't it?"

"Yes . . . yes, it will. Thank you, Alan."

He embraced her, but there was no fire, only a dull sense of heaviness.

"I will never forgive myself, nor forget. . ." He had to pause, take a breath. "But sometimes, with you, I feel that I could be redeemed."

"I'll try to help you, Alan." The words came out like pearls on a string, drawn indecisively out of a velvet box. "I'll help you as much as I can."

His hold on her became painful. "From now on, there can be only honesty between us. If I could ever trust anyone again in this lifetime, it will be you, and only you. You are my second chance, and my last one, do you understand? Honesty and truth, and trust—I can't have anything less. Do you promise?"

How could she do anything else? As she spoke the words, she felt herself being pulled under into inky blackness.

Chapter 34

ᘓᕽ

Joshua sat in front of his terminal the next afternoon, wrapped in stillness as he listened to the denizens of the Pit tease, laugh and patter on their keyboards: alien sounds leaching out of a parallel universe. How had he become so distanced? This was his department, which he had created from nothing, populated with hand-picked personnel and nurtured for years until it was respected throughout the world. The Pit was the closest thing he had to a family, and he had not realized until this moment, when it was too late, how much he had failed to take advantage of it.

True, he had tended to feel relaxed and social here, but it only ever went so far. Only now was he realizing that nobody would have minded if he had just been himself, if he had felt free to be grumpy or ludicrous, sedate or upset as the mood struck him. There had been no real need, here, to deploy the mask, to keep himself one step removed.

Until now. At the very moment that he was in extreme turmoil and desperate for an outlet, he had been forced to repress himself even more vigorously. Roz's warning was at the forefront of his mind, and he could not afford to relax his camouflage even for a moment. Bioinformaticians were highly trained in seeing patterns and inferring behaviour. If rumours began to circulate that there was something happening between him and Claire, the entire edifice could collapse—with himself at the bottom of the pile.

It was Claire's influence, he knew, that was making him recognize the poverty of his own emotional life. Ironically, as the secrets had tightened around her, she had loosened the truth from him—not just as an abstract concept, but as an interface through which everything could be processed. He could not imagine ever returning to a world where he could not be honest with her—where he could not love her, and be loved in return.

At the same time, Claire was working at the Raison, collecting samples in her usual trance. If she was aware of anything at all besides the glistening membranes and fluid-filled sacs of the scattered tissue below her needle, it was the relief that she'd finally been able to empty her mind of everything else: the secrets and lies; the intensity of Alan's grief and the immense burden of the promise she had broken before she had even uttered the words; Thursday's destructive experiment, probably the last one she would ever perform at NeuroSys. And threaded through all of it, her desire for Joshua, which kept sweeping through her like some shivery monsoon.

The sound at the door was so unexpected that she cried out, flinching away from the console as it were burning.

"Claire." Alan came over swiftly, put a hand on her back. "I didn't mean to startle you."

She turned back to the keyboard, typing rapidly with shaking hands. "It's okay—no harm done." She performed a few final taps to put the needle on standby and turned to him.

He pulled up a chair, looking her over with concern. "It's not like you to be so jumpy."

"I'm just stressed, Alan." Eminently truthful.

"Everyone's feeling the pressure, and this waiting around doesn't help matters. But the patient's daughter's instructions were very clear." He made a face. "It shouldn't matter—her mother is dead whether she's on a machine or not."

"People need to grieve in their own ways—there's a big difference between a warm body and a cold one." A difference he ought to know as well as she.

"Of course. Of course, you're right." There was a flash of pain about the mouth. No tactless jokes about old biddies any more, she saw—Alan was continuing to transform before her eyes.

"I'm off early, folks." Joshua paused in the door of the Pit's main space, jacket on and laptop case slung over his shoulder.

He was assaulted with cheerful goodbyes, waves and a few foam footballs, and felt again that twinge of lost opportunities. Turning away, he passed through the long dark corridor towards the stairwell.

"Wait, boss!"

Roz came pelting after him, the impact of her Jackbooted Thug Footgear echoing in the tight space. She grabbed his upper arm just as he was turning around.

"Boss . . . I just wanted to make sure. . ." She paused to catch her breath.

"What is it, Roz?"

She bit her lip, looking up at him. "Josh . . . don't do anything stupid, okay?"

"I'm only ducking off a bit early." He started to smile, then stopped cold at the look on her face.

"You know what I mean—please don't insult my intelligence any longer." Behind her sudden anger, he saw the sheen of tears, something he had never witnessed in their many years of acquaintance.

(After all that time, to think of her still as an acquaintance. . .)

He loosened her grip and took her hand between both his own, reading her fear like Braille.

"I'm sorry, Roz. I won't."

"Something terrible's going to happen, isn't it?" Her eyes searched his face. "I'm scared for you."

"I'm trying very hard to protect myself," he said slowly, after a moment, "but I'm not entirely sure I'll be able to."

"Are you sure she's worth it?"

"I'm sure, Roz. I've been looking for her all my life, but just didn't know it."

She paused. "And are you sure she deserves *you*?"

"I am." The smile that came over him was as involuntary as the revelation that followed. "I'm almost positive that she's been looking for me too."

"Okay, then." Roz rubbed her nose and produced a wily look. "You *do* know, boss, that if I didn't prefer women, I'd be dying of jealousy right now?"

"Cheeky." He leaned down and kissed the top of her head, and she squirmed free, slapped him forward down the corridor and threw in a jackbooted kick for good measure.

✤ ✤ ✤

"I've got an idea," Alan said. "Why don't we bunk off early and I take you to The Hague for an extravagant meal? You need a break."

She paused. "I was thinking of going back to Amsterdam tonight. I feel the urge to be home."

"But you were just there on Monday." He looked her over. "No matter—we can try out one of those trendy new places down your way."

"Actually, Alan . . . I was sort of hoping to be alone."

There was a cool pause, and then he stood up, strode over to the window, turned his back on her as he looked out over the green fields.

"I never should have told you," he finally said, voice controlled and even. "I should have realized how you would react."

"Oh, Alan." She stood up too, went over to him. CCTV cameras and the open door be damned—she put her arms around him, feeling the rigidity of his posture. "This has absolutely nothing to do with you." Another truth.

"Are you sure?" The need in his eyes almost crushed her.

"Yes," she said firmly. "I just miss my books. I need to read some poetry, Alan. I get like this sometimes—especially when I'm under pressure. It's how I deal with things." True in a different context, but close enough to keep her gaze steady. And she did intend to deal with poetry, in a very big way.

"I understand." He relaxed, slipping his arms around her and resting his chin on her head. They stood there for a few moments, eyes closed, each giving and receiving comfort for wholly unrelated issues, issues that would be grotesque to superimpose.

Claire cleared her throat. "How about I come back tonight, Alan? Let me just putter around my bookcases for a few hours, then I'll take the train. If I get my act together on these final samples, we can still have that late dinner."

"Thank you," he said, placing his lips briefly against her forehead. "I would like that very much."

✤ ✤ ✤

Joshua passed through the lobby, murmured a polite goodbye to the day porter and could not prevent his habitual glimpse at the upper right-hand corner screen. Because they were bathed by the late-afternoon

273

light, he was unable to avoid seeing Claire and Alan captured in their moment of quiet intimacy.

Yet not twenty minutes later, as he sat nursing this abrasion on the train, there was a bleep from his pocket. Pulling out his phone, he read the new message with disbelief:

I have to see you—7 at yours?

❦ ❦ ❦

Claire stood in her living room, breathing in the smell of the books, the smell that she had grown up with, that had followed her wherever she lived. If she closed her eyes, she could see her father standing by one of the shelves, smiling down at her. He was holding a book in his hand, and his mouth moved silently with some long-dead quotation or benediction, some aphorism or play of synonyms, some cryptic verse that she would need to grow into before the meaning could clarify.

Then, as if a switch had been thrown, the voice became audible.

"Now listen carefully, Clair de Lune ... this was written just for you."

"How could it be written for me? It's hundreds of years old, Daddy."

"Nevertheless..." He would give her his mysterious smile, the dimple by his mouth a parenthesis of affection. "I know he must've had you in mind. He must've known that one day you would be here to listen."

And the words would weave around her head and within her heart, from that day onward ever and for always meant only for her and her alone.

Claire felt tears press behind her eyes, and ruthlessly pushed them back. She didn't have much time, thanks to the change of heart that had goaded her into promising Alan she'd join him later. A change of heart inspired, she suspected, more by pity than by love. Pity, which surely must be the ultimate murderer of love. But it had not done the job, not yet. She was starting to be afraid that it never would. That she would be pulled in two. Or maybe that all three of them would, six aching whole-less halves and nothing the same, ever again.

She moved into her study, turned on the lamp and pulled out several sheets of creamy paper and her father's fountain pen. The fear of committing to a grown-up poem was already making her hands shake.

❦ ❦ ❦

Joshua felt like an animal, and his own house, a confining stable. He regretted that his great height made the pacing far too short to bring relief. It was too close to seven o'clock to leave the house, to race along the Amstel like a wild creature as he really wanted to. They had kissed, and there was no going back—stopping at that point tonight would surely be arbitrary, now that they had labelled it infidelity, now that the intervening time had amplified their last encounter beyond all recognition. There was no way that she could set foot inside his house without things taking their course, and he no longer had the strength to prevent it, any more than he could stop spring from turning into summer.

About ten minutes before Claire was due, he heard a metallic scuffling at his door, and then the soft plop of paper hitting floor.

Heart ramming inside him, he went to the front hall. A white envelope lay on the mat, glowing like a luminous underwater creature. Opening the door, he dashed out onto the pavement, but she was nowhere to be seen.

He swore, which for some reason came out in Dutch—such a blunt, efficient little word. She must've fled around the corner at a dead run to have disappeared so quickly, and he didn't dare go after her or call, in case Alan was there.

Filled with foreboding, he went back inside and picked up the envelope, which bore only his first initial in a fine hand. Flattened under a weight of impossible inevitability, he carried it to the sofa as he had so stupidly imagined he would soon be carrying *her*, watching her sink back against the cushions and draw him in, her dark eyes cloudy with desire.

He opened the envelope and extracted the two sheets of heavy paper, almost yellow compared to his own skin.

Dear Joshua

Please forgive me for not saying this in person—I've decided I can't come to you unless I've made a clean break. I don't want to taint us with further lies and secrets, tainted before we even properly began. If we are ever to be, it must be honest and open. And we would never have been able to resist this evening. I know that when I am standing outside your door holding this letter, it will be the most difficult thing I've ever done, to turn away when I know you are inside waiting to hold me. Maybe I will stand there for many minutes, thinking about your hands in my hair, before I gather the willpower to push it through.

Forgive me also for the enclosed poem, which is not, after all, an original. The prospect felt more like infidelity than what happened on Monday so, in the end, I offer you this substitute. It is not everything of how I feel about you, but only one part. I do not know if it would be possible to ever encapsulate that everything in a single, discrete attempt. Maybe some day, I will have the opportunity to try.

Meanwhile, please believe that I do love you.

Claire

Joshua scanned this wordsmith's code for patterns, for motifs, but it was seamless, utterly devoid of guarantee. From her, he would expect nothing less than the perfectly intentional. So carefully, the *unless* instead of *until*, *if we are ever*, *maybe some day*—all must be understood to be deliberately in the bitter moods of the conditional and of the subjunctive. The word *both*, hovering invisible just after the *I love you*, was somehow also penned. Even the decided split of infinitive, *to ever encapsulate*, spoke of the tenuous nature of this contract, inked on brittle paper when he had expected yielding flesh.

And he had only himself to blame for the last-minute intrusion of someone else's words—hadn't it been his honest question about Alan and poetry that had planted that seed in the first place? Or given the teacher of that honesty, did the blame go back full circle?

Prepared to be disappointed, he brought the second sheet to the front and began to read:

More and more frequently the edges
of me dissolve and I become
a wish to assimilate the world, including
you, if possible through the skin

like a cool plant's tricks with oxygen
and live by a harmless green burning.

He was surprised, having expected something old, something traditional, something made quaint by antique syntax and vocabulary.
Perhaps this showed him how little he knew her after all.

I would not consume
you, or ever
finish, you would still be there
surrounding me, complete
as the air.

Unfortunately I don't have leaves.
Instead I have eyes
and teeth and other non-green
things which rule out osmosis.

So be careful, I mean it,
I give you a fair warning:

This kind of hunger draws
everything into its own
space; nor can we
talk it all over, have a calm
rational discussion.

There is no reason for this, only
a starved dog's logic about bones.

He sat perfectly still as this stranger's words spoke to him, miraculously suffused with Claire's blunt delivery, her humour, and the
precise nature of the need he'd detected under her skin the last time
they'd touched. How was this possible?

Edward Cyrus, no doubt, would have been able to explain to him
exactly why it seemed that the poem had been written for Joshua, and
Joshua alone, forever and always.

And Claire Cyrus would have been too ashamed to explain to anyone
what had happened when she got back to Alan's house. But suffice it to

say that she flew into his surprised and eager embrace (and during which, suffered a few quips about the aphrodisiac qualities of a good poem or two), went to bed without any supper and tried to slake her unrequited passion for one man in the arms of another. Of such all-too-common endeavours, it is probably best to say as little as possible.

She of all people should have known that it wasn't scientifically possible to put out water with fire.

Chapter 35

❧

Thursday arrived with the infallible predictability of the billions of days preceding it.

Nobody came by Claire's lair that morning. The brain had arrived the previous afternoon by helicopter, and the entire company, having banded together to test modified Alzheimer's candidate drug NS3003, had more important things to do.

Some had worked through the night, and others had arrived fresh in the morning to relieve them. Whereas the Raison required living cells to test the drug, most of the other departments weren't so fussy. For them, the cells didn't need to be coddled, nurtured in a cocktail of growth factors and persuaded to settle down and grow in plastic dishes. They could examine fresh tissue taken straight from the organ, or sample the cells after only a few hours in culture—and these procedures were well underway by the time Claire arrived at work. Seeing the pre-dawn building electric with activity only increased her sense of unreality.

When the crickets began to sing, Claire broke with tradition and stopped what she was doing to listen. The room filled with the rhythmic pulsing, as punctual as always, and she recalled the very first time she'd heard their song, that long-ago September morning. Before Alan, before Joshua; before the idea, the accident and the regime of deception that had followed. Her new life then had felt on hold, just on the brink of opening up into a world of unknown freedom and possibility. What a contrast, she thought, to how it had all turned out—it was as if she had summoned up a black hole, and she and everyone around her was in the process of collapsing into it. But the cosmic tragedy was well in play, and she had no choice but to perform her allotted part.

The rumours began to sweep through the building as early at nine o'clock—NS3003 was working, people said, growing less tentative and more excited as the results continued to filter in. The extracellular fluid from the diseased brain had been clogged with aggregating SCAN/amyloid clusters, but increasing doses of the Son of Zapper had been just as effective as the parent drug in breaking them up in a test tube. Short-term, six-hour cultures showed similar promising results, tested by different individuals in independent laboratories using time-honoured biochemical techniques.

By lunchtime, the impromptu celebration had escalated into a full-scale party. Someone—people suspected Alan Fallengale himself—had spirited in crate after crate of champagne, and the canteen was seething with people. For once, Stanley said nothing about alcohol consumption on the premises. No one seemed to remember that Claire's tests had yet to be performed, or, if so, they were categorized as mere formality.

But Claire had not forgotten. The conviviality shot over her head without making even the remotest impact, and she stayed alone in her lab, preparing the Raison for its final battle.

If the normally staid Above Stairs was having a party, one could imagine the state of affairs down in the Pit.

"There you are, boss!" Roz sailed up, a necklace of fluorescent plastic flowers around her neck and a glass of champagne in each hand.

The music was throbbing so loudly that Joshua could barely hear her, let alone concentrate on his terminal, as people danced past in the darkened main space. Someone had strung up dozens of metres of fairy lights shaped like the letters G, C, A and T, abbreviations for the four bases of DNA, which blinked on and off in lurid asynchrony. His office, he had recently discovered, had been commandeered as a chill-out room, and reeked of marijuana, burning incense and microwave popcorn.

"Oops!" Roz fell into Joshua's lap, teetering over until he steadied her with a firm arm around her waist. "Brought one for you, boss."

"No thanks." He managed to deposit her on the adjacent chair without spilling anything. "I need to say sober."

"Why?" She peered into his face, downing one of the glasses and starting in on the second. "We've done *our* job—now it's down to the lowly biologists to do the mop-up."

He forced himself to smile. "Some of us have reputations to maintain."

She snorted, finding this amusing for some reason. Then she added, "Hey, I've just thought of something, boss!"

"What?"

"Son of Zapper. *Son . . . of . . . Zapper*. S. O. Z.—Sozzed!" She bent over in her chair, laughing uncontrollably.

"Listen, Roz, I'm trying to do a database search here."

She attempted unsuccessfully to focus on his screen. "I can't *believe* you're actually working on a day like this."

"Keeps the mind off things," Joshua said.

"So does this, my friend." She raised her plastic flute to him and then drained it in one swift movement.

After she left, looking for someone more fun to bother, Joshua returned his attention to the screen, which had actually displayed an empty desktop the entire time. He wished he had an excuse to go upstairs to see Claire, but assumed she would not want to him to seek her out. Meanwhile, the company continued to catapult towards its final reckoning, but he was convinced that, even if Claire's results were incriminating, nobody would possibly believe them in the current festive atmosphere. This gave him a feeling of surreal yet euphoric reprieve, like the postponement of an execution.

❧ ❧ ❧

Claire was curled up in the napping chair finishing the last of her sandwich when Alan and Ramon came in.

"Told you she'd be here, *hombre*," Ramon said.

"Why don't you join the party, my dear? I know you can't drink before your experiment, but there's no reason why you shouldn't enjoy yourself in the meantime. It's quite a scene downstairs."

"Everyone's been asking after you, *querida*—after all, if it weren't for you, none of this would be happening."

"I know. But I'd rather not . . . I'm too nervous."

"Nonsense." Alan took her hand and pulled her to her feet. "Everything is turning out splendidly. If anything, NS3003 seems to be *more* efficient than NS158."

"And Merriam just showed me some more encouraging results," Ramon added. "She's been testing the Son of Zapper on our standard human neuronal cell line and, as expected, not a whiff of RAJI-23's

281

harmful target gene gets turned on. So we oughtn't to expect those toxic side effects in patients."

"I insist, Claire. Just a few hours, then you're free to come back here and brood as much as you want."

❦ ❦ ❦

The canteen had cleared out considerably. Although empty bottles and glasses were still scattered about, the long tables were mostly empty, just older scientists having a quiet lunch or coffee, and those younger ones unfortunate enough to have important experiments to complete.

"Where'd everybody go?" Ramon asked, blinking.

Peter Klugg looked up from a nearby table. "The entire company is down in the Pit—or at least, trying to be."

"Why?" Alan asked.

"According to my students," Peter said, "it's too bright up here for a proper party. And Pelinore's apparently spent a large portion of his hardware budget on a decent sound system."

"Has he now?" But Alan just looked amused. "Shall we brave the fray, comrades?"

"I don't think I'm in the mood for that sort of. . ." Claire felt lightheaded at the prospect of seeing Joshua. Of bringing Alan into Joshua's domain.

"Ramon, we're clearly going to have to use bodily force."

Although Alan hadn't been drinking, there was an undercurrent of elation in his entire manner that made him seem years younger. He grabbed one of her arms, and Ramon the other, the men laughing as they escorted her across the long room to the stairwell.

❦ ❦ ❦

Joshua looked up at some point and saw an apparition on the other side of the improvised dance floor. Claire stood between Alan and Ramon, the men's arms about her shoulders. She looked unsound— dazed, pale and, as Joshua observed her more closely, sending out dull waves of unhappiness and tension. The men looked dazed as well, but only in the blithely bemused way of older men contemplating the excesses of youth.

Claire hadn't spotted him, probably because she was staring vaguely at the floor. He stood up and began to fight his way through the crowd, his body responding to a deep programme that was impossible to disregard. Halfway there, Ramon and Alan were tackled by Klaas, who was bearing a fistful of printouts and a no-nonsense manner, and Claire was left alone in the storm of flickering lights and thumping bass.

When she finally raised her head and noticed him, the look in her eyes was almost more than he could bear.

"You have no idea how happy I am to see you, *cariño*," he said.

The music was so loud that they might as well be speaking in a soundproofed room, but Spanish suited his feelings more than its utility in discretion. He touched her shoulder, scarcely a second, but it was enough.

Despite everything, she gave him a slow smile that somehow caught in his own throat. "You're still speaking to me?"

"Of course." He paused. "I'll admit that yesterday didn't exactly go as planned, but after I'd calmed down, it was clear that your staying away actually meant more than carrying on."

"I knew you'd understand."

"You'll always know where to find me." He felt himself filling up and spilling over, like a cup left out for days in the rain.

She nodded, battling to master her own emotions, and he couldn't help receiving the impression that he might not have long to wait.

"Claire, about your experiments. . ." He spread a hand, a hand that encompassed all the rampant jubilation around them.

She shrugged. "I know. It seems like a lost cause, doesn't it? But I've taken precautions."

"What do you mean?"

"Well, people can hardly fault the basic principle of the Interactrex, considering that it's jointly responsible for this entire alleged success story. But they *can* fault the logistics of assaying proteins from outside of cells—it's not designed for that, of course."

"How are you going to convince them?"

"I've made sure to have plenty of Alzheimer's mouse cell cultures seeded and at the ready. When it becomes clear that there are no detectable SCAN/amyloid clusters in the human Alzheimer's brain culture fluid, I can just show Alan that there *are*, in mice."

"Brilliant idea. Q.E.D."

"Let's hope."

"You know," he said. "In all the excitement, we've forgotten it's still a possibility that the first brain was an anomaly. And that all these celebrations really do herald a happy ending."

She shook her head. "Of course it's possible . . . but I don't believe it for a second."

⚜ ⚜ ⚜

Joshua was soon hauled off to dance by a smiling, redheaded colleague. And then Claire caught sight of Merriam across the room, a fluid wraith in an aquamarine dress, pale hair loose and falling down her shoulders as she laughed and pulled playfully on Alan's hand. Alan looked to be urbanely protesting—the clash of coercion and resistance—but Claire still grew hot with an unexpected surge of jealousy.

"Saved by my better half," Alan said, face brightening at her approach. "Claire, do tell Merriam how clumsy I am."

Claire's heart was beating out of sync, as if it were trying to waltz the tango.

"Only on the dance floor," she replied smoothly. "But it's sweet of you to entertain him in my absence, Merriam."

Her sea eyes burning with resentment, the woman moved off and Alan swept Claire up in his arms, a beautiful dancer after all. "It does a jaded old man good to witness your efficient brutality!"

"I feel as if I could tear her limb from limb." She was appalled by the violence of her unexpected reaction—and by the sight of Joshua over Alan's shoulder, moving gracefully with the statuesque redhead. The whole thing was degenerating into farce. "Can we please go back upstairs now, Alan?"

"But I'm having a lovely time." He bent down to deliver a lingering kiss, completely heedless of the rest of the company. And of course, on a day like this, no one would even notice. Except one very observant, very sensitive man.

She pulled away. "It's nearly three o'clock."

His feet came to a standstill. "You truly are dreading this, aren't you? Very well, let's go up to In Vitro and see if the cells are ready, then get it over with so we can celebrate with clear consciences."

"You *will* stay with me, Alan, won't you?"

"Nothing could keep me away. I don't care if it takes all night."

284

But Claire knew that clinging to him under these circumstances was about as effective as a drowning woman latching on to a slab of concrete.

Machines like the Interactrex are the eyes of modern science. Humans rely on them to see what they see without caring about the implications. Numbers on a screen have no interest in diseases like Alzheimer's or drugs to battle it; they pay no heed to the intense personal interest with which most scientists imbue their so-called impartial hypotheses. Machines don't "want" something to be true; they only tell their operators what, in the limits of their mechanical eyesight, lies before them in the physical world.

There are some researchers who are so enamoured of their theories that they refuse to believe any evidence against them. But a truly good scientist will heed the blind eyes of his instruments no matter how devastating their insights might be.

Claire did not complete her experiments until one in the morning, Alan with her every step of the way as promised. After he managed to recover from his horror and shock, he suggested driving back to Amsterdam so that she could be among her books, and perhaps somewhat comforted. He would have preferred his house for the same purpose, but for the first time in his life, he truly was more concerned about someone else than about himself. For the same reason, he did a fair job of hiding his feelings of panic and desolation, but once he had managed to calm her down and she had fallen into an exhausted sleep, he got out of bed and prowled around her moonlit flat, too disturbed to rest.

It may seem like a tremendous coincidence that of all the thousands of books in the room, he would happen to alight on that particular one. True, Claire had been dogged by such events her entire life, both the trivial and the deeply consequential, but Alan himself could not lay claim to more than his average share.

Maybe it wouldn't seem so coincidental to someone who knew that the book had not been returned the previous night to the long rows of colourful spines and thereby rendered anonymous among the multitudes. Instead, after Claire had consulted the book's unusual contents to refamiliarize herself with the rules of the game, she had been in too much of a hurry to remember to put it back, and it had been left carelessly on the otherwise bare coffee table. Having gone to the train station directly after dropping off her letter, Claire had not been back to the flat since.

Of course from then on, it was inevitable. Desperate for solace, Alan could not be blamed for turning to the book that his lover had so recently touched, blue and solitary and innocent on the smooth expanse of glass. And naturally he could not be blamed for letting the volume fall open at random, an act which is guaranteed to favour two pages between which a piece of folded paper had been inserted.

Alan had always been a curious man, which was one of the reasons why he was such a good scientist. He didn't understand Spanish, but in context, the meaning was all too clear. And though love letters can be years old, and therefore long since rendered irrelevant, this one looked especially fresh. Moreover, Joshua had been a colleague of Alan's for many years, four of them in very close quarters indeed.

And he had very distinctive, spindly handwriting.

Claire roused only briefly when Alan left her at dawn.

"Do you have to go?" She clutched sleepily at the sleeve of his coat.

Alan sat down on the bed, looking her over with an intensity that would make sense only in retrospect.

"I must speak to Stanley and Ramon as soon as possible," he said.

"Let me . . . let me come with you."

"No." There was a long pause. "I want you to take the day off, sleep yourself out. No point in endangering your health. I'm sure that most of the company will be off sick after that party anyway, and nobody will notice . . . or indeed, care."

If Claire detected the chill behind his words, she was too drowsy to give it much credence at the time, or to remember it later.

Alan leaned down and kissed her on the forehead, his lips cool as ashes in the grey morning air.

"Goodbye, Claire," he said.

Part IV

❧

THE GLASS HEART

Chapter 36

⚜

Joshua arrived at work the next morning at more or less the usual time. He was disappointed that Claire had not managed to inform him in some secretive fashion about the results as promised, but he supposed that Alan had been sticking close. He was more expansive than usual in greeting the day porter, using the chat to establish that Claire's lab, framed in its small CCTV square, really was empty.

Marta on the desk was also uncommonly talkative—in English as always.

"Not many in yet today, Dr Pelinore," she said. "Dr Fraser, of course, and the rest of the big guys, working all night to finish some emergency deadline. A handful of scientists—mostly old-timers. Your Ms Baker" —if Roz was here after the state she was in yesterday, there must've been some problem— "and you."

"Have you seen Dr Cyrus by any chance?"

When she shook her head, Joshua took the stairs down to the empty Pit. He had expected armageddon, but the place was spotless, set to rights by the long-suffering night cleaning staff. The faint whiff of grass in his office was the sole reminder of yesterday's excesses.

He finally found Roz in the narrow annex where the main servers resided.

"Thank God." She glanced up, pale and haggard. "What a day to be on call. Stanley paged me at fucking five in the morning—there was a power failure, the server's apparently been down half the night, and they've some urgent..."

"Roz, you're positively green. I can take over now—go home and get some rest."

"I'm halfway through the recovery procedure, and trying to resuscitate some files they needed two hours ago." She rubbed her eyes. "Take longer to explain what I've done so far than to just finish the job myself. But I'd appreciate your help."

Roz had just left the room in search of some support documentation when Alan Fallengale appeared in the doorway, clearly startled to see Joshua sitting at the keyboard.

"I was looking for Rosalind, about some lost files." He cleared his throat, rearranging his features into their usual pantomime of pleasantness.

"I'm on the case now," Joshua said. "We should have them in about ten minutes."

"Good . . . we're trying to rush through some paperwork about the clinical trial." Alan was studying his face carefully. "We hope that NS3003 can be swapped in for NS158 with only a streamlined rodent trial, on the grounds that the chemical modification is so minor."

"I take it that Claire's experiments went well, then."

"Actually, no. Unfortunately, the Interactrex proved ill-suited for sampling proteins from outside of cells. Of course it was never designed for that purpose, so Claire is not to blame."

"That's a pity," Joshua remarked. "Did you have any controls . . . such as Alzheimer's mouse cultures?"

He nodded. "Those didn't work either, so we know it's a technical failure. But thankfully all the rest of yesterday's data were so positive that her experiment wasn't really crucial."

"True." The computer beeped, and Joshua entered a few rapid commands. Out of the corner of his eye he could see Alan's weight shifting, his left hand worrying a silver cufflink—unconscious evidence of deception, both. The second human brain must have confirmed Claire's hypothesis, and they were covering it up for the moment—surely this was the real purpose behind Stanley's all-night meeting.

"At stressful times like these," Alan said unexpectedly, "it's good to know that one has the love of a truly good woman."

Naturally Joshua was too practiced to react. "I can imagine."

"Can you?" Alan paused. "Do you have a girlfriend at present?"

"I'm afraid that's none of your business."

"But you must've had your share in the past, such an interesting looking man like yourself—and have experienced how relying on someone you can really trust can keep you grounded ... even sane, sometimes."

"Figuratively speaking, you mean."

"Of course." Alan's eyes had taken on a derisive shape. "What do you think of my taste in women, if you don't mind me asking?"

Joshua slouched back in his chair, lazy and impenetrable. "I think it's markedly improved in recent months."

"You approve of Claire, then?"

"I'd say you've been very lucky there." *A lucky son-of-a-bitch.* His heart rammed against his ribs.

"That's what I thought, too," Alan said. "But it's so difficult to tell, isn't it? Things can seem to be one way, and then turn out to be something else entirely."

The two old rivals stared one another down, and the pair of green eyes was the first to blink.

"Do alert us the minute you've rescued those files," Alan said, turning to go.

When the stairwell door clanged shut, Roz slipped in, looking even paler than before.

"He is *so* onto you, boss," she said, eyes wide. "You are so in *seriously* big shit."

❦ ❦ ❦

Claire woke at sunset, disoriented and unsure of when and where she was. She groped around the space next to her and found it empty.

Then she sat up abruptly, the entirety of the previous day settling over her in a cold drenching: the gruelling ten-hour session on the Raison as she painstakingly ripped apart Alan's beloved theory, passion, brainchild and place in history, one needle-jab at a time. His unequivocal belief, once all the controls had been performed, the subdued way he had taken it—the simple kindness he had shown her afterward. Although she had been drifting away from him for some time, the incontrovertible evidence of his own feelings was certainly thought-provoking.

And there was another sensation teasing her as well, just beyond reach: a feeling that something else was slipping away, that something was out of control, that something had altered besides an important scientific principle.

Claire was suddenly desperate to see Alan, to see—what? *Something,* with her own eyes. To convince herself that this odd dread was the result of exhaustion and had no basis in reality. So urgent became her desire to seek out Alan that, after failing repeatedly to raise him on mobile, office or home lines, she launched off to Centraal Station without remembering her promise to inform Joshua about the final result.

✤ ✤ ✤

The rain was coming down and the world was in darkness by the time Claire reached Alan's door. Realizing she'd left her set of keys behind, she rang the doorbell.

After an unusually long time, Alan appeared in his dressing gown. She knew immediately that something was wrong. The deep freeze was creeping into her blood even before she caught sight of Merriam Clark lounging just behind, wrapped in a towel and flushed with blistering triumph.

"You wanted something?" Alan asked pleasantly as the rain dripped down her face. He made no move to allow her in. "I was too occupied to answer my phone, alas."

"I don't understand." *God, with anyone but her.*

Merriam began to laugh, and a look of irritation flashed across Alan's face. He didn't even like Merriam, she saw, which made it a thousand times worse.

"Please give us a minute," he ordered over his shoulder. "This won't take long."

The girl flinched before scurrying off like a servile dog.

"Tell me why, at least." Claire was flooded now with a sense of numbness, and the false calm it provided.

"I rather thought you might have a few things to tell me."

"I don't know what you—"

"Liar!" His voice cracked like thunder. "You've been lying to me for weeks. Joshua told me the entire story of your torrid love affair."

"He. . ." Claire put hand to face, the numbness splintering into pain and anger. *He couldn't have. He wouldn't have.* "And you promptly invited *her* round without even bothering to ask for my side of the story?"

"It wasn't necessary," Alan said. "Your side of the story has been written all over your face, only I've been too deluded to recognize it."

"We didn't sleep together, no matter what he's told you!"

"He's welcome to you," Alan said, cold as a vein of subterranean ore. "I made it clear I needed absolute honesty, and you have let me down. Can you deny that you have done so?"

She experienced a weird image in her mind: Alan, hanging over the edge of a cliff, grasping desperately onto her hand as she let him slip through her fingers.

Eventually, she whispered, "No."

"I'll box up your things when I've a spare moment. Now, if you'll excuse me. . ."

He made to close the door, and Claire pressed her hands against it, tears slipping down and mixing with the rain.

"What about *your* honesty, Alan?" She sounded desperate to her own ears, desperate and mad, blurting out the first thing that came into her head. "You swore on your mother's grave that you wouldn't break my heart!"

"My mother," he said, "is alive and well and dying of Alzheimer's in a care home in St Albans."

The door slammed in her face.

Claire let herself back into her flat. She sat on the sofa, heedless of her hunger and her damp clothing. Over and over she saw Alan's face, lost and falling, shrinking to a point in the distance. She did not think she would ever fully internalize the harm she had inflicted on this already damaged individual; she had coaxed him out of his armour only to slip a sword between his ribs. There was not enough remorse in the planet's worth of heaviness on her shoulders to compensate for this act that she could never undo.

But she had to do something—not acting now was unthinkable. In her shock and confusion, the only plan she could come up with was to attack the betrayal at its source.

Claire sent Joshua a text message, asking him to come over if he was free.

He replied: *On my way*, and Claire waited on the sofa, a dead thing crushed under the rubble.

Joshua climbed up the steep stairs, full of doubts and questions. Why had Alan been so suspicious that morning—did he know, or only suspect? Had Claire been careless? What did she want from him now—only to brief him about the experiment? The ink of her love letter was embossed in his memory: *I've decided I can't come to you unless I've made a clean break.* Had something broken? But her message had seemed abrupt, and the fact that he'd been summoned, not run to, was also less than encouraging.

Claire stared at him from where she sat across the room, motionless and cold. She reminded him of a fossil of a once-bright thing, trapped in mud for billions of years.

He crossed the room, reached for her. "*¿Qué pasó, cariño?*"

"Don't touch me," she said in clipped English, flinching away, and he froze where he was standing, hand outstretched.

Then she said, "You betrayed me."

Joshua dropped the hand. "I have no idea what you're talking about."

"How could you do it?" She was looking at her carefully folded fingers, not at him. "And then lie about it as well?"

"I'm not lying, Claire—I'm baffled."

Again his words failed to register—she seemed to be reading off some internal script. "I know that all my lies make it hypocritical to demand honesty from others, but I thought we had an understanding, Joshua. I *thought. . .*"

"If I've done anything wrong, I apologize." Despite himself, his voice sharpened. "But I haven't a clue what you mean. Please tell me what this is all about."

"If you thought it was an easy way to secure my love, then you were deeply mistaken. In fact, it's had the opposite effect."

A few pieces began to manoeuvre into place. "What has Alan been telling you, Claire?"

"And that's another thing: I can't believe you assumed he wouldn't pass on what you'd said! I thought you were cleverer that that."

"I get it now." Joshua paced to one of the bookshelves, simmering there a few seconds before striding back. "And did it ever occur to you that *Alan* might be lying?"

"But how else could he have found out?"

"You're a scientist, Claire—what do you think? Maybe somebody spotted us in Museumplein, or saw you leaving my house. Maybe one of our conversations at work was overheard. Or maybe you weren't as *clever* as hiding your emotions from him as you thought."

For the first time, a flicker of hesitation crossed her features. "But Joshua, what could possibly motivate him to—"

"Jesus Christ, Claire, use your fucking head! Because he hates me, obviously, and if I'd managed by some miracle to beat him at something, he had to make sure to destroy it." His fingers were curling involuntarily into fists. "It doesn't look as if he had to try very hard—you've done most of the work yourself."

Claire put a hand to her face. "I . . ."

"Alan did speak to me today." Joshua cut her off, his growing anger infusing into his voice. Why should he hide how he felt any more? Hiding had got him nowhere in life. "But I didn't say a single thing that would have divulged our relationship—he was clearly well informed long before he showed up. And as you no longer trust *my* word, you can ask Roz—she overheard the entire thing."

"I . . . I don't know who to believe." She looked up at him beseechingly.

"How about the person with the better track record?" His heart felt like an exploding star. "How about the person who's shown you unconditional loyalty? How about the person who risked his career because you were too cowardly to tell the truth?"

He watched her reaction, a reaction that filled him with malevolent joy and only fuelled his rage. "And yet you automatically assumed I betrayed you! Do you know how many years it might take for me to recover from what you've done to me?"

She just sat there, letting his words lash her, splotches of colour like bruises forming beneath them.

"Well? What do you have to say for yourself?" He was breathless, breathless and teetering on the edge.

"Nothing." The syllables slipped out, bleak and moribund. "I have nothing to say. I have no words—I am completely empty."

"At a loss for words? I'll give you words." His frantic pacing had brought him again in front of a bookshelf, and he reached over at random, grabbed a tattered, ancient brown book and hurled it in her general direction. She jumped out of the way as it smashed against the sofa and blasted into two pieces, with yellowed fibres and dust and pages fluttering down into the sudden stunned silence.

"I don't ever want to see you again," he said, as she stared at the broken book with complete lack of comprehension. "Not tonight, not tomorrow, not in ten years' time. Never. Again."

Out on the pavement, his rage bled into the wet concrete and wet sky and seemed to fill up the entire universe.

❦ ❦ ❦

After the second door that evening had slammed closed another phase in her short life, Claire didn't move for many minutes. When she did, she didn't touch the ruined book. Edging past it, she ran into her bedroom and packed her rucksack—thoughtlessly, unmatched socks and random toiletries, forgetting her toothbrush and mobile phone—before locking her flat behind her with shaking hands.

Chapter 37

꧁

Rachel took Claire in that night, asking no more questions when it became clear that Claire was unwilling to speak. Claire spent most of the weekend lying in bed in the spare room, sleepless yet almost in a dream.

On Sunday, she rose from bed and found her friend sitting in a window seat flipping through a glossy Stedelijk Museum catalogue and listening to jazz. Rachel's skin was honeyed in the sunset, the glass of rosé in her hand glowing like a foetal heart. And this was the moment when Claire realized that something was wrong inside her head, some impairment of basic processes. She seemed only to be able to register her friend's likeness as a visual image—the words to describe what she saw wouldn't come.

"Okay, darling?" Rachel looked up, her voice impossibly gentle.

"I'm sorry for all this."

"Nonsense. You can stay as long as you like. I do wish you'd talk to me, though."

"I'm ready, now. Can I help myself to something first?" She wandered over to the cabinet.

"Easy there, darling," Rachel said as the large tumbler filled with whisky. "You haven't had a proper meal for two days."

"It doesn't matter," Claire said, settling on a chair nearby and taking a long drink.

Rachel waited, and finally Claire said, "I've ruined the company. I've ruined Alan. Maybe Joshua caused that, but I'm not sure. Either way, I've lost both of them."

"Oh dear, it's worse than I expected." Rachel looked her over sympathetically. "I think you'd better start from the beginning."

After Joshua's fury finally burnt itself out, he fell into a heavy, dreamless sleep. On waking the next morning, and throughout the weekend, a sense of unreality tried to mould him into a state of denial. But he knew what he had been accused of, and he knew how he had responded, and he knew that his response had been appropriate. Everything had gone as it should, and he ought to be rejoicing in his easy escape, in the perfectly tidy break he'd summoned the will power to engineer.

But he didn't feel relieved. He only felt great sadness. It hung on him like the sort of pressure that turns green life into black coal, like a permanent new fixture on his giant's frame. He wasn't sure he would ever be able to stand straight again.

Rachel wasn't happy either.

"But darling . . . surely you ought to give him the benefit of the doubt. He's always shown great integrity in the past. For starters, he kept your ridiculous secret for months, at great personal risk."

"It's too much of a coincidence that Alan suddenly twigged at that particular moment," Claire said. "The night before, his love was . . . overwhelming. The next thing I know, he's shagging that. . ." Her voice shook, unable to choke back the blind, bitter anger.

"I grant you a precipitating event seems likely," Rachel said. "And the fact that Josh and Alan were both at work that day is suspicious. But. . ."

"What?"

"You're not going to like this."

Claire shrugged, having heard so many words that she was beyond caring.

"What if Joshua did tell Alan?" Rachel said. "Does it really matter so much?"

Claire put down the half-drained tumbler, confronting the charcoal gaze in disbelief.

"It's betrayal, Rach. How can you call it anything else?"

"People don't always behave like you want them to, darling." A trace of vexation crept in. "Haven't you considered the possibility that Joshua might have been driven to confront Alan? —driven by *you*? Nobody, even someone as controlled as Joshua, can be perfectly rational forever."

"I don't want to hear this." Claire couldn't get the image out of her mind, the brown book split into two at her feet.

"When people are pushed, they eventually crack. Cause, effect— something I thought scientists were conversant with." She downed the last of her wine, filled up the glass again. "Maybe he was *compelled* to tell Alan because it seemed as if you never would. And maybe that's a motivation you might want to forgive, considering the depth of feeling that's probably behind it."

There was silence in the room, and the joint absorption of liquid poison.

"It's too late anyway," Claire said. "Even if I wanted to forgive him, he hates me."

Joshua stepped into the specified bar that Sunday night, and Rachel raised a hand from her corner table. It was dark and quiet, just a few groups and couples, scattered candlelight and soft music.

"Thanks for coming." She inspected him, but Joshua made sure there was nothing to be seen. She was, he realized belatedly, the enemy now. "I was starting to think you wouldn't."

He sat down. "What is it you want, Rachel? If it's about her, I'm not interested."

"She's in a terrible way, darling."

"Good."

"Don't be a complete imbecile," she said impatiently. "You can't expect me to believe that you've turned off your feelings for her like a tap."

"Oh, I've plenty of feelings."

She sighed. "Listen, I know you've got cause to be angry, but have you tried looking at it from her angle? She's just destroyed her company and Alan as well. She's lost and confused—you should be patient with her."

"Alan, destroyed? Please."

She looked at him but said nothing, as if she wanted to say something but had decided not to.

"And she was given information, Joshua; whether she should have believed it is another question, but the state she was in. . ."

"I didn't tell Alan anything."

"I didn't think you had, to be honest."

"Is that why I'm here? Did she send you to probe my story for weaknesses?" There was the fury again, as if loosening it once had placed it on ready call forever.

"She doesn't know I'm here." Rachel fiddled with her teabag, the first sign of uneasiness he'd ever detected in her. "She's drunk herself into a stupor. I don't want to be away for long."

Joshua wanted to curse her and walk out. How dare she threaten his precarious balance? Instead, he just sat there and seethed, trying not to picture it.

"She's considerably younger than we are, darling." Rachel had raised her head again. "I know it's easy to forget because she's so precocious, but in some ways she's like a child. That's one of the reasons I like her—I like catching glimpses of the world through her perspective."

He warded off more memories and focused on his anger and hatred, coddled it, gathered it into a useful tool.

"But that same element can also make her painfully stupid," she said. "And I don't think she's had much experience with broken hearts—hers or anyone else's."

"Well, she's making up for lost time now—three for the price of one."

"I can see I'm wasting my time." She scattered coins on the table and stood up. "I thought you were a certain type of person, but I was obviously wrong."

Joshua sat there a few minutes after she vanished, probing himself for leaks and eventually concluding that the main flood barrier of his resolve had held. He had passed some sort of test: it could only get easier from this point onward.

✤ ✤ ✤

Claire was wretchedly, repeatedly sick, disgorging the spent secrets one after the other, mismatched tissue transplants that her body had finally decided to reject. Long after her stomach was empty, it kept trying to purge itself of the dark lies and the collateral damage they'd inflicted.

On Monday morning, Rachel called up NeuroSys and told them that Claire was too ill to come to work.

Claire sat on a riverside bench that afternoon, not her usual one but a seat further south near Rachel's flat in the Rivierenbuurt, just where the Amstel started to curve westward. Her internal chill was untouched by the sun, and she was bewildered by this strange, weekday aspect of her normal environment. Instead of swarming with the sleek club skulls, the water was spotted with elderly ladies and gentlemen slapping the green surface arrythmically with their oars, encouraged by indulgent young coxes. The street traffic was sparser and the entire city seemed similarly slow-paced.

Her brain felt sluggish, too. The alcohol had cleared from her system, and what was left was that peculiar emptiness of thought— at least, of words. Of images she had plenty: Merriam Clark, the sexual flush spread across the fine skin of her throat and chest like a sunset; Alan's closed face and cadaver eyes; Joshua's vivid hatred, more terrifying than she could have possibly imagined.

But the words—her constant companions since before words existed—seemed to have abandoned her for good. Not a scrap of poetry, not a metaphor or simile, not even a vivid prosaic description had come into mind since Joshua had hurled the book at her. If she'd been her normal self, she might have thought that she felt as if some-one had taken away her eyesight, as if she were still in that shadowy place before discovering Braille and the white stick.

At least she'd found the strength to prepare toast and a boiled egg, to keep them down, to take a short walk. The oxygen would have rejuvenated her if there were any red blood left to stir. Instead, she pictured her circulatory system as a network of gossamer tubes and sacs, filled with a colourless fluid, pumped around by an arti-ficial heart—vitreous, efficient, just keeping the minimal functions running.

Rachel came home early to check up on her houseguest.
"You're looking a bit better, darling."

"Sober, you mean," Claire said, pulling the blanket more tightly around her shoulders: a futile attempt to warm up her transparent, wordless insides.

"Will you be well enough to go to work tomorrow?" Rachel asked.

"I don't know how I can face everyone." Everyone—and particular someones.

"You've got to eventually, darling. And the sooner, the better." Rachel paused. "Are you still angry with Joshua?"

"I don't know." This was honest. "I can't seem to feel anything anymore."

❦ ❦ ❦

Well, and *was* she still angry with Joshua?

Because the words were gone, Claire tried to think about it in pictures, in a series translating loosely as follows:

She had misplaced every last bearing in the sea of her muddled actions and feelings and motivations, and now that sea had glazed over with a thick crust of pale ice, trapping her motionless in it, a bottle sheltering a message that would never get delivered, a glassy thing half stuck in ice, half exposed to the ruthless sky.

She didn't know if she was still angry with him. But somewhere underneath the rigid glass, she had a vague feeling that only he could save her, break her free and thaw her out and loose the message and make the words come back—make the brown book coalesce, fly backwards from the floor and into his hand, and from there into the bookshelf, his fury reversing until he had passed from anger to annoyance to puzzlement and finally to the concerned face and the outstretched hand and the sound of his voice calling her *cariño* when he'd walked into the room. And then somehow he might be able to stop the clock, before he'd backed his way right out the door and left her dead and alone on the sofa.

Was this anger, or lack of anger? Was this love, or lack of love?

She had no words, and without words, she could not distinguish.

Chapter 38

❦

Joshua sensed the change immediately, not a second after he had entered the building. It was sketched on the impassive face of the day porter, evident in the handful of employees he passed on his way to the stairwell, none of whom would meet his eye. The entire company knew about the affair, and though Alan Fallengale was hardly a popular man, group logic pronounced him the innocent victim.

And just like that, Joshua was a misfit again.

Down in the Pit, the atmosphere was marginally better. There was certainly a subdued feel to the morning social clamour, and he did catch people studying him in puzzlement, concern or surprise, but there was no underlying censure. Alan Fallengale didn't stand a chance on Joshua's home territory—if their beloved boss had done something wrong, there must've been a good reason.

Or more likely, it must've been *her* fault.

"We're going to the canteen for lunch," Roz said, later that day. When Joshua didn't look up from his terminal, she added, "And you're joining us."

"I was about to ask you to bring me a sandwich."

She positioned her mouth a few millimetres from his ear. "On today of all days, boss, you've got to show your face. Are you with me?"

He looked up at last, weighing the pros and cons of this folk wisdom.

Roz's voice dipped even lower. "I asked around . . . Claire's fallen ill, apparently, and Alan's in Rotterdam, negotiating some deal."

Joshua finally allowed himself to be escorted to the canteen, flanked by a group of brash, defiant colleagues and still so distracted by the thought of Claire being ill that he hardly noticed the awkward chill that seemed to spread out in waves at their passage. He came out of his reverie when Ramon looked up from his table and made brief eye contact. In that moment, Joshua was hit by the older man's anger and disappointment, and, most unusually, it was Joshua who felt the need to look away first.

✤ ✤ ✤

Roz poked him in the ribs, and Joshua looked up from his lunch to find Stanley Fraser standing behind him, his usual grey-suited, deceptively baffled self.

"Joshua ... sorry to disturb you, but I wondered if I might have a word with you in my office when you are finished?"

"Certainly." If Joshua hadn't been so startled, he might almost be amused by the look on Matt's face, who was sitting opposite. He thought fleetingly about the issue of downsizing.

"Take your time, lad." Stanley's tone was congenial, matter-of-fact as he strode away.

"It's been nice knowing you," Matt said.

"Shut it, moron," Roz hissed.

✤ ✤ ✤

"What can I do for you?" Joshua slung himself into what was known in company parlance as "The Hotseat." To be summoned there at any time apart from one's yearly assessment was seldom a good sign.

Stanley intertwined his fingers, steeple at one end and the loose thumbs tapping nervously, then leaned forward without his usual hearty preliminaries. "It's about the Zapper, Josh."

My God. It was finally happening. Joshua's anxiety about being told off for an ill-advised peccadillo distorted into something much more serious. Was the truth going to be disseminated in controlled concentric circles, to Department Heads and Senior Scientists first, as if any order could possibly stave off the inevitable rumours and outright stampeding panic amongst the troops?

"Tell me."

"Well, as you probably know, our financial status is fairly unstable at the moment." He took off his wire spectacles, then put them back on again. "Every month the clinical trial is delayed is a month later that we recoup our costs. The venture capitalists we're courting at the minute are highly strung."

Joshua nodded, not understanding where this was leading.

"We *had* been trying to cook up a plan to convince the regulatory bodies to let us take some shortcuts with the testing of NS3003."

"Alan mentioned something about that on Friday." Joshua began to feel his usual *déjà vu* as a suspicious pattern struggled to clarify.

"Well, he's determined to push for this shortcut because he thinks the chemical modification won't alter the drug's fundamental pharmacology—apart from the dosage, of course, but that's got to be established in a Phase I trial anyway."

The pattern rammed home, and the truth spread before him with breathtaking simplicity. Stanley didn't know about Claire's result. And he didn't know because Alan hadn't told him.

"Whereas Ramon feels more cautious and is reluctant to forego very extensive animal trials. I, personally, am on the fence."

"So what do you want from me?" Keep it steady, keep it calm.

"The Universal Aggregation Principle is my life's work. I think people forget that sometimes, with Alan and Ramon being so visible." Stanley took off his glasses again, revealing weary eyes. "And the Zapper is its culmination. As much as I want the company itself to flourish, the most important point, for me, is to make a difference to Alzheimer's patients, and to ensure that people are not harmed by any drugs that we eventually develop. Money is nothing next to that goal—a safe and effect cure for neurodegenerative diseases. What I *want*, Joshua, is a third opinion."

"But I'm no chemist or pharmacologist, Stanley. I'm not sure how a bioinformatical opinion will help."

"I don't ask you in your capacity as a computer wizard," Stanley said. "I ask you as the fourth most senior member of this company, as a colleague from the beginning—as someone I respect and trust. I know you've a reputation for intuitive thought, lad. What's your gut feeling?"

Silence filled the room. Joshua realized that if he wanted to come clean, now was the time. But he couldn't see a way to do it: the trap that he and Clare had devised was seamless.

"Personally, Stanley . . . I would advise caution."

The words probably sounded as lame and unconvincing to Stanley as they did to his own ears.

❧ ❧ ❧

After Joshua left Stanley's office, he went into the nearest toilet and stared at his black-and-white reflection. The eyes looked evasive. He was remembering another crisis, another meeting with Stanley, one February ten years ago. Ramon had been present as well—Stanley had known better, by that point, to invite Alan.

"I don't understand," Stanley had said. He was holding a letter in his hand, the letter Joshua had written to explain why he was refusing the promotion.

"I'm not interested in business," Joshua said. "I want to do this bioinformatics thing properly. Roz isn't enough—I need more people, Stanley, and space, and equipment, and if you let me have them then I'm going to be too busy to worry about anything else."

"But we *need* you, Joshua." Stanley put down the letter. "We're about to acquire seventy new people, lad. You've been with us since the start. We're a family now."

"I wouldn't be good at it."

"I don't buy it." Ramon spoke up for the first time, eyes sharp. "I'm going to have a twenty-person lab to run, but *I'm* not going to shirk my responsibilities. This is all about your bust-up with Alan, isn't it?"

"I don't know what you mean."

The subsequent stare-down produced the usual winner.

Stanley looked at Ramon, whose head was still bowed, then at Joshua, who had made himself stony and untouchable. Then he said, "You've obviously made up your mind, lad, so there's no point in wasting my breath."

"What about my budget request?"

Stanley sighed. "Of course I'll give you whatever you require."

❧ ❧ ❧

When Joshua returned to the main space of the Pit, the entire room turned around and quieted at his entrance.

"Well?" Roz verbalized the unspoken anticipation.

"A routine question for their big deadline," Joshua said, shrugging, and there was a collective cheer, a veritable fusillade of foam artillery, and someone nudged up the volume on the CD player.

"Thank God for that," Roz said, when he slipped into the free terminal next to her. "Meanwhile, the most incredible gossip has trickled down. . ."

She sounded more worried than delighted.

"Tell me," he said quickly.

"Apparently Alan's negotiations in Rotterdam are with the Dutch subsidiary of a big French pharma." She paused. "Apparently it's about the sale of equipment . . . one particularly large, expensive piece of equipment."

Joshua gaped at her before re-establishing control.

"People are saying it's because the budget is critical," she continued, "and the stroke project is going to get axed for the good of the whole. But *I* think it might have something to do with Alan trying to get rid of Claire."

He stood up. "Roz, I need to see you in my office."

For once, she got up and followed him without comment.

He shut the door, then allowed Roz to see every last manifestation of his mood.

"Boss. . ." She went over to him and put her hands on his shoulders, having to stand on tip-toe. "It's just a rumour. And even if it's true, and I'm right about his motivations, he'll never get away with it. It's almost impossible to fire someone in Holland—the employment laws are stupendous. Unless she'd done something wrong—and cheating on a member of upper management doesn't count. Even if they remove her machine, the law requires that she be retrained, repositioned. . ."

Joshua was shaking his head, and Roz dropped her hands. "What is it, Josh?"

"You'd better sit down. I've got something to tell you."

🌿 🌿 🌿

Roz was still staring at him, transfixed in horror.

"This is. . ." She stood up, ruffled her orange hair, smoothed it back and sat down again. Then, "But wait a minute, boss. You say that Claire never told you herself what the result was."

307

"As I said, things degenerated too quickly for that."

She crossed her legs, uncrossed them. "Yet she promised she would get word to you."

"Yes, but there were extenuating—"

"Maybe Alan wasn't lying. Have you thought of that?"

"What do you mean?"

"I mean, maybe Claire never *did* the crucial experiment. Maybe she lost her nerve at the last second. You said she was terrified at the prospect, right?"

"Yes, but Roz, that's absolutely not an option."

"Why not?" Roz's gaze had taken on a feverish glint. "Who would blame the poor girl for not having the courage to go through with the *coup de grâce*? Especially after that mother of all celebrations to the contrary?"

"No. I can't believe that, Roz. She promised me she would do the experiment. Given a choice between Alan and Claire, I know where the truth is more likely to sit."

"She'd been lying like a pro for months." Roz's face was expressionless.

"Not to me."

"How can you be sure?"

"I'm sure." Where was all this faith coming from, after the fury had seemed to kill it? Why were these tiny green shoots sprouting from the black mud?

"Maybe she went through the motions that night, put on a nice display for Alan, faked the technical problem and ended up with a hard drive full of meaningless numbers."

"My God, Roz. The hard drive." Joshua stood up without realizing he had done so. "I'd been thinking Alan was selling the Interactrex to prevent Claire from reproducing her results, in front of more reliable witnesses, at the next hospice death—so he could collect his milestone payment and quit, long before anyone found out the truth. But what if it's also to remove the immediate incriminating evidence?"

"She'd back up her work, surely."

"People are saying they didn't finish until after midnight, and Alan was probably extremely upset—taking time to burn a DVD was probably the last thing on her mind. And even if she did, she not in today, so how do we know Alan hasn't stolen those DVDs by now?"

"Slow down, boss." Roz stood up too. "So you aren't buying my hypothesis, I take it?"

"Listen to me, Roz." He took one of her hands in his, let his sudden calmness spread into the warmth of her palms. "Do you trust me?"

"More than anyone," she said. "Unconditionally. I know I give you grief a lot, but. . ."

"Good. Then please, can you just trust that my instincts are correct? If it turns out I've misjudged her on *this* issue, then I'll never ask anything of you again."

"Are you sure you're not letting love muddle your intuition?"

He sighed. "That's all over, Roz. It looks as if I was wrong about her being the one. But this is about honour, about doing the right thing for the company and for Claire's reputation."

She gave him a peculiar look, then eventually nodded. "I'll give her the benefit of the doubt, then. And I'll help you as well—I'll do whatever needs to be done. That probably goes for anyone else down here."

"I know that." He squeezed her hand, trying to think. "But we'd best keep this between us for the moment. What is the best way to rescue those files? Claire keeps her room locked, of course, and the Interactrex isn't connected to the server."

Roz freed her hand, put both of hers on her hips. "Leave that to me, boss."

❦ ❦ ❦

At 16:37, the Pit received an emergency call from one Dr Indira Malmuti, reporting that her connection to the server had unexpectedly terminated. Roz was careful to raise a fuss, complete with rather thought-provoking obscenities, until the entire Pit knew of her displeasure about being on call for a potentially lengthy job so close to clock-off time.

Dr Malmuti's workstation, it seems, held a crucial, half-finished report about the predicted crystal structure of NS3003 bound to amyloid proteins that upper management needed for its shortcut proposal, and for some odd reason Joshua, in his capacity as the System Administrator, was unable to access the file remotely.

The fact that the workstation in question was located in the adjacent room and next to the Interactrex 3000, separated by one flimsy wall, did not occur to anyone.

When Roz discovered the faulty internal cable, along with the architectural considerations that meant drilling access would be easier from

Claire's room, there was no question that the day porter would provide her with keys. Roz noticed that the Interactrex had been left switched on when she slithered behind the great bulk of the hot, breathy beast. The relevant region of wall happened to abut the back of the Interactrex's main computer casing, and Roz's activities with the faulty cable were completely invisible from the watching eye of the CCTV camera mounted in the corner.

At 20:14, just a few minutes after Dr Malmuti's file was finally restored, intimate digital information began to flow between the Interactrex's hard drive and that of the System Administrator.

"That's all of them," Roz said with satisfaction, reaching for the mouse. "Let's check that most recent file, created at 00:32 on Friday morning."

Joshua and Roz were both sitting behind his desk, and the office door was closed, even though everyone else had gone home.

"I doubt that it. . ."

And sure enough, an error message flashed up immediately:

```
The document 'ad_hu_000077.inx' could not be opened, because
the application program that created it could not be found.
```

She sat back, miffed. "What sort of file extension is that?"

"That's what I was trying to tell you," Joshua said. "Claire's data are formatted using the Interactrex's dedicated software. We've got to pull that programme and all its plug-ins as well, in order to read the numbers."

His hands had already started to rush over the keyboard, riffling through the Interactrex's brain. He felt invincible.

About a minute later, when the task bar indicated that only about forty percent of the programme folder had been copied over, the laptop emitted a polite ping and displayed a helpful dialogue box:

```
Network error: the connection to file server 'Interac-
trex3000' has unexpectedly quit.
```

Roz produced a string of syllables that were much less helpful and polite.

"Any ideas?" Joshua kept his voice calm as he failed for the fourth time to raise the Interactrex 3000.

"I did a quality job up there, boss. I have no idea what. . ." She paused. "Hang on, maybe this isn't necessary. Surely Claire's saved the original programme CDs after she installed the software. Most people store them in our library along with the documentation. Let me check. . ."

Meanwhile, Joshua was scouring through the various branches of the network, trying to determine the source of the cut-off, a tiny wriggling of panic beginning to burrow into the lining of his stomach.

Roz returned, out of breath. "They're not there, boss."

"Unlike most people, Claire probably knows how to use the documentation," Joshua said. "I expect they're in her room, on the shelves with her data folders. Do you still have the keys?"

"No, but Joop's on the desk by now, and he thinks I'm a sweet, traditional girl," she replied with a grin. "Back in ten minutes."

In actual fact, it took her less than one.

Joshua looked up, and the face of his head technician was blanched, making her orange freckles stand out like a serious medieval skin disease.

"I know why we've lost the connection," she said.

Chapter 39

⚜

The following day, Claire mounted the steps to the cube of NeuroSys at the unconventional hour of nine o'clock in the morning. Although arriving earlier would have circumvented some of the social disapproval—at least for a while—she had vacillated on Rachel's sofa for hours, gripped with fear and adrenaline, panic threatening just underneath, before finally gathering the courage to head to the station. Once she was on the train, though, it got easier: as most commuters know, the daily routines can be permeated with the sort of mindless inevitability that could only work in Claire's favour.

The day porter's face was able to communicate a great deal using the minimum amount of muscular adjustment.

"A note for you, Dr Cyrus."

Claire took the folder paper without meeting the woman's eye and hastened to the stairwell. On the first landing, she scanned the memo:

If you would stop by my office as soon as you arrive, I will be in the position to explain everything.

—Stanley Fraser, CEO

Claire began to feel a deep, wobbling sense of premonition, like a pebble dropped into a well that isn't heavy enough to sink in a straight line. She continued up the stairs with the intention of dropping off her rucksack and jacket, and stopped flat outside her lab.

The door was wide open, and the room—aside from a bit of dust and a few scraps of printer paper—was empty.

On closer scrutiny, Claire saw the crickets for the first time. Or rather, she saw their corpses, smashed into the floor by disdainful soles.

❧ ❧ ❧

Stanley, appearing more nervous than angry, looked up from his desk when Claire rapped on the open door.

"Come in, my girl, do come in and sit." He fumbled with his spectacles, only managing to hook his left ear on the third attempt. "I'm glad to see that you've recovered from your illness. I. . ."

One of the scientific world's most famous prattlers was at a loss for words.

"What," Claire asked slowly, "have you done with my machine?"

"Technically, Marjory ought to be present. . ." Stanley avoided her eye as he depressed the button and murmured a few words to his secretary.

I am about to get the sack, Claire thought to herself. The prospect filled her with an overwhelming sense of relief: it would be a fitting end in almost every way that mattered.

Marjory burst through the doorway like a slap in the face.

"Thank you for coming so *promptly* this time," she said as she settled in, arranging her papers with fearsome activity.

"It's not as if I could do any work otherwise," Claire remarked.

"Indeed not, indeed not," Stanley said. "And that's why you're here, so I can explain to you the situation that has lead to this rather drastic . . . this rather drastic and sudden. . ."

He looked helplessly at his Head of Personnel.

"Cost-cutting exercise," she finished with a bright, sympathetic smile. "I'm afraid that, given the current climate, all of the stroke work is going to be put on hold, and its affiliated personnel. . ."

"Fired," Claire said.

"Lord, no!" Stanley blinked. "That's definitely a last resort."

"Although redundancies are certainly conceivable in future," Marjory said, with a look towards Stanley.

"No," he continued, "your lot will be absorbed into the Alzheimer's work which, as you can imagine, needs all the help it can get for us to make this trial happen as soon as possible. You've plenty of old-fashioned biochemical expertise in your CV, I see." He rattled a sheaf of papers for emphasis.

"Surely the clinical trial's not going to go ahead now!"

Stanley looked at her uncomfortably. "Well, I admit that our opinions have been divided about animal trials for NS3003, but after much discussion, we've decided to convince the regulatory bodies for a streamlined procedure."

"But that doesn't mean we won't all have to pull together and work hard to make it happen on time," Marjory said. "Which is why your efforts in such a new capacity will be so appreciated."

The pebble had grown to a stone, and the stone hit the bottom of the well with a resounding impact.

"Alan didn't tell you, did he?" Claire said.

"I beg your pardon?"

"About my results last Friday."

"No, he did," Stanley said, frowning. "And most unfortunate too, that you were unable to sample proteins from the extracellular environment. Still, all the other work done last week was conclusive."

"I *was* able to do the experiment, as it happens," she said. The truth began to buzz through her glassy veins like electricity—intoxicating, empowering, unstoppable. "Alan must've misinformed you. There *was* no Universal Aggregation in the human Alzheimer's brain cultures: SCAN was secreted, but didn't bind to amyloid proteins."

"I beg your pardon?" Stanley repeated, blinking.

"While in contrast, the control Alzheimer's mice showed beautiful SCAN/amyloid clusters outside of cells. It's a species difference, Dr Fraser. The Zapper, whether it's 158 or 3003, in the nucleus or kept away, is never going to be able to cure human Alzheimer's disease."

There was a long lapse as they stared each other down.

"I don't understand," Marjory finally said, voice small and uncertain. Claire had almost forgotten that she was in the room. "What is she saying, Stan?"

Stanley slowly took off his glasses.

"It must be an artefact, a technicality," he said. "An anomaly."

"I doubt it," Claire said. "It's the second time I've seen it."

"The *second* time?"

She quickly explained about the first hospice death. "But I was too scared to tell anyone." Surely, surely the beauty of this belated truth would not be sullied by the harmless omission of Joshua Pelinore's name . . . just this once. "I was terrified, and covered up the finding."

"Covered up a finding!" Marjory exclaimed. "Why, that's—"

Stanley's palm cut her off, his eyes hardening into steel. "Alan said that it wasn't technically feasible for the Interactrex to measure extracellular binding. He told me he was there the entire time."

"Well, it *is* feasible. And if you don't believe me, you can ask my former colleague Dr Thor Ahrenkiel, who's been doing it routinely in Copenhagen on the other 3000 model."

"Alan is a very clever man," Stanley said, almost casually. "It is not like him to misunderstand an experimental result so severely."

"Alan must be lying, for reasons of his own."

Marjory's predatory eyes, with their clotted perimeters of mascara, began to narrow. "Perhaps this outrageous accusation has something to do with your personal life, Claire. Something to do with a certain PhD student in Dr Ortega's lab."

"Marjory, would you be kind enough to leave us now?" Stanley's tone was flawlessly correct and courteous.

After the door shut, there were a few more seconds of absolute stillness.

"Now you listen carefully, my girl," he said. "I don't give a rat's whisker what you've been getting up to in your spare time—I never have been bothered by affairs and gossip, as long as the work gets done. I'll even go as far as to say that I was personally relieved to hear that a nice girl like you had finally wised up to a shark like Alan Fallengale— an observation that you will keep to yourself until the earth cools, mind." He paused for air. "But I respect Alan's *scientific* talents immensely, and in matters apart from the fairer sex, he has always shown complete and irreproachable integrity. What you are accusing him of now is very grave indeed."

Claire nodded solemnly. "I understand, Dr Fraser. And I know it might be difficult to believe, but I don't want revenge, or to harm Alan in any way—any more than I already have. Why should I, when it was *me* that made a mess of things?"

She felt the pressure behind her eyes that should have heralded tears, but they seemed to have dried up forever.

"If what you're telling me is true, why do you think he might have done it?" His tone was entirely hypothetical—he didn't believe a word of it, she saw.

"Maybe he's in denial," she said. "God knows I was the first time around. Maybe he believes the Zapper might still work by some unknown mechanism. Maybe he thinks the brain is an anomaly, but it's too risky to bring the company down to let everyone know. Thanks to me, he was not aware of the first result."

"Steady on, hey?" Stanley passed her a tissue as if he, too, could detect the invisible tears. "But look here, as much as it's clear you're a decent and intelligent person, it's still your word against his. Have you any proof?"

Claire experienced several vivid images in her mind: her empty laboratory, with nothing remaining to cast shadows or shelter itinerant insects. Joshua's spindly handwriting, not spelling out love, but describing how to overwrite the files into oblivion. The stack of printouts, going up in flames in her kitchen sink, and the strangely satisfying way the DVDs had shattered into silvery pieces beneath her hammer, in a way that had brought into mind, at the time, a famous poem about a curse by Alfred Lord Tennyson.

"The only proof was on the hard drive of the Interactrex 3000," she said.

"Which would've been automatically wiped, for corporate secrecy reasons, before the workmen dismantled it last night." He seemed to think about what he'd just said, then carried on more thoughtfully. "Part of the superior deal Alan managed to swing in Rotterdam involved the haste with which we were able to provide the goods." He paused again. "Surely you've backed up your data?"

"Not on Friday . . . it was one in the morning, Dr Fraser, and both of us were devastated."

"Hmmm." Stanley put his glasses back on, stared into space for a while before making eye contact once again. "I'm afraid I'll require a good, long think about this, Claire. To be frank, I probably *won't* be able to take your word over Alan's. I certainly won't be able to justify it to the others."

"I understand," she said. "Do whatever you have to do. At least if the trial goes on with NS3003, it won't do the damage of the original compound. At least I've managed to save a few people a bit of pain and discomfort."

For some reason, this seemed to affect Stanley more than all her other explanations.

"Listen, my girl," he said. "In that act at least, you *have* done us a good turn . . . this is a matter of public record, and one which I will certainly attest to if necessary. It's only a pity you didn't come forward earlier with the other matter . . . but then, you're very young, aren't you?"

Tears should have been absolutely streaming down her face by now.

"And I hope to God you've just made an honest mistake about the Universal Aggregation Principle," he said.

"Me, too," she managed to get out.

"You are hereby suspended from duty with full pay until further notice," he said. "Go home, get some rest, and try not to worry. We'll be in touch."

Try not to worry . . . about as impossible as . . .

But no appropriate simile would come.

❧ ❧ ❧

Claire had two more errands to discharge before she left the building forever.

Alan was shocked to see her standing in his office. Ramon's expression was a good deal more complex: surprised, too, but also angry, sad and confused.

"I'd better go," Ramon said, getting up hastily.

"No, I'd prefer it if you stay," Claire said, and he sank back down, seemingly mesmerized by the authoritative quality of her voice.

"There is nothing you could possibly have to say to either of us," Alan said.

"Why didn't you tell Stanley and Ramon the real outcome of my experiment, Alan?" The indomitable electricity fizzed underneath her skin. "What are you playing at?"

"I have no idea what you mean," he replied smoothly. "I told them exactly what happened."

"What's she talking about, Alan?" Ramon demanded.

"You may have wiped all my data last night, but you can't hide the truth forever," she said. "Maxwell Bennett or Mads Thor Ahrenkiel would be happy to corroborate my findings. And the clinical trial is going to fail—why forestall the inevitable? Why give the patients false hope? Or worse, a placebo, when they could receive a more effective experimental drug? Why let Stanley axe the stroke department when it might be the only fallback?" She paused. "Is this something to do with the famous milestone payments?"

"Alan," Ramon said slowly. "What's going on?"

"The word has already spread that you had the unbelievable insolence to tell Stanley I was a liar," Alan said. "And all because you couldn't handle that I took a fancy to Merriam . . . for one night, at least."

"You leave that poor girl out of this," Ramon said sharply.

"What other lies did you tell Stanley about me after Marjory left?" Alan sounded almost pleasant. "He might not be so sympathetic when I tell him everything I know about *you*."

Ramon's face darkened, his eyes moving back and forth between Alan and Claire.

"Nothing you can say about me will make the Universal Aggregation Principle suddenly true again, Alan," she said. "You can get me fired, undermine my reputation with lies, make Ramon and everyone else hate me, but eventually the truth will come out. It always does."

"I *insist* that one of you tell me what the hell is going on!"

"You'll never believe me," Claire said to Ramon. "I've already accepted that Alan will win, but I thought I might be able to appeal to. . ." she turned to the other man, ". . .to some sense of decency."

"That's rich, coming from you." Alan's voice lashed out, a snake's tongue.

"I never meant to hurt you," she said, voice catching. She had worshipped words all her life, but it was only then that she realized how empty they were. Words only stood in for actions. "I've been stupid, and I'm truly sorry. But please don't take it out on the rest of the company."

"Get the hell out of my office," Alan said. "*Now*."

When Claire stepped into the main space of the Pit, the chattering and activity slowly dribbled out.

"I need to talk to Joshua," Claire said to Roz, who was sitting across the room, looking over a terminal at her with wide eyes.

"He's not in today."

"Why don't you leave him alone?" someone muttered. "Haven't you done enough already?"

"That's enough, Matt. I can see you in his office, Claire." Roz stood up, swept the room with a fierce gaze. "And as for the rest of you—get back to work."

Claire felt light-headed to be in this room that was so thoroughly infused with Joshua's personality.

"Where is he?"

Roz shut the door, shook her head. "I really shouldn't say."

"He's gone because of me, hasn't he?"

"Sort of. But that's all I can tell you."

Claire sank into the armchair, the chair where she'd shaken in fear and Joshua had looked after her until it was over.

"I don't blame you for not trusting me," Claire said.

"I have to trust you."

"What does that mean?"

"I can't tell you that either." Roz sat on the edge of the desk, gripping its rim on either side of her tensed body. "Listen, Claire, you've been a complete moron to accuse Joshua of betrayal—Joshua of all people!" She shook her head. "Still, I know how these things happen, and I don't hold it against you, honest. But as for his whereabouts now . . . it would be inadvisable to tell anyone. That lot—" she waved a hand towards the door, "thinks he's taking some well-earned vacation days."

"He's not at home, though, is he?"

"No. He's not even in Holland, so there's no point looking for him."

"Okay, I won't pry further. Only. . ."

"What?"

"Is he all right? Is he. . ."

Roz gaze seemed deep and troubled. After a pause, she said, "I can't tell you that either, because I honestly don't know."

"Look after him." She wanted to say *for me*, but it was no longer applicable. It never had been.

Chapter 40

❧

Joshua actually was all right, after a fashion, but mostly because he was heavily distracted.

"Good to meet you," Maxwell Bennett said, shaking Joshua's hand. "Your reputation precedes you ... our Bioinformatics Department refers to some of your algorithms as Holy Writ."

"Thanks for agreeing to see me at a moment's notice."

"If Claire's really in trouble, I've got unlimited time. Follow me ... mind your head through this doorway, son..."

Soon they had descended into the basement, and Joshua was staring at a vast, grotesquely enlarged version of the Interactrex, glinting under the feeble twilight of one greasy bulb, all patchwork and primitive parts, sprawled out and disappearing into shadows in every direction.

"I almost don't recognize it," Joshua said, awed.

"This is the Lady Jane," Maxwell said proudly. "And although they did a wonderful job in downsizing and jazzing up the commercial models, I must admit I prefer the original. But it does frighten off a lot of people."

"I can imagine." What he was really imagining was Claire, trapped in the dark and battling with this anachronism for four long years. But she hadn't been daunted—she'd slain the beast handily.

"Well, let's see what we can do with those files of yours." He slapped on the main console keyboard to rouse the Lady Jane's screen. Joshua pulled up a nearby stool and watched Maxwell feed the data into the computer.

"I'm afraid they won't be compatible."

"Don't worry, son, I get Interactrex files from Mads all the time ... the lad's impossible about trusting his own instincts, practically needs me to decide whether he ought to go to the gents. Not at all like Claire. You couldn't keep up with *her* for a second."

His fingers were moving rapidly over the cracked keyboard. "I finally had to write a programme to translate the damn files to Jane-ese so that I could hold Mads's hand with the least amount of bother on my part. One moment. . ."

He hit the return key, and the long strong of files with the extension 'inx' began to convert.

"This will take a few minutes," he said, running fingers through the mad tangles of his beard. "You mind telling me what this is all about in the meantime?"

Joshua gave him the very abbreviated version, leaving out key names and all references to the love triangle.

"Of all the asinine, unbelievably short-sighted. . ." Maxwell shook his head. "But if Claire tested it, you can bet that it was done properly. Have you notified Stanley Fraser?"

"No, I don't want to tell him until I've got proof . . . hopefully before Claire finds out about the cover-up and tries to do the job herself, empty handed."

"If her career gets ruined by this, I will personally fly over there and shake some sense into them." His voice crackled with anger, and in his microscopic reactions, Joshua read the protective response of a makeshift father.

"That's one of the reasons why I'm here," Joshua said. "Of course it's mainly for NeuroSys, but I wanted to clear her name at the same time."

"She's lucky to have a friend like you," Maxwell remarked.

Was she? Joshua remembered the hatred he'd hurled at her when she was probably at the lowest ebb of her young life.

"And you can tell Stanley Fraser that I'll gladly assay as many brains as he wants, in front of independent witnesses . . . okay, we're in business, son. Files all converted, uncorrupted and as tidy as you like."

❧ ❧ ❧

Over the next few hours, Joshua watched, fascinated, as Maxwell waded his way expertly through Claire's data. It soon became evident why he had insisted on doing the job personally rather than merely e-mailing the programme to NeuroSys; Joshua and Roz would never have been able to understand the information. Maxwell first had to

321

familiarize himself with her procedures, documentation and naming system, occasionally muttering statements like "clever girl, rerouting the Snakes like that ... ought to suggest it as a standard feature," or "oh, I see, EC stands for *extracellular*," or "would you look at those beautiful standard deviations!". He produced dozens of graphs and charts using an antiquated printer on the floor, and when it was all over, the two men hunched over the data, Joshua asking questions until he was sure that he understood enough to explain to Stanley.

"It's watertight," Maxwell finally pronounced. "All the controls have been done correctly, and everything was performed in triplicate with mice and human samples. The NS3003 compound does disrupt SCAN/amyloid clusters, but only in mice. And that's because your Universal Aggregation Principle only *happens* in mice, not in humans. In fact, it looks to me like beta amyloid can aggregate just fine all on its own. I'm afraid there's no other simple explanation: Occam's razor."

"But Maxwell," Joshua said. "I'm worried that Al—that they'll only claim that she didn't actually sample these proteins from outside the cell."

"Ah, but we *know* she did." He smiled. "Look here ... the background signature ... or lack thereof, is a dead giveaway. This looks just as clean as Mads's cerebral spinal fluid results. I'll make sure to make that clear in my final report."

"Report?"

"I'm not sending you back without a proper expert testimonial, son— no offence, but I'm bound to be more convincing than you."

"I appreciate it." Joshua paused. "Of course they could always claim that she didn't take samples from the right cells at all ... that the labels she entered into the computer don't correspond to what she actually did."

Maxwell rubbed at his unkempt hair in an absent gesture that reminded Joshua of Roz. "Well, you say she was observed the entire time, that this bloke was even around when she fetched the cells. So that person should have noticed if she'd been up to something funny."

"True." But Joshua, knowing Alan's eloquence, was not entirely convinced.

Maxwell paused, staring thoughtfully at Joshua. "Another thing. The observer claimed that Claire's experiments proved that seeing *any* proteins bind extracellularly was unfeasible."

"I heard him say it myself."

"He's made his claim now, so he can't change his story." Maxwell's smile took on an edge. "In the Alzheimer's mice, she's shown bona fide binding results from clear extracellular sampling." He slapped a hand on one of the graphs. "So it's *feasible*, all right. I'd say he's neatly trapped in a lie."

❦ ❦ ❦

Joshua took a train directly from Schiphol back to work and requested an urgent meeting with Stanley and Ramon, specifically stipulating that Alan be absent. Joshua was surprised at Stanley's immediate, unquestioning agreement to this condition, as if he already knew what Joshua was going to say. Even Ramon, he noticed, had lost his anger and was resigned to whatever was coming.

After the three men sat down, Joshua opened up his folder and began to speak.

❦ ❦ ❦

The worst part, for Joshua, had been Stanley's reaction—a slow crumpling, almost an ageing, as each graph and chart was pushed across the table. And then that deadened pause at the end, a full minute of silence. But Stanley didn't dwell in this state for long. Restored to his habitual energy, he buzzed his secretary to request an immediate private meeting with Alan Fallengale. An hour later, Joshua was called back to the office and asked to sit in with an emergency gathering of upper management—with Alan's absence hanging over the assemblage like an acid-green fog.

There had been much to hash over, both short and long term plans to be made. They decided to enlist Maxwell Bennett's help to reproduce Claire's experiments, when the samples became available. There was a general discussion as to whether the Zapper might still work in humans by some unknown mechanism—a prospect that seemed remote and therefore unlikely to sway the regulatory bodies. A committee was formed to determine whether any of the stroke work or other neurodegenerative disease projects might be mature enough to consider pushing as an alternative. But the overall outlook was unpromising; even successful companies were having trouble in the current economy, and one that

323

had probably lost its sole commodity didn't stand much of a chance. Stanley knew it, and so did everybody else.

Joshua had been struck by how bewildered people seemed without Alan. Although it was Joshua's first such meeting, it was obvious from body language that Alan had been a powerful guiding force, an essential element, in this operation. Joshua could even tell where he must have habitually sat, so frequent were the involuntary glances in that direction. Stanley, though outwardly brisk and decisive, could not hide the fundamental dissipation underneath. For the first time, Joshua internalized what Alan's worth really had been, even as he found himself more than capable of stepping into, and partially filling, those larger footprints.

After everyone else had left the room, Joshua paused just inside the door. Stanley was still sitting at the head of the table, staring at his notepad.

"I'm really sorry," Joshua said.

The older man looked up with a faint smile. "Thank you for joining in. I know you loathe this sort of thing, but would you be willing to attend these meetings from now on? There's bound to be a number of them, I'm afraid."

"Of course." Joshua was shocked that there'd been any question. He paused, then added, "Ten years too late."

Stanley stood up and extended his hand, completely free of irony.

"Welcome back to the family, lad."

Joshua wanted to speak to his department, but he needed some fresh air first. He slipped into the late afternoon rain and paced the narrow canal edging the campus of the fledgling industrial park. He was thinking about starting again. Where would he go, and what would he do? The one thing that seemed clear was that it was time to leave the Netherlands—it had nothing more to offer. He'd stay with the company for as long as he was needed and then—what?

It was a big world, and he was a capable man. He would think of something.

When he walked down the long corridor towards the Pit, he could tell that something was wrong. No music, no laughter. Of course the entire building, even the subterranean portion, would have heard the news by now—maybe they had all gone home.

But when he stepped through the door, he saw his people sitting there, clustered in chairs, drinking tea, talking quietly, not a single terminal in use.

"I'm glad you're all here," he said. "I've got something to say."

❦ ❦ ❦

Joshua went to his office afterwards.

He sat down at his desk, saw the spot where once, tulips not quite the colour of own his skin had pointed towards an invisible sky. He wondered, fleetingly, where Claire was, how she was. Maybe in a week or so he'd drop by, see if she'd accept his apology for losing his temper. Deep down, though, he knew he probably wouldn't bother. There wasn't much point; too much pain had lodged between them to regain even a patchwork semblance of their former friendship.

Roz tapped lightly on the open door.

"Nice speech, boss." Although she appeared tired, her smile was relaxed.

"You think so? I do hope they'll stick around for a while," he said. "Stanley might come up with one of his miracles yet, mesmerize an inexperienced venture capitalist with his relentless conversational skills."

"Well, we're bound to lose the odd undedicated one here or there, but the mood out there is fairly upbeat. Most of them are young and resilient ... not like us, eh?"

Joshua smiled too. Then, thinking of something, he rummaged around in his desk drawer and drew out a bottle.

"Fancy a drink?"

"Best offer I've had all day." She pulled up the armchair and collapsed into it. He filled up two glasses with *jenever* and they raised them.

"To the future," Joshua said, toasting his head technician with a flourish.

She echoed the sentiment before taking an appreciative sip. "So what are your plans if we fold?"

"Hmmm." The apéritif scorched his throat with its usual thoroughness. "I'm not sure."

"I thought you'd always dreamed of starting your own bioinformatics company." She looked him over speculatively. "This could be the perfect opportunity for you, boss. You've got an entire devoted department ripe for the picking—one who'd leap at the chance to work for you without an Above Stairs hanging over them."

"Hmmm." He could not deny that the thought had already occurred to him.

"Of course in the current unstable climate, it wouldn't be easy to raise the capital," she said, deflating a bit.

"I don't think money's such a big problem," Joshua said, with another smile. "But the thing is, Roz—business bores me senseless. I don't like the infighting. I'd just get caught up in the science and the entire enterprise would slide into the abyss."

"That's why you'd have to ask me to be your partner." Roz's eyes were bright and steady on his. "I love all that—you know I'm good at bashing heads, and I've always been keen to go back and earn an MBA. I could study nights, while we're getting established."

"While we're . . . Roz, are we still kidding around here?"

"I'm not—I never was. Are you?"

"Hmmm." Joshua took another sip, and felt the possibilities begin to open up inside him.

Chapter 41

Claire was starting to acclimatize to her new state of being. In pictures, but not words, she saw herself as having spent the last few days moulting a chrysalis. Only everything was in reverse, in negative. The casing had been made of warm, solid flesh, and what had emerged was brittle, transparent and flimsy, untouched and untouchable, a spent thing that could blow away with the next passing breeze. Her wordless metamorphosis was complete, and nothing could possibly harm her now.

It was Wednesday morning, and she was technically unemployed. Rachel's flat was a perfect environment for this advanced stage in her replication cycle, with its shelves full of oversized books of images—art, furniture, architecture, pottery, textiles, photography. She drank in the colours and shapes, trying to absorb them through her gauzy skin, to fill up the empty spaces within it. She could do this the entire remainder of her lifetime and never be complete.

✤ ✤ ✤

The afternoon slowly expired, bringing soft rains, damping down the city of Amsterdam and muffling sounds, smells and landmarks until all the edges were smoothed into a harmless blur.

Rachel had come home early yet again. Claire could tell that she was becoming increasingly worried about her.

"I wish you would talk to me, darling," she said, perching on the arm of the sofa where Claire lay.

Claire shrugged. "I'm fine. There's nothing left to say—I'm better now."

"You don't seem better at all. I think you're still in shock."

"Of course I'll be fired, and will need to decide what to do with my life, but I'll come up with a plan eventually. I always do."

"It's not healthy to repress everything. You can't just *decide* not to feel. And what about Joshua?"

"Joshua and I are finished. I've come to terms with that too."

"Look here, Claire, this is ridiculous." She hesitated, then pulled out a business card from her handbag. "A colleague of mine recommended an excellent therapist, a Brit, reasonably priced, offices just round the corner in Ceintuurbaan. I was thinking it might be a good idea for you to—"

"No! No, thank you. Honestly, everything's sorted. I've confessed all my sins and I'm free to start again."

"Won't you at least think about it? For me?"

Claire looked at her friend and finally took the card, its heavy stock gilt with the trappings of professional salvation.

"I'll think about it. By the way, I've bought all the supplies to make you a nice dinner, but after that I'm going home."

"I wish you wouldn't." Rachel pressed fingers into her knees. "I don't think you're ready to be alone yet."

Just then, the doorbell rang. Rachel went downstairs, and Claire could hear the murmuring of a familiar male voice.

"How did you know where I lived?" Rachel asked, and the voice continued, too soft to make out, except Claire thought she heard Joshua's name mentioned. "She *is* here, actually." Another rumble. "Let me ask first, okay? She's not exactly. . ."

Rachel's face appeared at the stop of the staircase. "Ramon Ortega, darling. Can he come up?"

"Yes, it's fine."

"Do you want me to stay with you?"

"Maybe it's better if. . ."

She nodded. "I'll be in my study. Just shout if you need me."

Ramon sat down, too overwhelmed to say anything for a good moment, a hundred different opening lines seeming to battle it out across his face and in his emotional brown eyes.

"You look awful," he finally offered.

"Thanks." She tried to smile, but faltered halfway there. She rubbed her frozen hands together instead, as if any effort could possibly ease her perpetual chill.

"I don't think it's possible to say what I'm feeling right now," he said. "I won't deny I was very angry with you, on a number of counts, and part of me still is."

Claire recognized then that he was using English deliberately to keep his distance.

"It's okay, Ramon. I understand." She managed the smile this time. "I broke your best friend's heart and you think I fabricated a problem with the Universal Aggregation Principle out of revenge. For all I know Alan's made up some story about me having a criminal record as well. Who wouldn't be angry?"

"You haven't heard, have you?" Ramon seemed to stop breathing for a moment. "Of course not . . . nobody knew you were here—and your mobile hasn't been working."

"Heard what? That I've been fired?"

Ramon told her everything, and Claire just sat, absorbing the story through her cellophane skin. Only one thing refused to clarify.

"Why would Joshua do that for me?" She looked up at Ramon at last.

"I had the impression that the company's interest was his main incentive." His brow wrinkled in puzzlement. "But I thought you two were lovers."

She shook her head. "Not really. Not technically, though I won't deny we were in love . . . but anyway, that's all in the past."

"But Alan said. . ." Ramon stopped. "*Qué idiota!* I am still trying to come to terms with how corrupt he really had become. I've had my suspicions for years, though I didn't want to admit it to myself. And with the way he changed under your influence, I had convinced myself that this loyalty had been justified. But. . ."

"Don't blame him, Ramon, for any of this. It's all my fault."

"Claire, really. How could it possibly be?"

Haltingly, she explained about Serena and the car crash, about the promise Alan had demanded, about how she was his second and last chance at redemption. About how she had been unable to stop herself from falling in love with Joshua, and how she had been trapped in her own web of lies, and that this had been the direct cause of Alan's ruin.

"He wasn't going to cover up the result initially, Ramon, I'm positive. And I know he didn't really care about the milestone payments.

329

It was only after he found out I'd been lying—something must've snapped."

"Unbelievable." Ramon stood up, went over to the bay window and looked out at the rain. His voice was tight with anger. "He had no right . . . *no right* to ask that of you, to lay such a responsibility on the shoulders of anyone, let alone those of a twenty-five year old girl."

"But—"

"No, Claire! Let's get one thing absolutely straight." He turned to face her, pale and grave. "The only person on this planet who bore the ultimate responsibility for Alan Fallengale's moral integrity was Alan Fallengale. And the fact that he tried to pass off this burden—forty-four years of dubious, wayward baggage—onto someone so unspoilt and ill-equipped as you is, frankly, disgusting."

She put a hand to her cheek, found it as cold as wax. "But he *was* a decent man, Ramon. I could see it. He was, before. . ."

"If there had been any decency, I have no doubt that you would've been the one to uncover it, even nurture it. But that doesn't change the fundamental point that he should never have forced you to sell your soul for his salvation. Do you understand?"

Claire tried to gather his words together, hold them in her hands, throw them onto the coffee table like dice until they came up sensibly. "Maybe a little. But I don't think I'll ever be able to forgive myself, all the same."

There it was again, that hole of darkness, inviting her to step in. It had been shadowing her for days, polite and patient.

"Truth and time, that's what's it will take," Ramon said. "Many of us will be coming to terms with what's happened for a while to come. Which is one of the reasons I'm here." He returned to the chair, sat down. "I need to know why you didn't trust me back in December, and come to me with the first result."

She thought about it, then shook her head. Before she'd shed her chrysalis, this conversation would have elicited yet more weeping, but the barren dryness was never-ending.

"I don't have the words to explain. I can't understand it myself."

He considered her a few moments longer before shrugging. "It's not really a fair question, is it, *querida*? Would I have done any differently at your age, in your shoes? Maybe not." His voice became gentle and the anger was gone. "And I doubt my bruised faith is anything that can't be repaired."

"I hope not. I can't bear the thought of your disapproval."

Both of them sat there a moment, just mulling things over.

"Incidentally," he finally said, "why didn't it work out with Joshua?"

Claire pulled the blanket tighter around her, a casing that she could never reverse time to crawl back into. "We had a fight. He left."

Somehow, this part of the pain wasn't a black hole one could escape into; it was an absence, a singularity, a void that her mind slipped around as a prism bends light.

"I see." He looked at her thoughtfully. "He's never been very good at fights. That's how he ended up down in the Pit in the first place."

"No," she said. "He said Alan didn't give him enough intellectual space."

Ramon snorted. "Alan never gave anyone space—he owned the entire universe! That's why we all learned to tell him to sod off—he'd move over if you kicked back. But Joshua refused—he just walked away. Of course he's a decent man, but we learned that he couldn't be relied on when things got stormy." He paused. "With recent events, I thought he was finally starting to change."

"I don't think so." She looked at her hands, pale and impotent.

"I'm sorry to hear that."

"And I'm sorry I let you down, you and Stanley and the rest."

"You told the truth in the end—and without a shred of proof to protect you." He reached over and patted her arm in a gesture very close to his normal affectionate briskness. "That took real courage—don't think we don't realize how much."

When Ramon got up to leave, she said, "What will you do if . . . when the company goes bust?"

He stood there, arms crossed.

"I've been thinking for some time how refreshing it would be to go back to Madrid, maybe return to academia," he said. "Try something new for a change. My wife would be thrilled and I've still got contacts. Of course this is a shocking situation, but there could be a positive side to it in the end."

"I hope so, Ramon. I hope it works out for you."

Later, as Claire left Rachel's building and walked down the pavement into the rainy darkness, rucksack slung over her shoulder, she paused at the first rubbish bin she passed and threw the business card away.

Chapter 42

❧

Claire let herself back into her flat, assaulted by stale air and the tang of rotting fruit. She flicked on the lights, put the grocery bag on the floor of the kitchen and opened up all the windows to the damp night air.

There was the broken book, still lying on the floor by the sofa. She was surprised to feel nothing on seeing this, but on second thought, was that really so unexpected? Nevertheless, she avoided dealing with it for as long as possible, putting away the groceries, throwing out expired bananas, watering the plants, charging her abandoned mobile phone. She checked her messages—all of them were from NeuroSys, which she deleted without even fully listening to.

Finally she knelt on the floor by the sofa and gathered together the broken binding, retrieved all the loose, yellowed pages and inserted them into their proper places. The presence of so many words was making her nervous. She spotted one last page, peeking out from under the coffee table, looked down to check its page number, and was just smoothing it into the book when one of the lines caught her eye.

The lost poem, tired of being lost, had decided to find her instead.

❦ ❦ ❦

Despite her shell shock, Claire was still able to appreciate the humour of this coincidence—should one categorize it as trivial or as deeply consequential? After she'd stopped laughing—a strange sort of laughter that echoed in the empty room and came back into her ears even stranger—she settled more comfortably on the floor to read.

The experience, on the whole, was disappointing. The words were flat, the emotions empty and the overall effect, decidedly anti-climactic. True, the description of the doomed knight was apt—skin of ivory, hair and eyes of the darkest midnight—and the plot was more or less what she had remembered: an honourable man, betrayed by the woman he loves, comes to a bitter end. But how she could have thought that this hackneyed, dead thing might have been a touchstone, a guide, a key to the secret heart of anyone, she'd no idea. This story had not been written for her and her alone. The one that actually *had* had been unfolding around her the entire time, and it was this that she should have studied, interpreted, tried to guide in the right direction. Instead, she'd followed words and shadows and secrets and ended up here, tasting the consequences of her bad choices and stupid mistakes like so much paper dust.

Claire went into her study, fetched some tape and repaired her father's book as best she could. After she'd returned it to the dark crevasse where Joshua had drawn it out, she went back to her restlessly precise tidying. It was when she was hoovering the last bits of fibre and particles of paper from under the coffee table that she noticed the second book, a particular blue book, sitting askew on the transparent surface.

She switched off the vacuum cleaner, silence roaring in her ears. She sat down on the sofa and picked up the volume thoughtfully. Claire always returned her books straight away—it was a habit of respect her father had drilled into her since she was strong enough to pull them from the shelves. She cast her mind back to that fervid evening, remembering when she'd taken the book down to look at Joshua's love letter. She could not, she admitted, recall putting it back, although she had a vague memory of tossing it on this table when she was searching for her keys.

Against her better judgement, she let the book fall open to where the note lay folded. But oddly, the pages shuffled by randomly, fluttering like bird wings, and did not alight by that special gravitation to any particular spot. Frowning, she flipped through the pages again, and then, in an act that would have shocked her father, turned the book upside-down and shook it unceremoniously.

The note was gone, and Claire, a scientist, accepted the facts. Occam's razor. The simplest explanation, and therefore the most likely, was that Alan had removed it.

The old Claire would have lost control at this point. But Claire was a new, glassy creature. She shelved the instrument of her own betrayal, put on her coat and quietly left the flat, letting the rain pour over her as she was absorbed into darkness.

❦ ❦ ❦

After the train arrived at Centraal Station and Joshua had peddled home in the pelting rain, he dumped his bicycle and set off for a walk along the river, too restless to stay indoors. His mind was unusually free of thought, just absorbing the environment: the spot-lit bulks of the Carré Theatre and the Hotel Intercontinental; the bridge lights reflecting starry curves into the water; a tram, shedding blue sparks like a passing meteor on the wires above.

Up ahead, he saw a figure sitting on a bench. As he drew nearer, the figure began to take on a familiar shape.

Joshua slammed to a halt, grip gone painful around the umbrella's stem. He stood there in the dark as rain galloped across the nylon dome and haemorrhaged down dripping from its metal teeth. He'd purposefully kept away, but still she'd washed across his path like ill-fated jetsam. And his first instinct was to run, as fast and as far away as possible, run away like he'd been running all his life.

Claire had been the only person in the past decade to draw out his violent temper. He saw before his eyes the arc of the brown book across the empty space of the room, and at that moment, he realized, with quiet clarity, that he had interpreted the patterns all wrong. The fury was only one half of the whole, only one part of the process. This had not been a tussle with a playground tormentor—he and Claire were adults, and their fight should have marked a beginning, not an end.

Did he love her or didn't he? That was the only question that mattered now.

❦ ❦ ❦

Claire looked up at his approach, gave him a faraway smile. "What a coincidence—didn't we first meet here?"

"God—you look terrible."

He sat down next to her, heart pounding. She was almost as pale as he was, and she was drenched, black hair slicked against her skull as if she'd

334

crawled up from the bottom of the river. And she was . . . slack, there was no other was to describe it, with a frightening deadness about her. She ought to be shivering, but she seemed somehow beyond that point.

"I'm fine." Her voice was slow and barely audible.

"Have you had a panic attack?" It was the only explanation he could come up with to explain her peculiar laxness.

"No. Just a few interesting revelations."

"You're going to catch pneumonia—how long have you been out here?"

"I have no idea." She smiled again, pupils strange and not quite focused on him. "I was just thinking about taking a swim. How it would feel to slip in, how dark it would be under the surface, whether the water would actually be warmer than my skin, how many minutes I could hold my breath. . ."

"Right—you're coming with me." He hauled her up by the elbow, and she didn't resist or say a single word as he put his arm around her and helped her stumble back to the gingerbread house. He stripped off her sodden coat in the entrance hall, steered her towards one of the guest bedrooms on the ground floor.

"Sit down," he ordered, and she sat. Her lips were blue in the light. She was still sitting there in the same position when he returned with a clean towel and an old fleece dressing gown. "Dry off and put this on—do you need my help?"

She shook her head, so he went to the lounge to light the gas fire and pour out a generous glass of brandy. He hauled the sofa closer to the fire and found a quilt in one of the cupboards. After a few minutes she appeared under the archway, a tiny pale snail in a shell ten sizes too large.

"Come over here," he said, and she came, trailing her shell, and sat down. He spread the blanket over her. "Drink this."

She did as she was told, and eventually she started to shiver, to shiver so violently that the liquid slopped in its glass bell, so he took it away from her and moved up close beside her, put his arms around her. She was shockingly cold, like an amphibian.

"My God," he said. "Have I done this to you?"

She started to laugh, a defunct-sounding laugh that was deeply disturbing.

"It's entirely self-inflicted," she finally managed.

He put his hands on her hair, but it was still drenched with water, so he fetched another towel and applied it vigorously as if she were a newborn foal. She sat motionless until he had finished, then lay back on the cushions as he combed his fingers through, removing all the tangles. She closed her eyes, colour slowly returning to her lips and her skin, and eventually her breathing evened out and she was asleep.

❧ ❧ ❧

"Lovely to hear from you, darling. Are you all right?"

"Yes, but I'm a bit worried about Claire." He shifted the mobile against his ear and glanced through the arched doorway into the next room, where her dark head was barely visible.

"Where are you?" Her voice raised a notch. "Where is *she*?"

"I found her in the rain acting a bit mad—I've brought her back to mine."

"I was afraid something like this might happen, but she insisted on being alone."

"I think I've caught her before serious hypothermia set in," he said. "Do you have any idea what's wrong with her?"

"She's in a deep state of shock, has been for days. I couldn't get through to her."

"Anything specific?"

"Everything, really—but mostly you, I would imagine. Although she's too stubborn to admit as much."

"I'll try to sort it out."

"I wish you would, darling. Any idiot could see that the two of you are madly in love with one another."

"You don't think it's too late?"

"Just sort it out, Joshua. And tell her I want to be head bridesmaid at the wedding."

❧ ❧ ❧

Claire was bathed in warmth, cocooned in a plush, comfortable nest. She had not felt this warm since ... when? Since before the doors slammed, one after the other. But that all seemed like a very long time ago.

She opened her eyes. The room was dim and ornate. She saw the gas fire, yellow and purple tongues writhing like an iris. She saw the chandelier, shards of crystal, each with its own fiery reflected core. She saw

336

Joshua, sitting on the other side of the fire in a high-backed chair under a lit lamp, a glass of brandy on the small table by his elbow, with another golden core floating within. He held a book in his hand, and he was lost within its words, the merest suggestion of a smile on his face. She could hear the fire steaming, the rain pattering against the ancient window glass, and most of evening came back to her, except that she could not quite recall how she had ended up on the riverside bench in the first place.

She felt completely at home here in this nest in this room with this man, a prospect that filled her with confusion, that seemed to tap against the door of her glass heart.

Joshua looked up from the page and met her eye, his smile somehow intensifying without actually changing shape.

"Feeling better?"

"Better doesn't begin to describe it," she said.

He closed the book with careful hands, set it on the table, returned the hands folded to his lap.

"You had me worried."

"I'm not surprised—you must've thought I'd lost it."

"Had you?"

"Maybe a little," she confessed. "But I think I'm a bit saner now." She paused. "You've forgiven me, haven't you?"

"Yes, for days now. I just lost my temper. Sorry about the book."

"Don't be," she said. "The shake-up did it some good."

He looked at her seriously. "And I'm sorry I walked out on you afterwards. I'll never do that again."

"I don't blame you in the least," she said. "I was wholly in the wrong, and I apologize—even if you had told Alan, my attack would have been unfair. But I found out how Alan knew, and it was down to my own carelessness."

"Apology accepted," he said. "And I'm glad I've been acquitted."

She was glad he didn't ask her to elaborate; she didn't want to think about Alan any more.

"I heard how you went to Stanley while I was in Liverpool," he said. "I heard you were magnificent."

"I heard how you and Roz siphoned off my data thirty minutes before the removals men showed up." She laughed, stretching her legs underneath the quilt and luxuriating in its warmth. "Your reputation as a man of mystery must've received a serious boost."

He chuckled too, then after a short pause, said, "Did Ramon tell you that the company is probably finished?"

She nodded. "What are you going to do?"

"I've got a few plans up my sleeve. How about you?"

"I've decided to leave science." At his look, she added, "It's not that I don't like it, but I think my true passion lies elsewhere."

"I had a feeling it might."

"I guess I've finally realized it's far healthier to commit up front rather than hiding behind some other profession."

"It sounds sensible," he said. "Will you become a professional poet?"

"I don't know, Joshua. I'm . . . at a loss for words."

"What do you mean?"

"I mean, I've literally lost my words. Ever since . . . everything happened. I'm afraid they've gone forever."

"Nonsense," he said solidly. "You've only had a bit of a shock. Be patient . . . they'll come back."

"Do you really think so?"

"I do."

She gazed into the fire, feeling an unexpected sensation. She thought it might be hope. "It would be a difficult step for me, though."

"Why?" When she hesitated, he said, "You don't have to tell me if you don't want to."

Slowly, with long pauses and a few digressions, she explained about her beloved father and his increasingly bitter life. She thought that maybe her body had somehow attuned to his over the past months, because she could feel his gentle influence acting on her even through the metre or so of empty air between them.

"Thinking back now, I realize he must've been clinically depressed. And it didn't help that we were always poor and that he couldn't seem to get a lucky break."

"Was he good?"

"Very. I'll show you some of his stuff some day. But he wasn't skilled at selling himself . . . he was very shy. And then. . ."

"What?"

Claire had never told anyone what she was about to tell Joshua.

"*Mamá* left him . . . us, I should say, when I was seventeen. She went back to Gran Canaria. I don't really blame her—Dad was almost unbearable at that point, had quit teaching and hardly ever left his room—we were just scraping by on benefits. She'd tried everything to get through to him, and then one day she'd had enough."

She was aware of his silent presence in the chair on the other side of the fire, strong and watchful.

"It was a relief to go away to Uni—it was a relief that it was so far away, I'm ashamed to say. I switched to biology my first year, and it was so exciting, so tangible ... so unlikely to lead down my father's path. I came back for Christmas that year, full of this new thing. Defiant with it."

"He must've taken it hard."

She felt that horrible laughter from the previous night crowd into her throat once more, but forced it back down.

"Yes; I wasn't even remotely tactful," she said. "I went down to the pub with some old schoolmates, and when I got back that night, I came into his room and found that he'd hanged himself."

After a few shocked seconds, Joshua said, "I'm so sorry, Claire. I had no idea."

"It was . . . about as bad as you can imagine. *Mamá* died a few months later, drowned in the sea. It was said to be an accident, but I've never been entirely convinced."

The clock on the mantelpiece ticked, and eventually Joshua said, "It wasn't your fault."

"I think I know that, most days. Except that if I hadn't been like that, maybe he wouldn't have . . . and maybe *she*. . ."

"Maybe, maybe not. You were just doing what you had to do— exerting your independence. Living your own life."

"I know. But at the same time. . ." She thought about cause and effect, something that scientists were conversant with. She saw her father's face, crumpled against the assault of her youthful scorn. She thought about Alan, refusing to give Serena her taxi fare. Things could happen because of one's actions, even if no one, strictly speaking, could be blamed. Things could change forever.

"You have to forgive yourself," he said eventually. "There's no other way. You've got to re-enter the world, take risks."

She nodded, feeling the empty sacs where tears should fill. Joshua would probably tell her to be patient, that those would come back too.

"Besides, history doesn't have to repeat itself," he said. "You can still be a poet if you want to."

"But how can one *be* a poet in this day and age?" she said. "I mean practically? I don't have a track record; I have no idea where to begin."

"I think you'll find that there are scientific procedures even for poets." He was looking at her fondly. "You can get another degree, get stuck in. There must be workshops, how-to books. You're very clever and ambitious—I can't imagine you'll have a problem making a start."

"Do you think I'll get anywhere?"

He waited a long time before responding.

"I have no idea," he said at last. "It's probably a long shot—but if you don't try, how will you ever know?"

She nodded, liking him all the more for not promising she *would* succeed.

"I think regret would've killed my father earlier than failure, to be honest—if he'd quit writing and got a better job, earned more money."

"It's good you've realized that," he said. "Some people never do."

She watched the flames shift in the hearth.

"But that's the thing that scares me the most," she said. "Because I'll have to have a real job at the same time, to live. And that's what really crippled Dad—being so divided and exhausted all the time."

"Move in with me," he said. "I'll look after you. I'm loaded."

"Oh, Joshua. . ."

"I'm flexible on locations, but if you fancy staying in Amsterdam, I've got an entire top floor up there, four rooms, completely unfurnished. I never knew what to do with all the space. There's plenty of room for you and every last one of your bookcases, room to hide whenever you want me out of your hair, room to think and breathe."

"I couldn't possibly sponge off you!"

"Why not?" he said impatiently. "Me not taking you in on financial grounds would be like eating a sandwich on the balcony and sweeping away the crumbs so that the sparrows couldn't get at them—that's how much of a dent you'd make in my estate."

"But it's the principle of it." She couldn't look at him. "I'm completely broken. It's too soon to tell how I feel . . . whether. . ."

"That's got nothing to do with it," he said. "I don't mind admitting that I'm still crazy about you, but if you're undecided, it doesn't matter. The truth is that you want to write, and I've got a pretty swanky garret going spare."

She finally raised her head to the unthreatening, matter-of-fact expression on his face. "I don't know if it's such a good idea, Josh. I'd have to think about it."

"There's no rush—it's a standing offer."

"I don't fully understand what you'd get out of it."

He shrugged. "I rather like watching the sparrows. They make me happy."

❦ ❦ ❦

Later that night, Joshua woke to find that Claire had left the downstairs spare room and was slipping into his bed.

"Afraid of the dark?" He put his arms around her and pulled her against him, feeling an ache of completeness like a fractured bone being set.

"No, just missing you," she said.

He moved his hand down her hair, her shoulders, her back, underneath the oversized T-shirt, testing skin and muscle and warmth, all reassuringly solid and quickening beneath his touch. It was such a relief that he didn't have to stop, that he could continue his sweep over the curve of her hip, along the swell of her thigh.

"I can't believe how good you make me feel," she said.

"This is nothing."

He found her lips in the dark, and when she eventually drew away, he could feel her little heart attempting to cope with the blood singing just underneath her skin.

"Before this escalates any further," she said, "I wanted to make sure. . ."

"It's okay, Claire, honestly."

"I've never had so much happen to me at once. I don't know how long it will take to heal." Her voice sounded impossibly lost.

"It doesn't matter, *cariño*. Even if this is the only time, it's what I want."

"Are you sure?"

Joshua had a choice of languages at his disposal, but in the end it seemed best not to use any of them.

And as for Claire, she felt the sea ice begin to thaw around her, popping and shattering with crystalline music, just a trickle at first, building slowly towards a mighty flood. The glass around her had long since melted away, and the message was loosed and vulnerable, ready to travel to wherever she might want it to go.

And then, in no particular hurry, the tide started to come in.

⚜ ⚜ ⚜

Joshua opened his eyes as sunlight fell across his face. He heard the birdsong, and knew immediately that she was gone.

He sat up and looked at the empty dishevelled space beside him, corroborative evidence. He wasn't terribly surprised, but it still made him sad all the same.

He pulled on a sweatshirt and shorts and went downstairs towards the kitchen. Then he stopped flat: Claire's coat was still hanging in the entrance hall. He padded over to the spare bedroom, and all her clothes were draped over the radiators where he'd arranged them the night before, and her shoes sat in two pools of water on the floor by the vacant bed.

As he looked at her shoes, a stray image flickered over top: a dark-haired figure slipping into the Amstel and disappearing beneath its black waters.

The house was suddenly holding its breath, cloaked in secret stillness. Not a whisper of life could be detected anywhere in the vast space of his domain. Awash in a sense of unreality, in a world where neither fear nor joy existed, he stepped into the corridor again and was alerted by a flow of cold air sinking down from the staircase. He went back up, passed the floor that contained his bedroom and kept going, all the way to the top of the house, where the final flight was a ladder.

That was when he heard it: Claire's voice, speaking soft words, repeating them, varying them as if trying them out for size, for shape, for heft, for impact. The sound was a gift that he could never repay. After a few more repetitions, the voice went quiet.

Carefully, very carefully, so that he wouldn't startle any sparrows, he poked his head up through the uncovered trap door into the main space of the garret.

Across bare floorboards and through the open French doors, Claire sat legs crossed on the balcony in a sea of sunlight, wrapped in the voluminous old dressing gown. She was writing furiously, using a computer manual as a support. Ever resourceful, she must have raided the recycle bin in his study, because she was using the spent detritus of his relentless database searches as paper—printed chains of DNA in patterns on one side, and on the other, her own growing lines of code, in many ways equally as mysterious. The words, he noted, appeared to be coming effortlessly.

After watching her work for the longest while, when she seemed to have reached a natural pause, he climbed the rest of the way up and walked over to the open doorway. She raised her head with a smile and a particular look in her eye. Of course he couldn't be entirely sure, but it just might be a look meant for him and him alone.

"I've got something to show you," she said.

The End